Players Ball

Playing Games II

You Only Get One Shot

Kendra Spencer

Cover Design: Marion Designs

Editor: Joy Nelson

This book is dedicated to Mary Holleran and the rest of my fans that read the original novel and wanted to know more about T. Thank you all.

A Piece of FOE

Honestly, I'm pissed,
Why didn't you fight?

My sisters need you
My brother needs you
Hell we need you

You are the glue that held us together
I didn't realize a lot of things
But I realize it now
Please come back

I can't physically, mentally, spiritually take away
their pain

I don't know what to do
I don't know how to help them

Come back or show me how
Our last convo was never supposed to be our last
Only the beginning

Please come back
I don't know what to do
How to help

I know you can't come back
I know you're really gone
No matter how much I try to deceive myself
I'm glad you are out of pain and in a better place

I will never forget our good and bad times together
Our bad times really showed me a lot
Cause it gave way to good times, which was a
blessing in itself

A lesson that I needed to learn

I'm going to miss you
I really am

I love you Trina Bridenbaugh
Thank you for being my stepmother
Helping to build me into who I am today

Thank you for being a great mother to my brother
and sisters
Thank you for being a great grandmother
Thank you for being a dear friend
Thank you for being an awesome family member,
daughter, sister cousin, and aunt

Your memory shall live on with us
You will not be forgotten

Rest in a peaceful paradise

FOE

T cut her car off and reclined back into her seat. Gazing off in to the distance at the sea of headstones assembled in the grass made T's mouth tighten as her lips twisted. She pinched the bone between her closed eyes. Being in the cemetery brought back another memory of a death, her older brother's. T shook her head to dispel the memories and reached for a blunt in her ashtray. Pulling on the blunt several times, T filled her lungs with the THC, exhaling before replacing it back in her car ashtray. Once out of the car T straightened her clothes out then started to walk towards Ronnie's grave plot.

With each step T took towards Ronnie's grave, her feet seemed to be getting heavier and heavier. Finally, she came to a stop in front of Ronnie's final resting place. A tear rolled down her face into the dirt as T looked at the up turned ground waiting for Ronnie's casket. Turning away, T went to sit next to Kenni's grave a few feet away from Ronnie's grave plot.

Letting out a sniffle, T began to speak to Kenni's headstone as if she were there next to her, "What's up Kenni. How y'all living up there?" she looked around. "Tell Ronnie's punk ass that was a bitch move she pulled but I still love her doe. What y'all had, had to have been love 'cause I know my nigga wouldn't leave me down here. That shit at da club doe that was fun. I wish we would have had more times like that. Our crew crazy as hell but I'll let Ron tell you our stories. Tell her to tell you some stories about when we was in high school before we hit dat eighteen bar."

Peering off into space again, she revealed a flask that contained alcohol from inside her suit jacket. She took a swig, "My nigga always had my back. Mafuckas in school already knew; you fuck with T, you fuckin' wit' Ronnie. You fuck with Ronnie, you fuckin' wit' T." A lump developed in her throat causing T to pause reflectively before swallowing to continue, "I can't believe y'all gone. All this mainly over Shyna. We should'a let Kim kick her ass when she volunteered. She took you away from her, made my nigga hurt core deep. Then took my nigga away from me. That's about a bitch if I ever heard one."

"Ronnie was my nigga. More than blood. Shit, she gone. Shit ain't gon' be the same no mo'. I feel like a part of me died. I love everybody else in our crew but Ronnie was my *nigga*. I don't know how heaven work, but I know y'all gon' see each other. So, when you see her tell her I miss her and shit ain't gon' be the same down here no mo," stopping T took a big gulp of the liquor before beginning solemnly, "I ain't know you that well but you was cool. You had spunk or fire, whatever da hell you wanna call it. That's probably one of the main reasons Ronnie loved you so much," T drunk some more. "Damn I'ma miss y'all. Y'all kept a nigga laughing."

Ma Dukes, T's mother and Moryah, Ronnie's mother walked up to T. "C'mon T they carrying her up now," Ma Dukes spoke to her daughter with Moryah hunkered under her arm.

Kim who was walking behind the mothers stopped at T's feet as the older women continued on. She stuck her chestnut hand out to T and pulled T to her feet, "You a'ight?"

"Yeah," T said brushing off her clothes. "I was just talkin' to Kenni about Ronnie."

"Oh," Kim said softly glancing at the headstone awkwardly as they started walking away from her permanent home. "You sure you a'ight?" Kim questioned looking at T sideways.

"I'm cool," T said exhaling in Kim's face.

Kim jerked back, "What you been drinkin' on?"

"Hennessy. Ronnie's favorite."

The two smiled and quieted down as more people flooded the cemetery to pay their last respects. They stood next to each other, T drinking silently with tears cascading down her face. A feeling of numbness overcame T as she shook the hands and gave hugs to the people trying to console her. An aching feeling deep within T exposed itself when T looked around the gravesite noticing people walking away smoking and laughing. Her gaze led her around her family of friends to watch Ronnie's mother Moryah being supported by her own mother. To see Chantel being held by her girlfriend Mya, Jay had a female with her as well who had wrapped her arms around Jay's back. Kim stood next to T, but she was on the phone declaring in a quivering voice that she was fine. T's somber gaze connected with Kenni's friend Layla whose watery eyes matched hers. Layla flashed T a smile. Before T could return it Arianna, Ronnie's sister, popped up in front of T. Arianna smiled mournfully and pulled T into a hug. She clenched Arianna tight closing her eyes as the tears seeped out wetting Arianna's t-shirt. When T felt Arianna take a slight step back she opened her eyes to discover, only their family of friends was still present along with Layla and Sayvonne.

T stepped back from Arianna and pulled out her flask again, tipping its contents onto the soil of Ronnie's gravesite.

"T!" Arianna exclaimed grabbing her arm.

"What?" T questioned back incredulously. "My nigga loved her some Hen, so you know I gotta marinate her grave in it."

Moryah chuckled sadly, "T, you is something else. No matter what we doing or where we at, you always make us laugh."

T smiled at her.

"Thank you," Moryah told her, her eyes watering as she held out her hands for a hug. The two embraced and Moryah said in a loud whisper, "Now I know you hurting, we all are. But don't go doing nothing off the wall. All of y'all," she looked around at her youngest daughter's "family" and Kenni's best friends. "I can't take no more funerals y'all," Moryah broke down but still managed to hug everyone before Ma Dukes ushered her to the car.

Arianna watched Ma Dukes sit Moryah, her mother as well, in the car before following her mother's example, hugging everyone. "Make sure you take care of T," Arianna whispered in Kim's ear then hugged T.

"Ooh do it again," T cajoled with a smile when Arianna kissed her cheek but sadness strained her voice.

The family of friends watched them leave then turned their attention back to Ronnie's gravesite. There was a long pregnant pause, as everyone except Layla consumed with their own thoughts running through their heads seemed to zone out while staring at the casket. Layla snuck glances at T who caught her more than a few times.

"T, you a'ight?" Chantel asked breaking the silence.

She looked around to see the family watching her. She plastered on a smile to mask the pain she felt soul deep, "Yeah man. I'm good."

"You sure?" Chantel's girl Mya asked.

"I'm cool y'all. Fa real I'm good."

The family gave way to another silent pause, which caused everyone to slowly drift back to their cars. One by one or two by two everyone rubbed the casket and went on to their car until only T and Kim were left. Kim's phone began to buzz feverishly in her purse vibrating against something. T glanced down at her but neither one of them uttered a word.

Plunking down on the ground, T laughed as a memory began to surface, "I remember the first time I met

Ronnie in seventh grade. I was new to her school and had pulled her gurl. We met up at a football game to fight and shit and one of her niggas was like y'all dumb fighting over a bitch. And we just got cool. Started talking and shit."

Kim smiled and laughed not really seeing the humor in the story, "I remember when I first met y'all."

Busting out with laughter T finished Kim's story, "We both tried to get on wit' yo' lil' sexy ass!"

"Hell yeah. Had you first bell, her second bell, and both y'all niggas fa lunch. Y'all was crazy!" Kim exclaimed laughing as a ton of memories hit her.

T's laughter slowly died away as she studied the white casket in front of her. "Them was the days man." She blinked back to focus when Kim asked her if she was ready to go, "Nah you go 'head. I'ma be there in a minute."

Kim stood over her and declared, "T, you been drinkin. You don't need to be driving like this."

Looking up at her T grinned, "Man I'm cool. I told you I was a'ight."

Folding her arms, Kim looked her over skeptically instead of responding.

"Kim. Go 'head. Invite ya gurl over. What's her name Cream?"

Smiling at the idea, she started to walk away, "A'ight. Turn yo' phone on." T took the phone out of her pocket and turned it on showing Kim. "I'ma call you if one of yo' gurls call and you call me when you leave here."

"A'ight."

"Holla."

Watching and waiting until Kim was out of hearing and sight distance, T sprawled out on the ground next to Ronnie's grave.

****

5

A vibration from T's pants awoke her; she didn't realize she had fallen asleep. T pulled her cell phone out of her pocket. She answered groggily, "Hello?"

"Where da fuck you at?" Kim shouted.

T took the phone off her ear and looked around, "I'm at the cemetery."

"What are you still doing there T? The funeral ended at three and it's going on seven."

Standing up, wiping her suit off, T picked up her flask and responded, "I fell asleep."

"We coming to pick you up," Kim said into the phone over the fumbling in the background.

Chuckling T declined, "Yo, I'm good," her phone beeped. "Hold on," T read a text message one of her female friends sent her. "Yo Tricia call me?"

"Yeah. 'Bout an hour or two ago."

"A'ight. I'm going over there."

"You sure you don't need us to take you?" Kim questioned with worry.

She let out a laugh hearing Kim's girlfriend do the same, "My car here."

"A'ight."

"Holla."

T walked over to Ronnie's casket and put her hand on it, "You know Ron, I was just bullshitting when I said I was gon' settle down a few months ago. Now though," she shook her dreads as a tear escaped from her eye. T looked towards Kenni's grave, "Maybe I need too. Life's short. I can't keep playing games with these hoes. Shit I should'a brought a bitch here with me too," T sighed heavily and patted the coffin. "I love you lil' bruh. And I'ma miss you like a muthafucka fam. I'ma come by again soon though. I'm about to go kick it with Tricia. I love you," she dropped a kiss on the coffin and started to walk off to her Monte Carlo while loosening her tie.

Popping open the trunk of her car T placed her suit jacket in it along with her tie. Rummaging around in her trunk for something she could place her flask in, she grabbed her book bag with a smile. "Ha. I'ma put this in here," said T putting her flask in the book bag. She patted her crotch where she had tucked her strap-on in her boxer briefs over her brief harness, "Love my new harness," mumbled T pulling out her cologne and spraying some on her wrists, neck, and midsection. T slammed the trunk shut, went to the driver's side of the car, and opened the door. She paused staring out at Ronnie's coffin then looked towards the sky, "I love you lil' bruh. And I miss the fuck out you already."

Before driving off T sent a text message to her female friend relaying that she was enroute to her house. Driving with one hand the other hand searched the compartments of her car. Her hands ran across a bag of weed, and she put it in her lap. Finally coming to a red light, she fished around for a pack of cigarillos. She sped off once the light turned green only to make a sharp left turn into a convenient store parking lot.

"Yo let me get a pack of White Owls," T spoke to the man behind the counter, still walking through the door.

"Two dollars."

T handed him a five-dollar bill and began to walk away. She turned around when the man called out to her. "Keep the change," she told him already splitting one of the cigarillos.

"Thank you."

Leaving the car door open, T plopped down in her car emptying the guts of the cigarillo onto the ground. T proceeded to break the weed back down in the open cigarillo and roll it up. Just as she held the blunt up for inspection, she noticed Layla coming towards her dressed in a pair of low-rise capri denim jeans with a red v-cut halter-top, a silver chain, and a black and red Cincinnati fitted hat.

She put the blunt in her ashtray only to get out of the car and perch on the hood to watch Layla approach her. Remembering the glances Layla kept casting her way at the funeral, T took in the view from head to pretty manicured toes adorned in black flip flops, "Damn you stay wit' a hat ma," T commented as Layla drew closer. "Who you trying to impress?"

Layla didn't respond at first, she just hugged T tightly. Feeling T stiffen slightly, Layla ran a hand down T's chest and pulled away, "You alright T? I'm sorry about Ronnie."

Staring into Layla's eyes T responded, "I'm sorry about Kenni. I've been better though, but you still skipped over my question."

Smirking Layla released T. She turned around and went into the store switching her ass. T followed behind Layla into the store, eyes glued to Layla's ass while Layla replied, "If I know you gon' be around, you," she glanced back at T catching her eyes glued to her ass. Layla moved towards the chips at the front counter waiting for T to come up behind her, "You stay around here?"

Grinning T replied with, "Hold on now doe," her eyes roamed over the back frame of Layla who had smiled, as she turned around to the man working the register, "You dressing to impress me?"

Biting down on her lip, Layla nodded hesitantly.

T sidled up next to her then spoke in her ear, "Well you doing a damn good job ma."

The man behind the counter watched the interaction between the two. Layla extended a dollar to him but he waved the pair on out the store.

"You on foot today?" T questioned not seeing her car in the parking lot of the one stop shop.

"Yeah. My car in the shop,"

"Well get in," T said, while opening the door of her black Monte Carlo for Layla. "It ain't no way in hell I'm letting yo' lil' sexy ass walk home."

Layla smirked and got in the car.

"So, where you stay?" T inquired hopping in and starting the car up.

"Off Beckenroff," Layla said checking out the interior of T's car.

They pulled out of the convenient store and T stopped at a red light.

"T?" Layla said.

T glanced over at Layla casually and before she could react, Layla was sucking on her tongue.

Chapter 1

"Kim, lemme call you back, ran into Layla," T said into her phone skipping a greeting, before Kim could say anything.

"A'ight. Bye."

Following Layla up to her house and in to her bedroom, T looked around the room. "You run track?" commented T looking at all the medals, ribbons, and pictures decorating the walls.

"Yeah. But that's not why I invited you up here," Layla answered, undressing quickly behind T and pushing her down onto her bed.

Inhaling sharply, T let her eyes travel down Layla's thick and curvy cocoa brown body.

Layla laughed. She crawled on top of T lifting her clothes and kissing along her flat stomach while unbuttoning her suit vest. Sliding further up T to sit on her midsection Layla leaned down, placing kisses all over T's face and neck while she unbuttoned T's shirt. Her hands moved down to unbuttoning T's slacks. Grinding her pussy on T, she slipped her pants down off her ass and pulled them to her ankles. Layla's hand vanished in her boxers rubbing against T's strap.

Swiftly T flipped Layla over and pressed a kiss to her lips. T's hand slid down Layla's thighs, sneaking between them to stir the pot of honey nestled in the grove of her thighs. With her head thrown back, gyrating her hips Layla moaned sensually. Yanking T's hand out of her snatch, Layla devoured T's fingers, licking and sucking each one individually until the essence of herself was gone.

T stood stripping the rest of her clothes off, "C'mere." Obediently Layla came meshing her body against T's.

T slapped her cocoa brown ass and left it there and with her other hand, tilted Layla's chin up and kissed her. They kissed voraciously, lips uniting with one another then parting only to meet again, alternatively tongues touched. Heat overcame the two in their haze as tongues tangled and danced all over each other's faces and neck, lips planted kisses here and there, bites parked along the neck of both individuals intensifying the need building between them. Kneading Layla's nipples between her fingers brought moans of pleasure out of Layla. One of T's hand escaped down to Layla's wet spot. She fingered her pussy for a minute then raised it to watch Layla ravage her fingers hungrily. T pushed Layla backwards on to the bed pausing to admire the beautiful sight of this cocoa creature playing with the wetness of her own pink. She bit her lip as her cell phone went off in her pants pocket ringing Tupac's I Get Around ring tone.

Layla moaned, dipping her fingers in and out of her pussy and tasting them, "You wanna get that?"

"Hell nah," T said bending down to kiss her. Her phone quit ringing then started back up, "The fuck man?" she rose to get up but Layla who had wrapped her legs around T pulled her back down over top her.

T smiled losing herself in Layla's lips, tits, thighs, and hips as she explored every crevice of her body with her tongue. Biting around Layla's hipbones T spread her legs apart caressing her thighs with her lips nearing the entrance

11

of Layla's den. T licked her own lips and scooted her tongue up between Layla's labia starting from the bottom of Layla's pussy.

"Ssss," Layla moaned biting her lip.

Positioning her tongue right above Layla's clit, she ran her flat tongue back down Layla's pussy. Subsequently a finger massaged against Layla's clit while another one dipped in and out of her opening. Maneuvering back up Layla's body brought her facial lips back to action. They began a match wrestling with their tongues.

Layla jerked her mouth away from T as her thighs tightened and a guttural moan escaped. Sucking on her neck T moseyed over to her collarbone doing the same until she journeyed across Layla's full supple cocoa brown titties, she flicked her tongue over both of Layla's nipples. Exhaling with pleasure watching T take her whole left titty in her mouth anxiously, Layla bit her lip. Their eyes met and T twisted Layla's one nipple in her fingertips, sucked her other nipple, and let a finger dance all over her clit at the same time. Layla began to sing a sweet song in T's ears when T switched her mouth to the right nipple suckling on it, pushed them together ran figure eights over her nipples then took both of them into her mouth. Fingers ran through T's dreads tugging, grasping at them amidst the quaking of Layla's legs.

Kissing, followed up with a lick down back to Layla's pussy, T glided her tongue between Layla's hairless lips again. A shot of wind blasted Layla's sensitive clit causing her back to arch. She looked down to see what T was doing only to find out as she watched T's strap about to get inserted. Briefly smiling at its girth Layla bolted over into her side drawer and handed T a condom.

T smiled looking at the Trojan in her hand; she rolled the ribbed condom over her strap and turned Layla back on her stomach. Teasing the corridor of Layla's pussy

12

T inserted her head guiding half of her strap in, extracting and delving deeper until all nine inches of her strap was inside of Layla. Creeping out of Layla's pussy T thrusted back into her making her cry out. A blow landed on Layla's ass cheek as T induced Layla's pussy with her strap, pounding it in to her. Screaming out in pleasure Layla threw her ass back loving the feeling of the balls slapping against her pussy.

"OOH SHIT!" Layla cried out with an involuntary dip in her back caused by T who had grabbed a handful of her hair and yanked her head back. "Fuck, fuck, fuck. Damn daddy. . . ooh shit."

Releasing Layla's hair T held onto her hips with one hand as the other hand rained blows on her ass rhythmically pummeling her dick in and out of Layla's pussy simultaneously. Collapsing forward yelling she was cumming Layla quickly gathered her strength and pushed T backwards onto her back. Sending a smile over her shoulder to T, Layla leaned forward and grabbed T's ankles. She rocked and rolled her hips backwards on T's strap with T pinching on her nipples and elevating her own hips in accordance with the way Layla moved. Layla's hand moved to T's thighs where she dug her nails in. She rose so T's strap was only an inch or so deep and bobbed up and down on it, twirling her hips on the strap, manipulating the head of her strap against her clit. T watched her with captivation then hastily pulled Layla down all the way on her strap, she lifted Layla and their hips collided mid-thrust bouncing off one another and engaging again.

Limply Layla fell off T onto the side of the bed. Rolling Layla onto her back T unfolded her legs, gathering her up by her ass T drove her dick in and out of Layla's pussy, grinding her strap down into her at times. Layla tried to wrap her legs around T but she wouldn't release her. Layla's eyes fluttered and rolled as her thigh muscles contracted. Attempting to run, T laughed holding Layla in place watching the inevitable.

"Fuck. Shit. Oh my god! T baby, ooh fuck. Lemme go, lemme go," Layla pleaded. "SHIT, SHIT, SHIT! DADDY OH MY GOD I'M CUMMING!" Layla exclaimed as a river of juices trampled out of her soaking the sheets.

Pleased with herself T eased the strap out of her. She slid a hand down to Layla's wetness and gathered some on her fingers to lick off.

"Damn baby," Layla panted.

T smiled as her phone went off again. She stood to retrieve it and answered, "Hello?"

"Where you at?" the woman she was supposed to go see asked. "I thought you were coming to see me."

Letting out a satisfied laugh T replied, "I am. Just give me a minute a'ight." *Might be awhile,* T added in thought as she glanced at Layla who had rolled over onto her side.

"Ok. I love you."

"A'ight."

"Bye."

"One."

Hanging up the phone, T licked her lips at Layla laying there butt ass naked on her side with a pillow in between her thighs, "Damn."

"You leaving?"

"Nah. Not unless you want me too," T said climbing in the bed, throwing the pillow out of the way.

Layla tilted her face up for a kiss; T dropped one to her lips. She broke away glancing at the clock, "My peoples gon' be here in a minute."

"Well I can't have you in trouble. Yo' peoples probably don't even know 'bout you," T stated retreating back out of the bed and putting back on her clothes.

With a mischievous glint in Layla's eyes, she watched T get dressed and led the way downstairs steering T by her hand. "But they ain't here yet," she remarked sitting T on the couch, sitting on top of her and placing one of T's hands between her legs so T could see how hot she was.

Beaming T kissed along on her neck. Easing Layla back onto the couch T knelt down and let her tongue take a stroll between Layla's lips for the third time. Skipping her tongue over and around Layla's clit, who was moaning sensually weaving her hands through T's dreads; T flicked her tongue across Layla's clit rapidly, engulfed Layla's clit with her lips, and shook her head. T started to write the alphabet on Layla's clit, halfway through, a car door slammed outside. T was tongue kissing Layla's pussy and Layla was humming and gripping T's dreads when they heard a key in Layla's front door and two people arguing.

Layla bolted upright yanking her pussy away from T. She grabbed T and took off towards the kitchen. She stopped pulling T at the back door and kissed her goodbye before pushing her out the back door.

T fell out the back door laughing. Layla however ran in the laundry room and grabbed a basket full of clothes she had left there to get washed. She searched frantically and found a robe to put on over her naked body.

"Relax baby. That could have been Sharon's people. You know they will park in our driveway if theirs is full," Layla heard her mother say.

Layla's stepfather retorted, "Yeah well-" he broke off hearing a car screech out onto the street. He looked out the window, "I see they moved now. I'ma go move ours into the driveway," he walked off and Layla came out of the room.

"Hey Mommy," Layla greeted her with a kiss on the cheek as she walked past her with a basket of clothes in her hand.

"You know anybody with a black Monte Carlo?" her mother asked.

"Nope," Layla said continuing to her room.

****

T breezed through the door of the condo she shared with Kim, who sat on the white sofa clad in a white tank top and white boy shorts with a blunt in her hand. Throwing her keys on the table, T strolled over to the couch to sit down with her roommate.

Kim glanced up at her, lighter in hand to light the blunt and shook her head, "Don't get comfortable. Tricia called and she told me to tell you when you get here that she is angry." T took a seat anyway; the two shared a laugh. "So, you got da lil' young gurl?"

"Aww man you already know sis."

Nodding absentmindedly Kim took a few long pulls off the blunt before passing it to T. Listening only enough to comment while T rehashed the night's events after the funeral the blunt was quickly finished. Immediately Kim began to roll another one.

The phone rang and Kim snatched it up. "Hello? Hold on," she held the phone out to T who wagged an index finger at her indicating no. Her lips curved up into a smile as her eyes followed her stud "brother" out of the door. "My bad but this a good ass blunt I rolled. A nigga feel proud."

Taking her sweet time over to the woman's house that had been jockeying for her time since the funeral, T stopped by a liquor store picking up a bottle of Hennessy hoping to lessen the chance of her being aggravated.

16

Picking up dinner for the both of them at a soul food place not too far from the female's house, she encountered a teenager selling weed and bought a bag from him as well. Finally, standing outside of her apartment building T buzzed the security intercom for access into the building and peeked at her watch registering it had almost been an hour since she left her own house.

"Tricia, buzz me in," T said into the speaker pausing briefly listening for a reply before pressing the speaker button again. "I picked up some dinner for us and I got us a bottle of somethin' to sip on," a few seconds passed and led her fingers to jab the button three more times in succession.

Subsequently, a door swung open with a woman emerging into the hallway with a pink scarf wrapped around her head, a too little white tank top, and pink pajama pants. "I'm coming!" she snapped sliding her feet into pink flip-flops. Opening the secure door the young lady muttered, "The thing broke."

As the female proceeded up the stairs without saying anything else to T, T grabbed her from behind pulling her close, "Damn. What's up to you too ma," murmured T nuzzling her neck with her nose. She squirmed out of T's grasp. "Oh, I can't hug you no more?"

Up a few steps the cream toned young woman responded, "Where the fuck have you been? You told me you were on the way like five hours ago!"

"I was drinking and fell asleep after everyone left."

"Bullshit. They wait on you to leave so they can put the coffin in the ground. They're on fuckin' site."

T walked up the stairs to her and turned her around gently by the wrist, "And I didn't fuckin' leave. What they gon' make me leave after I just lost somebody?"

The woman faced T with a look of contempt, "Whatever! I know you was with a bitch."

Glaring angrily T spoke in a calm, even tone, "I'm still in my fuckin' suit. I ain't even been home yet. Excuse the fuck outta me for mourning my friend's death."

She reached for the middle of her crotch, touched the strap, and let it go, "Why you strapped?"

"Wasn't it on when I met you? Didn't we make plans for me to come over here? Why you think I have it on? Look ma I'm telling you, if you don't believe it, fuck it! I was drinking at my brother's grave and fell asleep."

"Oh what the fuck ever! I ain't stupid. Fuck-" abruptly her words were cut short when T slammed her against the wall.

"Fuck what? Don't you ever think about disrespectin' my brother like that in yo' life bitch fuck you," T began holding the petite wrists in her hands. "I don't need this shit. My nigga just died playing games with females. You think I'm about to sit here and entertain yo' sadiddy ass? I ain't scared of commitment I just ain't 'bout to commit to yo' dumb ass. You already think you my bitch but know I got more hoes than a Rolodex," finished T harshly letting go of her wrists to walk down the stairs.

"T, I'm sorry," she apologized following T. "Where are you going?" questioned the woman to an unresponsive T who was taking long strides towards her car. The female caught up with T and grabbed her arm, "T, I said I'm sorry, damn. I didn't mean it like that. I thought you were with someone else."

T whipped around angrily, "You betta get the fuck off my arm, grabbin' me like you done lost yo' damn mind and shit. Bitch deuces!"

Limply the young woman's arm fell to her side, "T?"

They stared directly in to each other's eyes not saying anything, T taking note of the silent pleas in her eyes. Memories of their last few run ins with each other flashed across T's mind. The woman in front of her was needy, wanting all of T's time knowing she wasn't T's only girl but thinking they were in a relationship. T shook her head. She thought about Ronnie. It was time to let this woman go before she turned crazy. T broke the connection once her cell phone began to ring. Her lips curved up into a joker's grin, "What's good baby?"

Jerking her head back the woman in front of T opened her mouth only to pause as T's hand flew in the air to silence her. Smiling at the female in front of her, T got into the car listening to Layla tell her what happened when she left her house. T slammed the car door and turned on her radio drowning out the obscenities yelled by the woman she left outside her car.

****

Twenty minutes later T sauntered through her doorway once again. Kim glanced back at her with her curiosity watching T take a seat at the table without speaking to her, phone glued to her ear.

"Who you talkin' to?"

A smile dashed across T's lips at Kim's question, "Layla."

"Oh. Hey Layla!"

Once again a smile crossed her lips before she relayed to Kim that Layla said what's up, "Yeah you do… she da only fem in my crew… yeah we got a condo together… all she like is femmes."

Kim laughed listening to her brother's part of the conversation. She leaned over the back end of the couch, "Yo Layla!" T put her on speakerphone. "A fem and a fem is a beautiful thing! If I wanted a stud I might as well get a nigga."

Layla laughed, "A'ight. I hear you."

19

On the counter was a pack of White Owl cigarillos, Kim motioned for T to give them to her. Turning back around, she picked up a magazine that was on the table and placed it in her lap. Fishing a bag of weed out from in between her breasts Kim began the process of rolling herself a blunt.

An hour later Kim had smoked that blunt and now sat on the sofa alternating between watching "Belly" and throwing T, who was oblivious to everything except Layla dirty looks. Kim stood up angrily, "Yo T, I'm 'bout to go lay down after I roll dis."

T nodded distractedly from her spot on the sofa as her friend went to the table to roll up. Flashing T another irritated look, which she didn't even catch, Kim marched down to the garage to smoke. Promptly after the garage door closed the radio cranked up, so loud T couldn't hear the TV. Clutching the phone to her ear, T reclined back and propped her feet up on the table.

Coming back in from the garage and walking up the steps forty-five minutes later Kim declared, "Damn y'all niggas still talkin'?" Glancing at her quickly T sent her a smile before focusing back on whatever Layla was saying. Walking behind her Kim mugged her in the back of the head before continuing towards her room, "Y'all conversation about to end T. You know how I am when I'm trying to go to sleep!"

Ignoring her sister, T questioned Layla on the phone dubiously, "You ain't never been with a female? Damn what you take me fa? A lame ass nigga. Shorty you ain't gotta lie to kick it. I been around the block more than a few times I know that line baby gurl. Very well."

Their conversation carried them to two in the morning at which point Kim barged into the living room with a satin kimono covering her body and a silk scarf wrapped around her head, "If you don't shut the fuck up!

I'm tryin' to fuckin' sleep and I keep hearin' yo' happy go lucky ass! Damn you already fucked give her a minute to miss yo' ol' sprung ass!"

Chuckling T retired to her room.

"Thank you," Kim whispered rolling her eyes and whipping around to go back to her own room to sleep. Less than ten minutes later Kim stormed into T's room, "T, if you don't shut da fuck up dammit! Yo Layla no disrespect, I ain't T's mama or gurl but she gotta get da fuck off da phone! I'm tryin' to sleep and I can't cuz I hear her giggling ass up here in giggling like a fuckin' school gurl and shit! Y'all gotta say bye!" Layla laughing along with T who had put her on speakerphone during Kim's rampage only infuriated Kim more, "I ain't fuckin' playin'! T say bye fa I break that shit and you know I'm good for it."

"Take yo' insomnia ass in da otha room and go to sleep. Shit toss and turn all night like the rest of da mafuckas that got dat shit," laughed T with the phone still cradled against her ear.

"T I swear to God I will cut yo' ass right 'bout now."

"Man go in da other room, take yo' fuckin' medication and shit, and quit getting dat bullshit ass weed from Quincy!"

With narrowed eyes Kim replied, "T I'ma fuckin' slit yo' throat you keep fuckin' wit' me."

She let out a chuckle then murmured to Layla, "Yo I'ma quit fuckin' with her cuz she off like a mafucka fa real yo. I'ma holla at you tomorrow a'ight?"

"A'ight."

"Bye."

"Bye."

T flashed the phone at Kim so she could see the home screen and know that Layla was no longer on the phone. Growling slightly with exasperation, Kim retreated

21

out of the room and T threw a pillow at her. Finally, in her own room Kim stripped off her robe, stretched and slipped into bed. However, as soon as she had gotten comfortable in the bed she heard T's phone go off blaring T. Paine's "In Love Wit a Stripper" ringtone.

Kim exhaled through her nose, "One mo' time," Kim said to herself. "If that shit go off one more time," lucky for Kim it didn't and she was able to drift into a light sleep, which was penetrated by sounds of T in the kitchen along with keypad tones from her cellphone.

She leaped out of her bed not bothering to grab her robe and ran in the kitchen, snatching T's phone, reading Layla's text message, then texting her back, "This Kim. You will talk to T tomorrow. I promise you she will be right here and woke when you call or text her. I'm keeping her phone for the night so don't call or text back until two in da afternoon tomorrow. If you do, I'ma slit her fuckin' throat, true story. Goodnight," Kim spoke out loud for T to hear then walked out of the kitchen and back to her room.

****

Snuggled deep into her bed under covers and pillows Kim stirred at the ringing of a cell phone blasted T.I.'s "What You Know" ringtone. It was ringing and vibrating on her dresser. She checked T's caller ID and fell back in the bed. "It's yo' gurlfriend," said Kim to T who had entered the room.

"Which one?"

"Yo' player card lost talkin' to her all that long. Both y'all sprung as fuck off new pussy and new dick. You put it down on her and she put it down on yo' ass too," Kim told her laughing as the phone rang again.

Shaking her head no T scooped the phone up and answered, "Yeah," she tossed a blunt to Kim. "That's why yo' dog ears having ass couldn't sleep last night. You ain't have no good weed to carry you all night."

Kim gave her the finger and lit the blunt. She nodded her head yes to T indicating that she had some good shit. Smiling, T closed Kim's door. Taking more than a few more hits off it till it was halfway gone she put it in her ashtray. Glancing at the clock on her dresser caused Kim to let out a whoop of laughter. It was two o'clock exactly in the afternoon.

"New pussy a muthafucka," she muttered before drifting off to sleep.

Chapter 2

"So, what you getting into today lil' mama?" called out T from Layla's cell phone which lay resting in the middle of her bed.

Opening and closing her legs while smiling at herself in the mirror, Layla rolled over and said into the phone, "Linkin' up with you hopefully. My peoples gone fa the weekend."

"Oh true. So, what you tryin' to get into?"

Bolting upright, phone in hand she retorted, "Shit what you trying to get into? I know what I wanna do."

"Oh yeah? What's that?"

"What you think?" Layla rolled her eyes.

T let out a belch of laughter, "Oh ok. You want me to come beat dat pussy up?

A look of innocence flashed across Layla's face before a smirk appeared, "Maybe."

Laughter flowed through the phone lines again, "Shit you betta speak up shorty. A closed mouth don't get fed and a dry pussy don't get fucked."

"Oh my shit far from dry."

"Don't I know it doe?"

"You should come through right now so I can refresh ya memory."

"Shit you ain't said nothing but some words. I'm on my way."

"Whatever don't be bullshittin'!"

"Bullshit who? Gurl, if I said I'm on da way to beat dat pussy out da frame then you betta be naked and waiting on a nigga when I get there."

Rolling her hazel eyes Layla replied, "You want me to get it going fa you too?"

"Shit I ain't one of a dem lil' boys you mess wit'. I needs no help in dat area. But shit, if you gon' do it. Gon' head right now. Be my motivation," added T with a laugh.

Stretching one of her legs above her head Layla admired herself in the mirror; she smiled. Slowly placing her leg flat back on the bed she opened her legs, a hand sliding down to her pussy and a smile creeping over her lips. A French tip nail grazed across her clit and sent a shiver through her body. Layla grinned then began to rub her finger meticulously against her clit. Letting out a few contented sighs, she groaned and asked T, "Daddy, why you making me tease myself?'

"Shit I be there in a lil' bit. Gon' head keep doing what you doin'."

Layla's fingers parted her southern lips once more then froze and cocked her head, listening intently, "Hold on. I think somebody at my door," bounding up and pulling on a terry cloth robe over her bare body the knocks sounded again. She took off down the steps towards her front door.

"Damn. Who dat? Da police bangin' at yo' door like dat?" inquired T hearing the knocks.

Shrugging her shoulders as if T could see Layla answered, "I don't know," she walked over to the door, standing on her tiptoes to check the peephole. "It's Sayvonne," replied Layla swinging the door open and beaming at her mahogany slightly pudgy friend. "Hey girl! What's up?"

"Shit checkin' up on yo' ass. What's up? Who you on da phone wit' that you can't answer da other line?" Sayvonne asked coming into her house.

Snickering Layla replied, "T. She about to slide through in a minute."

Eyes flying to her gelled hairline Sayvonne's head jerked back in surprise, "T who?"

"Put me on speaker phone," cajoled T resulting in Layla placing the phone on speaker and handing the phone to her best friend. "Yo Sayvonne what's good!"

"Oh. That T. What's up?" greeted Sayvonne then chancing a glance at Layla. "What's good wit' y'all?" Sayvonne questioned.

Smiling devilishly Layla didn't respond but turned on her heel and ran up the stairs to her room.

"T what's good wit' y'all?"

T snorted, "Ask ya gurl."

"I did. She act like a cat got her tongue," called Sayvonne up the stairs where Layla reemerged dressed casually in a pair of tights and a somewhat larger shirt.

"Nah cat ain't got her tongue. Cat had my tongue da otha night doe. Cat was wet as hell too."

Blushing and biting her lip Layla passed Sayvonne to take a seat on the couch close to her friend. Sayvonne looked at her, "So, y'all dating now?"

"I don't know. Layla, baby we dating?"

Sayvonne looked at Layla for a response.

"Baby gurl?" prompted T after a pregnant pause.

"Huh?" Layla said softly.

"What we doing, we dating? We cooling it? What would you call it?"

"Nah we ain't dating. We just kicking it. I gotta see where yo' head at."

Opening her mouth to reply Sayvonne closed it shut as T spoke, "You know where my head wanna be at, in between them legs. Shit I'm about five minutes away too."

With a grin she stated, "You need to hurry up 'cause that's where I need yo' head to be at too."

Reclining back against the couch Layla's friend Sayvonne let out a whoop, "Ooh I heard dat. Look at y'all. T you betta not hurt my friend."

"How I'ma hurt yo' friend?"

"By doing you."

"Nah see that ain't even what's good ma. I ain't in the business of hurting nobody. Shit, a happy bitch breed a happy dick."

"Oh ok," Sayvonne murmured reassured slightly. She turned to Layla and muttered something incomprehensible at which Layla shook her head no.

"Hold on y'all whisperin' now. Layla, baby that's rude."

"My bad boo."

"It's cool. You good. Check dig I'm about to grab these rellos from da store around da corner from ya house so I be there in a minute a'ight?"

"Cool," Layla muttered then shot to standing up, "Hold on. I see you when you get here. Somebody at my damn door again."

"Damn you got the spot huh?" her voice called out to Layla's retreating back.

Not bothering to look out the peephole Layla flung the door open and her mouth dropped. In front of her stood a tawny complexion stud who was average in height with Cleo, Queen Latifah's character in "Set It Off" braids. The nasty scowl on her face marred her pretty features but fit in with the hard demeanor she possessed. She swung a trash bag from over her white t-shirt to drop it at Layla's feet.

"Here go yo' shit bitch. I don't know why yo' dumb ass ain't come get yo' own shit-"

"Brandy, you ain't gon come to my fuckin' house talkin' to me crazy! Bitch bye you can leave," Layla interrupted her leaving the bag where it was, waving her off.

Taking a step closer to where Layla stood in the doorway with her arms folded across her chest, Brandy sneered at her, "Hoe don't act brand new. I only been gone a fuckin' year and half. And I ah beat yo' ass like it was the day before I got popped. I ain't on papers hoe and I know yo' scheming ass had somethin' to do wit' it. Shit just don't forget you owe me bitch. Yo' ass is mines whether you like it or not until I get what the fuck you owe me," Brandy took a step back. "Yeah let dat shit marinate. I be back hoe," ridiculed Brandy as she started to walk away towards the sports car sitting in the driveway.

Sending a swift kick to the bag at her feet simultaneously Layla bit out harshly, "Fuck you."

Within two strides, the distance between the two was covered. Brandy gripped her shoulder pulling Layla close and sending an open palm towards Layla's mouth. Layla dropped to the ground, clutching her face, curling up into a fetal position. Brandy began to send lewd kicks towards every part of her body.

Charging into Brandy and knocking her off her kilter Sayvonne yanked Layla to her feet, pushing her behind her into the house, "What the fuck Brandy? Leave her alone! Take yo' crazy ass back wherever da fuck you came from!"

"What?" Brandy glowered menacingly.

"You fuckin' heard me!" Sayvonne hollered as the passenger in Brandy's car started to run up attempting to maneuver Brandy back to the vehicle. "I should call da police on yo' bitch ass!"

Ripping out of the arms of the passenger woman restraining her Brandy stalked towards Sayvonne with her eyes trained on her like a predator about to move in on its prey.

Standing without wavering Sayvonne began removing her earrings and bracelets letting them clang to the ground, "Keep coming bitch I got something fa yo' ass. I ain't Layla hoe."

Her steps didn't falter; Brandy drew closer and closer to Sayvonne.

"Let me call da boys so I can send yo' stupid ass back to jail where fuckin' animals belong," Sayvonne said picking up Layla's cell phone off the ground where she had dropped it in effort to relieve her friend. Quickly keying in nine, one, one, her thumb hovered over the dial call button. "C'mon dummy keep coming. So, you can get back to yo' lil' cage, locked up, no cash, and no freedom. Bring yo' lil' dumb ass on stupid fuck,"

Advancing stealthily towards Sayvonne, she took advantage of Sayvonne being distracted momentarily by a black Monte Carlo blocking the driveway and tackled her to the ground. Without delay, Sayvonne began throwing and connecting with punches directed at her. Sayvonne threw knees into her body.

Brandy caught Sayvonne's fist with one hand and seized the other wrist that darted to her face. She maneuvered Sayvonne's wrists so she held them both with one hand then laid a smack down on Sayvonne's lip splitting it. Brandy cocked back to punch her then looked around wildly as she was dragged off her, arms bent in a full nelson position.

"Bruh dats a fuckin' female yo. Calm dat shit down cuz. Sayvonne what da fuck going on man? Who da fuck is this? Where Layla?" spewed T releasing Brandy and extending a hand to her to help her up.

Clutching T's wrist Brandy snarled out and pulled T on the ground with her trying to roll on top of her, "Her pussy ass in da house nigga. Won't you mind yo' own fuckin' business bitch," she managed to connect her fist with the side of T's face.

T shoved Brandy away from, quickly rolling to the side and getting back to her feet. She faced Brandy who was now also on her feet and approaching her in a boxing stance. Hiking her pants up T's fists came up as well. Trying to land haymakers Brandy swung wildly leaving T to play defense as she dipped and dodged the blows. Once an opening presented itself, T hooked a left to Brandy's face and a rabid straight shot that knocked her on her ass. Wiping the blood from her nose Brandy jumped to her feet barging towards T like a wild bull. T weaved a few of the punches, caught a couple that landed on her face then snatched Brandy's arms and head-butted her in the face and pushed her backwards. On the ground once again, Brandy stood dazed slightly. T's chest heaved thinking the fight was over. Brandy stumbled to her car, yanked the door open reached under the seat and whipped around to face T.

Breathing slowly in and out deep breaths, T's jaw muscle flexed viciously. Now with regained composure Brandy looked livid with slits for eyes, jaws clenched, lips curled and growling obscenities. Brandy smiled evilly at T. She wiped the blood off her face.

"Oh you scared now nigga, huh?" Brandy taunted T. "Oh super save a hoe ass nigga. You gon' take a bullet fa these bitches too."

"You ain't shit dawg. I ain't never been Captain save a hoe but you put yo' damn hands on me, you pull a muthafuckin' gun on me. Oh, nigga I don't take too kindly to dat shit. And either you pull dat muthafuckin' trigga or I'ma beat ya ass black and purple. What's up? I ain't scared of no punk ass gun and definitely not intimidated by the bitch behind it."

Brandy's jaws clamped down together, her finger slid across the trigger. She pulled the trigger back only to discover it had jammed. Tossing it to the side, she spit out blood from the blow T just placed on her jawbone. She turned to face T only to be greeted by a hail of punches that she couldn't dodge. On the ground once again, T climbed on top of her letting fists and forearms loose to Brandy's face.

The female companion that accompanied Brandy tried to come to her rescue but T yelled threateningly over her shoulder, "Bitch you betta back the fuck up."

The woman froze and Sayvonne darted out standing in front of T's line of eyesight if she looked up, "T stop! The police coming! Let her go its over!"

"Sayvonne," T struck Brandy again, "back," again she struck her, "up,"

Three police cruisers came screeching onto the scene. The officers jumped out immediately and tore T who was still raining blows on a limp Brandy.

"She just jumped on her! All my cousin came to do was return some a Layla's stuff and dat bitch just jumped on her!" Brandy's accomplice wailed lying through her teeth.

One of the officers went to talk to her. Another one started towards Sayvonne and the rest of the officers struggled with T trying to get her into one of the cruisers.

****

"So, you say that one over there," an officer spoke to Sayvonne, jabbing a peach finger in T's direction, "T, was on the phone with the gurl in the house, Layla, when Brandy," he looked up at Sayvonne see if he had the right name. He continued when she nodded, "came over. Brandy gave Layla her things and proceeded to let her have it. Some name-calling and insults were traded between the two, which led to Brandy hitting Layla. Layla dropped to the ground and Brandy began to kick her at which point you ran outside and dialed us. You broke them up, told Brandy to leave, you were calling the police, and Brandy attacked you. The two of you were fighting when T arrived. T pulled Brandy off you and Brandy started a fight with her. Eventually a gun was drawn by Brandy. The gun jammed when the trigger was pulled and that is when their fight started all over and T overpowered her," the officer finished reading Sayvonne's statement. "And you swear all of this is the truth?" he asked in a monotone from his position in front of the young woman.

"Well the truth is what happened ain't it," snapped Sayvonne.

The policeman took a step closer to Sayvonne, "Three things. The loud mouth one over there," he pointed at Brandy's female companion that had accompanied her to Layla's house, "Brandy's cousin, Cherelle says T was already here and jumped on Brandy as soon as she knocked on the door and the gun you mention is nowhere to be seen."

With narrowed eyes, she quickly surveyed the front lawn and street hoping to see the gun poking out from somewhere, "Search her car. That is her cousin after all so she would be the one to have that or get rid of that. "

Ignoring her request the officer went to his next point flipping through his notes to get the right name, "Layla, you say is in the house but no one has answered the front door after repeated knocks."

Jerking her head back Sayvonne uttered out, "What the fuck?" while spinning on her heel to go confront Layla.

He grabbed her arm in a firm grip and twisted her around, "I'm not done talkin' to you yet."

Whipping back around to face the officer of the law, she snatched her arm out of his grasp only to spit out, "Don't you ever put yo' damn hands on me again. What da fuck is wrong with you? What da hell you got to tell me makin' you grab me all crazy?"

A sneer crept over his face before he spoke very slowly, "As you saw the one had to be carted away from the scene in an ambulance. The other was tasered in order to be retained and all she is saying is that she wants her lawyer. Now you say there is one in the house who is the cause of this but she won't answer the door. And the woman over there blames it all on the one that got tasered. Now I don't know if you ladies know the seriousness of what's going on, but if something were to happen to the one in the hospital like say she died, this could become a very serious investigation. Right now, we're looking at assault and battery but if that situation were to occur it could go to manslaughter, murder, you understand ma'am? Now when you two or three that are here are ready to talk and tell the truth, here's my card," he gave Sayvonne the car and started to walk away.

Eyes wide and frozen with shock Sayvonne gave herself a mental shake. She ran to catch up with the officer, "Wait. I can prove what I've been saying is true with or without Layla's help."

Turning to the young lady in front of him with a raised eyebrow, he pulled out his notepad once more, "I'm listening."

She pointed to her own car in the driveway, "That green Taurus in the driveway is my car. Layla's car is in the shop and her parents are away for the weekend. The red sports car that's parked directly behind me is the car Brandy arrived in. And that black Monte Carlo blocking the driveway with the keys still in it, door open, car running is T's car."

Peering from his first set of notes from Sayvonne to what she just said and back to the cars arrangement he smiled.

"And check Brandy's record I'm sure its long. She just got out of jail. She used to beat my friend Layla. Layla is the only link to all this."

Smiling once more, he pierced her brown eyes, "Well ma'am. I appreciate your honesty. Now would you be willing to come down to the station to write a statement? There's a tow truck on the way to come and retrieve the Monte Carlo. So, after that it would be great if you could."

Sighing Sayvonne nodded, "Alright. I'll be down there."

****

"I don't understand you sometimes Layla. I love you to death you like my sister. But I don't understand," Sayvonne confessed the next morning as she sat on Layla's bed watching her pick out something to wear. "You was getting yo' ass beat, I jumped in, T jumped in, police get here and take T downtown, but you can't even write a statement telling what happened? I mean damn you wouldn't even open the door when the police knocked."

Layla glanced back at her from her position in front of the mirror, where she was applying bobby pins to her hair, "I ain't no snitch."

Shaking her head sadly Sayvonne replied, "You can be dumb sweet most of the time but other times you just a dumb, cold-hearted, snake ass bitch."

"Whatever Von. You know you love me."

"What goes around comes around Layla."

34

Rolling her hazel eyes Layla countered with, "Like my eyes. Look Von watch," she pointed to her eyes, rolling them slowly for her friend to watch.

Chuckling lightly at her friends antics Sayvonne asked, "Where you need me to take you anyway? It's early as hell."

"To visit T."

"How you know she can have visitors this soon? This was just yesterday she beat Brandy's ass fa you."

"Duh I called, I know. And shit I ain't think she would be able to so fast either but hey what you know, she can, so I'm in there."

"She in there 'cause of yo' ass. I hope you at least coming to court Monday too."

Whipping around angrily Layla spouted, "Von, I ain't tell her to fight Brandy. She could'a stayed her ass at Kim's house!"

Shaking her head once again Sayvonne murmured, "I ain't never realize how much you and Kenni was alike till just now."

Mentioning Kenni's name caused Layla's hand to drop limply to her side. Her features visibly softened up, tears threatened to fall out of the brim of her eyes. Glancing back at Sayvonne through the mirror she admitted sadly, "I miss her."

"I do too," agreed Sayvonne brushing tears off her face.

The two paused, silently remembering the good ol' days when they were a trio.

"So, did they find Brandy's gun?" questioned Layla breaking the sad moment they each were basking in.

"Hell nah. Her whatever that female that was with her had to get rid of that quick. They even looked in her car. I don't know what she did with it.

"Damn Von. You fuckin' up you was supposed to peep dat. We could'a got her ass back locked up fa a lil' while. I thought you was the smart one," joked Layla.

Standing, Sayvonne threw a stuffed animal at her best friend, "Shut up and c'mon so I can take you to see T," the girls started to walk out of the room. "And when you gettin' yo' damn car fixed?"

"Soon! You love me, you don't mind and I owe you one too."

"Whatever. Love you too."

The women were quiet during the car trip; the radio was on but not overly loud like Layla's thoughts. She squirmed in her seat wishing she was going to visit T at her house. Feelings from their first sexual encounter washed over Layla's body. All over again she felt T's lips parading around her body, her tongue catapulting over her skin, those fingers prodding around in her. Layla rolled the window down, closed her eyes and her yoni gave a twitch as she remembered the feeling T provoked within her as her strap thrusted in and out of her pussy. Eyes springing open as she felt her snatch began to moisten, Layla was surprised to see that they were already there.

"A'ight. Call me when you ready. I'm about to go around the corner," Sayvonne directed Layla as she exited the car.

"I got you."

Lines were short so it was only a momentarily wait until Layla sat at a table in a room full of inmates and visitors, watching T approach her with a growing sexual excitement. She calmed herself internally. This visit was not about sympathy or pleasure. It was time to get down to business.

"You a'ight?" inquired Layla.

"I'm cool," responded T. "Who was that?"

"Who was who?" repeated Layla looking around, eyes skipping over Brandy who sat with a visitor also.

Smiling, T jutted her chin in Brandy's direction and let her eyes drift over to Brandy, "A'ight so what you an owl now? Who dat nigga is to you that I beat up?"

Turning all the way around to face Brandy, their eyes connected. Layla twisted back around to face T, "Oh... umm... that's my ex."

A smile dashed across T's face before she let out a guffaw, "Yo' ex? Damn ma-"

Interrupting her Layla spoke, "Look T before you say anything else let's just leave it at this. This pussy comes with a price. I mean honestly, like I just wanted to fuck you. So, we did. We fucked. It was great but truth be told you can't do shit else fa me. You can't afford me T," Layla admitted standing.

Another smile graced T's face. She glanced around the room spying the security guard conversing with another inmate then leaned over the table. Before Layla could react T's lips were on hers bringing back the passionate lust that overwhelmed her when they first fucked. Away from her mouth T's lips moved and her tongue slipped out running across Layla's lips and careening down her neck. A pool of desire developed between the center of Layla's legs while T played with her ear.

"What," breathed T, pinching Layla's nipples through the white, cropped shirt that covered her chest, and sending her other hand beneath the tights Layla wore. Her fingers dipped between the moist lips of Layla's vagina, rubbing against her clit. Fondling her pleasure button until she let out a few moans and her pussy began to ache with longing and anticipation, T removed her hand, placing it in Layla's mouth, "Makes you think you would have been special enough to see my money?" T snatched her fingers out of Layla's mouth, stood; taking a few steps away from

Layla then pierced her eyes with her own. "And who told you I ain't just wanna fuck? But you right it was nice while it lasted. That one time," laughing T sauntered away walking through the door that separated the inmates from the civilian world leaving Layla sitting with a wet pussy that screamed for T's loving.

Chapter 3

The moodiness of it being a Monday morning was broken as Kim let out a whoop of laughter. She sat in her Chrysler Sebring along with T who after a couple hours of court was released. "She said you can't afford her?" she guffawed, "Hell nah! Do she know who you is? Do she know what you do?" Kim cried out in disbelief at what T had reiterated about Layla's visit. T grinned silently prompting Kim to ask, "So, what you tell her?"

If possible, the Kool Aid grin T was already wearing broadened at her sister's question, "Check dig. The security guards wasn't paying attention so I reach across the table. I kiss her, start pinching her nipples and shit, I slide my hand down to her pussy cuz she had these tights on and I start playing with her. Hell she was already wet but I got her ass moanin' and shit then I put my fingers in her mouth and while she was sucking on my fingers I asked her like, 'What makes you think you would have been special enough to see my money? And who told you I ain't just wanna fuck? But you right it was nice while it lasted. That one time.' Then I walked da fuck away from dat hoe."

Laughter ripped from Kim's stomach out of her body, she clutched the steering wheel as she drove with watery eyes, "Dismissed! Fuck she thought."

"Right. Me pay fa pussy? Nah I don't even get down like that shorty crazy. I ain't never and I damn sho ain't about to start. Not when I look this damn good, stacks on deck, complete with a mouthpiece and vicious ass stroke game. Shit pussy always free fa me," admiring herself in the mirror T glanced at Kim to see her shaking her head, a smile playing on her lips. Closing the visor, she peeked out of the window to see they were passing the cemetery where Ronnie was buried. "Yo drop me off at the cemetery. I'm about to go holla at Ronnie for a few minutes."

"T, I don't have time to wait. I got a meeting I gotta get back too. You know that."

"I know it's cool. Don't wait. I be a'ight sis."

"What about yo' car?"

"It's only a few blocks away. I can walk."

"A'ight," Kim turned into the cemetery following the long, winding road until she was at close spot near Ronnie's gravesite. "Don't get in no trouble," she told her stud brother, watching her exit the vehicle.

"Shit I hope I do."

Pulling off with a beep and wave Kim left leaving T waving back. T tread carefully around the sea of headstones. She paused standing in front of Kenni's headstone. "What's up lil' sis? Sorry I had to hurt ya lil' friend's feelings but hey, shorty had it coming. She tried to offend me, is you crazy? Baby gotta come better than that. Shit she was good doe. Too bad that was the first and last time," stepping up T gripped the tombstone. "I'ma holla at you though. You know I gotta go holla at my nigga tell her 'bout ya girl," she let out a chuckle and walked away.

Once T arrived at Ronnie's grave she dropped down to take a seat. Pulling a blunt from behind her ear, retrieving a lighter from her pocket, T sparked it. Exhaling T asked, "Bruh, did you see that shit man? I know yo' ass seen that. She told me I couldn't afford her bruh. I'ma have to stunt fa dis lil' gurl let her know I can wear my closet and not wear the same shit twice," chortling loudly until she began to cough, T regained herself smoking and thinking about her first time with Layla. "She was good doe. Shit damn good fa real. I could fuck her six ways from Sunday ya dig. And her pussy tasted damn good yo," licking her lips at the memory she finished her blunt off quietly. Laughter tore from T's insides interrupting the sereneness around her, "You see me beat her ex ass? I went in on her ass soon as that shit jammed. Bitch betta not ever think about pullin' pistol on me again," she fell into another pause thinking what if the gun hadn't jammed. Ever so slightly, T shook her dreaded head; she stood up and touched the headstone, "I'ma 'bout to get up through doe bruh. I gotta go pick up my car. My brother gave me that you know I can't have them auction that off. I holla at you later fam. I love you."

As T made her way away from her brother's grave, she pulled a cigarette out of her pocket. She walked along the curvy gravel path spying a woman kneeling in front of a headstone a little ways away. T smiled to herself thinking about picking her up. Thunder sounded bringing her attention up to the sky. She shoved her hands deep in her pockets forgetting about the woman she saw and began to move faster.

"Hey, you need a ride?" a feminine voice called out from behind T.

Grinning T turned around. Shock passed over her face as she stared at Layla's friend, Sayvonne, smiling from the inside of her Malibu, "What's good yo," greeted T stalking over to the vehicle. Coming to a stop on the passenger side of the car, she leaned against it so she could see Sayvonne through the open window. "I'm cool on the ride fam but real shit I appreciate what you did and whatnot. You ain't have to write a statement for me and you damn sure ain't have to show up to court. So, thank you."

Rolling her eyes Sayvonne declared, "And you know what T? You didn't have to stop. You was coming to get some pussy not get mixed up in that shit. A different person would've kept it moving," T shot her a smile and opened her mouth to reply but Sayvonne finished with, "Now get yo' ass in the car. It's about to rain. C'mon."

"Thanks yo but I'm just about to go to the lot and pick my car up. I be a'ight walkin'."

Tsking with pseudo annoyance she snapped out, "T, get in the car for I put you in the car."

With a shadow of a smile, T opened the door and slipped into the seat. She reclined the seat to her comfort level then turned to Sayvonne asking, "So, who was you visiting up the way?"

Her fingers tightened on the steering wheel before replying, "My mama."

"Damn. I'm sorry."

"It's cool."

A quick survey around the interior of the car yielded confusion for T. There was a car seat in the back also her cd collection was at her feet. She picked it up and flipped through it noting it ranged from nursery rhyme CDs to Disney channel to Ludacris, T.I., Lil Wayne, and Ciara. Puzzled because she had never saw Sayvonne with a child she inquired, "You got a kid?"

Furtively Sayvonne glanced at her quickly. Returning her eyes back to the road she answered slowly, "Why would you think that?"

Holding up the cd case and pointing to the car seat in the back T gave her a comforting smile.

Checking out where she pointed Sayvonne answered, "Nah those my sisters, brothers, and boyfriend cd's. Few of mine mixed in."

Comprehension began to dawn on T, "So, yo' moms died and now you taking care of yo' brother and sisters by yo' self?" she deduced.

"Yeah," Sayvonne admitted. She paused then added, "My boyfriend and all four of us stay together. Ms. B used to help me out and Layla's peoples do if things get tight or anything like that but yeah. My mom's been gone two years now. So, it's just us. When my mama first died, they tried to separate us. I fought tooth and nail against that. No way was we goin' be split up in foster care somewhere when I was old enough to take care of us. Me and my dude wasn't even dating that long but he's a lil' older than me and he just stepped up. Hell he was helping out before that but he took it to the next level when she passed."

Nodding T peered at Sayvonne in a new light. She glimpsed the worry lines lightly marring her forehead, noted the slight dark shadows beneath her eyes, saw the tiredness in her eyes. Her heart went out to her then she looked at Sayvonne again, she spied behind the tiredness in Sayvonne's dark brown eyes was a glint of determination, noticed her square shoulders, peeped the laugh lines close to her mouth and became aware of the calm, robust aura that she gave off. "I'm glad you got a good dude in yo' life and people you can lean on. But if you ever need anything don't hesitate to call me yo. You got a good heart and a good spirit that shit rare these days. And you real. You a strong, black woman I like that in you. Make sure you call with whatever you need regardless of what it is. Kim and all of us love kids. Chantel, Lil' Buddy, she got a son too," finished T writing down her number on a piece of paper and placing it in a cup holder.

Sayvonne glanced at the paper and unlocked the car doors. "Thanks T."

Sending her that famous smile that showed all of her white teeth T told her, "No problem. You looked out for me when you ain't have too. You part of my family now sis. So, don't be a stranger."

Left speechless all Sayvonne could do was watch T walk away from her car with a heart that swelled with admiration. Tears welled in her eyes as she sent a silent prayer of thanks up to God and her mother for the amount of love that has always surrounded her especially since she's been without her mother.

****

Happily settling into her 2002 Chevrolet Monte Carlo SS, T smiled as she went through her car checking compartments to make sure her belongings were still accounted for. Running her hand across the dashboard the memory of receiving the car from her uniformed military brother who was deployed the next day flashed across her mind. The smile drifted as she reflected that was the last time she saw her older brother alive. Shaking her head and cutting the radio on T put the car in gear and began to drive out of the lot.

Away from the police impound she still marveled over the last conversation with Layla. With a smirk, T decided that she had a new destination in mind. Driving along she picked up her phone and dialed her voice mail. Deleting a few messages from a few different women brought a smile back to T's face.

Another feminine voice filled the car causing T to park in front of a large storage unit facility so she could listen to the articulated words dipped with sensual seduction, "I've been busy, but I've also been trying to give you your space since your friend's death. However," she let out a low moan. Listening intently T heard the discreet sounds of something sliding in and out of a dripping vagina. "I've missed you T. This pussy," a few more moans sounded, "she missed you. Listen," that familiar sound flooded T's ears as she listened to this woman play with her cat for their enjoyment. Several moans came out, a slight scream accompanied with some choice cuss words followed up by a groan and heavy breathing. "See what you do to me. I came, but I need you to make me squirt Daddy," pausing to synchronize a hum with some moans she said, "This pussy wet and jumping for you baby. When you get some time," exhaling she finished, "Come make me squirt baby. I need you."

The click followed up by voice mail prompts started as T sat there staring at the phone. Finally, she just ended the call. Letting out a low whistle T pulled out a cigarette and sparked it. "Damn Yolanda boah if a nigga had a dick I'd be splittin' bricks," rubbing her chin T finished the conversation or better yet the game plan to herself, "So, I'ma switch this out right quick and then go bust Yolanda open. Yes sir."

Entering in her access code T whipped around the facility coming to a stop in front of a large storage unit. She parked her car and exited striding confidently up to one of the doors. Unlocking and lifting the door T took a step back to reveal the vehicle, a white chrome 2007 Cadillac CTS on twenty-two inch spinning rims complete with tinted windows. Immediately she hopped in, pulled out, and parked the Monte Carlo in the storage unit. Back in her Cadillac, T retrieved weed and a cigarillo from the armrest. Rolling her blunt, she called the woman named Yolanda who had left the message on her voice mail.

"Fuck," she uttered when her voice mail came on. Quickly T ended the call and sent a text message.

Back to square one T smoked, driving along aimlessly thinking about sex. Yolanda's message had turned T on but now she wasn't available. Shaking her head T went down a list of women but couldn't anybody just take Yolanda's spot when it came to sex. Doctor when it came to business but playtime turned her into a sex deprived feline. The words sex kitten wouldn't do her justice. She was a trisexual, a sexually liberated individual; sex was an art for her. Again, T went down a mental list of females she knew would drop the draws right now. None compared again so T sighed with discontent. Catching sight of the mall she decided to go and see what fine specimen of women were shopping today.

Walking through the parking lot up towards the mall she sent smiles to all the women she saw. Her gaze drifted over to discover a little boy running through the parking lot zipping behind cars. Craning her head around she looked for the careless parent who didn't have control of their child. Catching sight of a woman clutching her purse, chest heaving up and down as she covered the distance in heels, with eyes glued to the toddler brought a smile to T's face.

The boy darted across the lot in front of a car, which in turn, slammed on its brakes and let out loud horn. T scooped up the boy who tried to juke to her right, "Yo, what's up lil' man?" she sat him on the ground but still held onto him, "Look you see this car right here? You just ran right in front of it. You know what would have happened if it hit you? Or what if that car didn't hit you? What if I didn't pick you up?" T turned them around to face the car they were standing in front of, "This car would've hit you. And I guarantee you it will hurt. It won't feel like this," T laid him flat on the ground.

A hand smacked him across the back of the head as soon as T put him back on his feet and punctuated with, "And its gon' hurt harder than that too."

They both looked up at the assailant. Slowly a grin began to spread across T's face as she looked over the boy's mother up close. Light bronze skin tone, sensual full lips that dared her to kiss, mine gray eyes, definitely, a high C cup filled the upper portion of her off white cat suit, and her small waist was accentuated with an ass that peeked around at T from the front. Dropping her gaze down low T grinned; sure enough, she had some pretty ass feet to match the rest of her beautiful physique.

"Thank you and for giving him the lesson too," finally the woman spoke after allowing T to view her from head to toe. She reached to take her sons hand who pulled away and ran behind T's legs, shaking his head no.

"No problem my nephew just a lil' older than him I remember how it was."

She smiled exposing a set of teeth that Crest 3D white had to influence. Turning to her son she snapped, "Deahlo, I'm not playin' wit' you. Let's go."

He shook his head feverishly, "No. You hit me!"

Grinning T caught the woman's eyes again, "I'm Timothy."

A chuckle slipped out from the women, "Yo' mama really named you Timothy or is that one of those stud things where you change yo' real *feminine* name to something masculine?"

"Right hand to God. I'll show you my ID. Mama wanted two boys. She said it was a unisex name."

Wetting her lips with her tongue, batting her eyes she took in T's appearance as well: the slightly frizzy dreads indicating that she kept them well groomed, her eyes didn't produce a suspicion of contacts so naturally her eye color was green, the woman's eyes ran over her shirt, shorts, and shoes. No stains, no scuffmarks, no hint of deterioration of anything. Peeping at T's fingernails she noticed even they were taken care of. She extended her manicured hand, "My name is Kiaysha."

Not releasing Kiaysha's gray eyes from her own, T brought the delicate hand up to brush her lips lightly across it, "Pleasure to meet you Miss Kiaysha."

No reply was given but a smile beamed at T before Kiaysha began to unravel her son from behind T's legs. Holding his hand firmly in hers Kiaysha looked back up at T, "Well thanks again it was a pleasure meeting you."

Suddenly breathless T's mouth dropped open and as she began to speak, her cell phone began screaming for attention with the help of rap artist Ludacris and one of his many singles entitled Money Maker. "Hold on," finally, T breathed just now aware of her own hand grasping the small wrists of the female in front of her. She let go and pulled her phone out quickly, "What's up sis. . . Yeah I'm good... at the mall. . . But yo let me holla back at you. I think I just met my wife. . . Bye."

Kiaysha struck a pose with her hand on her hips, "Really? You think you just met yo' wife?" she laughed, "Smooth. Real smooth Timothy."

Cracking another smile T shrugged, "Call me T but hey I'm honest. Why couldn't you be?"

Her lips twisted up together and she looked to the left as if thinking before her stone colored eyes darted back to T, "Well for starters you don't know what I prefer. Am I a lesbian, bisexual, or straight?"

"Doesn't matter."

"Oh really why not?"

"You standing here talking to me still."

"Touché. And how do you know I don't have a boyfriend, gurlfriend, married?"

Chuckling slightly T responded the obvious first, "No ring. Boyfriend, gurlfriend I doubt we would of got this far in our conversation without you mentioning that fact."

"And how do you know I'm not a cheater? What if I flirt and allow others to flirt with me with no regard to my significant other?"

Again, Kiaysha provoked laughter from T, "Nah. You ain't the type. You carry yo' self differently. You don't give off that vibe," T winked at her. "We damn sure wouldn't be playin' twenty-one questions. I'd have the number already."

T's last comment compelled laughter and a smile to join in together on Kiaysha's end, "So, what kind of vibe do I give off? Or how do I carry myself?"

Sliding her tongue across her lips T peered at Kiaysha, "Like a mature woman who has everything together. Goals, life, etcetera, etcetera," her words brought a smile to Kiaysha's lips. "But right now as of this moment. I personally think you just playin' hard to get," T teased her.

Those smoky colored eyes twinkled, "So, let's keep the game going. I'll give you my number," she paused watching T focused solely on her. "When you see me again. If it's meant to be we will," and with that she tried to turn and stride away from T.

Easily T caught up with her. She grabbed her hand and twisted her around gently to face her. "That was easy. Found you."

Giggling Kiaysha said, "No, you gotta wait till I'm outta sight."

Beginning to feel slightly exasperated T looked down at the beautiful woman in her arms, "I thought we were playing hard to get, not hide and seek?" Kiaysha opened her mouth to reply but T finished with, "How about I give you my number and you call me when you ready?"

Nodding she agreed. "Deahlo," she warned in a low voice at her son who was looking around the parking lot. "You know this is my son right? Not a nephew, god son or none of that."

"I'll show you a result before I ever give you an excuse beautiful. I don't care if he is yo' son. I love kids. Wait till you meet my nephew."

"We're a package deal. If you want me, you want him and his well-being comes before mines."

"It better."

"And he's also a handful."

"Most kids are."

Sighing deeply Kiaysha retrieved her phone from her purse, "Ok." she handed T the phone.

"Five-two-one, oh-seven-seven-four is my house. Me and my sister Kim share a condo. Seven-eight-oh, forty-nine- eleven is my cell."

Kiaysha smiled at her, "Ok. I'll call when I'm *ready*."

Leaning in close to her face, T spoke in a low tone near her ear, "I'll be waiting for yo' call tonight."

Guffawing Kiaysha finally said, "Smooth and cocky. Not a good combination."

T shook her head adamantly causing her dreads to move side to side, "Not cocky. Confidence."

"Umm hmm. I can think of a few other things. Time will tell how ever. It was nice to meet you *Miss* Timothy," she winked at T then began to make her way through the parking lot with her sons hand clenched in hers.

"Damn," T mesmerized at the sight of Kiaysha's ass swaying back and forth.

****

Several hours later a voice stimulated the erogenous zone of her ear as it insinuated, "Ain't this store a lil' too much fa you T? I mean you do gotta eat and pay half the rent or do Kim pay it all?"

Straightening up from where she was bent over in an urban store in the mall checking out the watch selections offered T turned her head to put a face with the feminine voice that was taking jabs at her. Licking her lips, she took in the sight of Layla clothed in a tight pair of jeans and a t-shirt that hugged her breasts, which in turn made the shirt ride up slightly so her flat stomach was exposed. Catching sight of the hat to match her outfit brought a smile to T's face. "Ha! I see you got jokes shorty. A lil' FYI though baby gurl that's my condo. I own it. Kim stay wit' me. The only time you don't pay bills is if you lucky or at yo' mama's house."

Sending T a scathing look as a response only brought another smile to T's face and a bout of laughter before T turned around pointedly ignoring the young woman in front of her. Raising her nose slightly in the air Layla paused to take a glance at the expensive watches that T was ogling.

A sales associate made her way over to the pair that was trying to appear oblivious to one another, but even before she stepped in front of the tall stud, she felt the electricity of their pheromones communicating fluently with one another. Blocking Layla from view, she held out a box to T, "Here you go T. You should find everything as detailed. And if there's anything else I can do for you just let me know," the older woman rattled off gazing at T with a look that said she could have the pussy right now however she wanted it.

Grinning T took the box from the woman allowing her fingers to brush across the chocolate woman fingers as well, "Thanks Miss," she checked her name tag, "Rhonda. I

51

will keep that in mind and you will be the first I come to see if I need anything."

T's words brought forth a smile accentuated with gold teeth, "Anytime," she reminded turning to walk slowly away from T while switching the little ass that her mother gave her.

Tearing her eyes from the sight T glanced at Layla and scoffed. Ignoring the stirring feeling Layla was causing in her libido. She turned to walk out of the store. With her back turned to Layla, she began to count silently to herself.

Staring daggers at T's retreating back, Layla waited patiently. Just before she could make it out of the store Layla rolled her hazel eyes and called out, "That's how you feel T?"

A smile flashed across T's face. It vanished as quickly as it came. She turned around standing stock still waiting on Layla to approach her. When it became apparent that Layla was waiting on the same action from T, T raised an eyebrow then started to turn around and leave the store. She heard Layla expel harshly and turned around to see the woman almost in front of her.

"What's in the box?"

Looking between the box and Layla, T smiled, "Oh dis right here? Just a lil' somethin' somethin' a nigga picked up. You na mean?"

"Is it for me?" Layla questioned sweetly batting her eyelashes innocently.

T tilted her chin, bringing her face closer as if she was going to kiss her, "Do you want it to be?"

Butterflies fluttered in Layla's stomach and her fingers tingled as she gripped the box, "What is it?"

Gingerly T unwrapped Layla's hands from the box, "Something for a nigga that can't afford you. Remember?" she winked a green eye at Layla.

Pouting Layla looked up at T, "Bae, you know I was just playin'. I don't doubt yo' hustle. I never have. I admire yo' style too much but what's a lil' fun without a lil' cat and mouse. Don't tell me you all up in Xxclusive, sales associates know you and shit but you sensitive. I know you like a good game of a gurl playin' hard to get," by the time Layla finished her spiel she had effectively succeeded in turning T on with light brushes and touches in all the right places while also managing to maneuver the box back into her hands. She tore the top off the box throwing it back against T's chest who caught the lid. Gazing down in the box revealed a chain dripping in diamonds, threatening to blind Layla's beautiful hazel eyes. Blinking rapidly she noticed the chunky bracelet to match. Abruptly T placed the cover back over the box; however, the images were engraved upon Layla's eyes. Staring up at T still, all she saw was the chain and bracelet ensemble. "How much was that?"

Brushing her dark lips against Layla's cocoa cheek T murmured, "Enough for me still to have money left over."

Layla's heart skipped a beat. Subconsciously she registered moisture developing down in her lower region. Feeling her lips began to slicken, her clit awakened with a jump, throbbing, as her hazel eyes remained glued to T.

Peering down at Layla, T saw all of the emotions flit across her face, "I see you later shorty."

Disregarding her words Layla fell in line with T, "How long you gon' be up here?"

Glancing down at the young woman a mental video fast-forwarded quickly. Excitement flooded down her body as feelings from a sex session with Yolanda collided head on with the heated hunger of Layla's and her own first time together. Layla wasn't Yolanda but she was a damn sure fast second. In contrast, whereas Yolanda was a deliciously curvaceous midnight skinned woman, Layla was a deep cocoa brown slightly slimmer but nonetheless well-proportioned woman. With Yolanda anything goes, she always brought something new to try to the table and never seemed to run out of energy. On the other hand, T couldn't deny the insatiable hunger Layla and she shared during sex as well as seemingly right now. The air around them seemed to crackle with sexual yearning and tension. *Yup*, T thought to herself. *I most definitely will tap that ass again.* "I'm about to leave now. I got what I came for."

"Can you give me a ride back to my house?"

Heaving a big sigh T rolled her forest colored eyes, "I don't know. I mean, I do gotta get home since its Kim's condo and shit. And you know I prolly ain't got no key...."

Biting down on her bottom lip Layla stepped closer to T. She scraped her fingernails across T's forearm, inhaling sharply at the zing of electromagnetism that shot through her upon touching T, "I'm sorry Daddy. Please."

Feeling the same current as Layla, she swallowed hard, "Yeah I guess I can do dat," T paused to look at her phone which vibrated and was about to ring. She checked her text message, "Yeah. Come on. We gotta leave now cuz I gotta stop by the club on the way."

Jerking her head back Layla stared at T, "Ain't no club open yet. It ain't even seven yet."

Smiling T tucked a finger under her chin, "So, what that mean shorty? They always open for me anytime."

"Oh you that special?" dubiously Layla remarked complete with a roll of her hazel eyes and a transient smirk.

Licking her lips. T leaned in close pressed a quick soft kiss against Layla's lips before retreating and casually muttering in her ear, "I own that bitch, I'm hella special."

"You shittin' me?"

Winking, T answered with a lie, "Yeah. Just a lil' bit."

Rolling those aesthetic hazel eyes, Layla sent her a playful push, "Ooh, you play too much."

"Wait right here. I pull da car up," commanded T from in front of Layla as they walked out of the mall doors.

"Ok."

Layla stood full of jubilation and nerves. Pulling in air, she calmed herself and sent thanks up. Chewing on her bottom lip reminiscing about their first time having sex almost caused a tidal wave in her jeans. *Superb sex skills and got some money,* Layla theorized mentally. *Now that's what I'm talking about. I did not wanna have to let go of that.*

Narrowing her eyes Layla tried to peek past the tinted windows of a Cadillac that had pulled up and stopped in front of her. Once unsuccessful she began to check out the spinning rims of the vehicle quickly calculating they were twenty-two inches. Deterred with not being able to see the driver of the vehicle she glanced at her cell phone for the time and swept her eyes through the parking lot. The hedonist feeling she had while in the mall with T quickly faded to exasperation. She turned about to stride back up to mall when someone shouted her name.

"Layla!"

Spinning back around her eyes scanned all around her for the familiar black Monte Carlo or the smiling face framed with dreads.

"Layla!"

Peering warily at the Cadillac, she watched as the window slid down. Ducking her head slightly to see the person inside, her mouth twisted up in a pout. Layla stalked back to the car and stood in front of the door glaring haughtily at the driver, "Why you trick me?"

"You want a ride or not?" inquired T revving the engine.

Quickly opening the car door and sliding in to the seat Layla looked around the ostentatious interior of the vehicle. Everything was customized, "When you get a new car?"

"Do it matter?"

"Well what you do with yo' old car?"

"I still got it. My brother gave me that Monte Carlo for my birthday before he died in Iraq. It was originally his but he got deported and I needed a ride."

"Damn fa real? I'm sorry."

A muscle flexed in T's jaw and she snapped out sarcastically, "Nah. Fa fake."

Not wanting to totally abandon the arousal she was feeling, Layla held back a retort. She didn't utter a word but instead stroked T's brown face with her pedicured hand. Once T suppressed her clenched jaw, she reached over and placed soft kisses down her jawline. Failing to earn a glance from T so that she could see the heat in her eyes Layla continued. Removing her seat belt, she positioned herself so she could kiss along T's neck. Sliding her tongue back and forth across T's neck she made her way up to T's ear and sucked it into her mouth. A shudder ran through T when Layla swept her tongue lightly behind T's ear.

At the red light Layla grabbed T's face and turned it to her, "Lemme show you how sorry I am baby," she didn't wait for a reply but instead kissing the juicy lips T possessed on her face. She sucked her bottom lip into her mouth and bit down on it.

As the light turned green, the two remained kissing oblivious to the environment. When a car finally screeched to a halt and punctuated their sudden stop with a beep only then did T glance up to see the green light and turn away from the provocative woman sitting in her passenger seat. T took a deep breath. An idea fluttered through her mind for when the two of them reached the club. Thankfully, she

56

was strapped when she got arrested and strapped up upon her release intent on getting some pussy, quickly.

A tugging of one of her hands from the steering wheel brought T back to reality. She looked to the right to discover Layla naked from the waist down clasping her middle finger and grinding her pussy down on the tip. T's finger was immediately encased with the sweet aroma of Layla's pussy. She slid her finger inside of her, drawing out a few moans from Layla as her finger moved in her. Her thumb joined the fray with empathy kneading against Layla's clit.

Once again, at another red light T removed her fingers sucking the juices off them. Layla lifted her shirt grinding on the seat in her absence and squeezing her nipples. A quick check in her rear view mirror yielded no cars behind her and none zooming up on her. Hastily she unclasped her seat belt and buried her face between Layla's legs.

Precociously T's tongue caused a storm inside of Layla. She tried to bring T's face deeper into her vagina, she gasped at the feelings T's tongue-lashing bestowed upon her. Her fingers pulled T's dreads, the orb between her pussy lips pulsated viciously in need. Layla's temper flared when all of the great feelings dissipated leaving her with an ache deep in her cat. Her eyes popped open, the awareness of being confined in the car, and her hearing slowly came back at the urgency of yet again another driver leaning on their car horn.

"We pulling in now," commented T noticing the lust burning in Layla's eyes.

Heaving a small sigh Layla concentrated on the wetness of T's face. She found herself licking her elixir off T's face much to T's enjoyment.

The car came to a stop and T turned kissing her passionately. She broke away abruptly to open her car door, "Come on."

"Let's do it out here," dropping her pants T looked up when Layla opened her car door coming around towards her but continuing to speak saying, "No, not in the car. Everybody then fucked in the car and on the car. Let me ride you on top of the car."

Grinning wickedly T stepped out of her pants but kept her shoes on. She pulled Layla to her and spun her around so her ass cheek was being poked by her strap. Suddenly, she picked Layla up and sat her on the hood of the hot vehicle opening her legs and suckling her pussy from the back.

"Ooh shit," moaned Layla peeking behind her at T while her back dipped and arms extended so she could grip the open space of the hood near the windshield wipers.

Separating Layla's ass cheeks that were bouncing softly against her face T trailed her tongue from Layla's clit all the way back to her perineum, which she tickled. Brushing her tongue back and forth against the diamond shaped area; T crept back to her hole sticking her long tongue inside.

"Shit," gasped out Layla at the sensations when T had pulled her clit back into her mouth holding it firmly and flipping her tongue against it.

Layla started to crawl up the car with T not releasing her pearl moving with her. On all fours, Layla's body trembled down to her toes and her juices came stampeding out of her. Snatching her pussy from T's talented mouth, she straddled the stud beneath her. A delighted moan escaped as T's strap filled her. She hit the base of the strap and froze.

Pulling Layla's legs apart, T held on to them keeping them at an almost straight line while Layla bent forward as if stretching. Gulping at the overwhelming desire overriding her at the sight of Layla's fat ass dancing up and down, in and out on her strap T caved into the desire meeting that plump ass with a thrust of her hips. Unable to fight the contusions from the intensity of their intimacy anymore Layla screamed out simply launching her ass back propelled by an orgasm. Sitting straight up she reached out and grabbed onto her ankles while gyrating her pussy down onto the strap with T emulating in sync the motion.

"Fuck! Ooh shit! God! Damn dammit T shit!" screamed Layla falling forward, her body quivering with pleasure well received.

Releasing hold of Layla's legs, she slid underneath her, removing the strap from her insides generating a moan from Layla. "C'mon ma," T gestured towards her to get down.

Shaking her head Layla looked at her through sex-glazed eyes, "I will get down, but I'ma just sit in the car until you come back out."

Smirking T helped Layla down and back into the car. She glanced around the back of the club surveying their surroundings before she closed the door but not failing to catch Layla's eyes close. A chuckle erupted as she turned to walk up to the clubs back entrance.

Entering the club and strolling like she owned it, which she did, with a smile painted her face. Hearing her employees in the employee lounge, she started to walk in when a Latino mixed white stud walked out. "What's good Jay," T greeted one of her stud brothers.

"Shit chillin' my nigga ready fa tonight. What you cheesing fa?" laughed Jay, the light illuminating her slanted eyes.

Giggling T proclaimed, "Layla in the car," with a Kool Aid smile.

Jay stared blankly at her.

59

"Ronnie gurl her best friend with the fat ass."

"Oh damn!" Jay said with a closed fist in front of her mouth. It dropped suddenly and she looked at T solemnly, "Hold on. I thought Kim said you got locked up over that bitch. She fake tried to shit on you. Her lil' gold diggin' ass. Shit I give her twenty to dip," she added. On after thought she sung her version of artist Dream's song "Shawty a Ten," "I will tip you. I will tip you."

Guffawing T ran the story of Layla and her encounter back to her stud brother, "I ran into her at the mall. She caught sight of a nigga in Xxclusive start talkin' that good shit when the lil' bitch in the store brought me my chain and watch. Oh my damn bruh, I think she fell in love when I let her glimpse that shit. She damn near forced the pussy on me. Her ass in the car now, don't know *what* to do. I put that dope dick on her."

Bursting with laughter Jay reminded, "Don't forget to tip her."

"Sheit," T sent her a look that said nigga *yeah right*, "Brush twice day. When you wake up and when you go to sleep. For best results, also after meals."

The brothers shared a laugh at Layla's expense and started into the vast room complete with its own small bar, lounging sofa and tables.

"Shit but on the real though, fuck dat. She good just looking at what bread get spent on."

"That's what up."

T nodded what's up to her group of employees before questioning Jay, "Who called me?"

Jay thrust a cream-colored chin to one of her coworkers that was watching them, but playing speed at the same time.

"Ha-ha!" the woman shrilled. "Pay up bitch. I won."

Smiling T made the way towards her bartender who was playing a card game with one of the studs employed there, "Stacey, baby you takin' Sean money already?"

Stacey laughed, "Money don't make itself daddy," she responded biting her lip at T.

"It damn sho don't," winked T at the paper bag brown woman, and then clapped the stud sitting across from Stacey on the shoulder. "Cuz how many times she beat you?"

The stud laughed embarrassed, "Five at twenty a pop playing spades, fifty on dominoes, twenty fa two games a speed, and ten at black jack."

Chortling T replied, "Nigga you got a gambling problem and it ain't working out fa you." Laughing the stud got up so T could sit down and talk to Stacey, "What's good ma?"

Batting her long fake eyelashes at T, she smiled revealing a gap in the front of her teeth, "Nothing, missing you. Wondering if you was comin' through after hours. I got something to give you."

Her tongue slithered out across her lips as she leaned in closer to Stacey, "Oh really? Well-" T was interrupted by the ringing of her cell phone, Crime Mob demanding for someone to Rock Yo Hips. Squinting her eyes at the number displayed, T wondered who it was for a second then another grin appeared.

"Go head and get dat daddy."

Leaning back in the seat, T answered her phone with her sexiest voice and not even attempting to deepen her already deep baritone, "Hello,"

The caller purred, "Hello to you too."

"Now look at you meeting expectations."

"Excuse me; do you know who this is?"

Stopping short of rolling her eyes the truth spoke in T's thoughts, *only gave my number out once today and everybody else in the phone, pussy especially got different ring tones ma.* Out loud and moving away from Stacey she declared, "Hmm let me think about it. I'm hoping you are this woman I met today. Beautiful light skin, sparkling gray eyes, in a cat suit with her son running through the parking lot. But you know, she said she would call when *she* was ready,"

On the other end of the phone lips smacked together but still T heard the woman let out a laugh, "Oh, whatever Timothy. You can't blame a woman seeking out good conversation. It beats the usual ay yo ma, what it do shorty, lemme holla at you,"

Grinning like a kid with his hand in the cookie jar and no one around T replied, "See and you called me cocky. I'm just confident that I'm different than everyone else."

"Oh is that so?"

"Yes ma'am," before T could say anything else a box crashed to the floor with loud glass breaking sounds punctuated with a string of curse words directed at Sean from Stacey.

"Umm are you busy? I can call back."

"Actually, I'm at work right now. I run my own business, a nightclub. I wasn't busy but now that one of my employees just dropped a box a liquor and my bartender is cussing her out, things are starting to get interesting," joked T.

"Well I'll let you go. You can call me back on this number if it's not too late."

"It won't be. I promise. I'll talk to you later."

"Umm hmm. Bye."

"Bye."

Observing Sean cleaning the mess and another employee filling out an accident report T strolled back over to Stacey. She slid into her a seat.

"Another lil' freak you got bagged up, huh?"

Wetting her lips T answered with a wink, "You already know."

"Well if you got time for me tonight make sure you come see me. And if you don't just know," she leaned forward so their faces was inches from each other, "I got mad love fa you. And you know I got yo' back daddy."

"I know you do baby and it's very much appreciated."

"Stacey, let's go!" shouted Jay from somewhere outside the room.

"I'll try to come through later."

"OK," Stacey grinned exposing that gap in the middle of her front teeth again. She kissed T on the cheek before walking out of the room.

Remembering Layla asleep in the car T rose and followed Stacey out the door. She made her rounds to her employees thanking them for their hard work as well as checking out that their duties were completed. She slapped hands with her stud brother Jay one last time and told her to call if she needed her.

****

"Wake up lil' mama," T nudged Layla whose eyes opened groggily blinking like an owl.

"Damn. Where we at?" she inquired with a voice thick with sleep.

Chuckling T laughed, "You at ya house shorty."

"Oh."

Peeping at her with laughter shining in her eyes T asked, "You gon' go in?"

She twisted around to face T and T had to check the loving gesture that almost occurred as she gazed at the beautiful young woman in front of her. She looked so

63

delicate and precious as an aura of sleep still surrounded her. T could only imagine how alluring she must be first thing in the morning after a night of sex. Biting her lip, she tuned in to hear Layla mumble.

"What you 'bout to do?"

"Hit the club."

"We just left the club."

"I know. I still got business to attend too."

"What about after the club?"

Shrugging she responded, "I don't know. Why what's up shorty?"

"I need you again."

The admitted femininity of her words caused a stirring in T's nether regions. She licked her lips with a rapid mind trying to figure out how to juggle Stacey and Layla tonight. "You need me?"

Leaning forward planting a soft inviting kiss on her lips, Layla murmured, "Yes daddy."

"Yo' folks home?"

"Yeah."

"A'ight. I tell you what. You can hit the club with me tonight. Go in the house, get dressed I swing back through and scoop you up but I gotta go get dressed too and shit."

Happy as a cat with a ball of yarn Layla grinned, "Ok baby. Don't have me waiting too long."

"I got you ma."

As Layla moved to get out of the car T cell phone began blaring from her cup holder. She silenced it but stared at the number with excitement brewing along with something else. T kissed Layla good-bye thinking of the woman, Yolanda who was calling her now. Watching Layla walk up the drive and enter her house, she knew she wasn't going to make it back to her tonight not with Yolanda calling right now.

Pulling off the curb she answered the phone as it rang for the third time, "What's up baby."

"What are you doing?"

"Driving."

"What will you be doing within the next twenty minutes?"

"You."

Yolanda laughed then in a more hushed tone she said, "Damn baby. You gon' start her back up again. Come to the north entrance of the hospital. I'm taking an hour and half break in twenty minutes."

"I'll be waiting with nothing on but my strap."

She chuckled sheepishly again before whispering, "Don't forget the handcuffs."

"I won't."

"Ok. I'll see you in a little bit. I need to check up on my patients once more."

"A'ight. Bye."

"Bye."

Chapter 4

Fresh out of the shower T sprayed cologne on as the finishing touches to complete her night fit. Before she could emerge from her bedroom, the door opened and in walked her sister Kim. She turned to face her accepting the blunt that was extended to her.

"Who you about to go see? I know you ain't get fresh for Layla?" questioned Kim.

A sneaky chuckle came out before she replied, "Nah but she gon' be salty when I don't show up though. Oh well."

"Then who you going to see?"

"Yolanda. I may swing by the club later doe and kick it wit' Stacey for a lil' while."

Shaking her head with amusement Kim said, "The freaky doctor right? Or should I say head doctor? You been a whore for so long I don't even know how she surprise you brah."

"Hey, you was once part of the club before you met Cream."

"Me and Cream ain't together."

"Might as well be."

"Whatever."

"I ain't retiring my card no time soon. I'm a proud whore," cajoled T. "Shit and I'm damn good at it."

"Don't I know it doe? New pussy the best pussy."

"You damn right sis," she handed Kim the blunt. "I gotta make moves sis. Pussy waiting! I gotta bust this bitch down at the hospital."

Kim chuckled, "Doc got a fat ass you should put ya finger in it one time for me."

In the living room now T glanced back at her, "You nasty but you know I got you doe," she walked out the front door.

Pulling out into her driveway T saw the time it was a little after ten. Her words from a previous conversation floated through her mind and she pulled out her cell phone calling Kiaysha back on the number she had called her from. Glancing at the time again, she hoped it wasn't too late. She couldn't wait to get in between Kiaysha's legs.

"I hope it isn't too late to call beautiful," spoke T as soon as Kiaysha answered the phone.

"No, you're fine. I just got Deahlo into the tub actually."

"Good 'cause I'm needed at the club tonight so I'll be working late but I wanted to call and hear your voice before it got too late and the night was over."

T heard the smile before she heard Kiaysha's response, "You're quite a smooth talker T."

Grinning at the fact that she had gotten Kiaysha to call her T instead of her government name Timothy she retorted, "Nah smooth is what skin should be. Me, I'm just honest speak straight from the heart."

"Oh really? Well your honesty makes a woman smile."

"Then you need to be talking to me more so I can make you smile all the time."

A bout of giggles reverberated in her ear, "Okay smooth operator!"

Grinning T licked her lips before replying, "Okay I see you got jokes, Miss Beautiful. So, tell me why are you single? Where yo' baby daddy?"

"Honestly, I just packed up and moved here from Texas. My mother and grandmother passed. Deahlo's daddy used to beat me so I left. What about you? Why don't you have a lady at your side?"

"Because we just met and I don't wanna rush you. Don't even worry about it though baby you mines already."

"Oh is that so?"

"You damn right."

"Whatever. What's the most important thing to you? And do not say me!"

Chuckling she responded, "Family. My group of friends none of us related by blood but blood couldn't making us no thicker ya dig? They are my family. My mama, Ma Dukes shit she they mama too."

"Okay mines is security. Whether it be job or a relationship. I need to be secure at where I am and what I am doing. No doubts or confusion."

"What do you do?"

"I work for the government. What inspired you to open a club?"

"My brother. We was like twins growing up only he had a few years on me. When I was in high school, he joined the service but every time he came home, he always made time to kick it with my niggas and me. They was all in the streets back then and going through things I ain't know nothing about. Ma Dukes was taking them in left and right. We was partying almost all the damn time 'cause a couple of them was hustling and still in school. One day he

68

told us, all of us like I'm not spending no more of this military money. I want y'all to do something with it and stay out these streets before y'all get killed. He told us to open a club. Made them promise they would leave them streets alone and made me promise to look out for them."

"Aww that's sweet! I know he's proud of y'all then."

"I hope so. He passed a year later during the war in Iraq."

"Oh, I'm so sorry."

"It's cool. Let's lighten the mood up some though," commented T as she pulled up to the north entrance of the hospital. "Tell me what's your zodiac sign, favorite color, favorite food, and favorite position."

"Ha favorite position? I guess you want that answer first huh?"

"Hey, I just threw that in with the rest you answer when you want too."

"Okay how about I don't answer it maybe one day if you lucky though I'll show you. Scorpio, green, and Italian."

"Okay that says about you freaky, you like money and you have a gift of gab," laughed T.

"I see you got the jokes now and no not freaky. Scorpio means I could be and if you got the chance to find out I'd be the best, duh. Green because I love how it compliments my skin tone. And Italian because.... I may have the gift of gab."

"See now look I was right," she looked up and spied Yolanda coming out of the hospital. Yolanda paused at the car door seeing T on the phone. "Well I'ma Pisces,"

"Oh so you like to have sex? Sex is a cure all for you?"

"Aye that's just what the internet said. I'm not responsible for the lies or for the truth of works not written by me. Guess you would have to just find that out huh?"

she watched Yolanda take a seat on a bench facing her while opening and closing her legs seductively.

"Whatever."

"My favorite color is purple because it means royalty. Surprisingly my favorite food is Italian too. Matter of fact you should let me take you out for lunch tomorrow. I know an Italian place downtown you will love."

"What's it called?"

"Cibo Di Venezia."

"Ok I can you meet there by eleven thirty."

"Alright. I'll be there by eleven fifteen."

"I bet you will."

"For you, I would be there waiting all damn day if I had too."

"Oh whatever!"

"Seriously. But I will have to talk to you tomorrow gorgeous. It's about that time now. I gotta get this paperwork done and make sure everything running effectively."

"Ok T. I'll see you tomorrow."

"Alright beautiful goodnight."

"Goodnight."

Hanging up the phone and waiting for the phone to lock itself ensuring that both lines were disconnected T slid the passenger window down gazing at Yolanda. She stared out at her succulent lips watching them part and mouth the word park. Without further ado, T whipped her car around until she found a parking spot.

"Follow me," Yolanda ordered with a finger accompanying her words.

As T followed the dark skinned woman, she reveled in her height and thickness. They were about the same height with Yolanda a half inch taller than 5'10. Even clothed in the slightly baggy doctor wear one could note the curves of her body, notice the protrusion her ass caused in her pants as well as the breasts trying to break free of the restrictive cloth.

Abruptly, Yolanda swiped a badge across the wall security and disappeared behind a door. Opening the door to slide in behind the woman T discovered they had reached a stairwell. Her white coat was draped over the rail and Yolanda was naked in front of a grinning T. Quickly T whipped the handcuffs off her belt loops. Yolanda positioned her arms above her head standing on her toes slightly as she reached for the next highest rail.

"Cuff me Daddy," she instructed erotically gazing at the stud in front of her.

Stepping forward to place the handcuffs around her wrists T felt her own orb began to pulsate between her feminine features under her harness. Catching sight of the flame of voyeurism evident in T's eyes brought Yolanda's tongue out of her mouth to glide up the side of her lover's throat and envelope her ear. A leg rose and rubbed against T before hooking itself around her.

Their lips crashed against one another, tongues fondled, pelvis's gyrated against one another, a hand slid between Yolanda's dripping pussy lips. T brushed against her clit with her finger and put it in her mouth to taste. She dropped her hand back down slowly caressing the dark nipples, twisting and pulling them, gripping that motherland ass, lightly careening her hand across those thunder thighs, parting the lush labia lips, sneaking across the pearl in the middle and diving inside the walls of her pussy.

Releasing pleasurably moans Yolanda lifted one leg straight up in the air so her foot was near her hands and pushed her groin out to meet the thrusts caused by T's hand. Licking her lips at the sight of her bronze fingers disappearing in the depths of her pink she watched with captivation only suddenly withdrawing her fingers to place in Yolanda's mouth and fall to her knees.

Two thumbs on opposite sides quickly migrated from the bottom of Yolanda's pussy to dipping inside of her separating the moist pair of lips to expose a hardened clit. Immediately T's lips devoured the gem sucking it into her mouth and flicking her tongue across it. Upon release, her thumbs continued the play massaging her from their own independent sides as her tongue escaped downward sliding into the leaky vagina tunnel tickling the g spot fleeing and coming back to do it again. One thumb stopped the ongoing fray following the route taken by the tongue, fingers eased inside of Yolanda's pussy once again; the other thumb stayed going strong stimulating her clit, and T's tongue tantalizing the piece of skin next to her asshole. A tidal wave of juices squirted out from her pussy and a string of curse words flew from her mouth, begging commenced.

Obliging with the request T dropped her pants after rolling on a Trojan man. Guiding herself in until she completely saturated the pussy she froze. Smearing a kiss to Yolanda's lip, she reared back and took flight, harassing her pussy with her strap. A door opened and closed from somewhere above amidst the vocal gratification T drew out from Yolanda. Thick legs enveloped T's waist, a warm mouth toyed with her earlobe until she shuddered deliberately thrashing inside of her.

Unbinding her legs from around T, she placed one foot on her shoulder, the other closely following up as she felt the surge of an orgasm coming. Aware of the pressure mounting inside of Yolanda, T ran her tongue over the bottom of one of her feet capturing her toes and suckling on them, a lone finger inserted itself in to Yolanda's ass.

"OH FUCK. . . SHIT!" she exclaimed. "I'M CUMMING. . . GOD DAMMIT I MISSED THIS DICK!"

Biting down on her lips T watched the orgasmic faces dart across Yolanda's sweat filled face before she felt her body go limp. She removed her strap from inside of Yolanda and stepped back. She unlocked the handcuffs, catching Yolanda who fell forward.

"Damn. How am I going to go to work after this?" mumbled Yolanda. "Once again T you have definitely wore me out."

"Hey, I aim to please."

Dressing quickly Yolanda took the used condom from T and dropped it inside of a zip lock bag that was in the front pocket of white lab coat, "And you do it so damn well," she checked the watch on her arm. "Shit. I have a surgery to get too," she pressed a kiss to T's lips and twisted her nipples then turned away from her retreating and leaving behind the words, "Next time I wanna play with you. So, be ready."

T watched her disappear out of the doors. She exhaled erotically satiated for the moment. Walking down two flights of stairs the stud exited the hospital. When she finally slid in her car and sparked the blunt in her ashtray, she sat there for a minute. Looking over the missed calls and text messages brought a smile to her face that her sex game was missed but tonight she thought, no worries fuck 'em she was going home and getting in the bed.

****

Licking her lips Kiaysha smiled across the table at T, "This has been a great lunch date T. Thank you so much for treating me."

Matching her smile with an ear-to-ear grin T responded, "No problem. I'm just glad you took me up on the offer."

"Well I was going to decline but then you brought me flowers and pulled out my chair," she winked at the stud across from her.

"Oh were you now?" laughed T. "So, you came all the way here to decline my lunch date to my face only to experience chivalry and decide to stay?" she bit her lip assuming a sad expression. "I feel so used."

Letting out a soft giggle, she remarked playfully, "In my defense I thought chivalry was dead!"

"Or maybe you just been talking to the wrong cats."

"Maybe," Kiaysha shrugged slightly and took a sip of the white wine on the otherwise empty table, "But on another note, I really love this place. It's amazing."

"I told you. I knew a five star Italian place."

Drinking in the style and layout of the restaurant Kiaysha nodded, "You did. I guess I'll have to give you extra points for that."

"Oh damn I'm getting points. What's the score to beat?"

A sly smile crept across her wet lips as she dismissed the question playfully, "Oh don't even worry about it. You'll know when your score is high enough."

"Is that so?" asked T unable to wipe the smile from off of her face.

"Why yes it is," Kiaysha winked at her.

"So, what was the last high score?"

"Umm...." Kiaysha dabbed her pink tongue out to moisten her lips as she pretended to think, "How about you tell me something about you that isn't necessarily so good? And I will think about telling you the answer to your question."

"Aww think about it though? Okay. I will take that. Every woman, every person may not be a fan of it but I do happen to smoke."

"Wow. I didn't expect you to say that."

"What you expected me to say?"

Kiaysha leaned back in her seat and put her arm around her chair. She lifted her chin as if to say what's up and gave T the Stevie J rat face, emulating his voice she said, "I don't have nothing. Everything about me is good girl."

The two burst out laughing together.

T shook her dreaded head in amusement at the "Love and Hip Hop" TV series reference, "Damn and hit me with the Stevie J face though. What you take me for mama?"

"Whatever. You know the game."

"Nah I don't beautiful. I keep telling you I'm not the average cat you would find yourself engaged in a conversation, light dating situation with," beaming at her T responded.

"Whatever Timothy! But see, if you would have told me what I expected, then I could've told you all the good qualities I've seen you possess that I like."

"What's stopping you now?"

"Nah. You feeling self already Stebbie," she let out a chuckle again. "How about you tell me what you smoke. Tobacco and or that green stuff too?"

One of T's eyebrows quirked in frolic as she answered, "See I can't tell you all that without knowing are you a lady officer of the law."

A snicker escaped from Kiaysha, "Why?"

"Because if you are, I may need to embellish a lot so you can arrest me. And I got weapons of mass destruction so feel free to search me."

A full-blown out laugh ripped from Kiaysha this time, "Well no in that case I'm not an officer."

"Well the offer still stands. We can get you a uniform and some cuffs and get it popping."

"Whatever! Answer the question," she demanded with a smile.

"I smoke weed and tobacco. That's it. Does that bother you?"

Shaking her head no Kiaysha admitted, "Nah. I used to smoke."

"Why you quit?"

"Multiple reasons. Job, kid. And it never really did anything for me. It was more so out of habit an escape away from the bullshit and abuse I was receiving. But to each his own."

"I can dig it. Your turn beautiful. What's something about you that isn't necessarily good?"

"Umm," she pretended to think about it staring up into space. Her eyes refocused on T with a playful smirk, "I can cook."

A blank stare washed away T's smile and she snapped out at Kiaysha's jest, "That's a definite plus!"

Vehemently shaking her head Kiaysha declared, "No, it's not 'cause I love to cook but I never get too. When I do food is always wasted."

"Maybe you just need someone else to cook for then."

Eyes twinkling Kiaysha beamed at her, "You think so?"

"I know so."

Grinning coyly Kiaysha broke their eye connection looking down at her phone. It was time to head back to work, "It's about that time for me to get back to work."

Immediately T stood. She pulled a hundred dollar bill out of her pocket and placed it on the table before taking Kiaysha's jacket and holding it open for her. Kiaysha smiled bashfully and slid her slender toned arms into the sleeves of the jacket with a slight blush creeping over her face.

"Thank you."

"No problem," softly T said into her ear.

"Do you need change back sir?" the waiter asked collecting the book.

"No, sir. The change is yours. Thank you for the great service."

"Thank you sir. You two enjoy the rest of the day and come back to see us soon."

"Thank you. We will."

The pair walked out together with T making sure to open every door for her. Once outside T snaked her hand around Kiaysha's petite hand grasping securely. Together they strolled towards the direction of Kiaysha's car.

"So, you're making dinner for us, was it Friday or Saturday?" innocently T asked.

"Who said I was making you dinner?" jostled Kiaysha.

"Either day is fine with me."

Playfully Kiaysha rolled her eyes and leaned into T, "Hmm I don't know. It depends on what you want. I have to go shopping."

"It depends on what I want?" questioned T with mock incredulously. "Are you on the menu because you won't have to shop for that?"

Stopping short of rolling her eyes but letting the grin expand across her face. Kiaysha fluttered her eyelashes, "No, I'm not on the menu Timothy. Try again," she came to a stop in front of her white Nissan Altima Sedan and leaned against the driver's side door.

Shrugging T told her, "I'm not picky. Make me your favorite dish."

"Chicken Ramen noodles?"

Smirking and boring her green eyes into Kiaysha's T replied, "If that's what you want me to eat. I'll eat it all up

77

and lick it clean," she finished licking her lips and staring seductively down at the woman before her.

The ends of Kiaysha's lips tugged begging to be released into a smirk of her own. Instead, she replied, "Friday. Eight o'clock."

T took her keys from her and unlocked the car doors. She opened the car door then placed a kiss on Kiaysha's cheek, "I'll be there. Text me your address."

"I will," she slid into her car sending T one last smile, "Thanks for lunch T," she placed her flowers on the passenger seat.

"No problem beautiful. Drive safe."

"I will. You too."

Closing the door T couldn't contain the smile if she wanted too. She was grinning like a whore that just walked into a whorehouse and anticipating Friday night like an inmate anticipates his release. She watched Kiaysha pull off until she couldn't see the vehicle anymore.

****

"Oh my God Von I think I'm in love!" blurted out Layla taking a seat on her bed staring at her best friend.

Sayvonne's brown eyes whirled with no interest and she continued to flip through the magazine in her hands, "With what besides money?"

Shooting up from her seated position Layla snatched a stuff animal from her closet and threw it at her, "T duh!"

Placing the magazine to the side one of Sayvonne's eyebrows raised and she met her best friend's eyes, "Now correct me if I'm wrong but didn't you just try to shit on her when you went to go see her in jail?"

Smacking her lips together, Layla rolled her hazel eyes, "Try? Umm I did. But that's beside the point. I seen

78

her at the mall the other day cashing out in Xxclusive Balla'z so you know I had to reel her back in."

"And?"

"And I put this good pussy on her. Had her eating me out on top of the hood," she smiled at the memory and her lips below moistened feeling the tenderness of T's lips.

"Wow! TMI thanks Layla."

"You should try it. The hood of the car what's up. Like seriously though oh my God. Her dick, her tongue! Oh my God!"

Staring sat at her best friend with a bemused expression Sayvonne went along with the conversation, "And you think you're in love?"

"Yes! I can't stop thinking about her. She got everything I need. She got the sex game on lock, appearance shit she always look flawless, and she look like money so I know she got enough cash to take care of me. You know I gotta have good ol' sam in a partner."

"S.A.M or sam? And what or who the fuck is a sam?"

Smacking her lips and rotating her eyes Layla replied, "Sex, appearance and money. S.A.M. I need those in a partner to qualify. You better bring something to the table."

"Okay whatever. So, you think you're in love with T? And how you think she feel about you?"

An offended look flew Sayvonne's way from Layla's face. She finished applying her makeup and confidently declared, "After you taste this pussy I'm the best and only pussy that matter out of the bunch," Layla went and retrieved a hat to match her outfit saying, "She feeling me though. I know it. You should have saw how she looked at me when she dropped me off. It was all soft, lovey, and tender like."

Smiling in bemusement Sayvonne shook her head, "So, why don't y'all sit down and discuss y'all like grown folks?"

Smacking her lips together Layla stood up, "I don't know. I may have to just do what I do 'cause she was supposed to come back through that night so we could step out to the club and never came," she looked at herself in the mirror. "I did go back to sleep though. Maybe I should let that one go let her slide this time 'cause she meet my S.A.M. requirements. She def still will owe me a night at the club though."

"Alright anyways! Sorry to out yo' whole lil' thought process going on but we are about to leave for a reason remember? I know you helping me shop now for his birthday but I need another HUGE favor."

"What is it?"

"One day and night. Keep the kids. You can stay at my house. We'll get a hotel room. I will make sure you have everything you need. Just give us a break from them for one night for Tre's birthday."

"What night?"

"Saturday."

"Aww Von!" she pouted looking at her friend she rolled her eyes. "Yay! Saturday night date featuring me and the kids!"

"Yes! Thank you girl. I appreciate it so much," Sayvonne pulled Layla into a hug from behind.

"You welcome. You lucky I love you."

"Whatever. Are you finally ready?"

"Yes, I'm ready mama. Dang! Come on lets go shop for your future husband."

"Hopefully."

"Uh definitely."

"Whatever."

****

"You ain't fuckin' with us tonight?" questioned Kim as she barged into T's room to discover her in her briefs and a beater staring at her open closet while smoking a blunt.

"Nah not tonight sis. I gotta date," she puffed on the blunt a few more times then held it out for Kim.

Taking the blunt from her hands Kim took a seat on the king size bed, "A date with who? You left work early the other day for a lunch date. This the same chick?"

Sheepishly T grinned, "Yeah buddy."

Handing the blunt back to her stud brother Kim reached across the bed and turned T's face to her. She held her face by her chin and inspected her nostrils closely, "Is yo' nose open bruh? Two dates, the fam ain't met her, have you hit yet?"

Swiping Kim's hand off her face T adjusted her strap in her draws. "Me and nose open don't even belong in the same sentence sis," she bounded up grabbing a pair of dark colored jeans, "You should know better than that but yo what you think?" she put a shirt on the bed over the jeans.

Glancing back and forth between her closet and the fit laid out on the bed Kim stood, "Do you really wanna wear those jeans? Cuz if so," she went into the closet and grabbed a different top draping it over the jeans. "That shit hot."

Grinning T passed the blunt back to her sister and began to get dressed with the top she laid out, "Smell that," she pushed her wrist to Kim's nostrils.

Kim inhaled the scent deeply, "If you ain't hit yet let her get a good whiff of that shit."

Cheesing like a kid in the candy store she went into her nightstand and grabbed the two blunts she already had rolled. She tucked them both behind her ears, "Yo you keep that shit sis. I'm outta here. I might swing through later if it ain't too late. If I text you tell Stacey to hang back she been waitin' for a nigga to come bust her ass down."

Laughing Kim nodded, "I got you bruh. Be safe and have a fucking... have a fucking."

Letting her belt sit in her belt loops unfastened, T stared at Kim's slanted eyes with amusement, "I know you ain't high yet. Nigga you mean have a ball?" she picked up a sack off her bed and slid it in her pocket.

Snickering Kim replied, "Hell nah. I mean have a fucking nigga. Have her fucking," she giggled, "And have a pussy. In ya mouth, hands somewhere."

Shaking her head T stepped around her feminine sister, "Whatever drunk ass. I see you later fam. Tell everybody I said what's good and don't forget Ma Dukes barbecuing tomorrow."

"I got you."

She walked out the door to her car and once settled in she took out her phone. T laughed to herself as she read a text message from Layla. Quickly she typed for her to call now.

"What's good lil' mama," she greeted Layla speeding off into the night.

"Hey Daddy."

"What you into this fine Friday night?"

"Nothing. Trying to find something to do. How about you?" questioned Layla.

Not tonight baby girl, mused T to herself. "Outside the club waiting on everybody to get here so we can have a meeting."

"You work there?"

"You could say that."

"You own it?"

"You could say that as well."

"Whatever T."

"Yeah but look everybody here now I'ma get back with you later on a'ight?"

"Will I see you later?"

Fleetingly a smile dashed across T's face as she sparked her blunt, "You might. How late you gon' be up?"

"As late as I need to be for you. Just call me."

"A'ight. I got you."

"Bye T."

"Yup."

T placed her phone down in her cup holder as she drove along. She smoked following the route to take her to Kiaysha's house. When she finally arrived, she placed the roach of a blunt into the ashtray and gazed at herself in the mirror.

Her slanted green eyes brought a smile to her face. She licked her soft lips and continued to scrutinize herself. Eyebrows arched perfectly, fresh line up, dreads freshly twisted, no unsightly acne bumps or marks on her clear face. She flared her nostrils and laughed. No boogers.

Smiling to herself T got out of the car. She spritzed herself down with cologne and popped a peppermint into her mouth. T reached into the back seat retrieving flowers and a bottle of wine. Looking around the neighborhood, she walked up the lit walkway to the front door and rang the doorbell.

"Shit! Hold on!" a voice yelled from behind the white door. A second later Kiaysha opened the door, "Hey."

"Good evening ma'am," drawled T extending the flowers.

Smiling sweetly Kiaysha took the flowers, "You know you only get points for the first and the surprise times you bring me flowers."

Stepping closer to her T whispered in her ear, "Did you know I was bringing you flowers?"

83

She turned to face the stud standing in her hallway, "No."

"Well I get points for a surprise then huh?" questioned T with twinkling eyes.

Kiaysha rolled her eyes but the smile on her face couldn't be erased. She watched T take off her shoes then led her into the living room. She gestured for T to have a seat in front of her flat screen television and handed her the remote. "I'm putting the finishing touches on dinner," she murmured into T's ear once T had sat on the couch.

Nodding and licking her lips T flipped through the stations settling on an R&B music station. She then looked around the immaculate living room. No trace or hint of a man had helped design or graced the aura of the house besides pictures of her toddler son. Knick-knacks mixed in with a few shelves, a clock and mirror were strewn neatly across the walls.

"Okay. Follow me," Kiaysha appeared on side of T.

Standing T followed her into the dining room. She took her seat and Kiaysha tied a napkin around her like it was a bib. Smirking T watched the woman maneuver from the kitchen back to the dining room. She placed two candles in the center of the table.

"I hope you brought your appetite."

"Yeah that's among one of the few things I brought with me," said T. Inwardly to herself she thought about the strap on dick that was also with her tucked into her draws.

"Close your eyes."

One of T's eyebrows lifted but she did as told inhaling the deep scents of the kitchen and the underlying femininity.

"Open your eyes," prompted Kiaysha with a hint of laughter.

Opening her eyes T stared at the table before her. A tray of garlic bread was in the middle of table. In front of both of their plates was a bowl of chicken Ramen noodles. Positioned next to their bowls of noodles was a full wine glass.

She tried to hold back her laughter but once her smile appeared the laughter emerged. "Well you did say your favorite dish was chicken Ramen noodles," T commented finally.

"I sure did. And I told you I could cook. You ain't never had no noodles like this before," bragged Kiaysha with a big smile on her face.

Grinning T reached out for a piece of garlic bread only to have her hand smacked down.

"Eat ya noodles first," she reprimanded.

"Yes ma'am," obliged T twisting her fork as Kiaysha rose from the table.

"You want some hot sauce?" she sat the condiment on the table next to T who shook her head no. "Okay well you've been a good sport," trailed Kiaysha removing the bowl from in front of T and the makeshift bib she had placed around her. "Here is the real dinner. Appetizer first," Kiaysha lifted the plate of garlic bread up placing it in the oven and sat a plate full of wings in the middle of the table.

A smile split T's from ear to ear, "Aww its cool mama. You ain't have to go hit up the restaurant down the street and get these wings for me," she assured her. "The noodles was bangin' just like you said."

Eyes twinkling Kiaysha smirked at T, "Whatever. Just try it. The sauce is homemade."

"I'm just saying I told you I would eat," she paused for dramatic effect. "Whatever you put in front of me. Lick it clean."

"Eat the wings then."

Nodding T picked up a wing then darted her eyes to the light bright woman across the table from her, "I will eat the wing, the breast, love the thighs."

85

Kiaysha rolled her eyes in response and made a point of picking up a wing to eat. She munched down on it making excessive noises that the food was good. Waving the bone in front of her Kiaysha sat it down and licked the sauce off her fingers careful to suck the tips. She grinned at T who was watching her intently.

"Yeah the sauce definitely good."

"You didn't even try it yet!"

"But the way you just ate it though," T shook her head and bit into her piece of chicken. As she chewed, she nodded in Kiaysha's direction. "Yeah these banging! I'ma need you to make this a lot," she commented in approval then made it a point to lick and suck her fingers dry as well.

The two continued to eat silence but their eyes communicated with one another fluently. Their eyes flitted to each other's and dashed away from each other bouncing around each other's face. Their mouths, lips, and tongues teased one another as after every piece they savored the sauce on their fingers. When the chicken was gone, Kiaysha stood brushing past T. She wiped the side of T's mouth with her thumb. Snatching her finger back towards her T pulled it into her mouth sucking the sauce off.

"Mm," exhaled Kiaysha biting on her lip and pulling her thumb from T's mouth. "You can have the garlic bread now," she bent down retrieving food out of the over, "Here is the main course."

"Are you for dessert?"

Chewing her lip Kiaysha couldn't suppress the smile, as she looked T up and down quickly while batting her eyelashes, "Dessert is prepared already."

T licked her lips seductively. Slowly as if she was viewing Kiaysha stark naked T ran her eyes the length of the woman in front of her. "I bet it is," she finally remarked.

A corner of Kiaysha's mouth lifted into a smirk, "You wish," she declared setting the tray of lasagna down onto the table. She removed the plates from the table that were used for the wings and put a new pair of plates down onto the table. Grabbing the wine bottle, she refilled both of their glasses. Kiaysha pulled one of the plates to her, she put lasagna on it, and two pieces of garlic bread then placed the plate in front of T. She did the same for herself with smaller portions.

"Thank you," said T.

"No problem."

"What kind of lasagna is this?"

"Does it matter? You eat everything remember? You're not picky," teased Kiaysha.

Grinning T responded, "Nah not everything but if it look good, smell good I just might bite."

A chuckle of laughter escaped from Kiaysha, "Oh is that so? Does mine look good?"

Looking from the lasagna and back to Kiaysha T winked at her, "It damn sure do. I can't wait to put it in my mouth."

Kiaysha eased closer to T. "Maybe you should try closing your eyes and just saying ah."

Dubiously T's eyebrow raised but she closed her eyes, opened her mouth, and said ah.

"I can't believe I'm doing this," Kiaysha muttered.

A vivid picture of a nude Kiaysha appeared in T's mind. Her eyes jumped wanting to open but she refused. That is until something warm rested in her mouth.

"Open your eyes," chortled Kiaysha.

T swallowed the food and opened her eyes staring at Kiaysha with a matching smile, "I knew it was going to be good but damn."

"Whatever. I'm glad you like it."

"Like it. I love it," she responded eating more of the lasagna and the added bonus of garlic bread.

"Thanks. So, you know you never did tell me why you are single."

Swiftly a thought of interviewing to hit the pussy ran through T's mind before she could answer. She cleared her throat then answered, "Haven't found the right woman honestly. Not too long ago one of my lil' brothers passed away playing between two females. She was in love with one and in lust with the other. Ever since then I've just really been looking at things with a different perception you know? Life short. I don't wanna lose that one due to something that should've been avoided. Hell I don't wanna not have an opportunity to meet that one either," scoffing T's eyes glossed over as she replayed a scene from the funeral. "You know it all became real for me as we put her in the grave. I looked around our lil' family and shit. Everybody had somebody you know to console them and shit. And I was just; I was just there mourning by myself."

Stroking her hand softly Kiaysha murmured, "I'm so sorry for your loss T."

"Thank you," T swallowed and blinked a few times barely aware that Kiaysha's hand had traveled from stroking her hand to stroking her whole arm. She smiled at her, "You easy to talk too ya know that?"

"Yeah. You don't always have to flirt with me," winked Kiaysha.

The wink came right back this time from T, "But I gotta make sure you know that I'm interested. You are beautiful, smart, silly, and I find you very attractive."

"Thank you. You know you're not too bad yourself. You could be handsome; I guess you're smart, and you a lil' silly."

Chuckling T inquired, "A'ight but do you find me attractive as well is the question."

"When? Who asked that question?" she grinned at T. "You never know though. I might. I might not."

Finishing off her plate T wiped her mouth with a paper towel and sat back a little, "I beg to differ with the latter."

"Oh is that so Mr. Timothy? How you figure that?"

"I'm here ain't I?"

Munching down on the last piece of food on her plate Kiaysha nodded, "That you are."

"There you have it then."

"Whatever. Are you ready for dessert or would you like more lasagna and garlic bread?"

"Nah baby we can move on to dessert," she bit her lip at Kiaysha.

Collecting both of their plates Kiaysha put a hand on the side of T's face, "Not that kind of dessert sweetie."

"Get ya mind outta the gutter ma'am and enlighten me on what's on the menu for dessert."

Rolling her eyes Kiaysha smiled, "Chocolate cake," she sat the dish down, "with strawberries covered in chocolate syrup," she placed that dish down as well then turned towards her cabinets to retrieve a couple of saucer plates.

T watched her cut pieces of the cake and place strawberries on each of their plates. She surveyed Kiaysha begin to eat her dessert quietly. She however did not touch her own.

"Do you not like chocolate or strawberries?"

"No, I love them actually."

"So, why aren't you eating then?"

Giving a slight shrug and a flirtatious grin T replied, "I can only eat both if I'm getting fed and feeding you."

A blank stare responded back to T's reply.

She inched her seat closer to Kiaysha's and took a forkful of her cake, "Open up," Kiaysha opened her mouth and T fed her a piece of the cake.

"My turn," Kiaysha smiled wickedly holding up a strawberry dipped in chocolate syrup.

Grinning T licked her lips and opened her mouth. When the strawberry touched her lips T let her tongue perform engulfing the strawberry and playing with it as if it was a clitoris. When she was finished all of the chocolate was gone off the strawberry. She took the strawberry from Kiaysha sucked on it briefly before eating and swallowing the fruit.

Wetting her lips, Kiaysha's eyes twinkled, "Was it good?"

"Not as good as you."

Laughing Kiaysha asked her, "Now how you figure you know that?"

Boring her eyes into Kiaysha's she questioned with a smirk, "Can I try something?" she inched closer to the woman.

Opening her mouth to respond Kiaysha was cut off by the prompt action of T's lips against hers. She started to protest but something awakened inside of her provoking Kiaysha to respond by pressing her lips to T's with vigor. Their lips crashed against each other again and again, as T stood compelling Kiaysha to come to her feet as well. Kiaysha wrapped her arms around the back of T's neck.

One of T's hand began to wander over Kiaysha's body caressing gently. Her hand came to rest on Kiaysha's hips where it paused. Abruptly, T's hand darted from her hips to underneath her jeans slipping beneath her panties and between her moist lips.

Kiaysha tried to pull away as she felt T's hands slide to her box and open it but T covered her mouth with her mouth again. As T began to massage her button all protests flew away from the scene. She gyrated her hips down onto T's fingers. A few moans escaped from her.

Moving her lips from Kiaysha's lips T kissed around her neck planting a seed of a kiss followed up by licking and sucking making the titillating temperature rise within the both of them. Covering T's ear with her lips Kiaysha breathed heavily as a groan accompanied with moans sounded while rolling her hips on the finger prodding against her yoni.

Her legs clamped together or T's hand. T directed the other hand to work her nipples through her shirt. Gently T's fingers pulled at Kiaysha's nipples. A low scream expelled from Kiaysha as her juices came charging out of her. Smiling T shed the clasps of Kiaysha's bra and went to unveil a breast but was stopped.

Breathing heavily Kiaysha smiled at T holding onto the wrist of the hand that was about to strip her of her shirt, "Wait," she took T's hand from between her legs and sucked her juices off of T's fingers who stared carnally. She dropped T's hand and moved away quickly. "It's time for you to go Mr. Timothy. You are too," she searched for the right words chewing on her bottom lip, "Talented."

Smiling T moved towards her, amused when Kiaysha skittered away putting the dinner table in between them, "You sure want me to go?" she asked gazing into Kiaysha's eyes which held the same amount of lust she felt.

Nodding no and speaking yes Kiaysha laughed, "See that's why you gotta go. Ump," she bit her lip sensually and shook her head. "I'll make you a plate to go with."

Standing with a smile T watched her dart around the kitchen carefully avoiding T and her space as she found the paper plates. T's eyes roamed over her body while she heaped food onto the plate. T's tongue took a mind of its own creeping out and sliding across her lips.

Holding out the plate between them, Kiaysha stared up at T, "Here you go. Text me when you make it home."

T took the plate and smirked, "No, to go kiss?"

Tucking a stray piece of hair behind her ear Kiaysha weighed her answer. T watched her unsure whether or not if she knew that her body was conveying yes. Finally, she bit down on her lip and shook her head, "Unh uh. You almost got me though."

Stepping up towards the woman so that there was no room between them T smiled down at her, "You sure?" she didn't wait for an answer but snatched Kiaysha's hand from her side and quickly placed a kiss on it.

"Damn you T," she murmured as she felt her resolve melting away once again. "Granny ain't raise no hoe," she took her hand from T's. "But you make me wish she did."

"I wouldn't think of you as a hoe if you gave in to what you want. We both two grown consenting adults."

A yeah right look plastered Kiaysha's face, "Whatever T it's not gonna happen tonight," quickly she placed a quick kiss on T's cheek and moved away. She opened her front door and with twinkling eyes, turned to T and said, "Why you think I ain't let you taste my juices?"

"Who said I wanted too?"

She rolled her eyes, "Whatever."

"So, it's just that good huh?"

"I don't know guess you'll have to wait and see huh?"

"Okay. I can wait but how long can you?"

Giggling Kiaysha lightly pushed the stud out of her front door, "Goodnight T. Text me when you get home."

Smiling back at her T nodded, "Yes, ma'am."

Settling down into the car T repositioned her strap. She pulled out of Kiaysha's driveway and cruised fidgeting with her strap more. "Fuck," she finally cursed realizing her sexual appetite was at full peak.

She grabbed her other blunt from the ashtray and sparked it in attempt to quell her raging hormones. Aimlessly T drove replaying the night's event starting with her getting into the car. She smirked realizing Layla had called. The smirk on her face from remembering Layla called her led to biting down on her lip. She checked the time. Eleven o'clock. She smiled. It was still early.

"What's good lil' mama," greeted T when Layla answered the phone.

"Nothing. Just got out of the shower. What's good?"

"You."

Laughing Layla agreed, "Yeah you right."

"What you about to get into?"

"Nothing. What you about to get into?"

"Depends. Yo' parents home?"

Layla rolled her eyes, "Yeah they here."

"Get dressed. I'm about to scoop you up. Bring a blanket or something too."

Her eyebrows raised inquisitively, "Why?"

"Lil' mama you trust me don't you?"

"Yeah,"

"A'ight then."

"Okay. I'll be dressed in a minute."

"Cool. I'm about to stop by the store up the street from yo' spot then I be der."

"Okay bye."

T hung up the phone on the young woman and parked in front of the store she had saw Layla at after the funeral. She walked in with her mind buzzing with anticipation. Moving down the aisles, she headed away from the convenient snacks part of the store onto the liquor section. She moved about not finding what she was wanting then strolled up to the counter.

"Yo lemme get a fifth of White Remy and a pack of Swisher rellos."

"Alright. Anything else?" the man behind the counter asked.

"Nah. That's it man."

The man eyed her warily and gave her a total. She gave him a bill and when he gave her the change back, she placed it in the tip jar.

Just as T walked out of the store her phone rang, "Hello?"

"I'm ready," said Layla.

"A'ight. I'm leaving the store now."

Once in the car T broke down a blunt and the weed completing the task of twisting it up while driving. She put the freshly rolled blunt in the cup holder and picked up the piece of a blunt she had left in the ashtray and sparked it. Pulling up to the driveway, she noted the living room curtains flutter before Layla emerged.

"So, where we going?" Layla questioned as soon as she got in the car.

"Somewhere special," responded T grinning wickedly. "Here hit this."

"I'm cool right now."

"A'ight. You remember that blanket?"

She held it up looking at T oddly, "Yeah."

T smiled wickedly, "We almost there."

Leaning back in her seat Layla didn't respond instead checking out the scenery of where they were going. T came to a halt in an empty parking lot. Scanning the empty parking lot Layla looked past the parking lot at a huge field with trees surrounding the outer skirts of the field. Slowly a smile spread across her face.

"Jim Hauser Park, is somewhere special?"

"Ask me in a couple of hours. If you scared we can bounce though."

"Scared of what?"

"I don't know you tell me lil' mama," grinned T getting out of her car.

Layla rolled her eyes and opened her car door looking across the hood at T, "I ain't scared of nothing."

"Good."

The duo walked to the middle of the field. T took the blanket from Layla and spread it out on the ground. She took a seat. Layla followed her lead sitting down as well.

"So, you ain't smoking with me tonight? You gon' make me face this whole blunt by myself?"

With a grin Layla replied, "I'll smoke with you this time. But you know you left it in yo' ashtray in the car."

"Yeah that shit was gone," commented T pulling another blunt from behind her ear. She sparked it took a few drags and passed it. "So, tell me lil' mama, you ever fucked at the park before?"

Grinning slowly Layla hit the blunt, "Nah."

"What you purpin' for ma? You know you been off to the side or got off in the parking lot."

"And if I was? Where you going with this anyway daddy?" she licked her lips passing the blunt.

Standing while smoking the blunt T bent down to pick up the bottle. She waited for Layla to get to her feet then the two walked to the middle of the open field. She laid the blanket down surveying the surrounding houses along the outer skirts of the field.

Layla took the bottle from T and dropped it to the ground. She stood in front of her staring seductively. Piece by piece she disrobed.

A flame of lust ignited within T as her green eyes ran over Layla's stacked young body. Her eyes sparked watching Layla touch herself and rubbing her own breasts, pinching her nipples. Slowly, sliding her tongue across her lips, she undid her pants and let everything fall to the ground until her strap was freed from its clothed confinement. Her hands on Layla's hip brought her closer to her.

Sexual urgency pushed the lips on their faces together over and over again, as Layla's pussy began coating itself. The fire brewing between her legs prompted her to not only just open them but also rub herself against the tool attached to T. She moaned with pleasure as T licked around her neck and her pussy grinded against the length of the shaft of the toy. A hand, not her own sped downstairs splitting apart her lips and teasing her insides.

An ache pounded from deep within her. She tried to replace T's hand with the head of her strap but the action was dismissed. Frustration led her to digging her nails down the tall studs back and biting down on her neck. Fervency washed over T steering her fingers away to hold up one of Layla's legs while she impaled her nether regions.

One foot high, one foot low didn't stop Layla's hips from meeting the stabbing sensation brought along by T's hips. Ambivalently, she kissed T's neck and collarbone, her hands roaming across T's chest pinching her nipples. Lifting her low leg inspired T to release her high leg and Layla locked them both around her lover's waist. As she hooked her arms behind T's neck, a wildness overcame her, which T kept pace with. The two humped themselves into a sex-crazed frenzy working the ladder up towards ecstasy and the after effect of sedation.

Groans ripped forth from Layla when her ass cheeks were spread wide, closed, and spread wide again while a strap penetrated deep inside of her. Her plump ass cheeks separated again only this time a lone finger slipped inside of her back door darting in and out keeping up with the rhythm their pelvises created. Begging moans turned into loud wails as the legs lock turned into a viselike grip, which didn't deter T from sending her dick inside of the trembling woman. Arms fell away, her back arched, and she withdrew her nails from T's back.

Dismounting Layla immediately dropped to her knees. She descended down on the chocolate strap on penis enveloping it into her mouth sucking her fluids off. Her hands went to T's ass guiding her hips to move faster until she was fucking her throat.

Slapping the trademark hat off Layla's head T gathered up some of her hair to hold in her hand as she jostled her strap in and out of her mouth. Layla shook her head free circling the head of her strap. She licked up and down the toy like an ice cream cone before turning over on all fours.

Suckling a finger into her mouth T placed it on Layla's pearl rubbing her finger in circles. She leaned forward dropped a glob of spit down the bountiful cocoa ass in the air. Concurrently her finger dipped into her chocolate star once again and her strap on toy filled the inside of her pussy.

The assault of ecstasy T created had Layla burying her face into the blanket moaning heavily. The strap fit snugly inside of her rubbing against every nerve friction in her walls. She began to scream out feeling the orgasm coming. She dropped her ass and cried out in pleasure when T followed suit bashing away at her walls.

T removed her finger from her asshole and tore her ass cheeks from one another. She watched her strap pelt in and out of Layla vicariously. Layla collapsed forward panting leaving a white substance covering T's strap.

Grinning wickedly down at the spent young woman dripping with sweat and cum T touched her tender lips. When the young woman screamed, T retrieved her bottle from next to Layla. She took a few swigs off it as she caught her breath. Layla leaned back onto her ass stretching her feet out in front of her. T passed the bottle.

97

"What you doing tomorrow night?" questioned T.

Removing the bottle from her lips Layla shrugged her shoulders, "Something with you," she guessed.

"Yeah, I still owe you a night at the club. I have yo' name on the list at the door for whenever you swing by."

Her lips curved up into a smile as she began to pull on her clothes. From far off police sirens sounded. Quickly the two gathered all of their belongings. T extended a hand to Layla on the ground and pulled her to her feet.

"Time to get the fuck outta here. Just in case," T said grinning.

Layla ran ahead of her to the car barefoot.

Chapter 5

Only a smidge of guilt twinged within Layla as she rolled over staring at her ringing phone looking at her best friend's name. She turned back over resuming her thought process of what she was going to wear to the club for T later on that night. The phone quit ringing then picked back up where it left off.

Showtime! Layla curled up in a fetal position clutching her stomach, "Hello?" she answered the phone in a voice straining with painful effort.

"Food poisoning Layla really?" Sayvonne's curt voice cut through the phone lines. "Are you fucking kidding me?"

Coughing back her laughter Layla stayed in character, "Von, I'm so sorry. T took me to breakfast this morning and when she dropped me off I started throwing up and shitting every damn where."

Sayvonne clucked her tongue on the other end of the phone, "Whatever Layla. What y'all supposed to link up later and get it in? I mean I know that's part of the reason I wanted you to stay with the kids too but you know damn well it's more than that. We rarely get fuckin' quality time together."

Her eyes rolled and flitted to the ceiling. She faked a few dry heaves, "Oh my God Von. I'm over here fuckin' sick as hell. And I'm on my fuckin' period. I couldn't fuck T if I wanted too tonight. I'm really sorry Von. If I feel better I'll call you later and let you know."

Expelling harshly Sayvonne bit out, "Whatever."

Counting down on her fingers from five, the two Layla sat quietly on the phone while Sayvonne simmered. She got down to one finger and smirked. Right on cue Sayvonne spoke.

"Do you need me to bring you anything? Are you okay?"

Smiling benevolently at her sister-friend's sensitivity, she politely declined, "I'm a big gurl Von. I got this. You worry too much."

"I know. I know but you the only sister I got left minus the rug rats."

She smiled wistfully at the mention of Sayvonne's brother and sisters. They embodied their sister and late mother in spirit. They weren't bad and were actually fun to be around. Just not more fun than a night filled doing the sexual tango with T.

"Layla? Hello? I asked what you ate. Are you okay?"

Dashing away from thoughts of an erotic dance with T, Layla heaved a sigh, "I'm fine Von. I just feel kinda disoriented."

"Alright. Well go head Lay. Call me back ASAP if you feel any better."

"I will sis."

"And if I find out you lying I'ma put my foot in yo' ass."

"Whatever! Ok mom."

"Hope you feel better. Love you."

"Thanks. Love you too. Bye."

"Bye."

****

"What you doing with yourself and ya son this beautiful afternoon ma'am?" T chatted away to Kiaysha while taking a seat at her kitchen table.

"I don't know yet. I'll probably take him to the park for a few hours sir. What do you plan on doing with yourself this beautiful afternoon?" Kiaysha bantered back.

"Enjoying the company of others at a social function."

"Translation?"

"Ma Dukes having a BBQ for the fam. So, I'm prepping these ribs to take over and gathering my greenery too."

Kiaysha chuckled, "Well that sounds fun."

"I can show you better than I can tell you. You're more than welcome to come."

Smiling Kiaysha shook her head then declined vocally, "I'm sorry Mr. Timothy. Deahlo and I have a date at the park today."

"Let me change your mind. It's a park not too far from Ma Dukes house, my nephew will be there so he'll have somebody to play with, and you will get to meet my family. Ma Dukes, my brothers and sisters."

"Do you always bring the women you're talking too around your family?" she questioned innocuously.

A side of T's mouth lifted into a smile, "My family always knows who I'm talking too. We are a very close knit group."

"So it is a habit to parade women you are talking to around your family this soon?"

"I didn't say that sweetheart. Regardless if we're talking, fucking or in a committed relationship my family already know about you, heard about you ya dig. Just in case somebody turn out to be crazy and try to take me out," cajoled T.

"Oh, so you think I'm crazy after all? And I'll try to take you out?"

T shrugged rolling a blunt, "I don't know. I mean. You know yourself better than I do. If the shoe fits," she trailed off.

The two laughed in unison.

"Whatever T! I'm just asking questions. Granny raised me to believe it means something to meet the family and a lady doesn't set herself up to be tossed away like last week's garbage from meeting the family too soon and becoming infatuated with the idea when in reality there is no title on anything."

"I can dig it. I know how y'all southern belles are."

"Oh do you now?"

"Why yes I do," T cut her sentence off listening intently until she heard the distinct ringing of her house phone. "Hold on for just a second mama."

"Ok," Kiaysha murmured.

Scurrying around the table to the counter T picked up the cordless phone, "Hello?"

Immediately she heard a female yelling in the background. She was screaming at the top of her lungs calling somebody a dumb fucker and screaming that she wasn't lying.

"Shut up!" a male voice finally roared at her. "Ay who is this?" the male voice mumbled at T.

The hostility in his voice made T's jaw clench. She walked away from Kiaysha on her cell phone moving towards her living room, "Nigga you called me? Who da fuck is this?"

"Tre," the man snapped drunkenly. "Why da fuck yo' number was in my gurl's car? Who da fuck is you?" Tre snarled in a drunken rage.

"I might be da nigga dats fuckin' yo' bitch. Who is yo' gurl Detective Tre?" added T with a laugh fueling his fire.

"Sayvonne."

Tsking with annoyance T walked back to the kitchen toward her cell phone. "Bruh you need to calm yo' drunk ass down. Get that bass up out ya voice bruh. That's my nigga. Her gurl Kenni went with my best friend. Tell Sayvonne T said what's good."

Tre sighed hard, "Oh yeah she told me about you," he said quietly. "Here go Von," he handed the phone off to Sayvonne smiling sheepishly.

"Hello?"

"Yeah what's good fam? You a'ight over there? Cuz got a jealously problem? I handle it."

Sayvonne expelled a hard breath of air through her mouth, "Nah I ain't pulled out my fuckin' hair yet. We both just stressed out. Ain't had a break from the kids in awhile. Then today his birthday so he came in drunk from work. And of course, Layla was supposed to have the kids for the night but no she has food poisoning. Wherever you took her to for breakfast this morning fucked her stomach up."

T walked away from her cell phone again this time to her bedroom, "Hold on I took who to breakfast for a date?"

"Layla?"

"Nah baby got her niggas mixed up. I ain't took her to breakfast shit I couldn't even do that for her."

"Say what? You ain't take her out for breakfast?"

"Look I ain't do for her," she began to walk back into the dining room, "I can do for you though. Ma Dukes having a BBQ and we all love kids like I told you so they can chill with me for the night."

"Huh? T I couldn't ask you to do that. Hell you don't even know the kids."

103

"Sayvonne I don't have too. I know your heart and I've seen you in action. Let me repay your kindness with my own. You said y'all need some alone time now I can dig that. So, I'm telling you right now you got a babysitter for the night."

"Are you sure? There's three of them. A thirteen-year-old, a six-year-old, and a two-year-old."

"If I wasn't sure I wouldn't be volunteering. My nephew eight. We know how to take care of kids," chuckled T.

"I don't know."

"You worry too much. They'll be fine. I stay on Bernard Street over by Kraus Park. It's a white caddy in the driveway. The address is 9972."

Sayvonne sent a silent prayer of thanks up to God, "A'ight. Thanks T. This mean so much to me," she responded happily.

"Aye anytime no problem it's all good."

"A'ight. Thanks again. Bye."

"Yup."

She placed her cordless phone back onto the base and retrieved her cell phone to hear Kiaysha chuckling, "Baby mama issues? Don't tell me you're a deadbeat."

"Ha there go yo' jokes again mama. Nah I'm just positioned to repay a favor that was done for me recently to a woman that was like the sister to my sister in law that passed."

"Aww look at you all sweet and whatnot."

"Yeah. Do to others as you would have others do unto you."

"True, true. Very true."

"But like I was saying though. My family is different. Yeah we just a group of friends really but we're the only family we know. We've all been through so much shit together it's crazy. We have values like you have but

104

it's important for us to meet and know who's talking to who not only for a just in case but you know just to know and get to know that person," T chuckled, "We all people persons."

Kiaysha snickered, "Okay. Whatever you say T. But I would like to see you this weekend."

"How about Sunday? We can go to a matinee?"

"That'll be fun."

"You damn right it will be. I get to spend time with you while in the privacy of a theater."

"And I'll be dressed like its arctic winter outside."

T guffawed, "Hey, I know how to behave myself. I don't know about you."

"Yeah we'll see."

"We will but hey I'ma call you later on mama. I gotta make sure the car child and teenager proof before she bring these kids over."

"Alright T. I'll talk to you later. Bye," giggled Kiaysha.

"Bye."

****

Sayvonne drove happily to T's condo with her brother and younger sisters in the backseat. Her boyfriend Tre sat in the front seat reclined back. In between the two seats, the couple held hands.

"Baby I'm sorry," Tre apologized to Sayvonne about his drunken rage and ran his free hand through his jet-black curly hair.

Flashing a smile at her boyfriend she replied, "It's cool baby. I know how you feeling, I'm stressed too. But that should be my problem they my family. All you wanted to do is love me. So, I'm sorry baby. My situation forced you into this."

Tre sighed. He placed Sayvonne's caramel hand on his cheek, "Von, I will always love you. We all are a family. And somewhere long, long, long down da line when we have kids I don't want you takin' da heat. I acted like a bitch cuz I was drunk. I'm sorry."

Opening her mouth to say something she was cut off by her thirteen-year-old brother Montae who jumped into their conversation saying, "No, it wasn't you Tre. I'm sorry… enough with the soap opera Von. You're both sorry. Can we get past that?"

Glancing up in the mirror at her smiling brother Sayvonne gave him the middle finger.

Montae rolled his eyes, "Whose house are we goin' to?"

"A friend of mine," Sayvonne supplied.

A blank look from Montae responded back until he sat up so his face was inches from her arm, "I hope so. But I don't think even *you* would drop me off at someone's house you don't know."

Yanking her hand from Tre's grasp, she flung it backwards at her brother, "Her name is T. Won't you go to sleep like yo' sisters?"

A grin flashed across Montae's face and he fell back laughing, "Newsflash," he exclaimed sitting up. "You're my sister. You're not sleep."

The three couldn't help laughing at Montae's antics and he continued saying weakly, "Back to you Bob."

Tre leaned forward and turned down the radio, "Hello?" he said into Sayvonne's cell phone. "She right here… yeah hold on," he passed the phone to Sayvonne.

"Hello," Sayvonne greeted.

"Hey Von. Where you at?" Layla greeted her friend.

With a roll of her eyes Sayvonne spoke dryly, "What's good Lay? I'm driving right now."

"Oh." Layla's mood seemed to drop slightly then just as bright as before she posed, "You still need me to baby sit? I'm feeling a lil' better now-"

"Nah I'm good," she responded curtly.

"You wanna chill den?"

Sighing Sayvonne flipped and took flight, "Layla Amorya, how da fuck you gon' lie to me? Fa what? On some shit like that? How long I been knowing yo' ass?"

"I'm lost. What you talkin' 'bout Von?"

"T!" Sayvonne cried out. "I talked to her earlier. She ain't take you out to eat no fuckin' where. And I know you probably gave it up to her fa nothing if you even seen her. If yo' fuckin' ass ain't lying about having food poisoning which I really hope you fuckin' do have so I won't have to face the reality of a lying bitch for a sister."

"Von, I-"

"No, Layla now is the time fa you to listen. So, shut da hell up and do dat. Cuz na mean no matter who it is, if you fuckin' them just because or 'cause a what they can buy or give you, I'ma still love yo' gold diggin', prostitute ways having, Trina mentality ass. I don't give a fuck what you do long as you safe. You like my sister. Shit you is. But you gon' lie to me like I ain't nobody? That's what's really good now?" she paused to see if Layla had something to say when she didn't respond she finished with, "Now if you don't mind which I don't give a fuck if you do right about now, today Tre's birthday. T watching da kids so I holla at'chu tomorrow."

"Hold on. How you get in touch wit' T?"

Sayvonne rolled her eyes, "That's all you fuckin' heard. You sprung den a muthafucka. You know dat? But anyways I called her."

"How she gon' answer da phone fa you and not fa me?" Layla spat angrily.

The usually soft big brown eyes of Sayvonne's flashed, "Maybe cuz she know I ain't tryna exchange ass fa cash or in yo' case giving it up fa free and wanting dough or to be treated like you her gurl when you steady talkin' slick to her. And what da fuck so wrong 'bout being in a relationship wit' somebody? T liked you fa real dummy but you let money control you. I bet she woulda settled down wit' yo' ass if you woulda acted right. So, like I was sayin' I get at you tomorrow Layla," Sayvonne replied tartly before hanging up. She expelled breath through her nose harshly.

No one said anything Tre glanced sideways at his girlfriend but didn't dare speak. The girls were still sound asleep. Montae gazed out the window pretending to be oblivious from the conservation that just took place.

The rest of the drive to T's condo was silent except for an occasional snore from one of the younger children sleeping in the back. Sayvonne pulled into T's driveway. She parked then turned to look at Tre.

"I love you," Sayvonne told him.

"I love you too baby," he leaned over to kiss his girlfriend.

Montae gagged from the back, "I think I'ma be sick."

Chuckling Tre kissed Sayvonne gently on the lips then opened his car door.

Stepping out of the driver side of the car Sayvonne opened the back door, "Simone," she shook her six-year-old sister's shoulders. "Simone!"

"What?" Simone whined. "Leave me alone," she whined fitfully in her sleep before going back to Dreamland.

"Simone!" she snapped at her then flicked her in her nose.

"Ow," Simone whimpered.

"C'mon."

Simone fought her for a minute then looked around curiously, "Where we at?"

"My friend's house. Her name is T."

Tre came up behind her "I got Chelsea," he whispered in her ear.

Sayvonne looked up and smiled at the sight. Tre was cradling Sayvonne's two-year-old sister in his arms as if it were his child. The diaper bag draped across his broad shoulders deepened the proud father look he had going on.

"What?" Tre asked.

Smiling she answered, "Nothin' daddy," she smirked at him turning her backside to him to walk up the porch.

Tre grinned at her words following her towards the door.

"A who gon' get me? How y'all gon' get da gurls and not me? Y'all like them better. I knew it!" Montae called out from the backseat of Sayvonne's car.

"Get yo' ass out da car," Sayvonne hissed at him.

Scrambling out of the car Montae joined the four waiting with bated breath for T to answer the door. When the ringing quit the door swung open to reveal Kim. She stared at them with a mask of annoyance and anger.

"Oh hell naw," Kim muttered. "T!" she hollered.

"Are you sure we're supposed to be here?" Simone muttered to her big sister.

Casually Kim leaned against the door with folded arms watching the small family in front of her and waiting for T to appear. Sayvonne glanced at Montae who was grinning broadly at Kim's chest poking through her short white robe. She stepped on his foot but Montae didn't even look up. Sayvonne glanced at Tre but he had averted his eyes from Kim's oiled body who was clad only in a robe to Chelsea, who he was bouncing and singing softly to.

109

Finally, T appeared behind Kim. Unlike Kim's barely clothed figure, T was dressed casually in a pair of jeans with a flashy belt and a white button down shirt with the first few buttons open.

Montae glanced at T then at Kim back to T then at his sister with questioning eyes. He even looked at Tre with a curious expression on his young face. His younger sister Simone stated the obvious question however.

"I thought you said T was a gurl. Who is this man?" Simone jerked her paper brown thumb at T.

A look of horror dawned on Sayvonne's face at Simone's words. She stepped on her sisters toes who glared at her angrily.

"Von, why you lie to da kids like that?" T playfully chided her. She pushed Kim towards Simone. "Dis my sister Kim. Y'all don't mind her we interrupting," T chuckled at Kim's expense.

Observing the adults exchange laughter Simone posed, "Interrupting what?"

Deftly Sayvonne stepped on her foot once again. And again, Simone looked up at her angrily.

"Grown folk bidness shawty," T said in an adopted southern twang causing Simone to smile. T turned to Kim. "Go head. I'm 'bout to take the kids out."

Kim spun on her heel and disappeared into the condo without a goodbye.

"What's good Von." T smiled at her.

Sayvonne beamed right back at her grateful for T babysitting, "Hey," she touched her boyfriend's arms, "This is Tre," the two shook hands. Sayvonne touched Chelsea's head, which lay on Tre's chest, "This is my youngest sister Chelsea. She two. We potty training her but we brought da diaper bag just in case," she waited until T nodded before going on, "This is Simone. She is a child recorder and says whatever on her mind without thinkin'. And I do mean whatever. She fearless."

Simone smacked Sayvonne's golden brown hand off her brown head, "No, I'm not."

Rolling her eyes Sayvonne continued, "Yeah whatever she a lil' con artist too so wherever you take her watch her closely," smiling she touched Montae's shoulder next, "This is my brother Montae, he a thirteen-year-old comedian. Why he look like he ain't make da basketball team I don't know cuz he the captain."

"Shit I do. He thought he was rolling wit' Kim not me," T ruffled his curly brown hair. "Maybe next time shorty. I tell her you like her doe."

Eyes bright and grin stretched from ear to ear he quickly said, "Ok."

T smacked her hands together and rubbed them together, "Alright, alright. Ladies and gent let's get moving."

Everybody turned and followed T to her Cadillac except Tre who went to retrieve the car seat for Chelsea. Once everybody was settled in the car and Sayvonne issued warnings and threats to be good or else the group said their good byes.

"Aye yo I'ma real cool muthafucka but don't fuck up my ride," T warned them.

Simone and Montae stared at her unfazed by the threat, "Where we goin'?" they asked in unison.

****

T smiled at the full drive way and parked cars on the street outside of her mother's house. Mentally, she matched the cars with their owners. Only Kim and Lil' Buddy were missing. She parked her car behind Jay's, another one of her stud brothers.

111

"A'ight now look," she began facing the two oldest children in the backseat. "This my mama's house. We welcome y'all as family to our BBQ but just so you know if you start acting disrespectful Ma Dukes won't hesitate to get off in yo' ass. She don't care who raising you. Ma Dukes is my mama feel free to call her Ma Dukes. And if you don't know, y'all are children you don't linger where the adults are. She got hella game systems and movies. We got a basketball hoop for you too homie if you wanna showcase ya skills."

They both looked unfazed and simultaneously said, "Ok."

She winked at Montae, "My sister Kim will be here in a lil' while too."

A slow grin spread across his face. Simone elbowed him in the ribs.

"Let's go ladies and gent," T said opening her car door.

The kids followed suit. T went around the car to grab the diaper bag and their baby sister Chelsea who smiled shyly at T.

The door was unlocked and the group followed T to the kitchen where Ma Dukes, Moryah, and Arianna froze staring back at them.

"Well this is new," Moryah, the mother of T's deceased brother Ronnie spoke first.

"Step DAD-DAY!" Arianna, the deceased Ronnie's paternal sister chortled.

Stopping what she was doing Ma Dukes went and rinsed her hands off then approached the children, "How are you young lady?" she asked Simone. "You can call Ma Dukes. What's your name?"

"My name is Simone ma'am and I'm fine. How are you?" she answered politely.

Ma Dukes smiled back at the other women in the kitchen impressed with the young lady in front of her. She turned back to Simone, "Well I'm fine ma'am thanks for asking. How old are you?"

"Six. I'll be seven next month. How old are you?" Simone asked unabashed.

Mothers and daughters in the kitchen hooted with laughter at the conversation.

"Hold on now baby. You can't ask a woman how old she is. That can be disrespectful."

Simone's brother Montae shot her a dirty look but she ignored him, "I'm sorry Ma Dukes. I wasn't trying to be disrespectful but you asked me first."

The kitchen exploded with laughter and smiles at the child's deduction of conversation.

Tickled with laughter Ma Dukes responded, "Well chile I guess you right. I apologize. I like you though so how about we bake you a cake for your birthday?"

"Can we eat it today?"

"Yes ma'am," Ma Dukes said and added, "But only if, you agree to help cook."

Her eyes ballooned, "Really? I can help."

"Why yes ma'am it's yours," Ma Dukes told her.

"What kind of cake do you like?" Moryah asked her then as an afterthought told her, "My name is Moryah honey."

"Hi Ms. Moryah. I like yellow cake ma'am."

"Alright well get on over here chile lets wash them hands and get ready," Moryah told her while cleaning off a section of the counter.

Turning to Montae as his sister ambled off to join Moryah, Ma Dukes stood in front of him smiling, "And what is your name sir?"

"Montae," he declared proudly with a big chest. "I'm thirteen ma'am. I will be fourteen in October."

Tossing a covet look back at Moryah she said, "Remember when these knuckleheads was fourteen?" She jerked a finger at T who had taken a seat on the table inching her way closer to a pie that sat cooling off. She smacked T's hand.

Moryah shook her head, "Yeah I remember."

Turning back to the young man in front of her Ma Dukes said, "Well alright Montae. I don't suppose you'd like to cook with all us women in the kitchen?"

A grin spread across T's face as the two shared a look.

He smiled sheepishly, "No ma'am."

"Lemme see, lemme see," Ma Dukes went to the open kitchen window. "Jay!" she hollered out the open window.

"You got the grill lit?"

"No ma'am!"

"Alright well wait a minute!"

"T, if you don't leave my pie alone! Yo' ass ain't never quiet and you mines don't think I don't see you inching closer to my pie!" Ma Dukes snapped at her daughter.

The room chuckled as T sat with the pie right in front of her now. T turned away from the pie. "Ma, don't nobody want that pie. It ain't even cool yet."

"Exactly why it's on the table. Take this boy outside and y'all go light the grill with Jay. Here these hamburgers and hot dogs ready to throw on."

Arianna ran her hands under the water quickly then swooped in and took the toddler from T. She clucked her tongue as they walked away from them, "I'm going to lay her down. She was sleep in ya arms pie stealer."

T rolled her eyes at her late brother's older sister who was older than all of their crew, "Thank you!" she called out to her.

Ma Dukes layered the table with the food that was ready to go on the grill once it was lit. She looked at T as the two filled their arms. "Don't y'all be smoking around this boy. Send him in here or let him go play basketball or something."

"Ma I know these things!"

She picked up a raw piece of chicken and flicked it at the tall studs retreating back.

"See you gon' want that piece later!" T called out.

****

The family of friends and the kids minus Chantel and Dreamz who never showed up sat outside eating Simone's birthday cake quietly. Montae looked around each person in the group studying them especially Arianna who was feeding his baby sister. He put his plate down on the table.

"Why are you all so nice to us?" his question barged out softly. "I mean I've never met any of you. My sister has never talked about you," his eyes widened and he turned to look T in her eyes, "is my sister okay?"

Simone stopped eating now staring also at T with a tender face but eyes bright.

She grinned easily at the two children in effort to comfort them, "Sayvonne's cool homie. She ain't in trouble, hurting, or nothing. But you know sometimes adults need alone time," she raised her eyebrows at him.

"Kids do too," Simone pointed out.

The family smiled. "Exactly," T nodded.

"Okay but that still doesn't explain. So, how do you know her? Why are you guys so nice to us?" Montae asked quietly.

"Well it's like this. Umm. Everyone here has known each other for a very long time. Has your sister ever mentioned Ronnie before?"

"That was Aunt Kenni's gurlfriend!" Simone answered brightly then sadly said, "But they both died."

"Well Ronnie was my brother-"

"But she was a gurl?" Simone interjected. "Sissy says she just dressed like a boy."

"As do I and Jay," she motioned to her Latino brother who was still eating the birthday cake. "We're really women but we call ourselves brothers-"

"You guys are weird."

The group laughed at her outburst and Ma Dukes high five'd the child.

"Yeah well anyway. She was my brother. In fact, Ms. Moryah is Ronnie's mother and Miss Arianna is Ronnie's big sister. But Kim, Jay, and I have another brother who isn't here. We all are brothers."

"And sister," Simone pointed out looking at Kim. "She doesn't dress like you guys."

"Thank you," Kim told her. "You tell that weirdo."

T rolled her eyes at Kim and looked at Montae, "Since Ronnie and Kenni were dating and they were pretty serious. We all looked at her like she was our sister."

"But she wasn't," Simone said.

"Simone, be quiet! Just let her talk," Montae demanded.

She stuck her tongue out at him but didn't say anything else. Just when T opened her mouth to talk she asked, "Do you look at Auntie Layla like a sister? Sissy said-" Montae clamped his hand over her mouth.

"Don't you ever shut up?" he shouted at her.

She bit him and he pinched her in return.

"Alright kids enough!" Ma Dukes said and they stopped immediately. "Your sister Sayvonne recently did

116

something very nice for T. So, we welcome Sayvonne and her family into our family officially because she didn't have to do what she did."

"What'd she do?" Montae asked.

Simone pinched him, "Quit asking questions. You being nosey."

He whirled around on her arguing back "you're one to talk" but then T's cell phone rang and they quieted down out of respect.

"Hello?"

"Hey T. How's it going? Everybody ok?" Sayvonne inquired.

"Yes ma'am. We at Ma Dukes house. We had a BBQ and baked a cake for Simone's birthday."

"Aww T you didn't have to do that."

"Yeah but hold on. I got a lil' lady that wanna talk to you," she handed the phone to Simone's outstretched hand.

"I MADE my cake," she declared proudly standing and walking away from the table.

Montae followed after her yelling, "You can't just walk off with someone's phone."

"I need alone time!" she snapped back at him walking into the house.

The group watched the kids with amusement.

Moryah looked at her daughter. "That was you and Ronnie when y'all was babies."

They chuckled again.

"So, what's up with Lil' Buddy?" Jay threw the question into the air to nobody in particular.

"Ain't none of y'all talked to her?" Arianna asked quizzically staring at the two studs and fem surrounding her.

The two studs and the femme Kim exchanged looks and in unison shook their heads no.

"Has anybody talked to her recently?" Moryah posed with worry in her voice. "What happened to checking in with one another?"

"I called her during the week. Everything was cool she was supposed to be here," Kim responded.

"Yeah I talked to her too during the week. She ain't returned none of my calls this weekend though," answered T.

"Well I talked to her yesterday morning. She was supposed to be bringing something special today," Jay told everyone.

"What about Mya?" Ma Dukes wondered. "Anybody tried her or heard from her?"

Jay lit a blunt with a smile. She chiefed it, exhaled and leaned up, "Y'all know how Lil' Buddy is. They might just be going through something right now. Arguing or something."

"So, what's the game plan?" Kim fired back ignoring Jay's statement.

"If we don't hear from her by tomorrow. Bright and early Monday we going over there. That way if they are arguing or something they had time to hash it out or whatever," supplied T.

Ma Dukes nodded, "Okay. Now what's up with you lady?" she looked at Kim.

Checking her surroundings puzzled that Ma Dukes was talking to her Kim asked, "I'm here what you mean?"

The studs snickered at Kim's expense as the blunt changed hands.

"Why you ain't bring Cream with you?" Moryah asked with exasperation.

"Why would I? She ain't my bitch, gurlfriend or nothing."

"Umm hmm," Ma Dukes muttered. "I don't know why you be playing with that gurl."

"Commitment   fear," Arianna   mumbled absentmindedly.

"She wouldn't be the only one here with that problem now would she?" Jay asked jovially but her eyes pierced Arianna's before bouncing around.

Arianna smirked standing up with the baby, "I'ma go change her, and check on the other kids make sure they ain't killed each other yet."

"Cool. Thanks big sis," nodded T.

Vigilantly Kim's eyes zipped from watching Arianna walking away from the group to Jay staring at the ground absentmindedly. She smoked her blunt pondering and missed the question Ma Dukes asked her. "Huh?"

"So, what do you call y'all?" Ma Dukes asked Kim.

Kim laughed shaking her head and passed her the blunt. She blew a smoke ring in the air, "I don't call us nothing. We just having fun. The roles and rules are well defined."

"Ok," Ma Dukes dropped the issue and leaned back in her chair. "T, here come the babies with your phone. Jay, finish this and then take that boy to let off some fireworks. Kim, find something to do with that lil' gurl or turn a movie on or something for her."

The three nodded waiting for the kids to approach.

"Sissy wants to talk to you T," Simone declared holding out the phone.

"Thank you," she took the phone from her petite hands. "Hello?"

"T, I can't thank you enough for this. They are having a *ball* at yo' mama's house."

A smile appeared on T's face at Sayvonne's words and she smiled even broader watching Jay and an excited Montae run to the garage to retrieve fireworks, "No problem. But hey when we hang up I'ma text you the address to Ma Dukes house. Pick the kids up from here tomorrow."

"Okay. Thanks again T."

"No problem. Enjoy ya'self tonight. I will call you if we need you."

"Okay. Bye."

"Bye."

T hung up the phone and smiled satisfied with being able to help Sayvonne out. The mothers glanced at her but didn't say anything instead focusing their attention on Jay and Montae. T raised a glass to her lips noticed it was empty and sat it down. She smiled wickedly switching her mother's cup and hers. She jumped up taking off to do fireworks.

****

Sayvonne snatched up her phone from where it lay crying in her car cup holder, "Layla, I'm not at T's yet! I'm still drivin'!" Sayvonne snapped at her best friend. "Bye."

Layla began to sputter protests before Sayvonne could hang up the phone, "Damn Von. Hold on damn."

"What Layla?" Sayvonne sighed exasperated,

Taking a deep breath Layla replied, "I just wanted to apologize fa how I been actin' lately. Dat shit wasn't cool Von. I'm sorry gurl. Forgive me?"

"Umm hmm," Sayvonne muttered through pursed pink lips as she noticed the address T had given her had a full driveway.

"Von, don't be like that. I'm serious," Layla pouted.

"Yeah whatever," Sayvonne said as she came out of the circle and parked behind a white Mustang. "But I'm at T mama house so hold on you'll talk to her in a minute," she heard the sharp intake of breath from over the phone and knew her best friend was smiling hard. "Yeah dats what I thought," she smiled and shook her head again. "Why don't you just admit you like her and wanna be wit' her?"

"Ok Von damn. I like her and I," Layla faltered.

Knocking on the white door Sayvonne muttered into the phone, "Lay, don't front."

Letting out a frustrated sigh Layla complied, "Ok! I kinda wanna be wit' her too."

"Now tell T dat. Here she comes now I think," she said glimpsing someone coming towards the door through the windows.

"Von, don't play!" Layla screamed at her.

Chortling at her best friend, she waited for the door to open.

"Uh-oh! Which one of dem knuckle heads you here fa?" Ma Dukes questioned Sayvonne.

Cutting out her laughter Sayvonne extended a hand to her, "Hi, I'm Sayvonne Jefferson. T told me to pick up my brother and sisters from here."

"Oh okay well c'mon in Miss Sayvonne. I'm Talina Martin. T's mother. You can call me Ma Dukes. I really appreciate what you did for my baby."

"It was the right thing to do ma'am," Sayvonne said as the two sat on the couch.

"That don't mean you had to do it. People my age don't even do what's right and wrong sometimes."

"Yes ma'am. I understand that but T also didn't have to step in. Like I told her, she could've just kept it moving. That was the least I could've done for her."

"I like you. How old are you?" questioned Ma Dukes with a smile. She leaned back taking in the woman before her eyes,

Before Sayvonne could answer T came striding into the living room in a black wife beater and long black basketball shorts, " Ma, it's too early to be askin' questions," T said while yawning as she sat down next to her mother.

Ma Dukes snatched up the pillow from beside her and smacked T in the face with it, "It's one o'clock."

Taking the pillow from her and placing it on her mother's lap T stretched out with a yawn, "Well den it's too late in the afternoon."

"You betta get yo' ass up fa I say what I wanted to name you."

As T hopped off her mother Layla exclaimed loudly, "What is it Von? Ask her."

T exchanged raised eyebrows with her mother, "Who is dat?"

Sayvonne rolled her eyes and extended the phone to her, "Who you think?"

Her lips curled into a smile as she took the phone, "What's good lil' mama," she greeted her in a deeper tone that instantly moistened Layla's panties. T started to walk off to her room.

Picking up a couch pillow Ma Dukes chucked it at her, "Hoe!"

From in the back somewhere T screamed, "Ma!" which set off a train reaction as Jay's snoring hit a peak causing Kim to scream, "Shut the fuck up before I suffocate yo' ass!"

"Oh y'all got a zoo up in here," Sayvonne commented laughing.

Chuckling at their antics Ma Dukes agreed, "Yeah. Now back to you how old are you?"

"Eighteen ma'am."

"Okay. You taking care of yo' brother and sisters?"

An old but familiar chill flew down Sayvonne's spine causing her back to stiffen, "What makes you ask that?"

"Chile, I'm not that old and it ain't too many tricks y'all youngins can get past me with. Kim, come over here all the time and I can always tell when she just got sexed right. And I know you did you are glowing Sayvonne! But last night your brother and sisters not once mentioned their mother or father, always you. And they were so worried," she paused to smile. "Now as I sit here finally getting to meet you. Baby, you look tired," Ma Dukes grabbed Sayvonne's hand holding on to it. "Now I ain't hitting on you," she joked. "And I ain't trying to be insulting by saying you look tired. I just mean I can tell either you are or you've been holding the world on your shoulders. Now ain't nothing wrong with that. Hell, that's what we black woman have always done. But it's nothing wrong with asking or needing help either baby."

Sayvonne looked down at Ma Dukes hand in hers just like her own mother used to do when she was alive, it was how they talked about problems, always touching. She began to breathe rapidly with thoughts of her mother beginning to flutter around. Sayvonne clenched her tongue between her teeth to stop the oncoming rush of tears, "My mama, my mother," she paused to swallow as tears began to fall, "she died."

Ma Dukes pulled Sayvonne into her smooth brown arms, "Its ok. I'm sorry. What about yo' daddy?"

Responding with a shake of her head no, she said bitterly, "Who knows where dat man at? It's just my boyfriend and me. My two best friends, their parents were helping out but one of them just had a break down. So, I'm helping her out anyway I can. And T told me she would help me out that's how she ended up with the kids."

"Yeah my baby got a good heart," she paused to smile, "All them do. You inherited all of us now. We all got yo' back. Tell T to give you my number. If you need anything and I do mean *anything,* you give me a call. You hear?"

Feeling foolish Sayvonne wiped her tears, "Yes, ma'am."

T came striding back into the room again, "Ma, how come every time I leave you alone wit' somebody you got 'em cryin' and telling you stuff they usually keep to they self?"

Her mother stuck her tongue out at her.

Montae however emerged from behind T, "You ok?" he asked his older sister while Simone and himself stared daggers at Ma Dukes.

The young woman shared a smile with the older woman. Sayvonne hugged the three of her siblings, "I'm fine. And y'all say thank you to Ma Dukes for her hospitality."

"Thank you Ma Dukes," Montae and Simone said in while their baby sister just smiled.

"Don't let it be the last time I see y'all. Y'all welcome anytime and I do mean that. These knuckleheads drop by whenever they want. Y'all part of our family now so next time bring yo' boyfriend so I can meet him," Ma Dukes said.

Smiling and nodded appreciatively she concurred, "Yes ma'am."

"And I been checking on Beaunna they might release her in a couple months," Ma Dukes added.

Curiously, Sayvonne looked at her wondering.

Ma Dukes sent her a wink, "Gurl I'm famous! You ain't know? I know everybody and we went to school together," she shrugged. "It's a small world. I saw what happened in the newspaper and T told me everything."

"Yes, it is ma'am. Tell Ms. B I'll see her soon hopefully this week,"

"I will."

"Ok thanks," Sayvonne said while ushering the kids out the door. "Bye y'all thanks."

"Ain't you forgettin' something?" Simone interjected with her hands on her hips.

"What?" Sayvonne asked.

Simone held up her cell phone, "What would you do wit' out me?" She rhetorically asked out loud as she hopped in the car.

Sayvonne shook her head amused.

Chapter 6

"That movie was hilarious. I'm going to have to get that," bemused Kiaysha as T and her walked out of the side entrance of the movie theaters.

Chuckling along T concurred, "Yeah. I gotta see that again."

As they neared T's car, Kiaysha stopped walking and looked at T. "You know every time I'm with you my cheeks hurt from laughing and smiling so much."

Biting down on her lip T grinned, "I know," she winked at her.

She rolled her eyes and smiled walking towards the passenger side of the car, "Oh whatever. Your big headed ass."

"Whoa! You cursing now Miss Lady?" inquired T as she opened the passenger door for her. Kiaysha slid into the seat. T winked at her, "I guess I do all kinds of things to you huh? Make you feel all sorts of ways."

Fluttering her eyelashes, she declined to respond and closed the door.

Giggling to herself T walked around the car door to the driver's seat. She settled down in her car cranking the engine. She looked at Kiaysha, "So, I take it that was a yes?"

Staring pointedly out the window Kiaysha responded with a grin, "Whatever. That wasn't a yes or a no."

Opening her mouth to reply she didn't but pulled out her phone from her pocket, "Hold on for a second ma. This my brother. I ain't heard from her all weekend."

"Okay."

"Yo," T said into her phone.

"Ay bruh I need you to come scoop me. Where you at?" a voice growled out.

"Just left the movies," T answered then with more concern, "What's good fam?"

An angry throat sound emitted over the phone before Chantel spat out, "Fuckin' psycho ass bitch Mya bruh. I'ma slap da fuckin' cuss words out her fuckin' mouth before they fuckin' form cuz. I ain't even tryin' to put my hands on her fa real fa real ya dig cuz a nigga don't need the fuckin' charge but she got one more fuckin' time man. One more fuckin' time to step in my damn face, mug me, slap me, punch me and I'ma beat da shit outta her and lil' buddy gon' be locked up down da way,"

"Damn. Yo, be easy folk. I got you. I just gotta make a stop on da way before I scoop you. A'ight?"

Chantel opened her mouth to tell T okay but instead she ended up yelling at Mya, "YO, GET DA FUCK AWAY FROM ME BITCH! I AIN'T GON' KEEP TELLIN' YO' ASS DAT SHIT! AND YOU BETTA NOT WAKE UP MY FUCKIN' SON! I'M LEAVIN'! TAKE YO' ASS IN DA OTHER ROOM!"

T heard scuffling in the background a slap then someone hitting the floor. She changed her mind at that time.

"Man nigga I see you when you get here," Chantel said into the phone and hung up abruptly.

"Damn," T rubbed her chin nervously thinking how their five-year relationship came to a screeching halt just like that.

"Is everything okay?" quietly Kiaysha asked.

Heaving a big sigh and shrugging her shoulders at the same time T responded honestly, "I don't even know. I would drop you off 'cause it's an emergency situation but ma I'm sorry. I don't think I got enough time. I gotta get to my lil' buddy. I will drop you off after."

Kiaysha smiled at her, "I understand T. It's not a problem."

Smiling back at her T spoke, "Thank you," then gunned the engine pushing towards her youngest stud "brother's" place of residence.

****

Twenty silent minutes later T was snapping out at Kiaysha to grab the wheel of the car while she jumped out of it still moving enraged at the scene unfolding in front of Chantel's house.

"Yo, Mya what da fuck?" T screamed out angrily looking at the damage done to Chantel's house through the busted living room window and her vehicle sitting on flats jagged holes ripped through the tires. Mya whipped around to face T who took a step back as a scare wave ran down her spine. T held her hands up, "Yo," she faltered at the full frontal sight of Mya complete with a steel baseball bat by her side. She could see every detail on Mya's chocolate face and that didn't help.

Mya's usually well-kept hair framed her face but now it stood up like the old school rapper Coolio's. She even had a track just hanging. An ominous fire of anger bristled deep in her pupils adorned by brighter stress red cry lines. Tear lines streaked from her puffy eyes down her makeup riddled face making trails past her quivering lips to her strong chin. Spots of tenderness stood out marking her face. Above her busted thick lips was a fresh sheen of moisture. She scowled at T.

"And what da fuck do you want T?" she cried out in a hard-edged voice that was laced with pain and broken because it was not her own. "Yo, ass probably knew all along and got da fuckin' nerve to be fuckin' callin' me fuckin' sis and shit."

About to respond T stopped watching Mya look past her. She glanced back to see Kiaysha parallel parking her car. Once she turned back to Mya, the scowl was replaced with a smirk.

"She new?" Mya questioned coldly but before T could answer Mya howled to Kiaysha. "YO DON'T FUCK WIT' DIS NIGGA! HER WHOLE FUCKIN' CREW FOUL AS HELL!"

"Yo Mya," vacillated T snatching her arm only to withdraw her hand when she felt blood leaking from it. Heaving breath out her tongue became captive between her teeth while her left jaw flexed viciously. "Where my brother at?"

"Dat BITCH IN DA HOUSE!" she wailed then in her anguish whirled around swinging the bat and smashing it through the back windows of the Jeep. The deranged woman walked around the vehicle swinging the bat into it. Once she went around it completely and was back to seeing T she cajoled menacingly, "Ain't you supposed to be saving her pussy ass? Calming me down or something?" When T declined to give an answer, she dropped the bat stalking up to T poking her in the chest. "Fuck you T! Answer me dammit!" she yelled shoving her. Again, T didn't answer so she turned back to the house. "You bitch," she growled out in disgust weeping heavily. "Bring yo' fuckin' ass out here Chantel!" she shouted again when she caught her breath. "Yo' brotha fuckin' nigga can't save you! So, just bring yo' fuckin' ass out here! Cuz it ain't no fuckin' way! No, fuckin' way," she lost her voice. Swallowing the tears piling up that she refused to let fall she bit out, "Five long ass fuckin' years," the tears finally pushed past the dam of Mya's refusal as she repeated herself, "Five fuckin' years. Gone," Mya crumpled in the driveway sobbing uncontrollably.

Shaking her head T glanced down warily at Mya then at her hand. She looked up at the house to see Chantel creeping down the driveway with her son Dreamz in her arms his eyes wide with fear and confusion. She let out a sigh meeting her brother's eyes and nodded for her to get in the car. T picked Mya up off the ground and hugged her tightly absorbing her tears, snot, and sweat.

Mya allowed T to comfort her for a minute while her body convulsed, hands wringing T's shirt. In a swift second, she twisted out of T's grasp as if T was contagious, "Don't you fuckin' touch me. You ain't no better than her," her red-rimmed eyes drilled a hole through T. "Shit you probably what caused all dis," her eyes hardened only to develop a steely glint. "Was dis yo' plan T? Is everything working out how you wanted? You know you ain't never want yo' so called bitch ass lil' buddy to settle down. So, congrats muthafucka she didn't. She still yo' trifling ass fucking around friend just like you. I hope y'all catch something. Nasty muthafuckas."

T held her hands up in surrender, "Mya, I don't know what da fuck is goin' on but I ain't have shit to do wit' it. I always respected y'all relationship and gurl you know lil' buddy love you," Mya scoffed at her words. "And yeah that's my nigga but she her own muthafucka. Whatever went down went down. She my lil' buddy before dis and still is but I ain't sign up for dis shit. Yo' ass den cut me and shit. Fuck dat. I'm out ma."

130

Mya's whole body bristled dangerously at T's words as her top lip raised curling distastefully, "I'm out ma. I'm out," she mocked T. "Well go head den. Run like a lil' bitch just like yo' nigga fuckin' brother."

T ignored her walking backwards to the car.

"And FUCK YOU T!" Mya hollered out watching T get in the car. She held up the middle finger on both hands as the car drove past her.

****

From inside the car T watched Kiaysha wave good night and enter her home. She sped off into the dark earliness of evening with only a glance into the backseat to see her nephew sleeping against the door. She tossed a bag of weed into Chantel's lap.

"Roll up Lil' Buddy."

Chantel didn't even look down at the weed. Seemingly, on automatic, she reached into T's glove department pulled out two grape cigarillos and broke them open with her nails. Diligently, she rolled her blunts while T called her mother.

"Yo, Ma what's good! I know I just saw you yesterday," an upbeat T greeted her mother, "No, ma'am I'm not in trouble. Lil' Buddy just hit me up not too long ago. She got a situation so I scooped her up. . . Yes ma'am she's okay and so is Dreamz. . .Cuz everybody about to meet at yo' house. . . Ha. Kim busy at the spot and she coming too. . . I'm 'bout ten minutes away. . . Okay. . . A'ight Ma. . . I love you too. . .See you in a minute," she hung up the phone and glanced over at Chantel whose muscles hadn't relaxed. "I'm 'bout to have Jay and Kim meet us at Ma Dukes house."

The youngest of their family nodded her head curtly but didn't voice a reply.

Exhaling softly to herself T called her sister. "Sorry to interrupt but Lil' Buddy got an emergency situation. So, meet us at Ma Dukes house," she didn't wait for Kim to answer instead hanging up immediately and calling their stud brother Jay. "What's good bruh? Everything cool down there?" T questioned referring to the nightclub Colorz the family owned.

"Yeah it's all good fam. Just the regulars in here sipping and chilling before the Sunday club crowd drop in. What's good with you? You coming in tonight?"

"Nah. You ain't staying either. Tell Stacey to hit me on da hip anything go down she in charge. Lil' Buddy got an emergency. We meeting at Ma Dukes house."

Jay repeated the words to Stacey and uttered into her phone, "Tell Lil' Buddy to keep her head up. I'm on the way to Ma Dukes now."

"A'ight."

"It's on."

As they came to a stop in Ma Dukes driveway, they noticed her standing on the porch waiting for them to approach. Patiently, T waited for her brother watching her cradle her son Dreamz like he was a newborn needing to be protected from the world. Ma Dukes beamed at the two studs when they got closer.

"Go on in and lay my baby down Lil' Buddy," she whispered to Chantel. "Then come back out and show me some love."

Maneuvering past the mother and daughter on the porch Chantel went inside the home to lay her only child down. T went in with her grabbing her nephew's favorite movie and turning it on inside his room just in case he woke up. They went back outside to a waiting Ma Dukes.

"What happened to your hand?" Ma Dukes shot grabbing T's hand once she was in arm's length.

"Mya cut her. I'm sorry bruh, I ain't even know she had nothing like that. I knew she had the bat," apologized Chantel.

Smiling easily at her baby brother T told her, "It's cool Lil' Buddy. You know Ma Dukes gon' get me right. I ain't tripping."

Ma Dukes moved away from the two inside of the house and returned with her first aid box. Opening it up revealed more than just the contents of a regular first aid box. Quickly, she wiped away the dried blood from her daughters wound, cleaned it out and placed a gauze pad over it. She sat it on the table that was a part of the front porch furniture.

"C'mere Lil' Buddy lemme look at you," she dictated. Chantel stepped forward and Ma Dukes took her chin in her fingers turning left and right looking at her face. She noted the red parts but didn't comment. Stretching her arm out and stepping back her gaze traveled up and down her frame looking for anything. When she was complete, she kissed her on the cheek. "Okay you look fine Lil' Buddy. Am I missing anything?"

Chantel shook her head, "No, ma'am unless you count the pounding in my head."

Popping open her first aid box, she tossed her a bottle of Tylenol extra strength. "She didn't cut you too did she?"

A bashful smile crept to her ears. She turned her head so they could see the back of her nugget, "I caught a vase to the back of the dome."

"Shit!" Ma Dukes sputtered. "Lemme go grab some water. Let me know if one of them fools pulls up before I come out."

"Damn Lil' Buddy," T said turning her around to inspect her nugget. "Bruh, what the fuck? When y'all start fighting like this?"

"Today."

"Aww man," she shook her head sadly. "How long yo' head been busted open like that?"

"I put some ice and sugar on it and shit for awhile but shit it's been long enough from the impact that I can finally fucking crash."

"Ma, Jay here," hissed T into the house as a 2006 Ford Mustang GT sped to a stop behind T's car.

The stud brothers watched their brother Jay exit the car, pop the trunk, and wheel up a cooler towards them. Jay and T slapped hands first. When Jay pulled Chantel in for her hug, she grabbed the back of her head and withdrew her hand quickly staring at the blood.

"Yo what the fuck?" she spat angrily grabbing Chantel's arm, twisting her around to view the back of her dome. "Who the hell did this shit?"

Ma Dukes stepped out onto the front porch ushering Jay to the side, "Mya," she answered simply.

A look of enigma draped across the Latino stud's face, "Mya?" Jay repeated.

Both of her stud brothers nodded their heads as a yes.

"What the fuck? What? Since when she start acting like this? Wait y'all was banging?"

A hand patted her shoulder, "Let me bandage her head up first. Slow ya roll with the questions baby."

Jay didn't say anything else but immediately lit up a cigarette offering one to T. Their eyes scrutinized the youngest of their family from head to toe while Ma Dukes doctored her wound. A red 2001 Chrysler Sebring Convertible LX came to a spot in front of the house parking on the street. The door flew open and Kim stalked up to the family in long basketball shorts and a white beater.

Kim stopped standing in front of Chantel, "Why didn't you call me?" she demanded to know.

A smirk appeared on Chantel's face when she looked Kim up and down pointedly, "You were busy."

Light giggles came from everyone else except the two standing in front of one another.

"Well you call me anyway next time. First," she poked her in the chest.

T tossed her cigarette sliding closer to Chantel. On the other side of her Jay stepped toward them as well.

"Kim, I love you but after everything I been through yo don't put yo' fuckin' hands on me right now."

"Done," declared Ma Dukes moving from behind Chantel.

Once Ma Dukes had moved out of the way Kim pulled Chantel into a hug, "I'm sorry Lil' Buddy," she apologized. "But you know I hate to see you looking like this fam."

"I know."

"Promise me next time you will call me first. Cuz you know T punk ass ain't gon' do nothin'."

A real smile of humor flashed on Chantel's face.

"Well fuck you too," said T.

They all laughed as Chantel nodded at Kim.

"A'ight well I'm out. Goodnight *ladies*. I gotta go make sure this boy stay sleep. Y'all move on towards the back," Ma Dukes stared at the three studs daring someone say something about being called a lady.

Everybody smiled bidding goodnight to Ma Dukes while moving toward the back yard. The arrangement of chairs from the barbecue stood unmoved from yesterday. Collectively, they took a chair regrouping them into a circle with the cooler in the middle of them.

"So, what's good lil' bruh?" Jay asked taking a blunt from behind her ear and lighting it.

"Man," she dropped her head into her caramel hands. "I fucked up y'all."

Kim lit her blunt hit it a few times and placed it in the opposite rotation of Jay's blunt, "What happened boo?"

One tear tumbled down Chantel's cheek before she lifted her face, "Y'all remember Breyanna?"

Saying Breyanna's name caused discourse through the whole group as they all began to speak their feelings about her at once.

"Hell yeah. Dat bitch tried to burn me saying she ain't have nothin'," T spat.

"And I beat her duck faced ass for fuckin' wit' my brother," Kim added.

Jay however broke the bashing to say, "But she had some good weed doe. And head."

T smiled as she remembered as well, "Yeah. Damn good head."

"Anyways Lil' Buddy, what about her?" exhaled Kim.

Chantel looked at them all as she took a hit off the blunt. She took in a little bit of air in before swallowing the smoke, "She da one that turned me out," she chiefed the blunt after that passing it to T. "After y'all graduated it was just me and Ronnie. And Ronnie eventually stopped coming. Me and her start kickin' it when I wasn't wit' y'all. First, we was just fuck friends na mean den we branched off into our own relationships and shit so we was just cool like."

"When did you have Dreamz?" Kim intervened. "I'm sorry shit!" she exclaimed at the dark looks T and Jay cast her way. "I love you Lil' Buddy and I love my nephew. I was just wondering like cuz nobody wanted to talk about it. And shit we talking about the past now."

Taking both blunts from behind her ears T sparked them at the same damn time. She puffed both of them then passed one to Kim. Jay leaned up popping open the cooler to reveal liquor and beer. She passed a beer to each one of her sister and brothers.

Gazing into the depths of Kim's eyes she admitted with a harsh scoffing laugh that ended before it started, "I was raped,"

"Damn. And dats dude's son?"

She nodded.

"He know?"

"Only y'all believed me."

"Damn my bad Lil' Buddy. I ain't mean to bring that shit up. I ain't know. Na mean when I came to da school and they introduced me to you I was a lil' put off like. Fa real a stud wit' a baby?"

Smiling sadly, she tossed the roach of a blunt, "It's cool."

"So, what happened Lil' Buddy? With Breyanna and shit?" T questioned.

"Oh yeah well we kept in touch all these years and shit. Like last week doe she asked could she come crash at da crib for da weekend. I was cool wit' it ran it by Mya she was cool wit' it. So, she came through," Chantel paused to chug half her beer. "Man that bitch got me wet as hell. I don't even remember what we was doin' before we start drinkin' and shit but we ended up fuckin'. And gotdamn Mya walked in," three mouths lost control of their lower jaws and dropped open hanging letting flies zoom in. "Exactly. And dat wasn't even earlier today dat shit went down. That was fuckin' yesterday," she growled out. "She ain't let me get no fuckin' sleep."

"Damn," everyone said simultaneously.

Nodding sadly Chantel downed the rest of her beer. The blunt was in her hands once more so she puffed puffed and passed it to T.

Kim found her voice first as she offered, "Well you want me to kick her ass shorty? It's nothin'."

The oldest of the group Jay and T snickered. Jay walked over to Kim laughing and draped her arm over Kim's shoulders, "Man you always tryin' to fight somebody."

Removing Jay's arm off her she retorted, "Well hoes should leave my fuckin' brothers alone."

"Nah. You just be wantin' to fight mafuckas," T teased her with a smile.

She extended her middle finger to T, "Fuck all y'all."

Everybody chuckled but the laughter broke off as they heard the screen door squeak open. They watched, waiting for Ma Dukes to approach. She glared at them from inside of the house still.

T bounded up towards her mother, "My bad Ma. We'll be quieter."

Ma Dukes waved her off sashaying out of the house towards the circle, "Yeah, yeah, yeah. That all sound real good but da weed smell real good. Jay, puff puff pass my way please."

"A'ight ma. You know you got asthma," cautioned T.

She passed the blunt to Kim and blew out a smoke ring, "Baby, I been smoking longer than you think. I can handle it," she began to cough. "Now I ain't never had no shit like dis," she wheezed out with watering eyes, "But I like it."

"See look. I'm all growed up wit' some Afghanistan shit ma."

The two laughed with the others watching their banter smiles plaguing all of their faces.

"So, what you gon' do Lil' Buddy?" Jay asked Chantel turning the conversation back to the reason why they were all present.

Emitting a deep sigh Chantel dropped her head into her hands, "Man ion even know."

Peering warily at the three studs Ma Dukes inspected each of their faces for a clue before looking at Kim who yielded no information. She searched their faces again. Finally, she stared at Chantel, "Set da scene."

Lifting her head up she brought her eyes to meet Ma Dukes. They stared at each other for a long minute without speaking. Chantel's jaw clenched then she revealed her error, "I always been cool with my first and she came thru fa da weekend got me drunk as fuck and we ended up fuckin'. And my gurl walked in."

"Well I be damned. Hand me yo' drink let me think 'bout dis," she snapped at Jay. The crew let out giggles but quieted down as Ma Dukes spoke again this time in a serious voice. "Is she worth it?"

"What you mean?"

"You know what I mean? Do you want yo' gurl back or not?"

"Ma, you know I love her. But this shit how she fuckin' acted tonight take the cake. I mean I know I fucked up and all but shit I don't know after this."

Laughing Ma Dukes responded, "Y'all young folk trip me out. You was with that gurl almost six years. She helped you and was there for you during a very hard time in yo' life but you don't know if you want her back. Lemme clue you in baby," she walked over to Chantel and rubbed her head then took her chin in her hand making her look into her eyes. "Sometimes when a woman hurt it will be like a hurricane ripping through your life and possessions and whatever else is around at that moment. All she telling you is that you've hurt her deeply but she still loves you and wanna be with you."

Swallowing a lump in her throat Chantel blinked back her tears refusing to allow them to fall. She moved

139

away from Ma Dukes sitting back stiffly avoiding everyone's gaze mouth twisted up.

Ma Dukes placed a kiss on her cheek, "Baby, you gotta quit holding so much inside. You gon' end up erupting like a volcano. There is nothing wrong with crying. Just like you need some good sex you need a good cry every now and then too," she straightened up to glance around the rest of her family. "I ain't too keen on missing another face. We all been drinkin' and smoking and don't need to drive. Especially you Miss Fast and Furious," a wink flew Kim's way. "Ain't nobody slippin' off tonight unless you plan on getting a ride or walking. Y'all get Lil' Buddy to vent some since Ronnie ain't here. Then y'all come in here and lay down for awhile."

Four heads nodded respectively, said yes ma'am and bid Ma Dukes good night. For a few minutes, there was silence between the family of friends. Kim raised her drink first and held it in the air until the others followed suit. They all drained the last of their beers onto the ground.

"We miss you, Ronnie," added T speaking what everyone thought before they all slipped back into the thoughtful mournful silence of their stud brother.

Sniffing Chantel wiped away the few tears that had managed to evade her efforts. "Ma, talkin' to us like she did when we was kids and after she beat our ass."

Jay started to laugh, "Nah y'all remember when she was outta town and she came back early and we had thrown a gay party?"

"And she went in T's room found her butt naked wit' five hoes," Kim added laughing.

"Shit don't hate me hate da game. Dem hoes served it up right. They are and forever will be the five heartbeats," argued T as they all began to laugh from their trip down memory lane.

Kim rolled her eyes, "Yeah whatever they wore yo' ass out I know dat. Yo' mama yelling at us, and you kept fallin' asleep on her."

"Here we go," Jay hollered out excitedly beginning to mock Ma Dukes. "What the hell? Everybody get da fuck out! Where's my daughter? Open T's door, close it back," she laughed. "Track all of us down sit us on da couch. Five minutes later five girls come downstairs happy as hell. They leave Ma Dukes go upstairs. T in da shower singin'."

Chantel took over at this point, "Ma Dukes say, what da hell wrong wit' you young muthafuckas. Kim, I thought you was straight?"

"And dats when I said no ma'am I like gurls too."

"And here come T whistling out the shower," Jay started again. "Nigga she beat yo' ass all da way downstairs and on to da couch."

T smiled slightly abashed, "Fuck y'all. Y'all den all got y'all ass beat by Ma Dukes too. Kim, you got yours when you got caught fuckin' at school. Lied to the principal and gave him my address and number. And you thought Ma wasn't gon' do nothin' cuz she ain't birth you?"

"Man dat wasn't funny. I got my ass beat twice fa dat."

"Shit mines was right before I got strung out. She beat my ass cuz she saw me talkin' to her ex dude dat d-boy. Den she beat my ass again when she found out I was strung out and again after I got clean as a reminder," reminisced Jay sadly.

"Shit me and Ronnie got in trouble at da same time. Dis when we was stayin' wit' y'all fa a min. We was supposed to been in school and Mama saw us following da thick twins home while we was skippin. She hopped out da car hit Ron hit me hit Ron hit me again and told us to get in da car. Da twins still laugh over dat shit man," chuckled Chantel at the memory.

141

"Well shit dats Ma Dukes fa you. Beat our ass wit' all da anger of a mad black woman then afterward talk to us with the patience and tenderness of a white woman," guffawed T.

They all laughed but stopped when the screen door opened. Dreamz walked out, "Ay y'all Ma Dukes said dat y'all ain't too old to get beat. She said y'all too loud."

His mother beckoned for him to come here. Chantel rubbed his head affectionately and gave him a kiss, "Tell Ma we will lower our voices. Go get in the bed lil' man. I'll be there in a second," she told him.

Dreamz nodded and ran back in the house.

"Dre, smart as hell to be so young. I won't be surprised when they put him up in school. " Kim complimented Chantel.

Smiling appreciatively Chantel stood stretching, "That's what happens when the family help raise a child. But I don't know 'bout y'all but we den reminisced about it and I ain't tryin' to feel another one."

Everyone laughed as they followed suit.

"Shit y'all need to catch up wit' me. I'm two ahead," Jay told them.

Rolling her eyes Kim hissed at her, "Get yo' ass up, and come in da house."

"Can I sleep wit' you?"

"You a have to start dressin' like me."

"Shit never mind den," Jay proclaimed faking disappointment as they followed T and Chantel into the house.

Upon entering the house, Chantel headed straight upstairs to her son Dreamz room. Her other brothers and sister continued on going down to the basement. They each took a seat at a portable table placed in the middle of the basement in front of a green futon with a mirror above it.

Jay slid her cooler next to her. She popped the lid and sent a beer flying to T and Kim.

"Y'all think they done fa real?" Kim wondered out loud to her brothers.

The two exchanged uneasy looks then Jay spoke, "You hadn't met us yet. But shit, it was bad. After Lil' Buddy found out she was prego she stopped giving a fuck about everything. Lil' Buddy was out there heavy in them streets. Man if it wasn't for Mya yo," Jay shook her head.

"Dreamz might not be here," whispered T. "She wasn't listening to nothing nobody had to say. Ronnie, Breyanna, Ma Dukes, us, and then Mya came along. After she had Dreamz, it was crazy. Her and Mya wasn't together officially but na mean Mya was always there for her. Before they even knew, they were unofficially officially a couple Mya pops had figured it out. And he a preacher so he kicked her out sap. Boom, Lil' Buddy turned right back to the streets leaving nephew with whoever wanted to keep him 'cause she felt like it was her fault Mya getting kicked out so she tried to get her a spot but Mya wouldn't take it which further pissed Lil' Buddy off."

"And Lil' Buddy had hoes. Even before she was like yeah I'm gay she had hoes," chuckled Jay. "Shit she fucked around with Breyanna for a minute even after we all was cool on her. Shit you could see they chemistry from the first time they met though," Jay said laughing.

"How Mya pull her away from everybody and the streets?" Kim asked.

Both studs shrugged as a response. T answered vocally, "Honestly we don't know. One day she was out there fooling wildin' out. The next day she said she was cool. She ain't have shit for sale, wasn't hitting no licks, Breyanna wouldn't even look in her direction."

Kim rolled her eyes dramatically, "Mya gave her an ultimatum. Her and no streets or Breyanna with the streets."

Mimicking Kim's eyes roll, Jay chided, "Great observation Kim. Damn I don't know why we ain't think of that,"

A lone middle finger flipped up into the air facing Jay sent from Kim.

Laughing Jay continued, "But nah real shit Lil' Buddy was keeping a lot of shit from us back then even me and we was the three amigos ha. If that's the case man, you know Lil' Buddy woulda just said that. Hell we asked."

"True," Kim mused

"Ay y'all know Lil' Buddy birthday coming up. Her lil' bro coming up on eighteen now. I think it's time to track the lil' homie down let him reconnect with Lil' Buddy," interjected T.

Simultaneously the two nodded.

"Yeah I got you. I can hire a private investigator or I can just ask around. But I'm on it," she turned to look at Jay. "What's up with you and Arianna bruh? I peeped that shit yesterday."

T raised an eyebrow and they clinked glasses together, "You wasn't the only one sis."

A halo appeared over Jay's head as she donned angelic features, "I don't know what y'all talking about," she said looking away from them. Devil horns began to stretch out her mouth into a smile once she took a sip of her beer.

"Aww bullshit!" chided T.

"Right! Her response, yo' response that LOOK you gave her. Then you staring at the ground zoned the fuck out. Be fa real bruh like we don't know you," added Kim.

Jay smiled bashfully. She leaned up on the table and her eyes ran to the ceiling solemnly, "Sorry Ronnie," she shrugged. "A'ight so, back in the day on the low me and Arianna used to fuck around."

Letting out an exuberant whoop of laughter T slapped hands with Jay, "Okay then my nigga! Shit big sis bad!"

Grinning triumphantly Kim yelled, "I fuckin' knew it! Boah you make me wish I would've tried my hand back in the day."

Sparks rose and Jay looked ominously into Kim's eyes while speaking lightly, "It was over sis. That Spanish fly had her on lock already."

"Shit you never know now though. Cream ass might get replaced," she baited her brother.

Scoffing Jay bit out bitterly, "Good luck with that," her jaw twitched ever so slightly.

Kim grinned, "Oh what's that? Does somebody still have a thing for her? What happened brah? Spill it?"

"Hold up, hold up, hold up," T halted the conversation holding up her phone. She stood up walking away from them and mumbling "Fuckers," when she glanced back to see the two still talking. "Hello?"

"Hello T? Are you busy?" Yolanda's sultry voice oozed over the phone.

"For you? Never," flirted T with a smile.

"Good. How fast can you make it to the east side?"

"How fast do you need me to be there?"

"Yesterday."

"Say no more. I'm on the way."

"Okay."

The two phones disconnected and T began whistling back into the other room where her brother and sister had ceased talking.

"Pussy calls?" Jay guessed with a smile.

T nodded grinning with excitement. "You know it," she downed her beer. "I'm outta here."

145

"Alright we ain't kids no more! I ain't covering for yo' ass," chided Kim.

"Did anybody ask you too? Ma know we grown and ain't about to stay here. One of us should stay though for when Lil' Buddy wakes up."

"I'll stay," Kim volunteered. "I already sent Cream home and Jay you need to get back to the club."

Jay nodded, "Alright sis."

The two studs hugged their sister goodbye and walked out of the house.

"Alright bruh. Be safe," Jay told T shaking her hand.

"You too bruh. Holla at me if you need me fam," responded T.

"I got you."

The two studs departed from Ma Dukes house in opposite directions. T drove along listening to an oldies R&B and hip-hop station. She sparked a blunt. A text message vibrated the cell phone in her pocket and she pulled it out to see Yolanda's message saying that the front door was open.

Inhaling deeply T walked through the open front door and traveled up the stairs following the scent of wet pussy and the moans of it being touched. She walked into Yolanda's bedroom to find her rich melanin body splayed across the bed biting her lip, legs draped across either side of the bed as she guided a double-headed dildo in and out of her vagina and ass concurrently.

"Damn baby. You couldn't wait?" T questioned with a smile. She began to undress slowly captivated by the stimulation Yolanda dealt to herself.

Yolanda revealed the concupiscence behind her brown eyes as she stared at T. A smirk drifted across her face. She held onto T's eyes as she brought herself to an orgasm pinching and twisting her nipples to help along the journey.

Once she was finished she rubbed the head of one against her clit and brought it up to her lips engulfing half the dildo. She tossed it to the side quickly after removing her juices from the toy and crawled towards T at the end of the bed. She came to T and grabbed her by her hips pulling herself up along her body until she was face to face with T.

"I'm sorry Daddy. I couldn't wait," apologized Yolanda pressing a kiss to T's face and then on her neck.

She lifted the shirt T had neglected to take off due to the trance of watching Yolanda please herself. Yolanda's lips cruised around T's neck and chest dropping off kisses and stopping to suck and suckle the stud's soft skin.

The hots overcame T from head to toe. She watched Yolanda's mouth move to enclose itself around her nipples. First one then the other. A gentle suction then a swift bite caused her libido to skyrocket with reverence.

With a smile, Yolanda gripped T's ass in her hands lips flying back up towards her mouth. Her breath tantalized T's ear as she told her, "I want to show you how much I appreciate you," she began to remove the strap on harness from T letting it slide to the ground, "After that you may appreciate me."

A broad smile stretched across T's lips. Peering down at the dark skinned goddess below her, she watched her partition her legs from one another so that she had a wider stance. Automatically T's head went back as a hand moved to conjoin with Yolanda's hair.

Down below in the center of T, Yolanda worked. She used her lips and her tongue in sync her plump lips sliding on and off the hardened flesh in her mouth while her tongue flickered like a hummingbird against it. Both of Yolanda's hands wandered to T's ass pulling and pushing her hips. Her tongue slithered down the inner moist areas of

147

T's vaginal regions. Pressing on she rolled her tongue between the skin separating a woman's two holes.

T jumped pleasurably a grin marring her face. Yolanda extended her long tongue letting it slide between T's ass cheeks. T groaned at the pleasure and bit down on her lip. She felt Yolanda go back to take her centerfold into her mouth again.

"Cum for me Daddy," Yolanda moaned playing with her own pussy as she ate T out.

The hands entangled in Yolanda's hair spread apart and grasped tighter than before. Yolanda allowed the hands to dictate where her tongue caressed the sexual sphere. T's ass cheeks tightened. Eyes clenched closed, ass cheeks flexing T groaned out and sputtered cuss words down at Yolanda.

"Fuck," she croaked out opening her eyes and looking down at the woman below her. "Stand up," she whispered.

Yolanda stood and T scooped her up lying her on the bed. She bent down and brought up her brief style harness so her strap on penis stood at attention. She held onto Yolanda's legs in the air and speared into her vaginal opening.

"OOH FUCK! Fuck this pussy daddy!" screamed out Yolanda from the drilling T imposed. "Oh my God! You so fuckin' deep daddy! Shit!" Yolanda sputtered breathlessly as T thrust in and out of her with her legs being held straight up.

The woman on the bed began to squirm backwards. T allowed her to do so and followed the pussy like a dog with its dick out. Once T was on the bed also, she pulled her back towards her by her thighs.

"Put ya feet in my chest," ordered T. "And leave them there. Don't move them."

Complying Yolanda began to moan and scream louder and louder due to the angle and depth of their position. Erratically her hands pulled at her own hair, pinched her nipples, and tried to hold onto T's thighs. T held onto her ass cheeks opening and closing them as she juked in and out of her pussy.

Hands back twisted in her hair Yolanda's mouth opened and a whimpering sound came out. T watched the pleasurable tribulation of an orgasm rock through her body leaving her trembling and chest heavy. T removed herself.

Automatically Yolanda's hand darted into the air, "Hold on. Give me a minute T. I can still feel you in my stomach."

Grinning T stood pleased with herself, "I'ma go grab a drink of water. You want some?"

"Yes, Daddy."

She went in the other room and returned with two glasses of water. She sat one next to Yolanda on the nightstand and downed her glass before sitting it down next to the full one. She slid into the bed next to Yolanda who was curled up in the fetal position. When T slid in next to her Yolanda drifted off toward her laying her head on her chest and holding onto T.

"T, I'm taking a leave from the hospital," she blurted out.

"Cool. What are you going to do with the extra time?"

"Well my divorce is final and I got fucked so I'm going to go to law school. Outside of that it's been a long time since I've had fun like real fun without having to go to work hung-over or worry about anything."

"What do you want to do?"

"Any and everything. I have the means to do whatever I want. Unfortunately, most people can't afford to go bungee jumping or something at the drop of a dime so

I'm lacking a fun partner. If you're willing I would love for you to partake in more adventures with me."

Smiling at the thoughts of all the new places they could fuck running through her mind T agreed, "I'm game. Let's do it."

Yolanda grinned and laid her head back down on T's chest stroking her body with her hand as her eyes closed.

****

"Thanks for meeting me beautiful. I'm sorry we had to cut our date short the other night," apologized T as she pulled out a chair for Kiaysha to sit in.

Obliging Kiaysha sat down in the chair of the Italian restaurant they had visited on their first date. T took the light jacket she had around her shoulders and draped it over the back of her chair. "No problem T. Obviously it was an emergency. I can't and won't be mad at that. How is your brother?"

T sat down with a sigh and shaking her head, "She will be alright," she said in an unconvinced tone.

Kiaysha peered at her quizzically, "Are you sure?"

A hard sigh expelled from T, "I hope so."

"What happened?"

A waiter drifted over before T could answer and began introductions and inquiring about beverage choices. T ordered a glass of wine for the two of them then waited for the waiter to bustle off before responding.

"She got caught up messing around with her ex, her first at that," one of Kiaysha's eyebrows raised but T continued on, "Don't judge her though Lil' Buddy ain't no cheater. Shorty manipulated and seduced her then her gurl walked in."

Her gray eyes spiraled in their sockets, "But why even put yourself in that situation? There is always a should'a, would'a, could'a. She should'a known better, if she would'a kept her dick in her pants, hell she could'a not kicked it with her ex."

Smiling with a shrug T poured their wine into wine glasses, "Hey, her gurl was cool with it."

Again, the eyes rolled, "Bullshit," she turned to the approaching waiter.

"Are we ready to order?" he posed.

Both of the women nodded their heads in response and T waited for Kiaysha to order first.

"I'll have a full chicken Caesar salad with ranch dressing please. Also, a minestrone soup," ordered Kiaysha.

"And for you sir?" the waiter questioned T.

"I'll start with a small house salad and the fish and steamed vegetables platter."

"Okay. That will be right out to you. If I can have those menus," he took the menus from T. "Thank you sir. I'll be back to check on you guys shortly."

"Now back to you," stated T with a smile. "You think my Lil' Buddy was stepping out on her woman?"

"Those are your friends. You know them better than I do."

"Okay but as for right now. Since you don't know them, it sounds like she was creeping to you?"

"Honestly yes."

"Alright. So, how about you meet my *friends* then? You will get to meet Lil' Buddy, have a feel for her personality, and ya mind can get changed."

A slight giggle escaped from Kiaysha, as she shook her head no, "Your friends that are your family? No thanks Timothy. Not at this moment. Even if I did meet Lil' Buddy that doesn't mean my mind would change either. I

151

mean just from one encounter or even several encounters you never know what the next person is capable of. Hell from your personality I could guess you would be a cheater."

A look of affront dressed T's face, "Hold on mama. My word is bond always," a crooked grin flew across her face. "I ain't never stepped out of bounds on a female when it's just me and her on the court. You dig?"

Again Kiaysha's eyes rolled, "Hmm. Says the single, fast talking, charming, handsome gentlewoman across from me. I wouldn't be surprised if you had a slew of women jockeying you for a ride."

"But I'm single," crooned T.

She sipped her drink, "And that's exactly why I do not want to meet your friends, family whatever. I refuse to just be one of those women."

"Slow down ma. I was using your words. I mean but if I did have a slew of women I'm single though."

"Yeah single free to mingle. But meeting family is supposed to be an accomplishment that you know you're working towards something. And being that you have a slew of women I could be replaced at any time right?"

T winked at her, "I don't know depends on the player and of course how the woman rock."

"Well what type of player would you be?" she asked sweetly and batting her eyelashes.

Biting her lip T leaned forward, "I wouldn't be a player. I would be me. An honest single free to mingle individual. What about you how would you rock? Would you pull out all the tricks of the trade, grade A shit or would that be a gradual process of unraveling ya freak flag?"

Spying the waiter coming towards them with their food Kiaysha's eyes fluttered and she sat back in her seat, "If you're lucky one day maybe you will find out."

The waiter placed their food in front of the couple, "Here you are. Is there anything else I can get the two of you?" he looked at each of the woman who both declined. "Okay well ladies. Enjoy the food I will return in a while to see how everything is going."

They nodded at him.

Kiaysha watched T begin to dig into her food without touching her own. T looked up at her and smiled. She dabbed her mouth with her napkin and looked at Kiaysha.

"What's up?"

"Did you bless your food?" asked Kiaysha.

"Huh?"

"Did you bless your food?"

"No, can we bless our food together?"

The two joined hands across the table from one another. T followed Kiaysha suit as she bowed her head and closed her eyes. "Thank you Lord for this food that we are about to receive. Amen."

"Amen," murmured T.

Quietly the two munched on their salads not looking up at one another. T filled their glasses after she had quickly finished her salad. Halfway through hers Kiaysha began to play with her food pushing the salad leaves and chicken around with her fork.

"T when was the last time you went to church?" she pried.

"Never."

"Oh. I haven't been in awhile. Do you know what religion you would be?"

"I don't know. Ma Dukes wasn't big on religion."

"Would you go with me one day?"

"Sure why not?"

Kiaysha grinned from ear to ear.

An awkward silence draped across their table once again as they finished their entrees and waited for the waiter to come and collect their tables. Once he finally did, the two of them declined to dessert. T's phone began to buzz excitedly on the table while waiting for their check to arrive.

"What's up mama...Private investigator...for who?....Who hired him....oh....alright....yes ma'am....in a minute ma....no ma'am I'm on a lunch date....personal," she grinned over at Kiaysha, "My mama said hi."

"Hello ma'am," answered Kiaysha sweetly.

"You hear her ma?...alright....yes ma'am....Ma, I will be there as soon as you let me off the phone...alright....okay....See you in a bit."

"Private investigator?"

A playful grin broke across T's face, "Let me find out you ear hustling."

"Whatever. Is it a secret why you need a private investigator?" teased Kiaysha.

"Nah. Lil' Buddy's birthday coming up. We throwing her a party and trying to track down her lil' bro since he turning eighteen this week."

"Why didn't she keep up with her little brother herself?"

"It's complicated. Lil' Buddy had a lot of fucked up shit happen to her in her life. One of those an estrangement from her brother."

"Oh. Well that's sad."

In agreement T nodded and stood up taking the check from the waiter, "Shit you don't even know a quarter of it ma," she pulled out a fifty dollar bill to cover their cost and pulled Kiaysha's jacket off of her chair to place the jacket on for her.

"I'll take your word for it," murmured Kiaysha as the two strolled out of the restaurant towards their cars. "But I hope everything does work out for her."

"Thanks ma."

"No problem. When is her birthday?"

"In a couple of weeks but her lil' brother's birthday is this week sometime, I believe."

"Oh ok. Well I hope you catch up with them. If I was her I would be beyond happy to see him," she pulled open her car door.

"Hold on Ma. Show me some love before we part our separate ways," chastised T. She slid her arms around Kiaysha pulling her close to her chest. T went in for a kiss on the lips but Kiaysha turned her head and she caught a cheek instead. She started to say something but her phone began to ring again and without looking, she knew it was her mother.

Kiaysha slid out of T's arms into her car with an impish grin, "Alright T. Get to your mom's house safely."

Nodding to the woman in her car T smiled and walked away heading to her own car answering her phone, "Ma, I'm leaving the parking lot now. I just got in my car," she said with eyes trained on her vehicle. "Alright bye," T unlocked her car doors and climbed into her car.

Thirty minutes, one blunt, and two cigarettes later T was entering her mother's house using her key, "Ma," she called out.

"In here,"

"Ok baby. We in the kitchen," Ma Dukes hollered back.

T dropped her shades down over her face and walked into the kitchen. She took a seat at the table across from an older gentleman. Ma Dukes placed two plates of food down in between the two.

"Jeff Hinton, this is my daughter Timothy Martin," said Ma Dukes.

The two shook hands firmly.

"Okay well Timothy as I was telling your mother I received a phone call from a Ms. Kim Fields inquiring about setting up our services. She says you guys are looking for a Tyriq Thompson," he waited for T to nod then asked, "And why would that be?" he gazed at T sternly.

Taking off her glasses T met his gaze head on, "His sister is one of my best friends like family blood couldn't make us any closer. She hasn't seen her brother since she was sixteen due to a situation her mother never got past. Mother and daughter estranged she took Tyriq with her and forbade the two from speaking to one another. She even followed up with a restraining order."

"And the situation?"

"It's not my place to tell. It's very personal. But I assure you it's nothing illegal. Tyriq is turning eighteen this week and his sister Chantel's birthday is next up. It's just time for a reconnect now that Tyriq is old enough that if he wants to be in his sisters life he can choose too not his mother."

The private investigator shot a look at Ma Dukes who was earnestly listening to her daughter speak and nodding along sincerely.

"Okay. Well if at any time I expect this isn't what you've said I won't hesitate to end our dealing and go to the police."

Ma Dukes laughed, "That's fine."

"Okay now what can you tell me about the kid?"

"Tyriq Austen-"

"Denise Austen," Ma Dukes jumped in, "Is his mother's name she graduated from West High. Chantel Thompson is her daughter's name. Their old address around when Timothy and Chantel were teenagers was

156

1894 Triangle Lane. Tyriq probably went to Rosa Parks elementary,"

"I think he used to play ball. I know football and soccer for sure. But I think basketball was his thing," interjected T.

"Anything special? Tattoos, scars, injuries?"

The two shrugged.

"He was eleven when she got kicked out," said T.

The investigator closed his notepad, "One more thing do either you know if the mother ever remarried? Is Austen her maiden name? Are you positive the siblings share the same last name?'

Staring at each other both mother and daughter shrugged.

He nodded reviewing his notes, "Okay well I will be in touch soon with one of you. I have a list of six women I can call."

"Yes sir. Any one of us will be fine to contact," the two stood and T shook his hand once again. "Thank you sir for your services."

"No problem. You guys enjoy your day."

"Umm excuse me Mr. Hinton, please take something to eat. A sandwich, fruit, bottled water."

As if that was her cue T moved away from them grabbing a paper plate.

"No, thank you ma'am," he politely declined.

"Mr. Hinton, did you know it's rude to refuse food from the owner of a house while you are in their house. Now I didn't do anything to it. It's just common hospitality that's what you do for people. Now please," she insisted.

T flashed a plate in front of him, "Turkey or ham? Ma feels like she has to feed everyone that comes into our house."

"Umm turkey. Thank you," he stammered taking the plate consisting of fruit, veggies, and a sandwich.

157

"Thank you again ma'am," he said accepting the bottle of water as well from T. "Thank you. You all have a great day."

"T go lock the door."

She bounded up to lock the door and came back out to see Ma Dukes putting the lunchmeat, fruit, and veggies away. "Hold up Ma! I ain't get none."

"Didn't you just come from a lunch date?"

"Yes ma'am."

"So, you ain't hungry then," Ma Dukes said.

Quickly T snatched a handful of baby carrots before she could put them in the fridge, "Whatever Ma. Will you twist my hair up for me?"

"Ugh. Why don't you do it like you always do? I will do the front and braid it back for you in a couple big braids."

"Ok that a work Ma."

Immediately T took a seat in a chair munching on her carrots. She pulled the hair band out of her dreads and let them fall past her shoulders Ma dukes left the room returning with locking gel and spray.

"Ma, can I ask you a question?"

"Well being that you just asked me one. I guess you could ask me one more," Ma Dukes replied with a smile.

"When do you think a female should be brought around the family? Like is there an appropriate time?"

"Depends on the individual. Me personally I want you to at least have a name and a face. Now don't get me wrong every lil' random cum catchin' Courtney or hoeing Heidi don't need to meet the family. If they do happen too then that's by chance. But as for the ones you spending more time with than the average chick like Layla. I think it's important for us to have a name and a face just in case especially if you have an emotional attachment like Kim and Cream. Hell I don't think nobody met her."

158

"I did awhile back by chance. She a pretty big girl. But what if Cream didn't wanna meet the family unless it was official?'

"Then that's some stupid shit. If my family is a huge part of who I am and I'm dealing with you but you can't deal with them we can't be official. Shit that's a deal breaker for me if you can't accept my family."

T smiled thinking along the same lines as her mother.

"Tilt ya head baby. Now come on tell what brought this about. You ain't just bust out with this question for no reason," said Ma Dukes.

"You right Ma. Honestly shit I been entertaining the idea of settling down. I thought about it a lil' bit after Ronnie funeral but now this shit with Lil' Buddy and Mya. Entertaining these hoes got my brother six feet under and the other one hurting like a bitch."

"Well you gotta do what's best for you Timothy. I know it would seem like I groomed you and had groomed your brother to be a player. But really, I just wanted to make sure you didn't get hurt by any lies or games a female run. I didn't want you to have to depend on a female to cook, clean, cash or nothing. And I have no doubt in my mind if your brother wouldn't have passed he would be married right now. I know I'm not and I don't plan to be but if the right man came along. I would give him an honest chance. And you need to be able to do the same without the extra women."

"A'ight," she rubbed her chin.

"Alright my ass. Spill it," demanded Ma Dukes.

"Spill what?" innocently T asked.

"The beans girl. Which women is who and don't wanna meet the family?"

"The chick I was at lunch with earlier when you called. Lil' Buddy and Mya saw her the night they broke up. If they even remember. She don't wanna meet everybody until its official."

"Well how can it ever be official if you never really meet your family? Have her come over tomorrow. We can have everybody over play some spades and bones, BBQ and the whole nine."

"She," T stopped talking to look down at her ringing phone. She answered, "What's good Ma."

"Hey T. How are you?" Yolanda's sultry voice flowed over the phone.

"I'm doing good. Ma Dukes twisting the locks for me."

"Oh okay well if you ever need me too I know how to twist them too. What are you doing tomorrow night?"

"Ma Dukes having a get together. Spades, dominoes, food, drink. Why? What's up?"

"Well tomorrow is my first official day of break. I was wondering if you wanted to celebrate with me," pouted Yolanda.

"Oh well shit come through baby. It's cool."

"Okay. Just make sure you text me the address. Okay?"

"A'ight. I got you Ma."

"Okay see you tomorrow."

"Yup."

"Bye."

"Was that the one?" inquired Ma Dukes.

"Nah and neither is this," said T with a smile as a text message from Layla came through.

"Well who was that?" Ma Dukes asked.

"Hold on Ma," T mumbled texting Layla back to say she would be over as soon as Ma Dukes finished her hair. "Ma you almost done?" questioned T closing out of Layla's text message and reading Kiaysha's text message.

"Yes chile! Now which one of them things you then invited over here?"

"It don't matter remember. I kick it with her on the regular," joked T.

"Timothy," Ma Dukes yanked her head.

"Damn Ma. Its Yolanda, the doctor," complained T.

"Thank you. Now you finished. Are you going home or to Yolanda's house?"

"Neither. I'm going to Layla house."

"Okay well be safe. And wrap ya strap baby," said Ma Dukes kissing her daughter on the cheek. "I see you tomorrow baby."

"Alright ma," called out T leaving the house.

Chapter 7

"Come around back?" rhetorically T questioned out loud reading Layla's text message. She adjusted her strap on underneath her pants and got out of the car.

T crossed the street making sure to take in all of her surroundings. As she began to meander through the backyard, she hiked her pants up slightly in case of patches of mud. She came to a stop in front of Layla who was in the doorway posing clad only in her lingerie.

A grin split across T's face, "What's good Ma."

"What's up daddy," purred Layla stepping closer to T. She kissed her on the cheek while her hands went in opposite directions. One slipped under her jeans to wrap around the strap on penis tucked in T's draws. The other hand traveled up T's shirt to the back of her neck pulling her closer so their lips could meet.

Their lips and tongues danced and frolicked with one another again and again. Layla broke the kissing off and stepped back from the doorway. She pulled T along with the one hand that held onto the strap.

Layla paused at a full service bar, "Would you like a drink?"

"Whatever you serving," grinned T.

With a wicked grin, Layla removed her hand from T's strap but only to leap on the center of the bar. She whirled around and pulled out a shot glass and a bottle of whiskey. Layla poured the shot then leaned back on the bar placing the shot between her thighs.

A slight chuckle escaped from T before she dived down towards Layla's knees marking the inside of her knees as the starting point for a trail of kisses. Light caresses and soft kisses accompanied the kisses left along her thighs. She took her tongue and circled Layla's thighs with her tongue before wrapping her lips around the shot glass and tossing the shot back. She sat the glass down with her mouth.

Reaching out to take a hold of T's face, her tongue slithered out and across T's lips. Slowly, Layla's tongue traced them again. The top lip first followed by her bottom lip, which she pulled into her mouth giving it a bite before releasing it. She grabbed the hem of T's shirt and lifted it up over her head. T pulled the shirt completely off and unbuttoned her jeans letting them fall to the floor.

"My turn," murmured T grabbing the bottle of whiskey and pouring herself a shot.

She took a step away from Layla and tucked the shot in the harness of her toy smiling widely at Layla. Layla mimicked her grin and shed the lingerie off her body. The curvy feline in front of her went from standing to dropping down swiftly in front of her legs open. She smiled up at T then kissed along her left hip licking and sucking. Bouncing on her toes, she bypassed the shot kissing and licking until she reached T's hip on her right side. She circled around her hip with her tongue and bit down on it.

"Ooh," squealed T with a smile of pleasure.

Sending T a smile, she ran her tongue from the head of the strap towards the base. She dipped her head grabbed the shot glass and tossed it back. She rose in front of T who furtively pressed a kiss to her lips clamping down on her nipples and twisting them.

"Ooh baby, baby, baby," begged Layla, "One more shot," moaned Layla.

"One more," T rolled one finger between her pussy lips flicking across her clit as she did so.

She sucked Layla's juices into her mouth who in turn hopped backwards on to the bar. Quickly Layla poured a shot and laid out spread eagle on the bar. T smirked watching Layla secure the shot glass between her pussy lips. Once it was yoked, she dived down suckling on Layla's clit. Trotting away her tongue went to the shot glass to lap up a few sips of liquor and went back to caressing Layla's pearl.

"Ooh shit T," moaned Layla touching her throbbing clit. "Daddy," she begged when T moved her tongue away.

Transitioning from clit to shot back to clit made her bud pulse painfully beseeching only T's cunnilingus. Finally obliging T scooped up the rest of her shot and tossed it back standing looking at Layla with a smile on her face. Hazel eyes fully blazed with lust stared at T.

"One more shot remember?" laughed T pouring her shot.

Careening herself off the bar, she strode over to T grabbing the full shot glass. She pulled T to the other side of the room where there was a piano. She pushed T backwards onto the piano and climbed on top of her straddling the stud. Layla tossed the shot back and threw the glass across the room.

Layla's hands stretched all the way up T's body followed by her wet kitty, which she lowered onto T's face. She grabbed a handful of T's dreads pulling her head back over the edge of the piano while she rode her face. Layla controlled her pelvis rocking, rolling, and twirling her hips on T's tongue. When T slid a finger in her ass, she flinched cum squirting out of her. With cum still drizzling from her center T flipped her over and propped her up so her ass was in the air. T chucked her strap all the way inside of her causing another typhoon.

"Wait, wait, wait," moaned Layla sliding the strap out of her.

Taking a deep breath and tossing a crooked grin behind her at T, she climbed off the piano. Layla sat T down on the piano bench. She slid in between T's legs and uncovered the piano keys. Softly her fingers began to push down on the piano keys bringing forth melody while her hips swiveled seductively encasing T's strap on penis.

Flipping her dreads back from her face T kissed along Layla's neck and behind her ears. She licked behind her ear as well before taking it into her mouth, "Alright. Don't stop playing," ordered T.

Unable to reply Layla tossed her head back and gyrated her hips down on T with a moan. She bit her lip and turned her sweaty face to look back at T, "Okay daddy," she moaned.

Their thrusts collaborated while T inched towards the edge of the piano bench. T's hands gripped the edge of the bench and slid it back. She extended her hips all the way up using the strength of her arms for the exertion of exercise an called dips as her strap propelled all the way inside of Layla during the process.

The first dip made her miss a note from the sultry melody her fingers were strumming on the clavier. T noticed and delivered a punishing thrust of her hips. Biting down on her lips, she tried to recover, to keep strumming the pleasure felt within her into a pianistic melody. The dips and the agile movement combined from T deterred her from the keys and coaxed her into pausing to cum impetuously, scream loudly, moan heavily and squeeze her eyes tightly. Only when the harsh punishing blow came did she attempt to keep on playing.

165

"Fuu-ck," she whimpered. "Fuck this pussy Daddy. Fuck this shit," she took her hands off the keys and stood leaning over the piano.

T pulled her two steps back then pushed her face down towards the ground and took her legs in her hands placing them around her hips. She locked her legs around T's waist and slid her hands out a little further on the floor. T's hands slid to her hips guiding their movement so that depth met force as her strap shimmied in and out of her.

"Damn T... shit daddy... oooh fuck... I'm cumming again," announced Layla with a stiff trembling body that T took control over delving all of the cum from inside of her.

"You a'ight shorty?" murmured T after her last convulsion while kissing her sweaty body.

Still basking in the climatic glow Layla shook her head no, "I need you to pull out baby. But I don't want you too," she admitted with closed eyes.

"Brace yo' self shorty I'm about to pull out," warned T. Once Layla nodded, T slid her dick out of Layla.

"Ooh!" Layla moaned eyes popping open.

"You cool shorty?"

"Yes Daddy," she sighed pleasurably and kissed T's lips sweetly.

"Lemme get something to wipe down my strap shorty."

Darting her eyes downward laughed a little, startled to discover along with her juices there was blood also on the strap. "Damn you was deep," she muttered walking away gingerly and up the stairs to the laundry room. She returned with a damp rag and began to clean off T's toy.

"Thanks shorty."

She kissed her, "No, problem daddy," she said carefully walking away to put the rag back in the laundry room. She came back downstairs to find T fully clothed. A sad feeling swelled in the pit of her stomach. "You ain't

166

gotta run right out T. I'm home alone," she smiled again kissing her willing her to stay.

Softly T kissed her back and broke away "Nah I'ma slide on up outta here shorty."

Something within Layla broke but with a smile plastered on, she gave one last kiss to T, "Okay daddy be safe."

"You already know," she jogged out the way she came in leaving Layla looking after her forlorn.

****

"Hello?" Sayvonne answered her ringing telephone. "Hello?" she repeated groggily.

"I'm tired of this shit," slurred Layla on the other end of the phone with an empty whiskey bottle in hand. "She came over here and fucked me. Fucked me good Von. And fuckin' left," she spat out bitterly.

"Layla, are you drunk?" wondered Sayvonne.

"So, what if I am! Least the alcohol will help me sleep and cope with being alone," argued Layla. "Cuddle up with my bottle," she wrapped her arms around the empty liquor bottle.

Sayvonne sighed moving the phone away from her mouth she nudged her boyfriend, "Tre, Tre. I'm going to Layla's house baby. Call me if you need me anything."

"Whelp! I got friends! My sister come stay with me. She ain't the one that fucked me but she knows I don't wanna be alone right now," declared Layla her voice ringing loud and clear from Sayvonne's cell phone.

Covering his head with a pillow Sayvonne's boyfriend muttered, "Love you too baby tell Layla to be quiet," he complained before resuming snoring.

Chuckling Sayvonne whispered, "I'm on the way over sis," while slipping on a pair of sweats and a shirt.

167

"Thanks Von," she said and in another breath. "I'm sorry Von. I'm drunk in my feelings. You were sleep. I hope I didn't wake the kids up."

"Layla, you didn't. It's ok."

"You sure?" she sniffled.

"Yes sis. Now stop crying. Why are you crying?"

"You are a great sister friend," admitted L.

"Is that why you crying?"

"No."

"Then tell me why you are crying."

"Cuz I'm all alone," whispered Layla sniffling again.

"Well we're like fifteen minutes away from each other and it's been eight and there is no traffic so in two more blocks and like two minutes I will be there and you won't be alone."

"You know what I mean Von. Kenni had Ronnie still got her now. You got Tre. Who do I have? Who do I have Von?"

Sayvonne didn't say anything.

"Exactly. Nobody."

"Open the front door Lay," Sayvonne said gently as she pulled in the driveway of her house,

"All I wanted was for her to stay. Just this one time. Every fuckin' time she leaves right after."

"Did you unlock the door?"

Layla flung the door open revealing her stark naked body.

"Why are you naked?" Sayvonne questioned hurrying inside and closing the door.

"Cuz. I took my shower and then I just couldn't. Why didn't she just stay? I have the whole house to myself."

"Who?" Sayvonne asked wrinkling her nose, as they started downstairs.

"T who else!"

"Oh I'm sorry."

"S'not yo' fault. Why didn't she just stay? I told her she could," Layla asked plopping down on the couch.

"Umm. C'mon lets go upstairs and lay down and finish talking," she held out her hand for Layla.

Begrudgingly Layla took her hand, "We fucked on the piano. She fucked me while I played or tried to play."

"Well I guess the kids can't come play on the piano any time soon," joked Sayvonne.

"Whatever," smiled Layla.

"Alright go head. Lay down," instructed Sayvonne pushing Layla into her room.

Flopping down in the bed Layla started to ask, "Will you-"

"Yes, I will light your aromatherapy, sleepy, relaxation candles," finished Sayvonne. "I've been knowing you a long time Layla. I know."

"Do you know why T didn't stay the night with me?" asked Layla with lowering eyelids.

Sayvonne covered her friend up with the comforter and stretched out onto the comforter holding Layla, "Well for starters you should have been direct. Tre and I are very direct with one another especially about our feelings. You can stay if you want is like if you ain't got nowhere else to go. I guess."

"I said you ain't gotta run right out. I'm home alone."

She rubbed Layla's head and nodded, "Has she ever stayed the night with you?"

"No," was her wounded reply.

"So, maybe next time you should say something along the lines of stay the night with me daddy. I'm home alone. I want you. I need you to stay with me tonight," joked Sayvonne imitating Layla's voice. "You ain't going nowhere after that session."

"Whatever."

"Did you ever tell her you was feeling her more than a lil' bit?"

Again, a no came from Layla.

"Well it's time to fess up to that my darling. Never have I encountered this drunken side of Layla."

Yawning widely and at ease with her best friend next to her comforting her Layla muttered, "Whatever."

"Yeah take yo' ass to sleep. I will be here in the morning when you wake up. Don't expect me to touch downstairs it smell like twelve cans of bounce dat ass down there."

"Love you sis. Thank you," Layla giggled,

A genuine smiled graced Sayvonne's face as she stroked her best friends hair, "Love you too lil' sis," she kissed her hair. "I can't wait till you find true happiness," she muttered to a sleeping Layla.

****

"I come in peace," yelled out T the next day as she entered the home of Chantel, Dreamz, and Mya, which currently only Mya resided in.

Mya came around the corner with a smile, "Whatever T," the two hugged like siblings. "I'm sorry for everything I said to you the other night especially for cutting you."

"It's cool sis. You was in yo' feelings in the worst way," she winked at her. "But you did almost hit a main artery I bled all the way to Ma Dukes house," commented T with a jokers grin on her face.

Instantly tears spilled forth from Mya's eyes, "Oh my god T! I'm so sorry!"

A shameful feeling spread throughout T as she took Mya in her arms and wiped away her tears, "Whoa sis. Wait hold on. I was just joking."

"No, you're not T! I'm so sorry!" cried out Mya shaking her head.

T smiled shamefully pulling back and showing Mya both of her hands, "See look no scars Mya. You didn't even cut me that deep."

She wiped her eyes and shoved T away from her, "Jerk."

"Sorry sis. Bad joke wrong time."

Her stud brother's girlfriend nodded in agreement.

Sliding her lanky frame onto the couch T peered up at Mya's soft features, "How you holding up sis? You alright?"

Biting down on her lip Mya attempted to say yes but the liquid began to fill Mya's eyes and seep out. Her head swayed to answer no but she rubbed her hand over her chest against her heart, "It hurts."

Dolefully T nodded, "Do you think y'all will be able to move past it or is this the end of y'all relationship?"

Liquid began to fill Mya's eyes threatening to pool over as she stared into T's green eyes, "Honestly T I don't know. I've never felt this pain before and it hurts. It hurts really bad and really deep."

"I'm sorry you had to experience this Mya but you know Lil' Buddy love you and wanna be with you. Alcohol a muthafucka though. The right amount can get you in the wrong shit."

"I know and I really didn't want her to come over for the weekend. It was suspect to me. I know they still talked emailing each other back and forth but I was fine with that. Chantel let me read the emails whenever I wanted. I was trying to show her I trust her by letting them hang out," she admitted painfully.

"Don't take this the wrong way Mya. But y'all been together almost six years. How can either one of y'all not trust each other?"

Softly Mya laughed, "T the length of time together doesn't mean if it's been awhile you won't have problems, old problems at that. Problems don't define your relationship. It's how you solve them."

"So, how can I help solve y'all problems?" cheesed T.

"You can't T. I wish big brother could too but you can't. This is something me and Chantel will have to fix or end."

The reality that their relationship could be over caused T's eyebrows to knit together, "If y'all broke up-"

"Yes, I would still be there for her emotionally, physically, mentally, and spiritually. You should know that." Mya finished for her. She sighed, "Hell I couldn't not do for her. Even now, I'm pissed off still. But I want her to come home. I miss her and I love her. Hell I'm sorry and she cheated," she finished shaking her head.

"Cool come to Ma Dukes house then. My doctor chick coming through. We gon' play some spades, bones, and shoot the shit."

Mya smiled, "I wish it were that easy T. One day when you finally fall in love you will understand as much as I miss her and love her right now and crave her being with me I really sincerely hate what she did and has done to our relationship. I don't think we could be in the same room without fighting yet."

"Alright. That's cool. But what about for her birthday? You know we tracking down Tyriq for her? I don't care if the lil' nigga outta the city. He will be back on her birthday."

"I will be there. No drama. And I won't be staying the whole time."

"Cool. Works for me sis," she stood. "Call me if you need me. Okay?"

Stepping into a hug Mya squeezed her tight, "I will T. Thank you."

T kissed her cheek, "Love you. Keep yo' head up."

"Love you too T and don't be giving me your cooties. Make sure Chantel is okay for me please."

She smiled at her and gave her a nod that she would. At the front door she saluted her, "Will do ma'am."

As soon as T walked out the door, her phone notified her of a text message coming in from Yolanda and an incoming phone call from Kiaysha. She chose to answer the phone first. "What's going on beautiful?"

"Hey T."

"How you doing this beautiful day ma?" flirted T starting her ignition and pulling off from Mya's house.

"A lil' tired from work but nevertheless I'm fine. I actually wanted to hear your voice."

"Look at you being all honest and open. How about I slide through and put you to bed? No pun intended."

"You would love that. Pun intended."

"So would you mama. You would damn sure be missing more than my voice."

"Umm hmm. You talk a good game Timothy. *Anyways*," she stressed the word for dramatic effect. "How would you put me to bed no pun intended?"

Before replying T texted her mother's address to Yolanda, "Aww I can't tell you all of that ma. That's along the lines of showing. One thing I will tell you though is that I would soak your feet and rub them for you."

"Oh really now? What are you doing tonight?"

Unable to stop smiling T said, "Getting ready to rub yo' feet?"

"Whatever Timothy! We're about to get off the phone and I will *dream* about you doing that and *maybe* one day you can make that a reality."

"Give me a time and I will."

"Whatever. So, anyways, what are you doing tonight really?"

"Missing you while me and the family plan Lil' Buddy's birthday party over drinks. Hopefully the PI will call tonight he said he would let us know this week what he has or hasn't found."

"Oh okay," yawned Kiaysha. "Well have fun Timothy. I'm about to crash with my son and take a nap."

"Alright ma. Sweet dreams about me rubbing them feet."

Kiaysha giggled, "Whatever. Bye Timothy."

"Bye ma."

Pressing the end button on her phone T opened her door to see her nephews frowning face. She looked up curiously at the doorway to see Chantel and Jay smiling and smoking watching them. She looked back at Dreamz, "What's up nephew?"

"Uncle T you not supposed to have a woman wait on you," Dreamz criticized.

Feigning ignorance T questioned, "What woman waiting on me nephew?"

"You see her. Look around," Dreamz stated and walked off.

Grinning at her nephews departing back T looked away to spot Yolanda sitting in a white BMW. She strode over to the car. At the driver's side, she lightly rapped on the tinted windows to get her attention, "You waiting on me sexy?"

Yolanda grinned at T. She removed her fingers from her vajayjay and licked the skeet off her fingers. She opened the door, "No daddy I was just entertaining myself."

Immediately T stole her fingers and sucked them, "I'ma entertain you later."

Batting her eyelashes and looking at T flirtatiously she responded, "Don't I know it Daddy? And you always treat this pussy right. I can't wait," she spoke pulling T's earlobe into her mouth and giving it a light bite before releasing.

"Damn you make a nigga not even wanna go in now."

"We have time. Come on let's go in and party."

Biting her lip T lead the way in.

****

"Ay shorty cool as fuck bruh," Jay announced to T as they stood in the kitchen making plates. "She fit right in with the best of shit talkers, us."

Grinning T responded, "Oh yeah. She can talk that shit but you see she can back that shit up. She bust you and Kim's ass in spades."

"Whatever! I had to let her win. I did that for you," spouted Kim as she walked into the kitchen grabbing beer out of the refrigerator.

"You ain't do that shit for me. We kicked y'all ass fair and square," joked T.

Looking up from her plate with a retort on her lips Jay's words were stolen as Arianna came out of the bathroom with a silly drunk smile plastered over her face. She asked her instead, "You want a plate? You look like you feeling it over there."

Arianna stood staring at Jay with an impish grin, "I can hold my own Jay, but yes I would like a plate."

Kim walked into the kitchen observed the two briefly then walked over to the counter to stand next to T. She took a piece of chicken off T's plate not taking her eyes off Jay and Arianna.

"What all you want on yo' plate?" continued Jay oblivious to the rest of the fam in the room.

Shrugging she replied, "What all can you handle carrying?" her eyebrow raised.

A smirked appeared on Jay's face, "Gon' and chill out yo. I got you."

Sauntering drunkenly away from everyone in the kitchen Arianna called out, "T I love your friend!"

"Somebody feeling it," cracked T.

The three burst out laughing and followed suit into the basement where the rest of the family plus Yolanda were drinking it up. Upon entering the basement, they realized they had stumbled upon a drinking game.

"Alright. Alright. Have you ever had a threesome?" Yolanda asked.

"You must not know my children gurl," Ma Dukes laughed as the three studs and Kim took a drink.

"My turn, my turn," Arianna yelled out. "Will you ever have a threesome?" she asked looking pointedly at Yolanda and winking at T.

She met her question with a drink and a smile then turned to T, "Baby I would love to have a threesome with you. Let's add that to our list of things to conquer."

T nodded, took a drink, and smiled. She raised her glass at Arianna, "I got one. Will you ever fuck with someone in this room again?"

Every pair of eyes in the room watched Jay down her drink including Arianna's. Jay brought her eyes to stare at her and with a wicked smile Arianna slowly tipped her glass back until it was empty never taking her eyes off Jay. Ma Dukes let out a whoop of laughter.

176

"Y'all got that one over on me!" Ma Dukes clapped her hands.

Arianna giggled and put a finger to her lips miming shh. "Alright I'm almost drunk fam. I'm headed home. Love y'all."

Immediately Jay jumped to her feet, "You not driving home drunk yo."

She laughed, "Watch me," and bounced out the door with Jay following.

Yolanda peered at T, "I think your friends need to fuck each other's brains out."

"Damn Doc that's yo' diagnosis?" Chantel questioned laughing.

She nodded her head, "Damn right."

Kim excused herself from the room with her cell phone glued to her ear. Ma Dukes stood up going to Lil' Buddy for an embrace then stopping in front of the couple, "Well Miss Yolanda it was very nice meeting you. You are a joy to be around and you fit right in with our crazy family. Hope to see you again lady," she hugged Yolanda. "T, keep in mind that the baby is here."

Kissing her mother's cheek, T winked and murmured, "I got you ma. Love you good night."

"Good night ladies."

"Alright y'all. I'm about to lay it down with my son," Chantel leaned back in her chair tossing her drink back, "Y'all get down with the nitty gritty. It was a pleasure meeting you Yolanda."

"It's been great meeting you all too. Next time I will have to bring my drinking games over."

"It's on," Chantel called back over her shoulder.

After Chantel left the basement, only Yolanda and T remained in the basement with their drinks. T led her over to the futon abandoning their drinks on the table. T sat down on the futon and Yolanda straddled her grinding her hips to a beat only she could hear. She dipped her head and placed her lips onto T's.

Their lips smashed against one another with turbulence. T's fingers whisked off underneath her shirt toward her nipples twisting both hardened areolas. Her lips moved on to kissing on her neck and sucking. She dropped one hand away from her girls to unbutton and unzip Yolanda's jeans. Lifting Yolanda by her ass, she pulled the jeans off her hips.

Holding onto T's ankles Yolanda bent backwards lifting herself into a bridge so T could pull her jeans off her and get a look at her edible arrangement while doing so. Once her jeans were off and decorating the floor, she flipped back up into the straddling position but seated on T's thighs. She unzipped and unbuttoned T's jeans until she could slid her dick out to encounter her pussy.

Engulfing T's strap with her pussy Yolanda worked it until it was all the way in. She began to gyrate her hips with T's face buried into her chest. She pinched T's nipples while working her hips. Leaning forward she kissed, licked and sucked along T's neck and ears moaning heavenly.

A shudder went down T as Yolanda's lips grazed one of her sexual stimulation zones by her ear. She grabbed two handfuls of ass ripping them away from each other and bringing them back forth. Yolanda's fingers raked down her back and T's hip shoved her dick inside of her while opening and closing her ass cheeks.

"Fuck daddy," whimpered Yolanda. "You making me come already...ooh shit...." her hips went into cruise control driving its way up to an orgasm.

T held onto her hips moving with her continuing to thrust her dick inside of her while she attempted to retreat. Yolanda pushed down on T's chest and rose up so her clit was positioned right on the tip of the strap on penis. She nuzzled her clit against it a few times then dropped her ass all the way down onto it. Fingers grasping her ass cheeks T lifted her halfway up her strap and guided her back down. Her pinky finger drifted into her chocolate star darting in and out.

"Shit," Yolanda moaned out. Her body convulsed and tightened. Trembling her eyes rolled back to the back of her head. "Fuck," she stuttered with the insides of her vagina still jumping. She collapsed forward on T. "I hope I wasn't loud."

"You wasn't."

"Can we finish at my house? I think you fucked all the liquor out of me."

"Let's go."

Chapter 8

"Good morning Daddy," greeted Yolanda coming into her bedroom with a tray of breakfast for T.

She grinned looking at the crepes, fruit, and orange juice Yolanda had prepared, her stomach grumbled in response. "Good morning Ma," she sat up so she could begin to eat her food.

"Sit back. I will feed you," ordered Yolanda.

T sat back obediently unable to wipe the smile from off of her face.

"Have you ever been canoeing or zip lining?" Yolanda questioned while feeding T.

"Nah. How about yourself?"

"No but I know of a place where we can go. It's about an hour or two away if you're down."

"I'm down."

"Really?" inquired Yolanda sitting back with a grin on her haunches.

"Hell yeah. Let's get dressed and get to it!" she wolfed down the remnants of her plate.

"Whoa! Slow down tiger. Chew," laughed Yolanda. "Do you want more?"

Swallowing the food in her mouth T nodded her head once, "Hell yeah. That just hit the spot in the best way."

"Do you want anything else along with this? I have bacon, sausage, and eggs but didn't know what you prefer?" Yolanda laughed bounding up to get T more food,

"I love all of that baby. You bring it to me I'ma eat it," called out T rolling over to check her cell phone to see what notifications she may have missed.

"Don't I know it," Yolanda called back as the kitchen began to sizzle and drift food aromas back to the bedroom tickling T's nostrils.

"Thirty percent?" T shook her head staring at her phone. "Shit my shit gon' be dead by the time we get there," she checked her messages and phone logs once again to discover she hadn't missed anything. Then she sent a text message out to the family letting them know what she was about to do and go and that she would stop over Ma Dukes later in the evening to pick up her charger. She also added in Yolanda's number just in case they needed to reach her.

"Here you go T," offered Yolanda coming back into the room with a loaded plate of food this time layered with sausage, bacon, eggs, fruit, crepes, and another glass of orange juice.

"Did you eat?" questioned T looking at her portions.

Nodding earnestly she answered, "Yes, while you were sleeping."

T grinned at her dubiously, "I don't believe you shit you gon' have to help me finish my plate."

"I'm fine."

Scoffing T gathered some food on her fork, "Open up."

Daintily she licked her lips. Seductively she opened her legs with a sexual grin.

"You know I will feed that too but open ya mouth woman. You barely ate last night when we was drinking

181

and I ain't see you eat nothing this morning. You will be sharing this plate with me."

"Alright T," she gave in accepting the food.

The two finished the plate off together silently feeding one another. Yolanda took the dishes in the other room and T followed her. She grabbed the dishes from her at the sink and began to make the dishwater.

"You cooked. I clean. I got the kitchen. Go head and get dressed Ma," said T.

"Thank you T. I will go get dressed but first while you were sleep I went somewhere and got you this," she went into the hall closet and retrieved a bag from a store. She pulled the contents out to show T that she had bought her an outfit for the day with shoes, socks, and draws to match. "Do you like it?"

"Hell yeah."

She kissed T on the cheek and grinned, "Now I'll go get ready."

"Cool. I'll be up in a lil' bit."

"Ok daddy."

****

"Hey you cool? I ain't heard from you in a few days?" questioned Sayvonne as soon as she heard Layla pick up her ringing cell phone.

"I'm sorry gurl. I been in my feelings these last couple a days and embarrassed as hell too. I'm so lucky you are my sister. Thank you gurl," admitted Layla.

"No problem. You know that. You in yo' feelings and embarrassed about T?"

Layla sighed heavily with discontentment, "You know it."

"I take it you haven't talked to her then," mused Sayvonne.

She expelled again before answering, "No, but I been trying to reach her all day. Her phone going straight to voice mail."

"Umm hmm. You been trying to call her to tell her how you feeling for real?"

"Yeah," lied Layla.

Sayvonne rolled her eyes, "You are such a bad liar Layla."

"And you know me so well."

"So, let's add this up. You got drunk and got in yo' feelings. You been hibernating these last few days because you in yo' feelings. You embarrassed that you in yo' feelings. Three points. And you don't think you should talk to T about anything?"

"I mean what I'm supposed to say Von damn. Hey, T I like you. Will you be my gurlfriend? Yes or no? I don't do the chasing. I get chased."

"Doesn't seem to be that way to me right now."

"Whatever. She want me too."

"Sounds good but why don't you just be logical and keep it real with her."

"Cuz I don't know what to say!"

"Say what's in yo' heart Layla duh! Do you like her?"

"Yes."

"Do you wanna be with her?"

"That would be cool I guess?"

"Layla."

"Fine yes."

"Do you wanna be in a relationship exclusively with her? Meaning neither one of you has anyone else besides each other?"

"Yes."

"Now look at all that conversation we got of where you can start and go. All it took was you being real with yourself."

"Whatever."

"Will you talk to her now?"

"Yes, Von."

"Like right now?"

"I will send her a text so she will call me when she get her phone charged up."

"Alright. What you gon' say?"

"What I need to?"

"And what's that?"

"I miss you. Duh!"

"Alright well I gotta get these kids cleaned up. We still got some dinner left over if you want me to bring you some."

"Nah. I'm fine boo. Go head."

"Alright sis. I love you."

"I love you too sis."

****

"This was an awesome day," commented Yolanda licking her ice cream cone as T and herself walked around the river downtown.

T smiled in concurrence, "That it was. Never thought canoeing and zip lining would be that much fun. I'ma have to plan a trip and take the fam. Show them what we been missing out on."

"They have campsites as well so you can grill out and or camp out too."

Stealing a lick from her ice cream cone T said, "We should of did that," she winked at her.

"Next time. Let's do it."

"Bet."

184

"Beautiful night out eh? You ladies enjoy your night?" a man's voice called out to them from the dock where his ship was idling in the water.

"Yes, it was great," Yolanda spoke politely to him.

"Well end it the right away. If you haven't had dinner at Nick Marriners, where all of our products are caught daily you haven't ate down on the riverfront. Come on in order your food. I'll give you a buzzer for when your food is ready. Explore the art of this here beauty, gaze out on the river, and listen to music in our classy lounge room. We're only here for thirty minutes before pulling off again. What do you say ladies?"

"You wanna go?" T asked Yolanda. "You haven't ate so I know you hungry."

Yolanda grinned, "Let's go," she beamed tossing her ice cream cone and holding onto T's arm as they started over to the boat.

The man clapped, "Welcome aboard ladies to the fabulous Nick Marriners. I am the Nick Marriners and I will be your guide and hostess for this evening," he said jovially welcoming them onto board. He stopped walking in a brightly lit hallway where pictures of food matched the menu selection. "Look around and let me know what you two would like for dinner."

The couple looked around the walls and ceiling with amazement. Each wall was different. One for appetizers, entrees, and desserts all with a seafood theme. Drink specialty's and prices were on the ceiling but instead of having to crane your neck back there was reflection glass on the fish tank so it looked like fish were swimming with the names of drinks and prices.

"I know what I want," murmured Yolanda to T.

"Go head get whatever you want ma. I got it," offered T.

The owner and hostess whipped out his notepad, "And what can I have my cook fix up for a beautiful woman ma'am?"

"I will have fried oysters with green tomatoes, corn, no vinaigrette, and no okra."

"How about an appetizer? Dare I say raw oysters with two glasses of champagne?" he wiggled his eyebrows at the couple in front of him.

The two woman looked at each other and T nodded, "That's fine. I'll have the shrimp, and crab finger scampi but I would like to add lobster to that as well."

He nodded. "Yes, yes," he wrote their orders down and smiled handing T a buzzer, "Follow me. I will take you to the lounge room where there is live jazz music playing. Your server will deliver your food here. Once your appetizer is prepared, the buzzer will vibrate and flash until a server turns it off. Your main course meal you may eat in the lounge room or out on the deck but I do ask that you please tell your server immediately after receiving your appetizers." He opened a double door for them ushering them into a dimly candle lit area where a lot of couples populated the area around the stage some eating, some conversing, some listening and some dancing to the music. "Please follow me," he gestured to them leading them towards a table on the out skirts of everyone else in a darker section of the room. "Here you are ladies. Your food should be with you momentarily. Thank you for dining here tonight at Nick Marriners we hope to see you again soon," he said and walked away with a smile.

"This is really nice. I honestly had a few reservations at first," admitted Yolanda.

"You thought we were going to be the inspiration for the next scary movie?"

Yolanda shrugged, "Honestly yes. I've been down here plenty of times and never stumbled across the place."

"Maybe you weren't meant to yet," winked T.

"He was still creepy at first."

"You think I would let something happen to you?"

"No. I actually feel very secure and safe when I'm with you like you wouldn't let anything hurt me or even attempt," T smiled at her words and Yolanda finished with. "It's a nice feeling. Haven't had that in a long time."

T reached out and took her hand. She kissed her open palm beginning to make a path up her arm, "I'm glad I can make you feel again ma."

She closed her eyes as her nerve endings began to tingle awakening with pleasure. She slid her tongue out across her lips wetting them slowly. "Thank you T," she breathed airily. "For everything."

The tall stud stood up pulling Yolanda to her feet as well. She nestled her close to her chest and began swaying to the music placing light kisses on Yolanda's neck and shoulders. Once their lips touched a surge of felicity shot down the two woman's bodies welding them tighter.

The feminine counterpart moaned grinding against her masculine partner, "Daddy I need it right now."

"Ahem," someone cleared their throat. "I have a tray of oysters and champagne for the two of you," the waiter declared.

"Yes, could you place that on the table and when you deliver the main course we will be outside on the deck."

"Yes sir," he nodded. "Sorry to intrude. Please enjoy your appetizers. I will be back in awhile to check on you."

T nodded as he pivoted and walked swiftly away. She slipped away from Yolanda and into her seat leaving Yolanda standing whose eyes flashed at her. T smiled at her.

"Did you hear me daddy?" Yolanda questioned.

187

Without giving recognition to her words T picked up an oyster from the tray and sucked it provocatively while staring at Yolanda, "Wait," she picked up another oyster.

With reverence, she watched T play with the oyster an intensity mounting within her as she gazed. She slid into her seat and leaned forward staring into T's eyes. "Don't stop eating the oysters," she ordered and tossed her glass of champagne back.

Quizzically T looked at her until Yolanda disappeared from view and under the table. T grinned feeling her pants becoming unbuttoned. She lifted up slightly so Yolanda could yank her undergarments down her legs.

With T's undergarments out of the way, Yolanda dropped a kiss between the inside of both of T's knees. Her tongue swept up her thigh littering kisses all over. She clamped down sucking on T's inner thigh until she could hear the soft groans T uttered out. "Keep eating those oysters," she demanded with one hand jerking T's strap on harness out of the way. She took that down her legs as well while the other hand scratched lightly up T's other thigh.

Once the toy was out of the way, Yolanda split apart T's pussy lips and began to suckle on T's clit. The sound of a fist slamming into the table brought a smile to Yolanda's face. She pushed T's legs as wide as they would go and dropped her tongue down low tickling her hole before coming back up and pulling a lip into her mouth. One lone finger prodded against T's clit circling and flicking against it. Yolanda abandoned the left lip to pull her right one in her mouth just as T's hand flew underneath the table. She pulled her lip out of Yolanda's mouth grabbing her face and grinding her vagina on it. At T's urging, Yolanda interacted with T's clit not failing to let her finger partake. Her tongue stroked butterfly flicks against her clit while her finger scratched a spot down below.

"May I take your tray" Yolanda heard their waiter come back and ask T. She listened for T's response but didn't hear any so she smacked her leg and devoured her clit wholly in her mouth.

"Yes, yes," stammered out T to the waiter who was looking at her curiously while T concentrated on an orgasm she felt building up within her.

"Would you like more champagne for the lady?"

Chewing on her lip T spit out, "No thank you."

"It's on the house courtesy of the owner," he smiled at her.

"Yes," breathed T. "No," she snapped back out. "That is all for now thanks. Bring our main course out to the deck," she rushed him away and leaned back in her seat disregarding if he was there or not and taking Yolanda's head in both her hands coating her face with cum. "Damn Yolanda," groaned out T biting down on her lip.

Peeking her head out from under the table between her legs she smiled, "Napkin please."

T grabbed Yolanda's head from between her legs and pulled her up and pressed a kiss to her face. She cradled Yolanda's face in her hands and slowly licked herself off Yolanda until her face yielded no more traces of her essence. She slid the table back, "C'mon let's get outta here."

"Where do you wanna go?" Yolanda stood with a question and twinkling lust filled eyes.

"Follow me."

She led Yolanda outside of the lounge room and up to the deck of the river where no one was watching the beautiful scene of the moon gleaming down on them as they sailed across the river. T brought her to the edge of the railing and stopped with a wicked smile. She picked Yolanda up and sat her on the edge of the railing.

"Don't let me fall," warned Yolanda.

"Baby you trust me with ya body but you don't trust me with your life?"

She stared in her eyes, "I trust you," she opened her legs.

Quickly T undid her pants and slid her strap on dick out. Whipping a condom from her pocket, she rolled it on and dived into Yolanda's pussy. With Yolanda's legs wrapped around T's waist and both hands gripping the edge of the railing, slowly, T pumped working her eight-inch shaft in and out of her twat. The two kissed tenderly with the moonlight highlighting their sexual escapade.

"Ooh shit Daddy," moaned Yolanda. "Ah... don't let me fall... don't let me fall," begged Yolanda. She removed her vise-like grip from the railing to go under T's shirt and scratch along her back.

"I got you," grunted T driving her strap into Yolanda's garage only to reverse and dart back in.

She went below Yolanda's dress and separated her ass cheeks. T delved passed both sets of her labia uprooting her insides. She drew high pitch screams and moans of pleasure from Yolanda but didn't stop her hips from their duty. Again and again, her rod pierced her insides refusing to let up. Her speed picked up but her back didn't falter. With every stroke, Yolanda felt every inch of the tool.

"Ooh shit! Fuck fuck fuck! Oh damn T!" Yolanda began to scream hysterically.

There was a slight buzzing in T's pocket but not enough to deter her from navigating her johnson as she watched Yolanda begin to climb the ladder of ecstasy. She watched Yolanda's face contort with the pleasurable pain that only an orgasm could bring. Her legs tightened around

T, her hips went into overdrive, and her toes curled on T's back.

"Oooh shit," groaned out Yolanda gutturally as her body shuddered. Limply she held onto T with her head resting on her shoulders. "Damn T," she sighed. "You just took everything from me. I just wanna go to bed...with you...damn. You dangerous."

"Am I? Am I really now? Or did I really just make you delirious?"

"T the waiter is here with our food."

Glancing back over her shoulder T asked, "Hey could you get us a few boxes?"

The waiter nodded, "Certainly. Also, there is a large party on its way out here."

T smiled in appreciation and watched him go back inside the ship before the two pulled themselves together.

True to his word, a large loud party walked out on the deck momentarily and he packed away their meal.

Chapter 9

"Lil' Buddy, you been talkin' to Mya?" T questioned her brother and passed the blunt to Jay.

Chantel slid up in her chair and placed her beer can on the table on which they were making a beer can pyramid. She beckoned Kim next to her to hand her another beer. "We have na mean but it's just been on some cordial shit."

"Lil' Buddy you fucked up. You know you gotta make amends," chastised Kim.

"Fuck that," Chantel spit out harshly. "Did you see my car? My house? Shit me?"

Kim shrugged, "What you think was gon' happen when you scar a woman's heart? If she didn't do shit she obviously didn't care."

She rolled her eyes, "So, what's up bruh?" she directed at T.

Jay snickered, "Clean change of subject two points for Lil' Buddy."

"You do need to talk to her Lil' Buddy. Y'all been down for too long to let this break y'all. Fuck the car, fuck the house and bruh you know she was gon' put her hands on you. Shit you probably woulda put yo' hands on her if the shoe was on the other foot," T said and Kim nodded in approval while Chantel looked bored as if she wasn't listening. "But, I'm feeling a change of subject too."

"New topics? New topics?" Jay banged her beer on the table.

T and Kim exchanged a look and a smile before T asked, "Nigga what happened when you took Arianna home? Y'all gon' kick it or nah man?"

Slowly Jay grinned, "So, y'all just turn that on me now? That's what we do?" she nodded and took a sip of her drink. "Kim, when you gon' bring Cream around the family and start acting like that's yo' gurl?"

"She ain't my bitch so therefore she has no reason to be around my family," retorted Kim.

"Yeah alright."

"Alright my ass Jay!"

The three studs laughed at Kim's expense.

"Aye sis is you mad or nah?" chortled Chantel.

"Fuck you," she spat with a smile back at her.

"Five points for Jay for the change of subject and drawing fire from yo' ass," commented T.

"What the fuck ever T! Why you ain't brought the one chick around you met at the mall. We all know you been going on hella lunch dates with her," jabbed Kim.

"Man I ain't even fucking with shorty like that yo," T said and looked down at her phone to see who was calling. "Hold on turn the music down Jay."

The three shared looks among them as the music was turned down low. T answered the phone and they all leaned forward straining their ears to hear who it was. Jay pressed pause on the music to cut it completely.

"T you gon' play yo' hand bruh?" Jay called out to her with a smile.

"Shut up man," T cajoled back at her then into the phone she said, "Yo."

Someone sniffled then Kiaysha's voice somberly asked, "Sorry I didn't know you were busy."

"I'm not. I'm just shootin' the shit with the fam. Kickin' it," T responded puzzled.

"Oh."

Kiaysha didn't say anything but T listened to her sniff a few times. "What's wrong Ma?" T questioned standing up and leaving the garage.

"Nothing," she replied in a very small voice.

"Bullshit."

"I'm fine," she took a few deep breaths, "I'm fine, but I would be much better if you could just come hold me," her voice trailed off getting lower and lower.

A warm feeling began to spread in her belly as the ends of her lips begin to stretch to either side, "You promise to talk to me when I get there?"

"Of course I'm not just gonna ignore you," Kiaysha laughed.

"Nah. I mean I wanna know why you crying and don't give me that tough gurl shit. When I get there and wrap my arms around you. You gotta tell me what's wrong."

She sighed, "Okay."

"Have you ate today? What about yo' son has he?"

"We're fine. He ate earlier. I'm not hungry if I get hungry I can whip something else up."

"Alright ma. I'm on the way."

"Thank you T."

"No problem."

T walked back into the garage with a silly grin and grabbed her keys off the table.

"Where you going?" Chantel asked T with a big smile.

"Kick it with shorty for a minute," T answered with a wicked grin.

"Which one?" Jay asked.

"The one I met at the mall."

The two studs and Kim burst out laughing immediately. Kim was the first to stop laughing and she looked very seriously at Jay, "Man shit Jay, I ain't even fuckin' with shorty like that."

Her comment sent the others back into laughter.

"Man whatever. I holla at y'all when I get back or something."

"Alright bruh," Jay extended her hand to her followed up by Chantel and Kim.

****

"Ma what's wrong?" blurted out T enveloping Kiaysha into her arms as soon as she opened the door to her home. T lifted her off her feet carrying her into the living room and taking a seat with her on her lap on the couch. "Ma, what's wrong?" gently T asked again.

No verbal response came but Kiaysha sniffled and buried her wet face in T's shirt.

"Is yo' son okay? Did somebody hurt him?" inquired T.

She shook her head no.

"Did somebody do something to you?"

She shook her head no again.

T opened her mouth to say something else but Kiaysha lifted her tear streaked face and pressed a finger to her mouth cutting off her vocals. T stared down at Kiaysha watching her lower lip tremble and the water begin to well in her eyes. She stroked her face gently before dropping a kiss on her forehead.

Once T drew her lips away from Kiaysha's forehead, she opened her eyes and sighed heavily. She gazed up at T, "Thanks for coming over."

"No problem. I told you, you can count on me ma."

"If you say so," she jabbed weakly with a smile.

"I'm here ain't I? Now it's yo' turn to uphold yo' end of the bargain. You supposed to be tellin' me what got you over here tearing and snotting up my shirt?" she winked down at the woman in her lap.

Unable to resist the urge Kiaysha let out a chuckle while rolling her eyes. She looked up at T's broad smile and quickly grabbed a handful of her shirt and wiped her nose with it.

"Alright. You know I'ma get you back right," T guffawed.

"What you going to do Timothy? I'm in my feelings right now so I get a pass," cajoled Kiaysha.

"Oh is that so?"

"Yes."

"Sike," T said and twisted Kiaysha's nipples drawing a moan from Kiaysha who instantly curled closer and squeezed her legs tighter.

She eased her eyes open, "T,"

Hungrily T dropped a kiss down to her lips. Eagerly Kiaysha kissed her back wrapping her arms around the back of T's neck. One of T's hands slipped between Kiaysha's thighs and ran up to her center stirring her thin pajama pants against her pot of honey.

"Ooh," Kiaysha moaned out grinding her hips down onto T's fingers. She turned her face and grabbed T's fingers with her mouth sucking one then two of them into the moistness of her mouth. She let T's fingers drift out of her mouth and sat upright pushing T against the back of the couch she straddled her.

T pulled down the front of Kiaysha's pajama pants and got her first glimpse of her rosebud. Quickly, both hands delved in stimulating her from two different sides brought on by the strumming of her fingers. Her fingers switched and her thumbs took on a wax on wax off caress

196

against her flower while her middle fingers dug inside of her.

Working her hips like a corkscrew, she roved, winded, and threaded onto T's fingers. Her own hands zipped under her cami pulling on her own nipples as her toes began to curl. Kiaysha's eyelids began to flutter until she was unable to keep them open. One hand managed to hold onto her breast twisting her nipple while the other clenched T's shirt. She exhaled softly twitching as her bodily fluids began to abandon her.

"Mommy?" a child's voice sent a charge through Kiaysha propelling her away from T and dragging her shirt down to stand and face her three-year-old son. "Mommy, you pee-pee on yo' self," he pointed at her pajama pants where the wet spot was.

She snatched a pillow off the couch and held it in front of her, "Deahlo, why aren't you sleeping?"

"I was."

"Then go back to sleep," she ordered.

"Okay Mommy," he said and walked away back down the hall towards his bedroom.

"Fuck," Kiaysha cursed collapsing onto the loveseat next to her. She looked up to see T sucking her fingers quietly. "Damn you T," she said with amusement.

"You got them last time," she stated with a shrug of her shoulders.

She stood up walking past T and smacked her with the pillow she just held in front of her. T reached back and tapped her ass before she got out of her reach.

"You better stop," warned Kiaysha with a threatening finger accompanying her words.

"Or what?"

"Don't play with me Timothy," she called back disappearing in her laundry room.

"I did that already," she stated back touching her wet shirt. She took it off and walked towards where Kiaysha was. T stopped when she saw the boxers shorts Kiaysha had traded her pants for, "Damn."

The woman turned around to see T in her sports bra and her eyes skidded across her scarcely tatted, sculpted body. She smiled at the view, "T," she began to protest but T was already in motion lifting Kiaysha into the air sitting her on the dryer. "Wait, wait, wait baby. Wait, wait," moaned Kiaysha trying to fight the sexual urge that was mounting within her.

Ignoring her protests T began to kiss along the side of Kiaysha's neck while grinding against her. Kiaysha succumbed to the pleasureful desires her body demanded. She grabbed T's face in both hands kissing her on the lips. She bit down moaning on T's bottom lip when T pinched her nipples. Gently T pushed her backwards onto the dryer and lifted her slightly so she could take off the boxer shorts Kiaysha wore.

"Baby wait. My son. I can't do it while my son is awake," she whispered in her ear with her earlobe still in her mouth,

A shaky breath left her frozen body as she quelled her raging hormones. She exhaled again and eased off the temptress sitting on the dryer.

Eyes slanted with lust, Kiaysha licked her lips and dipped her finger between her dripping center. She let out a few soft moans until T drew closer again at which point she placed her fingers in her mouth, "I want to too baby, but not while Deahlo is here."

Holding onto Kiaysha's eyes, T sucked the nectar off her fingers and backed away from her. "I just wanted to let my shirt dry because it got a lil' wet," she held it up.

Reclining backwards on the dryer, Kiaysha licked her lips taking in the view of T's toned body, "Hmph."

"You like what you see?"

Hopping off the dryer with a roll of her eyes, she grabbed T's shirt, "Maybe," she put it in the washer. "Come *hold* me while we watch a movie."

The two snuggled close together under a cover and settled on a scary movie. On their best behavior, the couple watched the movie silently; touching on a PG rated level. Halfway through the movie Kiaysha turned the volume down, "Today is the day my grandmother passed," she put a hand on T's chest and lifted herself staring into the studs green eyes. "Hold on. I really like you T. I don't just give my body to anyone. So, please don't make a fool outta me."

A kiss on her forehead followed up with, "I won't. Tell me about yo' grandma," was the assurance Kiaysha brought forth.

Memories played on her face as her eyes gave way to a different place and time and her lips curled into a wistful smile, "Maw Maw was the best. Maw Maw loved to cook. People would come from all over town just to get some a Maw Maw's cooking, especially after church. And if it was a BBQ, everyone in town showed up. We all wanted Maw Maw to open a restaurant but she never wanted too. She was content with feeding people. She didn't ask people for nothing in return. Hell we never paid for groceries. People used to bring by groceries for Maw Maw just because and Mister Clemons or old man Clemons as we used to call him ran the grocery store in town and he loved Maw Maw's cooking. His wife had died long ago. I think he only stuck around for Maw Maw's cooking especially after Papa passed. When she passed old man Clemons did too not too long after."

"She taught you how to cook then I assume?"

"Yes, it is def safe to assume that," she smiled up at T.

"Do you think she would of liked me?"

199

Chewing on her lip, she stared at T debating within herself before a grin exposed itself, "I think she would have. She would have been wary of you though as well because you're flashy and have a slickster's mouth. She would have had more words for you than me though."

"What you mean?"

"Maw Maw was a sweet old lady but she was a thug too. She carried a forty-five when Papa was alive and a three eighty after he passed. Shit the dope boys and Maw Maw was on a first name basis after Papa died. Weed was her vice. A lot of them she helped raise so they were already at her beck and call anyway but for the ones that she didn't raise and the ones that she did she still went over and beyond stopping beefs, making them put at least some of the money back into the community. She fed them, clothed them sometimes hell she even stashed and made a few deliveries for a few of them."

"So, was yo' baby daddy one of those?"

Sharply she exhaled and snapped out, "You know it. I met him when I was sixteen and hot in the ass. He was a few years older than me. He respected Maw Maw at first. He waited until I was eighteen, in college and out her house before he made his move. We start dating fell in love blah blah blah. Shortly after Maw Maw died I don't know what happened, what changed within him but he started getting physical. My mother tried to help me but she was so heartbroken about her mother that she really couldn't help me. She passed away six months later. Maw Maw, old man Clemons, and Momma. You know they say death comes in threes. Well anyway he moved me further away from the town I grew up in because people still had love for Maw Maw's granddaughter and were catching wind about what he was doing to me so he had prices on his head."

"How you get away from him?"

Kiaysha smiled wryly, "Deahlo. When I went into labor, he tried to take me to a hospital the town over but I ended up almost giving birth in the backseat of the car on the side of the road. An ambulance showed up he tried to direct them not to take me back to our hometown but it was closest so that's where we ended up. And of course, people at that hospital knew I was Maw Maw grandbaby word spread. Niggas start showing up showing love to me and giving him those looks. They let him sign the birth certificate and walked him out to the car. They didn't kill him cuz he in jail right now but he never came back for me and I never heard from him again. His mother calls every now and then."

"They put the fear of God in that man," laughed T.

"I guess so."

"Tell me about yo' mama or are we gonna go down this road again in six months?"

"Who said you was going to be around in six months?" Kiaysha shot at her with a smile.

"Oh you don't want me to be?" she dropped a kiss down onto her lips.

"Mmm," she moaned, "Maybe. Thank you for coming tonight."

"I told you it's no problem ma."

No more words were said. Kiaysha smiled and gripped onto T a little more tightly after turning the volume back up on the television. Eventually the movie ended up watching them. T woke up to discover herself stretched out alone on Kiaysha's couch with a fleece throw partially covering her long body. She peeped the clock seeing she wasn't out long but it was well after ten now. T yawned and stretched herself into standing. Gazing around until she spied her shoes, she crept down the hallway quietly.

The first door she nudged open made Deahlo look back at her with a smile. He ran to T hugging her legs, "Mommy room there," he pointed. "She sleep."

"Cool thanks lil' man," T gave him a handshake. "I'ma go say goodnight to yo' mama and leave okay?"

"Okay," he retreated back to sitting directly in front of the television where he was watching a movie.

T pushed open Kiaysha's door and she licked her lips immediately upon discovering Kiaysha laying across her king size bed half of her naked body covered. Her eyes darted across the neat room looking for anything besides the mirrors that decorated to gain insight about the woman lying across the bed. The room was neat and put together however. Everything had its own proper order from her vanity mirror filled with all the smell good essentials, to the extensive shoe collection hanging on the door of her closet, all the way to the bed, which was enticing within itself.

She crept over to the beautiful feline and dropped a kiss on her forehead, "Goodnight beautiful."

On her way out the door, T stopped to tell Deahlo she was leaving. The little man followed her to the door and locked up after her. T smiled with the door behind her as she thought of the shoes he was filling as man of the house even at such a tender age. She continued to her car and once settled in she pulled out her phone to discover she had missed phone calls and text messages from everyone in her family.

She called Jay back first, "Bruh, what's going on? Everything cool?" fired off T revving her engine and whipping out of Kiaysha's driveway.

"Yeah everything cool bruh. The private investigator called though. He got a location on lil' bruh."

"Oh true. Where at?"

"College party. He just had his last b-ball game and won."

"Cool where y'all at? Y'all ready?"

"Yeah. We at the house waiting on you to bring yo' ass fam."

"Alright I'm on my way. Y'all be outside I'm like five minutes away. I thought something was going on so a nigga raced away from shorty house headed home."

"C'mon sis. T about to pull up," Jay spoke to Kim.

"Cool. You got the info in yo' pocket right?" Kim questioned.

"Yup. Grab dat bag and that bottle."

"A'ight."

As soon as T jerked to a stop in front of her home, the garage door began to rise revealing Jay and Kim. They hurriedly hopped into the car. Jay placed a cooler in the backseat along with Kim and hopped in the front seat with her phone out illuminated from her GPS directing her on where to go.

"When was the last time either of you seen him?" Kim questioned her brothers.

Jay and T exchanged glances.

"Lil' bruh was prolly like twelve last time I saw him," said Jay.

"I don't know if I ever officially met him," commented T. "I remember Lil' Buddy used to dip out early some times. I remember her walking a few times with a kid and a basketball. We went to a game once but her mama ended up spotting us and getting us thrown out."

"I remember that," Kim said. "So, what's the game plan? What if he don't remember us?"

Jay shrugged, "We all got pics of Lil' Buddy and we all know everything major that happened to her."

"And what if he still ain't tryin' to hear us?' T questioned and exchanged a smile with Jay. "Get his attention," the two studs nodded and smacked hands together.

****

The two studs and fem got out of the car in the college district of the city smiling and looking around. College kids were hanging out everywhere chilling on cars, walking down the street, on the front porch drinking. The house they headed towards had people on the lawn and hanging out on the country style porch. They got in line for entrance to the home.

"Five dollars apiece," said one of the college boys but staring lustfully at Kim.

Stepping into his ambiance Kim shook her head with a smile, "We not paying to get in. We just brought the birthday boy a present," she nudged Jay who popped open the cooler to reveal a cooler full of liquor and on top a basket with a basketball pendant on it and a wad of cash.

The boy looked back up at Kim smiling, "Thank you."

Annoyance flared as her hips smacked the lid closed, "You're not the birthday boy sweetie," she stepped in his face. "And if you can't point me in the direction of Tyriq then we can find him ourselves."

"Shit I don't wanna be the birthday boy if that's all you got for him. After you find him, come back and see me. I got a present for you though," he grinned at Kim as she led her brothers past him.

"Alright. What's the plan? Divide and conquer?" Kim asked pulling a blunt out from between her breasts.

"Nah. I don't think he gon' be that hard to find," snickered T reminiscing.

"Not at all especially if he was like us," chuckled Jay.

Shaking her head at her brothers Kim added, "Y'all was some nasty fuckers," she sparked the blunt looking around the room of drunk patrons.

"Damn baby," Jay smiled at a passing woman.

The woman turned back and sent a smile her way but kept walking.

"Yo I'm about to see if shorty know where Tyriq is," said Jay but before she could walk off Kim grabbed her arm.

"Put ya pink thing in. Let's find lil' bro first," she grabbed T's wrist as well. "Now watch a woman work."

T and Jay passed the blunt between the two of them and cracked a beer watching Kim stumble through the crowd reassembling her outfit to show some more skin. She walked up to a dude engaging him in conversation flirting and laughing with him quickly. He tried to kiss her but she dipped it and hugged him. She whispered something in his ear and when the two parted the boy had a smile on his face and Kim's finger was telling her brothers to follow her.

Up the stairs to another floor of the two family home, the two stood outside the door with Kim and the boy. He glanced uneasily at the two studs backing Kim. He eyed their cooler with questions in his eyes.

"I'ma bounce," he stated backing away from them slowly.

The three watched him walk away with a look of disgust.

"Good thing we ain't doing no harm to lil' bruh bruh cuz not only did yo' pussy ass give up his location, you ain't even got the balls to make sure we ain't trying to do him no harm," Jay spat at his retreating back.

Boom! Boom! Boom! T knocked on the door.

"What's up?" a male voice questioned back.

"Open the door Tyriq," Jay said. "It's family bruh."

"I ain't got no family," he muttered back harshly.

"You got a sister named Chantel," T pointed out.

"She our sister too so you our family," Kim finished.

"I don't know what you talking about. My sister died a long time ago and I ain't feeling these crack head ass games you playing," he ripped the door open staring angrily at the group.

"Ain't nobody playing no games bruh bruh," Jay told him stepping up. "You don't remember me? I don't expect you to remember these two fools."

Tyriq however wasn't looking at Jay he was looking past her at his own group of friends crowding the end of the hallway. "Nah. I don't know you bruh. And it's time for you to get up outta here."

With her cell phone extended T stepped in front of Jay and Kim, "If you really want us to leave bruh we will. But take a look at this video and tell me this ain't yo' sister. Yo' sister ain't dead lil' bruh I don't know where you got that idea but here she go with yo' nephew Dreamz."

Unsure of what to do Tyriq looked at the woman who was standing behind his back and the crowd that was on the other end of the hall. The young woman behind him nudged him to take the phone. He reached out to take the phone hesitantly from T. He pressed play and immediately all of the adrenaline fled from his body as if he was punched in the gut. Tears welled in his eyes but he didn't take them off the screen where he was watching his sister and nephew interact. "It's good y'all," he waved his group of friends in the hallway away and backed into the room. He dropped on the couch. "Where is she?" he asked suddenly staring at T then Jay and Kim.

"She stay in Primrose. I'll give you her number," T started but he interrupted.

"How y'all know my sister again?" he inquired again staring at them intensely.

The scrutiny of his gaze brought a smile to her face, "She family. You probably too young to remember us. I'm T, that's Jay and this pretty lady Kim. We been knowing yo' sister since high school but we older than her. Do you remember her hanging around somebody named Ronnie?"

Tyriq scrunched his face up, "Yeah," he nodded. "She used to always be with Ronnie especially when she snuck out at night. She made sure I remembered Ronnie number and hers before she snuck out every night. Why y'all ain't bring her? Where she at?"

Upon the look of pain that crossed T's face Jay stopped rolling her blunt and took over the conversation to inform Tyriq, "She passed bruh."

"Damn. I'm sorry."

"It's cool."

"So, how I know y'all ain't trying to set her up or nothin. Niggas change after high school?"

"Not real niggas lil' bruh," pointed out T.

Kim whipped out her cell phone, dialed a number and placed the call on speaker, "Chantel Thompson!" she yelled when someone picked the lineup.

"Kimberly Fields!" shouted a voice back.

"What's up Lil' Buddy? What you doing?"

"Shit chilling with Mya and Dreamz watching a movie."

"Aww send me a family pic. I'm glad y'all back together."

"We not but I will snap chat you."

"Okay cool. Tell her I said hi."

"Mya, Kim said hi. She said what's up sis. Ay you know where Jay and T is?"

"Nope but I gotta hop off here though Lil' Buddy. Love you. See you soon."

"A'ight. Love you to sis goodnight. Call me if you need me."

207

"Fa sho."

"Believe us now?" smirked Kim staring at Tyriq.

His eyebrows stayed furrowed together, "So, why y'all come for me? Why didn't she come? Why ain't she been came for me?"

Jay told him honestly, "Bruh, she was fucked up for a long time about it. And that's my word. Y'all just alike so she kept a lot of shit in even from us. But there was times we were all together like at yo' basketball game."

"What game?"

"It was an AAU game out of the city," T started.

"You was playing for the Tigers," added Kim.

"Aww man I was young then. My mama made me quit the team that day. I didn't even finish my game," murmured Tyriq.

"At halftime she stormed into the locker rooms wearing a Tiger shirt and black jeans," Jay told him.

"How you remember what my mom wore man?"

Sadly, Jay smiled, "It was the first and last time I ever saw her. First time I saw you up close not hella far away bouncing a ball too. Towards the end of the half yo' mama spotted Lil' Buddy."

"Who?"

"My bad. Chantel. We call her Lil' Buddy."

"Oh."

"Look lil' bruh," T stepped in handing him the blunt but giving it to Kim when he declined. "We came here because we knew it was yo' eighteenth birthday. It wasn't easy tracking you down. We had to hire a private investigator to do so,"

"Is something wrong with my sister?"

"Nah. Not at all man but you know you legally a man now so you can do what you want. You can make the choice of who you want to have in yo' life and who you don't want to have in yo' life. Ya dig?"

208

Tyriq shook his head no.

"Hate to say it like this but I'm guessing you don't know. Yo' mama had a restraining order out on Lil' Buddy your sister, but with you no longer a minor you file your own restraining order or don't file it."

He collapsed back on the couch. His woman came from the back and approached him. She sat behind him on the couch rubbing his back and whispering in his ear.

"We also brought you a birthday present," Kim reminded him pulling the cooler forward.

Slowly, Tyriq lifted his wet face and looked at her. He lifted the top to reveal bottles of liquor. What immediately drew his eyes however was not within the storage area of the cooler but a pocket that on top had a zippered part with a long white box speaking out on which he could see his name. Tyriq unzipped the pocket and ripped off the top box to reveal a basketball pendant and chain full of diamonds. He grinned then noticed the cash. He looked down at it and back up, "Where did you get this money from?" Sadly, he packed the necklace away. "Its dirty money ain't it?"

"All money is dirty nephew," Kim told him with a laugh.

"Not if you work a nine to five instead of ducking out from twelve," he countered.

"We own a club."

"Cool." he grinned. "So, why y'all ain't bring my sister if everything is fine with her?"

"We throwing a surprise birthday bash and we want you to be the surprise guest of honor," answered Jay.

"Bet. I'm down. When and where?"

"On her birthday. Ma Dukes house. You ever been to Ma Dukes or met her?" T questioned him.

"Nah not that I can't remember."

"It's 3433 Moosewood Ave. Here put yo' number in my phone and I will text you and remind you," she extended her phone to him.

Quickly, he saved his number to her phone and handed it back, "Thanks y'all for tracking me down," he told them earnestly then picked up new piece of jewelry. He wheeled the cooler between them. "I don't drink or smoke though so y'all can keep the liquor."

All three of the adults grinned at the newly eighteen-year-old man in front of him. Jay took hold of the cooler. One by one, they slapped hands with Tyriq.

"Lil' Buddy gon' be so proud of you," Kim told him.

His heart swelled with pride and in anticipation of reuniting with his sister then it began to deflate, "Is she still in the streets?"

"Nope," Jay answered.

"Y'all don't wanna stay for the party?" he asked.

T chuckled, "You up here nephew and it's yo' party. Shit not to mention we been then turned every chick out in this muthafucka."

He guffawed, "Alright. Well y'all be safe."

"Fa sho nephew. We see you soon."

Chapter 10

The next afternoon Sayvonne took a deep breath and dialed T's number while watching her baby sister play on the floor. "Hello?"

"Yo what's good fam. You alright?" T greeted Sayvonne jovially.

"Yeah. I'm good T. Thanks for asking," she bit down on her lip. "But umm do you have a minute to talk?"

"Fa sho. What's going on?" asked a concerned T.

"Layla," Sayvonne said simply hearing the smile stretch across T's face over the phone.

"What about her?"

"She really likes you T. Like really likes you."

"That's what's up. I really like her too. Like really."

Sayvonne sighed, "T you know what I mean. Now I know you got a lot of women to entertain,"

"Hold on ma before you go any further. You right I do know what you mean. I'm glad you put that lil' bug in my ear too 'cause honestly I have been thinking about settling down too. But you know it's hard to find the right individual the one that completes you."

"Yes, it is but you can't be scared to try it T. Everything you do in life is a risk. So, is a relationship. You're risking a lot of factors within a relationship," grinned Sayvonne.

"I can dig it. But yo tell lil' mama to come up to the club tonight. I will make sure she on the list to get in."

"Okay. Thanks T."

"No problem fam."

The two lines disconnected and Sayvonne grinned pleased at her handiwork. Whether they went for it or they didn't T knew how Layla felt now. The rest was up to them. She dialed Layla's number. "What's up sis?"

"Nothing. Just laying down watching TV," morosely Layla answered.

Holding onto her sister's hands, she led them to her car, "Ew gurl you stank booty? You ain't washed yo' ass yet?"

"I ain't doing shit today. I'm on my Bruno Mars lazy ish."

"If I was you I would get up and start my lil' routine as if I was going out."

"But I'm not. So, why would I?"

"Cuz I just got off the phone with T and she said she got you on the list for tonight if you wanna kick it with her at the club."

Adrenaline surged through Layla and she shot off the bed whipping her closet door open, "What am I going to wear?" she exclaimed pulling out a pair of jeans holding them up to her and throwing them on the bed. "Von, can I borrow yo' red shirt?"

"Do you know many red shirts I got?"

Drunk with giddiness Layla laughed and tossed another pair of pants onto her bed, "Yeah. I got half of them. I just need something sexy."

"Well look in yo' closet."

"What you think I'm doing?" she pulled out a short red dress and held it up to her body then draped it across her bed.

212

"Hmm. I don't know then," Sayvonne pursed her lips together coming to a stop at a red light. She handed Simone the pacifier who in turn plopped it into Rachel's mouth. "Have you even talked to her about yo' feelings?"

Her smile faltered, "No, but I did call her and she ain't never return my call but obviously she thinking about me if y'all was talking and she had you pass a message to me. I'ma talk to her tonight though fa sho."

"Umm hmm."

"Fa real."

"Yeah alright. Well you better call me and let me know what happened afterwards."

"You know I'ma call you sap with good news sis. Well text you so I don't wake nobody up. But lemme go ahead and get ready fa tonight."

"A'ight sis. Stay focused please. I love you be safe."

"You know it and I love you too sis. Bye."

"Bye."

****

Sitting in between the legs of her girlfriend who was braiding her hair, Brandy stared at the laptop screen scanning through the jobs that she had put an application in at but hadn't heard from. "Baby, won't you call them," her girlfriend said from over her shoulder pointing to a job-requesting bouncers at a club.

"What I look like?" tsked Brandy with annoyance.

One of her girlfriend's hands dropped out of Brandy's wavy hair and the other jumped to the side of her face and mugged her, "Like you need a job so call them."

With a scowl on her face, she spat out, "Don't fuckin' mug me again."

213

"Baby, we den fought time and time again. I be a'ight plus the makeup sex is crazy. So, do what you feel I ain't neva skurred," she moved Brandy's head back. "Tilt ya head back."

"Call 'em and give me the phone."

A smile graced her face as she dialed the number for Brandy. Upon the phones lines connecting she handed the phone off to Brandy, "Here baby."

She took the phone and straightened up away from the hair weaving fingers, "Hi, I'm calling about the bouncer position...Uh-huh...Yes...No...Tonight...Nine-thirty...Yes,   that's   fine...Brandy...Ok   see   you then...Thanks...Bye," Brandy hung up the phone and looked at her girl. "She told me to come in for an interview tonight at nine thirty."

Squealing with excitement her girlfriend wrapped her arms around her kissing her and wrestling her to the floor. Her girlfriend's lips changed citing a new source of need she was feeling.

Brandy kissed her chocolate neck drawing moans from her. She worked her way up to her ear and murmured, "You gotta finish my hair first then I put this in yo' life before I leave for my interview."

Instantaneously her girl let up and pulled Brandy back into a sitting position. She grasped her hair and began to braid.

****

"What's good Daddy." Stacey greeted T as she walked in to find her alone in a back room of the club that had been dubbed the smoke room.

"Shit what's good baby," T flirted passing the blunt to her. Stacey accepted it and T spoke again. "You got my back tonight?"

214

Smiling through the smoke Stacey told her, "Don't I always baby," she exhaled and passed the blunt T's way who declined so she could watch Stacey smoke again. "And Jay got a bouncer interview at nine-thirty tonight."

"You know I think it's sexy as hell when a female smoke. Especially when she got sexy full ass lips like yours."

"Give me a shotgun," Stacey said with a wicked grin.

Taking the blunt from her T hit it once and flipped it around placing the lit end between her lips. She beckoned Stacey closer. Stacey slid closer and wrapped her full lips around the blunt. Smoke began to fill her mouth and T watched her chest rise as it did so. Once she jumped back, T flipped the blunt around and hit it a few more times before she exhaled.

"Shotgun got you feelin' it huh?" commented T with a smirk while Stacey coughed.

The tip of her pink tongue slipped out wetting her lips, "Nah it ain't the shotgun I'm feeling but I'm definitely feeling and wanting something."

Maneuvering one leg over the bench so that they were now open T grabbed onto Stacey's hips and scooted her closer. She kissed her hungrily while her hands went under Stacey's shirt to palm her titties and pinch her nipples. T leaned back against the wall and Stacey straddled her draping her legs across T's while grinding on top of her.

"Ahem," someone coughed. "And dis would be one reason most companies don't let you blow on the job."

Dropping her head and expelling a breath T glanced up at the stud, "Sean, fa real?"

"I am. It's a line up the street and we open in five minutes," Sean complained not wavering from T's gaze.

"I'm trying to get my smoke on too before we open. Shit at least a lil' hit," she looked at Stacey seductively.

Stacey stood, "Well lemme go get ready," she drifted away from T.

Still smoking T watched her leave waiting until she was out of the room. Once she was out of the room T pushed off the wall getting off the bench. She walked over to Sean and slapped the joint out of her mouth, "From now on this a no smoking facility. You light dat back up you fired."

Sean sucked her teeth and followed her boss out the door to work.

****

Wolf whistles and catcalls began to break out from the end of the line Jay worked with Sean. The calls continued as a young woman clad in a Catholic schoolgirl outfit blended in sexuality approached the front. Both studs smiled appreciatively at her.

"Damn," Sean mumbled no longer working.

Letting the last person go on in after patting them down Jay stepped up next to Sean. "Layla?" she sounded surprised. "Damn shorty."

"Hey," she grinned ignoring Sean who was following their conversation back and forth like a tennis match.

"What's good baby. I'm Sean," she side stepped Jay and extended her hand.

Raising an eyebrow and making a blank face at Sean, she uttered hi and turned back to Jay.

"Nigga you gon' find yo' ass fired. She ain't fa you cuz. Get back to work," Jay ordered glaring at Sean.

Grimacing Sean turned back to the next customer in line without another word.

"C'mon ma," she ushered Layla in after mean mugging Sean. "Her punk ass, nigga just don't know if dis interview go right she ass out."

Unable to respond Layla basked in her seventeen-year-old sexual appeal, which oozed through her, attracting stares from everything with eyes. She drank in the immensity of the club. Her eyes lit up at how stylish the club was laid out.

"C'mon bring yo' lil' hot ass on up in here."

Eyes roving over to the bar where they were heading they connected with T's. T had a woman in between her legs whispering in her ear but once her eyes locked onto Layla's they never left the honey suckled female. She politely excused herself from the female in her ear and started towards Layla.

The two stud brothers exchanged daps then Jay left to go back to work. T turned her attention back to Layla who looked like she'd been dipped in honey and tasted oh so sweet. She kissed her cheek. "You tryin' to start a riot up in her baby?" T commented admiring her outfit.

She took a step closer to T and whispered in her ear, "Nah I just want you to tear dis pussy up."

"You ain't said nothin' but some words baby," she looked toward the bartender. "Stacey, slide me two double shots of Goose."

Stacey nodded and a minute later both T and Layla had downed their drinks.

"Hit me wit' two more," T called out.

She slid the drinks their way and went back to assisting the other customers while the two cheered and tossed their drinks back.

The alcohol kicked into effect making Layla feel more and more loose. She sat on T's lap slow grinding to the beat of the song. T kissed around the back of her neck strumming her clit underneath her skirt. Layla moaned. She turned to face T and kissed her once. She kissed her twice and didn't stop. Instead, she pushed her backwards onto the bar and mounted her.

"Hold on Ma," laughed T holding onto Layla's hip. "Dis a place of business. Let's go upstairs."

Layla dismounted and straightened her clothes out. She bit her lip and bucked her eyes giving T an innocent look before responding with, "Yes daddy."

****

Brandy got to the club earlier than scheduled for her interview. She paid the ten-dollar admission fee so she could see what type of atmosphere she would be working around. Upon entering Colorz she was immediately impressed. She nodded to herself as she pictured herself working here. What was not to love? An upscale joint filled with hood niggas and sexy bitches. After hitting the dance floor a couple times, she headed over to the bar.

"What's good boo? What you want to drink?" Stacey came to her service immediately.

"What it do baby. I ain't drinkin' ma. I'm here for an interview," Brandy grinned at her.

"Okay. What's your name?"

"B Jacobs."

Stacey smirked. "Like I ain't gon' find out yo' name sooner or later if you 'bout to start here."

"True, true," she winked at her. "Guess you have to wait till dat time den."

"Anyways," Stacey rolled her eyes playfully then turned to call out to another stud down at the end of the bar. "Ay Sean! Tell Jay she got a B Jacobs here to see her.'

Sean glanced at Stacey then at Brandy, "For what? What position she 'bout to have?"

Tsking she replied, "A possible future employee. Now can you please tell her?"

"I thought-"

"Sean, will you fuckin' tell her and enjoy yo' last day!" Stacey exploded interrupting her.

"What?"

"Fuck it," Stacey growled. She came around the bar angrily, "*You* watch the bar and I'ma tell her then. And all my shit betta add up right tonight too nosey muthafucka."

****

T slammed in and out of Layla's pussy with long deep strokes. Layla placed one leg over T's shoulder while the other leg T held down hostage as she beat it up. Thigh muscles tensed and her fingernails dug in T's back.

"Oh shit," Layla moaned sweetly in T's ear, which turned into a scream.

Slowing her pace T calmed herself but thrusted into her with just as much intensity.

"Fuck T," she moaned biting her lip.

Leaning down T fed her lips to Layla. They began to kiss hungrily at first then with more urgency as if their lips needed to touch. She wrapped her legs around T and began to pull her inside of her. She picked up speed and switched from kissing Layla's lips to biting and sucking her neck. As T licked around Layla's spot her back arched and toes curled.

Layla whimpered with pleasure. She took T's hands and placed them around her neck to choke her. The hands around her neck enticed her even more and she eagerly met T's hip movements. The two winded together as if they were made for fucking one another, fucking like there was no tomorrow only this moment.

Keeping one hand on her throat the other hand wound into Layla's hair grabbing on tight while T lengthened her stride so she seeped out and dove back inside of her box. She cocked her head at an angle retreated to the head of her strap and pummeled back through her insides. Grunting she took the hand off her neck to put one of Layla's legs back on her shoulder. Her hand went back to Layla's neck applying pressure as she beat the wet cat.

The two switched positions so Layla's rotund ass was in the air. Upon assuming the position, Layla placed one hand on the wall. In one fluid motion, T smacked her ass, yanked her head back, and sent her strap on penis deep inside of her. She pumped from behind watching Layla's ass work. Laying a smack down on it, she watched it jiggle and slipped a finger inside of her chocolate star.

"Ooh shit daddy keep it in there," panted Layla pushing T backwards.

One finger inside of Layla's ass while she rode, the other hand and fingers took turns teasing her clit. They flicked back and forth against it and darted away making a wet path to her nipples where they twisted them rolling them back and forth between her fingertips. Running back down to her clit they massaged kneading against it. Juices came tumbling out of her once again.

Removing her juiced slicked fingers, she fed them to Layla. T leaned up biting and sucking around her neck. Once the young woman gave in T pushed her face down. She maneuvered her body so that she was hitting Layla from the side on bent knees. They humped themselves into a frenzy until they both just lay there panting with exhaustion.

After catching her breath, T rolled over to the side of the bed and began putting on her clothes.

"T you tired?" she inquired with a smile while laying on her side.

Leaning over T kissed her lips and deepened it with her tongue, "Never dat baby. But I gotta check on the club make sure everything cool. But we most definitely gotta finish this."

Quickly Layla flipped T over so she sat butt naked on top of her, "We can't finish right now?""

"Just let me make sure everything good shorty."

Sliding up T's flat chest she murmured, "They got yo' cell phone number daddy. They a call." and with that Layla lowered herself onto T's mouth. T allowed Layla to ride her face as she palmed her ass and pinched her nipples. Then she eased Layla onto her back so she could bestow a tongue-lashing.

****

The two sexually satiated beings exited another back room T had turned into a private freak room. A vibration started against buzzed against T's thigh. She grabbed Layla's hand, "Go tell Stacey she da bartender to make you a drink on the house. And order me a shot of Goose while I make sure everything good."

Grinning happily Layla agreed, "Ok daddy," and then pushed T against the wall and tongue kissed her before walking away.

She watched Layla walk away with a smile as her eyes were entranced by her fat ass. Her phone buzzed against her thigh again. "What's good," she greeted the caller after sliding her phone out of her pocket.

"Hey. You working," Kiaysha's melodic voice flowed through the phone lines.

"Yeah ma. Why what's good?" T slapped hands with a stud walking past.

"You own a club right?"

"Yeah," answered T posting against the wall watching Layla dance for her while at the bar.

"So, when are you going to invite me out to see it?"

"When you have a babysitter for yo' son."

"What if I told you I had one right now?"

"Then I would say bring yo' ass," laughed T. "You need the address?"

"Actually I think I'm here," she giggled nervously. "I googled some hot spots since I had a sitter for the evening and stumbled across this spot that I think may be yours."

Looking at Layla one last time T walked out of her line of sight heading towards the front door. "Lemme find out you stalking me."

"Oh. Whatever. Don't flatter yourself. I needed to let my hair down and have some drinks and this club just *happened* to be all over Google. So, I decided to check it out. Hell it might not even be your club."

"Uh huh. What's the name of it?"

"Colorz? I think. I'm not quite sure. There was a rainbow over it and then someone almost crashed into me."

"Oh ok. Yeah that's not my club. Go head on up to the front though. I got a friend at that door tonight. So, just let them know T sent you."

"Oh. You got pull like that at even at other clubs?"

"Whatever ma. Just make sure you tell her that."

"I just hired a bouncer. She a lil' small for da position but she know a lot a people in here. She ain't no bitch nigga fa sho look like she can handle herself," reported Jay walking up to T.

"A'ight. Take her up top. I'll be back in a few to meet her," dictated T.

Jay nodded, "Alright."

Whipping out a small bottle of cologne T rubbed herself with it on her neck, behind her ears, wrists, and beneath her belly button. She took a piece of gum from her pocket and slid it into her mouth. "You at the door ma?" questioned T hearing her argue with someone.

When Kiaysha didn't respond and T recognized the voices she sidestepped a few people and blocked the entrance to the club. "What's up we got a problem?" she snapped out at Sean who was exchanging words with Kiaysha.

Sean turned around to see T, "Nah. I just thought cuz she da second girl-"

"Next time don't think," T cut her off. "This my place of business. I can let as many women in free as I want too. You out here arguing with a line up the street man."

"Yeah. A'ight," the brown toned stud turned her back to T to the next patrons in line.

Laughing T gestured the women to the inside of the club, "Nah. They in free too since you worried about it enough to hold my money up let's spend yours. Oh yeah and this the, third, fourth, and fifth female I let in free tonight."

Exhaling sharply she didn't say anything and T ushered in the women along with Kiaysha who sat back on her heels watching the exchange.

****

"Ain't it funny how we keep runnin' into each other?" Brandy sneered in Layla's ear from behind her.

The words she was about to speak to Stacey whisked away from her as a shiver ran down her spine. She closed her eyes and let out a slow breath before turning around with a smirk plastered on her face, "Ain't following me against yo' probation or something you gotta be on?"

Guffawing as if Layla told a joke she cut it short quickly, "Shorty, you is not that damn bad and yo' pussy ain't no damn gold mine contrary to what you think."

"You wasn't saying that when you was fuckin' me and keepin' me caked up," retorted Layla with slits where her eyes were.

Scoffing Brandy took a small step back looking around the club then took a bigger step forward into Layla's personal space, "You gotta pay to play. Ain't nothin' free remember?" her Cheshire cat smile was the answer so Brandy barked out, "And since we talkin' about it, it's obvious you been fuckin'. Where my money at? You owe me."

Licking her lips and lifting herself off the stool she stepped into Brandy, "I don't owe you shit," she said and walked away.

"Da fuck you just say to me?" bit out Brandy yanking her to her chest. "Da fuck you just say to me Layla?"

"Yo, y'all good?" inquired Jay as she walked up on the two.

Dropping Layla's arm but sending her a violent threat with her eyes she nodded and looked at Jay with a clean slate for a face, "We good cuz. We go back. This was my shorty back in the day," her eyes crept to Layla's daring her to say anything different or more.

"Cool," Jay nodded with her eyes on Layla. "The boss ready to meet you B. Layla stay here looking sexy. I know T ain't leaving you unattended for too long," complimented Jay with a smile.

At the mention of T's name, a smile appeared on her face, "Okay. Tell my daddy to hurry up," she said out of spite and shooting an evil glance at Brandy who walked past her following behind Jay.

The two fell in line with one another as they neared the upstairs VIP section of the nightclub where T was waiting with their crew and Kiaysha. She stopped the light skin stud before they walked into the secluded area, "Dig I see you and Layla got some relationship history but dis a place of business we real cool but we don't be on no shit up here fa real but havin' a good time. So, whatever drama y'all got call her ass later. Don't bring that shit to work so y'all both catch charges. And dig Layla got history wit' us too," she stared into her eyes until she nodded. "Cool. Come meet the nigga that sign ya checks from now on."

Immediately Brandy's light-skinned features darkened hardening with tension. She stared across the room into the face of her source of animosity, which happened to have the same mug on her face. From across the room she watched T motion towards the bar and leaving the woman at her seat, she got there first. The anger dissolved from her face by the time Jay and she made it over to join T at the bar.

"So, we meet again? I'm good if you good. This a place of business. Hoes don't mean shit to me," said T sending a wink over to Kiaysha who was seated with a drink watching them.

Business. Money. That was a language Brandy understood. She exhaled and responded, "Cool. Glad to see bitches don't run you."

T laughed, "Nah never that it's no fun," the newly hired stud joined in with the laughter. "So, you game for this job?" she asked seriously sipping her drink.

"Fa sho. I need one and dis joint cool right here."

In agreement T nodded, "It ain't no foul shit up in here. Save the drama fa yo' mama but not my mama ya dig. We just kickin' it having fun. Na mean niggas get beside they self sometime but I expect my security team to fully handle it so we can go on having a good night. I ain't never

225

had to shut the doors cuz of some bullshit and I pride myself on that."

"I can dig it."

"Layla give you any shit while you here just holla at me."

"Fa sho."

"A'ight. Now I gotta get back to my date. Consider tonight yo' first night on the job. Let that bitch nigga know she been replaced. As long as she ain't on no bullshit, she can stay and kick it. If she get on that mess put her ass out," T said referring to Sean who was leaning over the railing looking down at the crowd.

She nodded walking over to do her job.

"I don't trust her not at all but I'm sick of Sean bitch ass," admitted T to Jay who nodded and followed the other two studs back downstairs.

****

"Nah. I'm good," Layla declined another offer to dance while she danced in her seat at the bar with a shot of Goose next to her.

"What you waitin' on the President to ask you? You betta go have a good time," muttered Stacey as she hurried past her to assist another patron.

She rid herself of the response she had lined up when she spotted T coming down from the VIP and began to excitedly primp. Layla raised her skirt and poked out her cleavage while dancing exotically waiting on T to look her way. However, when T did look her way it was only briefly. Abruptly, she stopped dancing and zeroed in on T's hand intertwined with another woman's.

"Look at you. Over here hatin' like a muthafucka," Brandy spoke up from the side of Layla.

226

An eye roll accompanied her sharp reply, "Whatever," she glanced her ex up and down briefly before asking, "You wanna dance?"

Mock surprise written all over her face Brandy questioned, "What? I get to dance with you your Highness?"

She rolled her doe eyes again and grabbed Brandy's hand leading her onto the dance floor. Layla led her close to where T and Kiaysha danced then stopped and began to seductively dance all over Brandy. Brandy half smiled as she held onto Layla's swaying hips while Jay watched from afar.

J. Holiday's single Put You to Bed rang out through the club and Layla turned to face Brandy. She settled in close to Brandy grinding slow with her head on her shoulder. Layla kissed along her face.

"You eva think 'bout us?" Layla wondered out loud without raising her head.

Refusing to get caught up in the moment she looked down at the woman in her arms and looked away, "Yeah but I think more about da shit you owe me."

Layla sighed. She lifted her head to kiss Brandy sweetly before taking her butter colored ear lobe into her mouth, "What if I had a way to pay you back?"

"And what's that?" Brandy asked gathering more of Layla into her arms while lowering her face into the crevice of her neck.

She stepped back to look at Brandy, "T."

****

Holding on tightly to Kiaysha, T glared over at Layla and Brandy. She was watching their "romantic" moment unfold before her eyes. Scoffing quietly to herself she kissed Kiaysha's neck as she noticed Layla stop dancing step back and say something to Brandy before kissing her.

"I'm glad I got to see you tonight," murmured T into Kiaysha's ear.

"Are you sure you didn't wanna spend more time with female number one that you let in the club free?"

Her head cocked, "Huh? As long as the category ain't got my mama in it you da number one female in my life ma."

"Uh huh. Sound good. I remember what your friend said at the door."

"Hold up she not a friend. Not even an acquaintance. She a fuckin' employee; was a fuckin' employee."

"Hmm even worse. And what about your friends sister?"

"What you mean?"

"The night our date ended short and you had to pick up Lil' Buddy. While I was parking the car her gurlfriend hollered out not to mess with you. That your whole crew is foul."

A knot twisted uncomfortably in T's stomach, "She was outta her mind at the time with that shit with lil' bruh. I ain't sayin' I'm no angel and I have no problem saying I haven't been in a committed relationship. I ain't scared of it just ain't found the right one. I'm searching for her but in the meantime I'm free to mingle."

"How many women have you mingled tonight?"

"None."

"Are you sure? The chick in the catholic get up won't stop staring daggers at you and me," pointed out Kiaysha.

She did a two-step so she was facing the direction Kiaysha just was and looked up to see Layla's hazel eyes glaring at her. T moved around again, "Honestly, I fucked her once in the past."

"What's the past with you T?" asked Kiaysha stepping out of her arms. "The hickey on your neck says it wasn't too long ago." She walked away from T towards the exit of the club.

Touching her neck and glaring at Layla who smirked and flicked her off delayed T going after Kiaysha. When she finally did catch up with her in the parking lot, she placed a hand on her car door to close it. Kiaysha turned to face her begrudgingly.

"Yes, what is it T?"

"Look ma I'm sorry."

"For what? Getting caught or shall I say caught up because you are single."

"Kiaysha I like you. Like I really like you ma."

"Funny way of showing it Timothy. I like you too. But it seems the only obstacle in the road is that you *like* a lot of other women too. I have to go get my son," she tugged at the car door underneath T's palm.

"What I can do to show you I'm serious ma? That I'm serious for real."

Pursing her lips together and tapping her foot with annoyance she said, "You can start by not being an even bigger asshole by holding me up from going to get my son and opening the car door for me like the gentleman that I know you can be."

Smiling at the compliment T opened the car door for Kiaysha who slid into the vehicle and cranked the engine, "Maw Maw reminded of one of her sayings in a dream last night. She used to say you wanna know what a whore is like. Meet her in her whore house," she paused to laugh. "I never knew what that meant until tonight. Thanks for the clarification Timothy," she slammed the car door shut and pulled off.

Sighing T watched her pull off until she couldn't see her anymore. Shrugging off the sad feeling, she whipped her phone out with a new thought, *Oh well onto another piece of pussy.*

****

A vibration awakened T from her sleep. She rolled over to grab hold of Yolanda's body but she wasn't there. Her eyes popped open glancing around the room. The quick eye survey of the room yielded nothing however as soon as it became apparent by the humming and singing that Yolanda was in the kitchen. Again, something vibrated. T looked at the nightstand next to her at her phone and checked to see who was calling her. She smiled Kiaysha was calling her early or rather T was waking up late upon seeing the time. She answered the call.

"What's good ma," she greeted her warmly with a yawn.

"Let's skip the formalities and let's be honest. I like you. I'm feeling you. I want you. But I'm not stupid and I refuse to play Booboo the fool for anyone. I know you probably laid up with another female right now so I'll make it quick. After this phone call based on last night's events T. Don't call me again unless you ready to come correct. I'm through playing games," she hung up the phone on a baffled T as quickly as the conversation began.

Walking into the room with a tray of food Yolanda came to a halt seeing T's face, "T what's wrong? Why do you look so shocked?"

'Cause shorty just blew my mind and a nigga still lightweight sleep, T thought to herself before shaking herself mentally, "I'm good baby. Still sleepy. You wore me out last night."

"Me wear you out? Nah. I don't believe it."

230

"Oh but you did though."

"Or I had some help," she pointed out the hickey on T's neck.

The feeling of deja vu began to drape itself around T. She opened her mouth to say something but Yolanda placed a forkful of pancakes in it.

"Chew T," commanded Yolanda laughing. "Listen baby. We're both single and having fun. I'm not upset. It be like that sometimes. Don't let it happen again but I'm fine. Hell you should have brought her with you last night."

"Next time I will."

"I wasn't playing at your mother's house when I said lets cross out a threesome on our list of fun shit to do. I'm down for whatever, whenever."

Chapter 11

Boom! Boom! Boom! Sayvonne knocked on Layla's parent's front door as the sun beamed down on the back of her neck.

The front door swung open slowly. Layla's mother smiled at Sayvonne and unlocked the screen door, "Hey Von. How you been?" she greeted her holding the door open. "How y'all doing? Y'all alright? You need anything?"

Smiling appreciatively she declined, "No, ma'am. We're good right now. I'm blessed to be around caring people. Kenni's umm boyfriend's friend's told me they would look out for me as well."

"Hey now! I guess you been dubbed they honorary lil' sister."

"Yes ma'am. Layla too."

A roll of her hazel eyes accompanied by a laugh came from Layla's mother, "Yeah right her lil' hot ass. I know they ain't thinking lil' sister."

If you only knew how true that was. Sayvonne thought laughing nervously. "Lay upstairs?"

"Yeah mad as hell and moping around for some damn reason. She ain't came out all day."

She jogged up the stairs thinking to herself, *Probably still got a hangover.* At Layla's bedroom door, she turned the knob but it was locked. Sayvonne knocked on the door impatiently.

"I'm fine Ma. I'm not hungry," Layla called out from within the room without opening the door.

"Who said it was yo' mama?" questioned Sayvonne with a smack of her lips. Silence answered her question. "And I'm not yo' daddy either Lay," she said with a touch of patience in her voice as if Layla was slow at understanding.

The door flew open however once Sayvonne entered she slammed it shut and locked it again. She didn't say anything to her best friend but instead stretched out across her bed gazing at the television advertising commercials. She pretended not to notice Sayvonne's eyes scrutinizing her.

"Uh what's wrong wit' you?" Sayvonne finally asked.

Again, Layla didn't answer her.

"Okay.... How was yo' date at the club wit' T?"

Flipping around dramatically onto her side she spat out, "Fuck T."

Instantly Sayvonne took a seat at the edge of the bed, "What happened?"

Sitting up angrily and through the water in her eyes she bit out, "Cuz when I first got to da club she was all on me-"

"What you end up wearin'?"

Her smile cleared the liquid that had made her hazel eyes shine, "A good bad gurl outfit. I jazzed up the catholic uniform."

"So, I take it y'all fucked?"

Layla rolled her eyes again but couldn't hide the smile that appeared as the memory replayed itself, "Yeah but listen to dis right. Right after, I mean, right, after, we get done she sends me to the bar to get some drinks. I'm at the bar a good twenty, thirty minutes declining all these offers to dance. Tell me why she come down from VIP wit' another bitch. And looked at me like I wasn't shit."

An uneasy feeling began to settle in Sayvonne's stomach while her mouth prepared honesty, "Well Lay, it ain't like you her gurl. And you know she carry a team a females."

Anger shot through Layla lifting her to her feet, her hazel eyes ablaze with fire she yelled, "SO! That don't mean she gotta be an ass. What she invite me down there for if she gon' have another bitch up there? And be all over her ugly ass."

"Oh you jealous?" she suspected with amusement.

The fire in Layla's eyes combusted viciously, "Whatever! Wasn't nobody jealous of that ugly ass frog faced bitch."

Sayvonne laughed, "Layla. You know it's not too many times when you cuss like a sailor right?"

"Whatever! Fuck you Von you takin' her side."

"It ain't no damn sides to take Layla."

"Whatever," she turned her back to her best friend.

A small chuckle escaped from Sayvonne as she stood calmly, "Look I'ma drop some sense on yo' ass and den I'm out. You making yo' self her honey dip because whenever she want it, you give it to her. Of course, that's all you is, is pussy to her if you giving it up like that. Just like when you look at her and see dollar signs. You just mad you got played again. Open yo' fuckin' mouth and try talkin' to her. See where da fuck that get you. See you when I see you," Sayvonne retorted and left the room.

Spinning around on her heel Layla watched her best friend stalk out of her room with an open mouth.

****

"Yo, Kim peep dis I been thinkin-" stated T coming into the living room and sitting at the counter in their kitchen.

"Shut da fuck up T! YOU, been thinkin'? Aww hell nah," Kim clowned her after pressing pause on the TV.

She laughed, "A'ight I fell into that one. But dig this. I been thinkin' like I know I been saying it but for real, real shit. I'ma settle down."

The movie resumed playing and Kim tossed a pillow at her, "Selfish ass. Who gon' be my drinkin' partner?"

"Fa real sis. I'm serious right now," T said laughing.

She pressed paused on the TV again and put the remote down. Kim swayed over to the counter where T sat on a stool. Kim rolled her eyes watching T watch her walk up to her with a big grin on her face.

"That's why yo' bitches be think we fuckin' around," she punched T in the arm.

"Shit you know you sexy. I'm just giving you my opinion."

"You been telling me since high school. I think I then figured it out that you like what you see."

"Damn right I do. That's why I'ma keep complimentin' you."

She laughed and rolled her eyes, "Whatever," she pulled a stool around the counter so she could sit in front of T's face, "Alright now what got you thinkin' 'bout settlin' down? Or should I say who? And please don't say Layla."

Laughter burst forth from T at the mention of Layla, "She salty at me fa right now but dig Kiaysha, Yolanda," she made a face and shook her head. "You know I fucked Layla last night in the back room? Well shit she ended markin' my ass and then Kiaysha came through. Long story short I ended up Yolanda bed last night. So dig I'm laid up in Yolanda bed, my phone start ringing. I answer its

235

Kiaysha she talkin' like you know I peeped the hickey. I ain't stupid. Come correct next time you wanna holla at me."

"Well hell naw she ain't stupid," giggled Kim.

"Anyways soon as she hung up Yolanda comes in with breakfast and we get to talkin'. She talkin' da same shit. She peeped the hickey but she don't care. Shit she told me she down fa whatever, whenever and that I should'a brought Layla back to the house for us."

"Hell nah. Tell her you graduated from threesomes what freshman year?"

"Hell yeah I was fuckin' both them hoes from eighth grade up to freshman year. Every time I went up a grade I upgraded and added another bitch."

"So, you feeling Yolanda?" posed Kim.

T couldn't contain the grin that began to stretch across her face, "Shit what's not to like. Baby got her own everything. She don't need me for shit but like when I make that pussy gush like a water hose. Shit she fit in the family and she just as freaky as I am."

"True, true."

"But then on the other hand I still ain't hit Stacey yet."

"Y'all can hit her together?"

"Yeah but the first time solo. Shit that's her audition," joked T. "And I want Layla and Yolanda together sis! That a be some player shit I settle for. Baby gurl got some good pussy. Layla thick but Yolanda grown woman thick. Layla a freak but she just barely wiped the counter off of Yolanda's freakiness. And I still gotta hit Stacey," laughed T.

"Bruh you makin' this out like this a reality show."

"And you know it shit. This is important business. The scores been fluctuating I'm just waiting to see who win. Shit dis T's lucky lady we talkin' about not Flavor of

236

Love. She gotta pass all parts like the kids taking them proficiency tests."

"First never is they called that anymore old ass," she got up from her seat and drifted over to the couch. When T looked away, she threw another couch pillow at her. "Second, you a conceited ass."

"Yo, I'm just sayin' shit. Yolanda, Stacey, Layla. Yes."

"You know what T I'm through with you and this conversation. Go get some rellos and beer. I got some Cali dro in da back."

"So, why you ain't get no Cali rellos or beer?" she questioned picking up her car keys. She smiled at the finger her sister presented her. "Aye I'm going ain't I?"

"Get the leaf shit!" Kim called out to her.

"Man I know what you like," she yelled back.

Cruising to the convenient store bumping Lollipop by rap artist Lil Wayne she smoked a cigarette. Upon pulling into the parking lot, T noticed a familiar figure at the counter of the store. T smirked and whipped into a parking space.

She walked into the store and approached Layla at the counter, "What's good shorty."

Without turning to face her Layla rolled her eyes and didn't say anything.

"Don't go nowhere," commanded T with a smile and a touch of her elbow. She strolled to the beer cave to nab a cold case.

From her position at the counter Layla waited but once she caught sight of T approaching her again she walked out of the store.

"What's good Mike," T greeted the man behind the counter.

"Shit, chillin', been a slow day. Shorty on da team?" the man behind the counter asked.

237

"You know it. Yo, let me get a grenadeer with that."

"I got you fam. Its seven thirty-five."

She gave him a ten-dollar bill and as the cashier dished out her change he looked out the storefront, "I see shorty still waiting," he laughed.

"She knows what's good for her," said T joining in with the laughter. "A'ight man. Stay up," she walked out the door and casually strode past Layla who was sitting on the windowsill of the store sipping an Icee.

"What do you want?" Layla snapped at her when her car door opened.

She glanced back at her, "Nothing."

Layla jumped to her feet and flew towards T like someone lit a fire under her ass. "So, what you tell me not to go nowhere for?"

Ignoring her T sat her beer in the front passenger seat. She took a seat in her car.

"So, you not even gon' say nothin' for dissin' me at Colorz?"

"Nah," T started her car engine and stared at Layla who blocked her from closing her car door.

Something incomprehensible growled out from Layla and she spun on her heel walking away from T.

"Layla!" yelled T to a female who didn't turn around. "Shorty, come here!"

"Yes, T!" she shouted whipping around to glare at T. "What do you want?"

"Come here and see."

Visibly she sighed with a big heft of her shoulders, "What?" she crossed her arms over her chest.

"Bring yo' ass here!"

Like a shot, Layla was in motion once again. "Don't you fuckin' cuss at me!" she poked T in her chest.

With a calm voice and a lick of her lips T asked her, "What you gon' do about it?"

One of her open hands swung up towards T but she caught her by the wrist. The other arm came up hand open and extended as well but T caught that one as well. T pushed her backwards down onto the car lying on top of her.

She stared up at T willing herself to hold onto the anger she felt as her pussy began to stir and scream for T's attention. Her heart thudded in her chest as she thought about the last time they were this close. Layla's breath began to labor as her pussy jumped in wanton need for need. She tried one last time to ignore her pussy's heart beating furiously between her lips and focus on the fact that she was mad at T but all was lost when T touched her lips to Layla's.

One by one, T let her wrists. They kissed feverishly. Layla wrapped one of her legs around T's back as T began to nibble on the side of her neck.

"Yo, I don't mean to interrupt y'all but get the fuck off my car," a storeowner replied with a cigarette in his mouth.

"My bad," apologized T to the storeowner and easing off Layla who smiled bashfully and hurried to her car with her head down. T followed her. "You wanna roll with me?" she asked from outside of the vehicle Layla sat in.

"I do," admitted Layla chewing her lip squirming in the driver's seat. "But we need to talk. It's something I wanna talk to you about."

Quickly, T cast a mental check over her body to discern if she had any unwanted signs of an STD. She didn't have any so she relaxed. "Dig how 'bout I follow you home and you can come kick it with me and Kim?"

She chewed her bottom lip debating on whether to go or not. If Sayvonne would advise her to or not. Layla glanced up at T's smiling face, "Alright."

"Lead the way then shorty."

"Like you don't know the way," called out Layla.

She sent a smile over her shoulder.

Fifteen minutes later of the dog following the cat home put T in her car watching Layla park behind an SUV and high stepping towards hers.

"A'ight. Let's go," said Layla slamming her car door shut.

She whipped off the residential street, bent a corner, and slowed to the appropriate speed limit. T turned the radio down to a whisper, "So, dig what's on ya mind lil' mama? What you had to talk to me about shorty?"

"Umm...." her voice faltered. She turned the radio back up. "Umm...." Layla sputtered again drawing T's attention now as she clasped and unclasped her hands. She took a deep breath and squared her shoulders. "I like you T," Layla finally admitted. "Like I really like you. I was salty as fuck the night you left and I had the whole house to myself. I wanted you to stay. I was pissed at the club seeing you with that ugly bitch after we had just fucked. Like I mean we both was freshly fucked, cum still wet on the both of us. What the fuck? And I know I put a hickey on you. I didn't do it on purpose but shit honestly that's how I feel."

Slowly nodding and grinning T commented back, "So, you wanna be my shorty?"

"I don't wanna be yo' main, yo' bae, yo' shorty none a that," she looked away from T staring out of the window. "I wanna be yo' only."

T allowed silence to seep into the car and fill up all channels of communication. She pulled into her driveway, cut the engine, and placed a hand over Layla's. "Honestly, I been thinking a lot about being in a relationship. Only spending time and my attention on one woman. Before I left me and Kim was just having that conversation," she kissed Layla's cheek and whispered in her ear. "I'm glad you feel the same way I do," she whispered and then hopped out and around the car to open her car door for her.

She exited the vehicle watching T carry the case of beer to the front door and followed her inside with shock freezing her vocal cords and spreading a warm sensation in her stomach.

"Sis, we got company!" shouted T then turned to her. "Kim, be walking around here naked and shit like she live alone. Only her and them damn moles covering her body," joked T.

Kim stalked up to T and mugged her in the head, "Fuck you lying bitch."

Chuckling T told her, "Chill we got company. Behave sis," she bantered back.

"Whatever bitch," said Kim with a roll of her eyes. "What's up Layla," she greeted her and immediately went to open the beer and put it away. "You get that rello?" she asked T.

She handed it to her and Kim cracked a beer and gave it to her in return then opened her own.

"You want a drink? We got some other shit in there. Not just beer," asked T sliding her hand into Layla's.

"Nah. I'm cool," Layla declined.

"Gurl, you can turn down the liquor but don't act like you too good to smoke with us. Assume ya smoking stations please," ordered Kim to the both of them and walking out of the kitchen.

"Where y'all smoke at?" inquired Layla watching Kim walk away from them.

"C'mon," said T tugging at her hand.

She followed behind the two concealing her excitement and curiosity. Her ears barely registered the repartee of the "siblings." Her mind however was wrapping around the words of T. The admittance that they were thinking along the same lines all along. Mentally she patted herself on the back knowing Sayvonne would be proud of her spilling how she really felt.

Upon entrance to the garage, she stopped in her tracks. One side of the garage yielded a parked car. The other side was a different story. It was decorated as if it were a room in the house. In the middle of the open space was a black rug with a weed plant on it. Against the wall in front of the rug was a black sofa. To the left of the sofa was a boom box sitting on a crate. On the other side of the couch was a small folding table and two stools perched next to it.

"Go head have a seat," Kim beckoned her gesturing towards the couch.

"You sure you don't want nothin' to drink shorty? I know we got some goose down here," asked T when she sat down.

She grinned wickedly remembering the double shots of Grey Goose she had. "Yeah. Can I have a shot?"

"Where da shot glasses at sis?" T grinned at Kim.

"Hmph. I guess dreams do come true," muttered Kim as she handed T the shot glasses and turned on the stereo.

T poured the three of them shot and gave them out. They all tossed them back and Kim lit her blunt from seat directly in front of them on the sofa. Layla declined when T tried to pass her the blunt so the two smoked half of the blunt with all three of the women quiet.

"You quiet shorty. You nervous or something?" commented T accepting the blunt her sister passed her.

"Nah. I'm cool," answered Layla.

"Man hit this Cali cush," Kim extended the blunt to her without hitting it herself. "C'mon its gon' get you right ma."

She smiled looking at the both of them quizzically but not replying.

"C'mon now shorty. I know you know fuckin' while y'all both high is the shit. Gurl don't act like you don't know and don't wanna hit this shit," jested Kim with a smile.

Laughing softly Layla accepted the blunt. She hit it too hard and backed off it coughing heavily and holding it out to whoever took it.

"She told you this was some Cali shit now. That ain't no reggie shit that's some loud baby you ain't gotta boof it we got enough," said T.

"My bad," giggled Layla.

Time continued on with the three of them passing the blunt between them silently. The THC kicked into effect within Layla making her relax back into T who had her arm draped over her shoulders. Within her state of highness, she began to realize her pussy was getting wet. She moaned as T became aware of her rising hormones of her own and began kissing around her neck.

"T give me a shotgun," demanded Kim who was watching the two intensely.

She stopped the charades on Layla's neck, "Bet," she lifted Layla slightly. "Watch this shorty. I'm about to fuck her life up."

Kim smirked handing the blunt to her brother. T hit the blunt once and flipped it around placing the lit part in her mouth. Her sister leaned forward wrapping her lips around the blunt and T began to fill her lungs with smoke.

"Watch a boss," uttered out Kim swallowing the smoke and going back for more.

Again, T filled her lungs up. This time when she was full up however she backed off the blunt with closed eyes and squared shoulders holding it all in for a minute. She exhaled slowly as T hit the blunt the correct way.

After emptying her lungs Kim stared at Layla, "You want a shotgun?"

She nodded with a smile and Kim came towards her.

From next to Layla, T watched the weed exchange with her eyes roaming over Layla's body. They scoured over her and her libido tweaked excitedly in anticipation. Her cell phone went off when Layla backed away from the blunt. She checked the caller id and handed the phone out to Kim with a grin, "Set dat up for me sis."

She jumped up and looked down at the phone and back at Layla, "Cut ins," she said and walked out of the garage.

She turned her attention back to a coughing Layla and rubbed the small of her back. Once the young woman finished coughing T turned her around to face her and kissed her softly. Layla's emotions jumped awake and took over. She wrapped her arms around T pushing her backwards on the sofa. When T's tongue traversed out of her mouth, she wrapped her plump lips around it sucking on it.

T stole her tongue back and laid kisses along her neck covering them with glides and flicks of her tongue. She tucked the kisses along with bite marks until she was positioned behind Layla's ear. One hand entwined in her hair tugging her mane back as T spoke in her ear. "If you ain't down with what's 'bout to go down then just leave ma. I got a friend that wanna meet you. Hell, she wanna see you, me, and her together. But if you ain't 'bout that life just say the word."

Layla paused, "Daddy I ain't never ran from an opportunity to bust. If you want me to stop something just tell me so."

"I don't want you to stop doing shit. I want you to keep up," said T and kissed her lips again.

"Damn bruh. You having all the fun," complained Kim coming back into the room.

"Roll another blunt and take what you want. Shit sis you know I'ma sharing, giving muthafucka," said T lifting Layla upright.

"You roll. Mami on her way," she said handing her the weed and her phone.

"T what you got to eat? I got the munchies," said Layla snapping out of her induced state of mind.

"Shit you ain't as hungry as me ma. I'm starving," she stated before swiftly moving towards Layla and opening her legs. Kim unbuttoned her jeans and attempted to pull them down an uncooperative Layla.

"I told you keep up if you 'bout that life. We share in this family," said T as the scene unfolded in her front of her and Layla stared at her.

Sliding the jeans under her ass along with the draws Kim tossed them to side and told her, "Layla, you won't even be thinkin' 'bout T when I get through with you."

"Get the fuck outta here Kim! My head game way betta then yours," she blurted out amidst the young woman's giggles. "Look even Layla know that's why she laughing."

"You wanna bet on it?"

"Do what you do sis but remember I can do it betta. Run me yo' five when it's all said and done."

"That's all you got is five. Empty yo' pockets big bruh."

"You don't want me to do that."

The studs "sister" rolled her eyes, "Whatever. I take yo' lil' punk ass five for right now to prove my point," Kim agreed and with a swoop of her neck she cut off the continuous giggling emanating from Layla pulling moans from within her as she played in the middle of her.

Without hesitation, Layla's hands flew to her head. Instinctively, she spread her legs wider pressing her head into her center. The sensations she drew with tongue on

245

clit, stirring inside of her, and the plumpness of lips suckling another set of lips and her button had Layla inches from an orgasm that quickly.

When her thigh muscles tensed, Kim backed out, "Now you see how she had me right. Tell me she ain't loving this head game," bragged Kim while the young woman searched for Kim's mouth.

"Fuck what you talkin' about. Watch out so I can finish this job," T handed her the blunt and they switched positions.

Sensually, Layla moaned feeling the familiarity of T's mouth take over. She hissed as her tongue cruised against her spots and screamed out in pleasure when the casual approach was replaced with ruggedness. T sucked her clit in her mouth allowing her tongue to wheel around her clit then devour her it sucking the leaking juices down. Two fingers exposed her hole.

Intensity vibrated from Kim as she watched the two while smoking her blunt. She sat the blunt down and came up behind Layla running her fingers through her hair. She eased her head back leaving kisses along her neck, in doing so she shed her bottom attire. Once Layla kept her head tilted backward eagerly receiving the attention her neck was drawing, Kim lowered her trim dripping pussy down onto her open mouth.

"Go head and handle that for me boo," moaned Kim toying with the both sets of their nipples.

Layla's tongue slithered out of her mouth and tasted Kim's juicebox softly. She explored moderately using only her tongue. As T brought her closer to an orgasm, she abandoned her own task in her mouth to call down pleasurable verbs and nouns to T.

With one hand in her hair, she yanked Layla's head back and covered her mouth with her pocketbook. "You started it you gon' give me mines now handle that shit

246

shorty. Make me feel what you feeling and don't be a lil' bitch about it."

She tried to nod but Kim pinched her nipples harshly. She retaliated with biting down on the pink button in her mouth. Kim however didn't flinch but moaned her delight and ground down on her face. Feverishly, Layla tried to keep track of what T was doing and duplicate the motions of her tongue on Kim with her own orgasm about to burst forth. Slowly, she moved away from pleasing Kim to releasing what she felt.

"Wrap yo' lips around it," directed Kim.

Kim spoke it but immediately T did so to Layla pulling the knob in her mouth and humming on her pearl and flicking her tongue against it rapidly. Layla flinched wanting to cry out from pleasure but Kim countered her move stifling her would be screams by riding her face. Her dam burst. Kim rode the wave of her orgasm working her hips into a frenzy until she was tender.

"Damn," Kim said pulling her pussy from Layla's mouth.

"That's my line," responded Layla when T stood from in between her legs.

"No, baby. That's definitely my line. I walked in on this and had to start playing with my damn self," declared Yolanda from her seat on the stool where she sat stark naked and a trench coat littering the floor.

A grin slid over T and Kim's face as they stared at the curvaceous woman in front of them. T turned to Layla, "Layla, Yolanda. Yolanda, Layla."

The dark toned naked woman smiled approvingly at Layla. She pulled her to her feet and cupped her ass, "You're cute," Yolanda told her with a naughty grin after kissing her. She moved to Kim and kissed her on the lips groping her body. When Yolanda finished with her, she placed her fingers in T's mouth to suck off and kissed her as well with a tongue exchange. "Shall we continue upstairs?"

"I wanna smoke again and another shot," announced Layla.

The three females smiled at her. Yolanda sat down next to her and handed her the bottle. Kim sparked the blunt. T sat on the other side of Layla and began to roll another one.

"I'm matching but only this one time," said Yolanda retrieving from her purse a bag of weed and cigarillo pack.

Both Kim and T lit their blunts and placed them in opposite rotations. The next hour passed silently with the group of women getting lifted and their sexual drives filling the room. Blunts gone weed smoke still swirling around them. T lifted herself out of the haze to drop a kiss down onto Layla's lips. Her fingers flirted with Layla's nipples and she peered over to see Yolanda and Kim getting to know each other as well. She smiled.

An unrelenting spike of hormones exploded within Layla and she quickly shed her top gear and tugged T's shirt over her head. Fumbling with the stud's jeans, she hurriedly cast them down to T's ankles. She freed the strap and immediately bobbed down on it sucking it into her mouth.

Grinning with erotic bliss T throat fucked Layla and stared over at a doctor and her sister 69ing on top of Kim's covered car. Abruptly, Layla stopped what she was doing to rise in front of T. She straddled her facing her and began to ride. T averted her eyes and brought her attention full force back to Layla.

She stood up jabbing her rod in and out of Layla. Not one to merely be fucked Layla took the dick thrown inside her and in return used her hips to try to knock the stud off balance. She put her plump breasts in T's face for pleasure as well as to try to distract. T arched her back never breaking stride and took one of the hardened areolas into her mouth. She bit down on it holding it captive between her teeth while her tongue flickered across it.

Across the room, the other two women rose off the car with heavy breathing and sticky thighs. Kim went for her weed on wobbly legs. Yolanda however moved toward T and Layla. She slipped on the couch and eased behind T unnoticed. From her view, she watched T's ass clench and unclench as she thrust in and retreated out of another woman's pussy. She snaked her hands up T's thighs until they reached her hips. She held them there for a moment learning the pace. Note taken she pulled apart T's ass cheeks and slid her tongue between her cheesecake. T groaned euphoniously launching her strap on penis harder into Layla's love canal. Weed smoke trailing behind her Kim joined the trio and slipped a finger inside of Layla's ass.

"OOOOHHHH SHIT! OOOOHHHH SHIT!" screamed out Layla overcome with pleasure pelvis on automatic as she bounced on the pogo stick inside of her. "OOOOHHHH T! FUCK!" her hips mellowed to a slow grind. One last shudder escaped her; she opened her eyes and extracted her nails from T's back.

The pack of women eased out of one another. Yolanda went to Layla who had meandered down to the sofa with a freshly fucked face. She lifted her off the couch with a kiss of her lips. T and Kim took a seat on the couch passing the blunt back and forth watching the thick women in front of them touch each other's bodies with their fingers, mouth, and tongues.

With ease and not missing a beat, Yolanda scooped up Layla and spread her down onto the rug. She stayed between her legs placing her clit on the young woman's and began to mesh their clits against one another. One finger ducked into her opening bobbing in and out.

"Fuck!" Layla screamed out. "Ooh shit! Fuck!" she moaned with tense legs hands attached to Yolanda's ass trying to meld their clit into one.

Chancing a glance behind her Yolanda bit her lip at T, "Fuck, Daddy put it in please. Please," she begged.

Like a shot, T was off the couch balls deep inside of Yolanda. Hands gripping her hips she led their sexual tango into winding. Yolanda forced Layla from underneath her scooting her up until her breath was tickling the young woman's pussy. She wrapped arms around her thighs and plunged in mouth first.

From her seat on the couch, Kim watched the trio get theirs over and over again while she smoked a blunt and played with her hard nipples. She put the cocktail down in its ashtray and straddled Layla's face muffling out her chorus. She sat facing T at the beginning of the line stretching her hands out and fiddling with the feminine women's nipples.

Kim gripped Layla's head assisting her on what spots to hit and manipulating the spot so the spots could get hit how she liked them. Layla not in control of her upper body nor lower body as Yolanda held her legs and her face was buried in her pussy bringing her over the edge of an orgasm brought her fingers to Kim's and pulled them roughly. Yolanda took the onslaught from T and delivering what she felt by her mouth to Layla.

A domino effect sparked. One by one liquids gushed from each of the women and they all began to disband. Yolanda was the last to push T's strap out and once she did, she flipped around and began to suck her juices off the toy until there was no more.

The stud grabbed a fistful of hair and pumped into Yolanda's throat as if she were still in her pussy. The gags from Yolanda intensifying the mounting feeling she was chasing. Her eyes squeezed tight ass muscles flexed as she began to cum from throat fucking the doctor on her knees. Yolanda ripped the toy away and parted T's lips with her tongue drawing out more of her secretions and sucking them down her throat.

"Fuck," T finally groaned opening her eyes. She surveyed the women with a smile on her face. She dropped down next to Yolanda with heavy eyes feeling the erotic electricity smoldering.

****

Finally back at home three sexually fulfilling days later. Layla stretched out across her bed sighed contently. She leaned up and turned on the radio to sing along with Mary J. Blige who was searching for Real Love. The song gave way to another and Layla's thoughts turned to her best friends. One, she lost who had real love the other she wasn't on speaking terms with.

She imagined Kenni's voice in her ears and a smile crossed her face. She knew Kenni would have made one of them give in and a feeling within her whispered that the deceased would have pressed down on her the hardest. So with Kenni on her mind Layla turned down the radio and called Sayvonne.

"Hello?" Sayvonne answered wearily.

"Hey Von. You alright?"

"I'm cool. I think I caught some shit from Rachel."

"Oh," Layla said softly. "What's wrong wit' you?"

"I don't know, Lay. I'm sick," Sayvonne rattled off. "I keep throwin' up. My head hurt, I'm runnin' a fever off and on. I sound like a fuckin' advertisement for Benadryl.'

"Well since I haven't been behaving like you ARE the best sister friend in whole world how about I get my mama to make you her soup and I take Rachel off yo' hands for a few hours?"

"Fuckin' suck up," she paused waiting to see if Layla said anything then wheezed out, "Hurry up and tell yo' mama I said thanks."

A smile crossed Layla's face once again as she felt Kenni's insistence began to recede, "I took yo' advice wit' T."

"And?"

"I ain't sayin' nothin' else till I see you," said Layla jumping off the bed to gather some clothes and a towel.

Sayvonne smacked her lips together, "Alright well hurry up. I'ma lay down till you get here."

"A'ight."

"Ma!" hollered Layla from her doorway. "Ma! You still got some soup on the stove. Von sick!"

"Alright!" her mother yelled back. "It's on the stove for you when you leave."

"Thank you!"

****

"What's good Ma," T's flowed over the speakers as Layla drove to her best friend's house.

"Nothin'. Headed over to Von house," she answered with a smile and warmth spreading through her body.

"Damn shorty. You don't stop do you?"

She giggled, "Well Von sick and I was being a bitch to her before you gave me my medicine so I gotta go make amends. I'ma take her baby sister off her hands since she's not feeling good."

"What's wrong with her?"

"She said she feel like a Benadryl advertisement."

On the other end of the phone T guffawed, "Well tell her to feel betta. I'ma let you go though shorty. I just wanted to hear that sexy ass voice before I head to this meeting."

Butterflies took flight in her stomach and her heart fluttered, "Okay baby."

"A'ight."

"Bye."

Ten minutes later, she stood outside of Sayvonne's apartment building pressing a button repeatedly while waiting for a buzz from upstairs to unlock the secure apartment building. She expelled and looked up at the second floor to see through the open curtains and see Sayvonne sleep. Layla hit the buzzer again. Sayvonne didn't budge.

"Open da door," she finally called out and pressing the buzzer again.

"Shut up!" a voice yelled back at her as the buzzer sounded allowing Layla to open the door.

She entered the apartment building and went up the steps to apartment 403 turning the knob immediately only to discover that it was not unlocked. "How you ain't gon' have the front door open?" Layla complained again. "See I could have been in by now," she kidded hearing Sayvonne unlock the doors.

"You also could have been slapped in the mouth by now too," bit out Sayvonne when she whipped the door open.

Layla smiled pulling the retreating Sayvonne into a hug, "Aww I quit messing with you sis. Just cuz you sick," she kissed her on the cheek. "Where my brother in law at?"

"In his skin. Where my soup at?" Sayvonne answered from where she had plopped down on the couch.

She forked it over and watched Sayvonne tear into the container.

"Tre at Montae's game. He took Simone wit' him. Rachel playin' in her room."

"Oh ok," Layla sat on the love seat and picked up the remote beginning to flip through channels.

Tilting the container up Sayvonne gobbled down the last little bit. She sat the dish down with a smack of her lips. She fluffed her couch pillow and got comfortable. "Alright so spill it."

"Huh?" said Layla a grin slowly expanding over her face.

"Huh my ass," she snapped out while stretching. "If you can huh you can hear me. Now spill it."

"Well," Layla laughed tucking her feet under her on the couch. "I told T. I ain't just wanna be her cuddy buddy that I wanted a relationship."

"And?"

"She said she had been thinking along those same lines."

"And?"

"And we spent like two nights together. I went to her house. She been randomly calling saying lil' sweet stuff to me all day. Like earlier she called on my way over here saying she just wanted to hear my voice."

"Did y'all make it official?"

"No, not yet but I can see the difference in us already though."

She sighed not wanting to wipe the smile off Layla's face, "That's what's up sis. I'm proud of you for getting ya feelings out."

"Thank you," she kissed her cheek.

A loud wail from the other room signified that Sayvonne's little sister had woken up. Sayvonne's hands shot to her ears cupping them. She patted Sayvonne's thigh and walked to the back room.

"Hey boo," Layla cooed at the baby. Her niece laughed and raised her little arms to be picked up from out of her crib. "What you doing all that cryin' for mamas? Yo' sister sick boo you gotta be quiet."

An out pour of baby language streamed from her then finally, "Von?"

"You wanna see you sister?"

In a reply, she wiggled fitfully fighting to get down now that she was free from the confinement of her crib. As soon as Layla sat both feet on the ground, she took off running into the living room. Layla cursed under her breath taking off after Rachel trying to make as little noise as possible.

"Rachel!" Layla hissed scooping her up from the kitchen where she was at the bottom cabinets attempting to pull out all the pots and pans. "C'mon mama. Let's get dressed. You and me gon' go somewhere."

"Go!"

"Ssh!" she quieted the baby. Layla took her over to the sleeping Sayvonne. "See look sissy sleepin'."

Rachel mimed her older sister laying her head against Layla's chest and snoring lightly.

"You better wake up we gotta get dressed so we can go."

Her little eyes burst open and a smile shone across her face, "Go," she whispered.

"Yeah. Come on lets go lil' mama."

****

Sayvonne stirred fitfully in her sleep. She rolled over on the couch scooting closer into its warmth. Someone knocked on her door and she put her hands over her ears. The person knocked again.

"Use yo' key Lay!" she yelled raising her head and dropping it back down on the couch with a heavy sigh.

The knocks sounded again.

She heaved another sigh and pulled herself off the couch. "This better not be a fuckin' solicitor. This is a no soliciting community," Sayvonne grumbled wiping her eyes as she neared the door. "Who is it?" she threw the door open and mouth dropped open in surprise.

"Did we wake you?" greeted T with a smile.

"What's good Sayvonne?" Chantel smiled at her.

"Hey y'all," she smiled bashfully opening the door wider for them to come in.

The two studs followed her inside and found seats. T on the loveseat Layla had previously occupied a couple hours ago. Chantel sat backwards in a kitchen chair.

"A lil' birdie told me you was sick. So me and Lil' Buddy brought you some get well gifts and to make sure you was ok."

"Oh thanks y'all," she pulled the covers back around her makeshift bed of the sofa. "But I'm fine," she paused to burp and hold her chest. "Sorry," Sayvonne smiled. A split second later, she was in the bathroom vomiting.

"Bless you!" Chantel called back hearing her sneeze back to back.

"Thanks."

"You got allergies?" Chantel questioned when Sayvonne came back into the living room and sat on the couch taking deep breaths.

"No."

"You ain't allergic to nothin'?" T interjected.

"Nope. I'm thinking it's some shit I picked up from Rachel. She was sick all last week."

"Damn. Shit I know what that's like," Chantel muttered shaking her head.

She laughed, "Your son is the cutest."

"Thanks."

"What you had to eat today?" asked T.

"Layla brought me some soup over."

"Okay cool. Well we just had lunch and I brought you some shit back to help ease ya belly," she put the bag down on the living room table and began to pull its contents out.

"T I probably can't even keep it down. I've been throwing up all day. Hell the soup just came back up."

"Eat a lil' bit at a time then."

"We got you a vaporizer too," said Chantel setting the machine up on the dining room table.

"Aww thanks y'all."

"No problem," both studs said simultaneously.

"Did Rachel have all the symptoms you got now?" Chantel questioned after the vaporizer was up and running.

"Hell nah! And if she did it didn't stop her bad ass from rippin' and runnin' all over the damn apartment."

She laughed, "Hey better than Dreamz. He acts like he gon' die when he sick even a cold.'

"Tre is the same way. That's how I know Dreamz learned it from you," Sayvonne told her.

"You right about that," Chantel laughed.

"Alright Von here you go," T came out the kitchen setting dishes down. "Ma Dukes special sick remedy hot chili. I already crumbled up crackers in it for you too. And this a hot toddy with a lil' bit of ginseng in it too."

"What's a hot toddy?"

"Tea, honey, cinnamon whiskey, cough drops, lemon juice."

"Oh ok. Thanks y'all."

A car horn beeped outside and they all looked out the balcony to see Layla and Sayvonne's baby sister walking up to the door. The buzzer sounded. Sayvonne pressed the entry buzzer to let them in.

"How did y'all get in?" she asked curiously.

"One of yo' neighbors," Chantel answered.

Layla opened the door and Rachel came sprinting in tackling her sister. She put her little brown hand on Sayvonne's forehead, "Better?"

Sayvonne kissed her hand, "Yes. I feel a lil' better Rachel. Thanks."

"What's good lil' mama," T greeted Layla who was froze on the spot staring at her.

"Hey," smiled Layla.

"What's up Layla," greeted Chantel.

"Hey Lil' Buddy."

The two studs looked at each other and stood up. One by one, they hugged Sayvonne. Chantel made sure the air purifier was out of the toddlers reach. T scooted the table closer to Sayvonne so she wouldn't have to get up to get her food.

"Make sure you drink that tea while it's hot Von," advised T on her way out.

"Will do thanks again T. Thanks Lil' Buddy," she waved bye to them jovially.

"Call me later Ma," T ordered Layla before disappearing out of the door.

"Alright Layla," Chantel said leaving out as well. "Lock the door ladies."

From her position in Chantel's now unoccupied seat, Layla watched the two studs exit the building and get in T's car. She peered out watching them until they pulled out of the complex. Casually she stood meandering to the loveseat and taking a seat tucking her legs underneath her.

"So, what brought T by?" she questioned nonchalantly.

"You told her I was sick," answered Sayvonne with a smile and winking a tired brown eye at her.

258

"Oh yeah," a fake smile graced her face while she suppressed the jealously rising dangerously within her. "What else?"

Sayvonne put the dish of chili down and eyed her best friend suspiciously, "What you mean what else? They brought me a vaporizer, chili, and a hot toddy courtesy of Ma Dukes."

"Ma Dukes?"

"T's mama."

"Oh," she sighed. "Alright well I'm about to lay Rachel down and get up through too. Call me if you need anything sis."

Now stretched across the couch Sayvonne watched her through sleepy eyes take Rachel to bed kiss her forehead and leave out the door.

"I got the lock sis!" Layla called out.

She smiled and gave way to her dreams.

Chapter 12

"So, what does Lil' Buddy like?" Yolanda questioned T while the two of them walked around the mall.

She shot her a sideways glance of curiosity, "Is that what we here for? And here I thought we were here for me."

The woman laughed, "It's not always about you baby. Yes, we are here for your friend. I can't come to the party and not have a present for the birthday boy. So, what does she like?"

"Pussy, money, and weed," answered T simply with a laugh.

"Besides the obvious."

"Nah for real. You don't have to do that," she told her solemnly. "Lil' Buddy a real private person. She probably wouldn't even accept it if you bought her something."

"That's why she won't know and if she asks you say you bought it."

"I already got her gift."

"So, she will have another. How about matching hats and shoes for her and her brother?"

Unable to contain the grin from spreading across her face T acknowledged it was a great idea without saying so. Instead, she just followed behind the woman into the hat store. The couple quickly found a hat for the two siblings that matched their laid-back attitude. They were in and out the shoe store with fresh kicks for them and back in T's car in no time.

Time passed pleasantly and they found themselves outside of Ma Dukes house. T grabbed the bags and led the way into her mother's house. Music drenched their eardrums, their sense of smell was overpowered by the aroma of food and spices splashed with a slight stench of weed and mixed with liquor.

The two walked into the kitchen to find Ma Dukes slaving adding to the party food she already had spread across her island. Kim was putting jello shots in little cups. Jay sat at the table rolling blunts from three different bags of weed she had on the kitchen table.

"What y'all got in there baby?" Ma Dukes called out to T.

"Yolanda got Lil' Buddy and her brother matching hats and shoes," she informed her family.

Everyone looked up in surprise with grins jumping on their faces.

"Damn. Word? You ain't have to do that ma," Kim told her.

"Hey, what's a party when you show up empty handed? I had to get her something," answered Yolanda.

"You damn right," cackled Jay.

Ma Dukes flicked water on her, "Shut up chile. Thank you Miss Yolanda. That's a very sweet thing for you to have done."

"No problem. Now how can I help here?"

Again, the family was tacked aback with surprise. Ma Dukes however laughed and steered her out of the kitchen, "We got this baby. Y'all go on downstairs and decorate that. Get that all set up for her."

261

"Yes ma'am," Yolanda grabbed T's hand and they headed down to the basement.

****

"Shot up!" Kim declared holding her shot glass in the air while waiting for the rest of her family to join in. "Happy birthday Lil' Buddy! I love you fam!" she said when everyone had joined her.

"Thanks," laughed Chantel.

Everyone touched glasses and tossed their shot back.

"Ma, somebody at the door!" Dreamz screamed from the top of the basement.

Immediately T stood, "I got it," she told them walking up the steps to her nephew. "Who is it nephew?"

Dreamz didn't reply he stepped back from the basement and closed the door then leaned in close to T, "Its Mya," he whispered. "Is that cool? That she here?"

A grin maneuvered over T's face, "Yeah man," she stopped him at the front door. "Just because they going through some things right now don't mean they don't love each other. You feel me?"

He nodded, "I understand."

"What's up sis," greeted T opening the door for Mya.

She smiled and tucked her hair behind her ear, "Hey T. What's up Dreamz?"

He hugged her legs tightly, "I'm glad you came."

"Oh. Why is that?"

"Because Ma still loves you and I love you. Y'all need to see each other and talk. Not tonight though. No talkin'. Tonight it's party time for Ma cause it's her birthday."

"Aww," she hugged him tighter. "Thank you Dreamz. I still love Chantel too."

"I know it," he said and walked away into the kitchen. He came back with a bottle of water for her. "Here you go. And just in case," he winked at her pulling a beer from behind his back, "I brought you this too."

"Aye where mines at sir?" T asked.

"Nah man. You grown. My services are only for the ladies."

"Oh okay nephew. I see how it is," T pushed him a little as she walked past him.

"I still love you Uncle T," Dreamz responded with a smile and walked away from them to his room.

Mya followed T into the kitchen. "So, is her brother on the way? What's he like?"

"Yeah. I thought you was him. He should be here any minute. He texted me awhile ago and said he was on the way. He a real cool lil' dude," T laughed. "A grown up Dreamz or a male Lil' Buddy."

"Oh Lord."

"Nah. He cool."

"That's good!"

"Yeah," she paused hearing the doorbell. The pitter-patter of footsteps meant Dreamz was running to the front door.

"Who da fuck?" Dreamz cursed from the other room.

"Dreamz, watch your mouth," reprimanded Mya.

Peering out the window T turned to Mya, "That's him."

"Who?" Dreamz asked.

T opened the door with a broad grin, "What's up lil' bruh bruh," she greeted him pulling him into a hug and nodding respectfully at the woman he had brought with him.

"What's up T. T this my gurlfriend Saniah. Saniah, this is T one of my sisters friends," said Tyriq.

"Nice to meet you," his girlfriend replied.

"And this is Mya," T put a hand on her shoulder. "Lil' Buddy's wife."

Tyriq grinned, "Sis in law. Well it's a pleasure to finally meet you."

His girlfriend and Mya shook hands as well smiling at each other.

"And this lil' dude right here," commented T with both hands on Dreamz shoulders. "Is yo' nephew Dreamz."

Staring down at his nephew Tyriq's eyes widened. He looked Dreamz over from his head to his shoes. He reached out for a handshake.

"You ain't my uncle nigga. I don't know you," spat out Dreamz looking at his hand distastefully.

"Dreamz!" shouted T and Mya.

"Excuse us," Mya said snatching Dreamz hand and leading him to the kitchen.

"I'm sorry. He's usually not like that," T said. "But come on man let me take you to ya sister and the rest of the fam," she lead them downstairs.

They trooped down the steps quietly. Chantel had her back to the staircase but everyone else began to fall silent. Yolanda slipped away to turn down the radio. Finally, Chantel turned around.

"Aye T back!" drunkenly Chantel yelled. "Shot up!" she demanded. "Who you brought with you man? Who is them?"

Ignoring her questions T simply moved out the way as Chantel crept closer.

All eyes were on Chantel and Tyriq. The two siblings stood facing each other staring at the grown up versions of each other. Their eyes drunk in the sight of one another after seven years.

His eyes roamed over his sister. Gone was her hard gangster like exterior. Laugh lines were prevalent on her face. Her attire, her hair, her nails, the fact that she gained some weight showed she is being taken care of nicely.

She stared at her only brother remembering the kid who always had her back first who was now a man built like he was Ford tough. Automatically a hand ran over his fade just like back in the day.. His smile lit the already bright room. Chantel noticed how straight his teeth was, his fronts had grew back from childhood. The woman behind him stood close. She nodded at who was obviously his girlfriend understanding she was his rock, his vice through all the madness.

"Sis," Tyriq finally uttered.

They embraced tightly holding on to one another for dear life. Tears avalanched down their faces. I love you's and I miss you's were exchanged repeatedly.

"Where's my son? Where's Dreamz?" Chantel asked looking up around the room.

"He's right here," Mya declared stepping into her view with Dreamz in front of her. She bent down and whispered softly in his ear.

"Mya," Chantel reached for Mya and her son at the same time. "Mya, this is my brother Tyriq. Tyriq this is my rock," she introduced them. The two shook hands again smiling. "Dreamz, this is my brother Tyriq your uncle. I haven't seen him in a very long time. Ty meet ya nephew."

Staring down at his nephew Tyriq didn't say anything or move to give the little man that held an angry face dap. A sharp pinch from Mya made Dreamz straighten his face out and say, "Sup."

Chantel beamed with happiness. She threw her arm around her baby brother steering him around in a circle, "You was too young back in the day. You didn't meet anyone besides Ronnie. She gone now but she here in

265

spirit. I know it," she spun him around to Ma Dukes. "This T mama, Ma Dukes, T, Kim, Arianna, and Jay. We was thick as thieves growing up and still is. This is my other family bruh. This who took care of me and helped me to be who I am today."

He shook each of their hands and gave hugs to the ladies. Once she was finished with her introductions. Tyriq introduced his woman, "This is my girl Saniah," he smiled at Chantel. "My rock."

"Presents!" Yolanda yelled weaving through the family and placing a bag in the newly reunited siblings' hands.

"Why he get something? It ain't his birthday," Dreamz spoke up.

Ma Dukes flicked him in the ear as they each took out the same pair of shoes and a matching hat.

"Foe?" Tyriq looked at his sister puzzled while staring at the embroidery. Chantel offered no explanation for the acronym however.

"Family over everything," T told them smiling. She looked around the group, "Family ain't always yo' blood and blood don't always make you family. Foe is about the ones that's close to your heart no matter if they blood or not. You know you can always count on them."

"Foe," the group repeated the foreign word smiling at one another as their meaning spread through them.

"FOE!" they all shouted and grabbed for their drinks.

A drink was pushed into his hand by his sister. Tyriq smiled at Chantel and said, "I usually don't do this but," he shrugged with a smile and tears in his eyes looking at his sister, "Foe!" he shouted and tossed the drink back with everyone else.

****

"Alright drunk asses! C'mon! Let's get this cut cake!" Ma Dukes shouted out over the music and loud commotion caused by intoxicated people.

"Did I hear cake?" Dreamz smiled from the top of the stairs. He whizzed down the steps and stood in front of the cake next to his mother but staring daggers at Tyriq who was on his mother's other side.

"Move boy," Ma Dukes ordered. "Lil' Buddy, you ready to make a wish?"

She grinned, "Fuck a wish. I'm happy right now."

"Chile, you betta blow these damn candles out and make a wish," snapped out Ma Dukes. "T cut them lights."

"Yes, ma'am."

The lights went on and the family gathered around the small folding table holding Chantel's birthday cake. Ma Dukes lit the candles. Everyone began to sing the rhythmic version of happy birthday. Chantel looked around at everyone's faces illuminated by the flickering candles. She felt whole again with her family of friends, reunited with her brother again and Mya there watching her. She blew the candles casting away the only light in the room.

"Get off my ass dude!" Dreamz shouted amidst the darkness.

At once, the lights were flipped on to reveal Dreamz standing and staring oozing hatred in Tyriq's direction. However, the look Dreamz was giving his uncle was nothing compared to the malevolence clothing Tyriq's face as he stared down on his nephew. He shrugged his girlfriend's hand off his arm.

"What the fuck? Hell nah!" he spat out. "Hey, I understand you don't know me kid but you need to be careful on what come out yo' mouth. I ain't that type of dude and I ain't never been and you don't know what you speaking on lil' nigga. I get it cool you don't like me. You ain't no toddler or a baby and I wasn't around then but believe me it wasn't by choice. I do anything for my sister and I always have her back. Don't disrespect me or yo' mama with that foolishness man. That's some bullshit. What the fuck?" he ranted grabbing his jacket and pulling it on.

His woman followed him out of the patio door talking quietly to him.

"Fuck you! And stay out!" Dreamz shouted running to the patio door and locking it. He ran back to stand next to Chantel with his chest poked out.

No one moved nor said anything until Chantel smacked Dreamz in his mouth. Mya leaped forward to go to them but Ma Dukes stopped her. Yolanda whispered in T's unresponsive ear and crept upstairs.

"Sit down," Chantel thundered quietly at Dreamz.

Kim slid a chair behind the boy and Chantel took a seat in front of him.

"That was for cussing. You ain't grown don't you ever cuss in my fuckin' presence. You see all these women in here. Watch yo' mouth in a woman's presence," Chantel took a deep breath and heaved a big sigh. "Dreamz, you are my son and I love you no matter what. Tell me the truth did he touch you just now?"

"I don't like him. Who is he? If he my Uncle how come I never seen him before? I'm not calling him uncle," said Dreamz folding his arms across his chest.

"Dreamz," she began calmly. "Yes or no? Did Tyriq touch you?"

He looked around at the group poking his bottom lip out, "I just want him to leave. I don't want him here."

"Dreamz."

"No," he answered with his head down and tears fleeing down his face.

"So, what do you need to say?" Chantel asked him looking up as Tyriq and his girlfriend came back in.

"I'm sorry!" Dreamz screamed. "I don't like you!" he ran up the steps crying.

She moved to get up but Mya put a hand on her shoulder, "It's okay. I got him. It's your birthday and your brother is here. I'll stay upstairs with him," she kissed Chantel's cheek.

"Thank you," Chantel said. She stood and went over to her brother. "Tyriq, I'm sorry bruh. I don't know what's gotten in to him. He usually not like that at all. He admitted that you didn't do it."

He nodded curtly.

"Shot up?" asked Jay holding the bottle. "Let it go, kill the tension, back to the party?"

The room smiled and the seriousness withdrew slightly.

"Let's get it. Lil' bro, Miss Saniah y'all down?" Chantel asked.

His girlfriend smiled and looked to Tyriq whose facial expressions were shifting from pissed off to smiling. "Let's go foe."

****

Layla rolled over and knocked her phone off her nightstand. She stretched and looked around before reaching down to retrieve her cell phone. The phone lit up and Layla squinted at the only light in the pure darkness. She had a missed call from Sayvonne at three fifty-six in the morning. Layla dialed her number back. "Hello?" she said groggily into the phone where the ringing stopped.

The person on the other end of the phone sniffed and Layla heard Sayvonne choke back a sob.

"Von? What's wrong?" Layla bolted upright.

269

No response was given only the soft cries from Sayvonne then a click.

She stared down at her phone in disbelief. Layla dialed her best friend's number again. While it was ringing, the phone alerted her to a text message coming through. The voice mail kicked on prompting Layla to hang up. She opened the text message from Sayvonne. It read:

I'm good. I love you. I promise we'll talk later.
Call and say it.

"Hello?" Layla answered her phone.

Sayvonne sniffed, "Hey gurl."

"What's goin' on Von?'

"Nothing. I'm good sis. I love you. I promise we will talk later."

"What is it? What's wrong?"

"It's about me. I'ma jus-"

"Where Tre?" Layla interjected her mind racing rapidly through different scenarios her friend could be going through.

"Holdin' me," Sayvonne said softly. "But like I was sayin', I'ma pray on it and go on to sleep."

"Sis, I'm up now. We can talk."

"It's cool. I'm good. I don't wanna talk 'bout it right now."

Sighing Layla relented, "Okay sis. Promise we'll talk?"

"Promise."

"A'ight. Good night sis."

"Night."

****

"Why you wanted me to ride to the store wit' you? We went to the store. You was quiet. We back at yo' house and you still quiet. Why?" Layla questioned Sayvonne after she came out of the store with one bag and insisted that Layla ride and wait for her in the car.

"Cause," Sayvonne replied.

"Von, last night, early this morning, whatever, you called me late as fuck cryin'. I thought we were supposed to talk. You ain't been sayin' shit but cause, every time I ask you a question."

Her fingers gripped the steering wheel and she sighed, "I know Lay. I'm sorry," she apologized with tears welling in her eyes.

Quickly, Layla stretched out her arms and wrapped them around her sister friend, "Sis, what's wrong? You startin' to scare me."

"Open the bag Lay."

Quizzically, she looked from Sayvonne to the bag and then picked it up from its spot on the back floor. Layla opened the bag pulling out a box, "You pregnant?"

Silent tears cascaded down Sayvonne's face, "I don't know. I think so. The test says so! I been takin' my birth control. I ain't missed a fuckin' day. I can't have a baby right now, Lay. Shit is hard enough."

Snapping out of her trance Layla placed the bag on the floor in the back seat, "You don't know fa sho boo. Chill out."

"The fuckin test say so Lay! I know my body. I know I got all the symptoms of a pregnant female."

"Okay Von," she sighed with dejection, "But you know whatever happens you got support. You ain't in it alone. You know me and my fam gon' help you out."

She wiped her eyes, "It's just the wrong fuckin' timing Lay. Tre, been workin' hella crazy hours to keep us straight. Another baby," she moaned. "I miss my mama."

"I hear you sis. But just calm down you know it ain't no use cryin' over spilled milk."

Sayvonne nodded attempting to refrain from letting the tears fall from the well of her eyes. "You right," she wiped her nose sniffing.

"You need another sis?" Layla asked holding out a few napkins she retrieved from her glove department.

"Thank you."

"You want me to go in wit' you?" Layla offered moral support.

"Please."

"C'mon," she smiled encouragingly at her "sister."

The two young women exited the car and walked up to the house as if everything were normal. Sayvonne stopped at the door to stare at her friend. Layla pulled her into a hug and kissed her cheek.

"C'mon gurl. You know he love you. Everything gon' be cool."

She took a deep calming breath. Sayvonne unlocked the doors and walked into the house to discover her thirteen-year-old brother Montae sprawled out on the couch watching television. Simone, dance walked around the living room and as the girls moved further into the apartment they saw Tre preparing lunch.

"Hey baby," Sayvonne walked up to him turning his face and pressing a kiss to his lips. "Where's Rachel?"

Tre dipped a fish in flour, "What's good baby. What's up Layla," Tre said then turned back to his girlfriend. "I sat her in front of the TV with a Barney marathon recorded."

Faking a laugh Sayvonne looked at Layla nervously, "When was that?" she stalled from telling him the news with a question.

"'Bout an hour ago."

"She probably asleep now."

"I will go check on her," Layla offered giving Sayvonne a coveted look that told Sayvonne to quit beating around the bush and get to it.

Sayvonne gave her a dirty look back as she watched her disappear into the back of the apartment. "Montae, can you and Simone go in the other room for a minute I wanna talk to Tre. You can leave the TV on," she told him before he could began to protest.

Montae sucked his teeth rising off the couch reluctantly. He grumbled past Sayvonne to push his dancing younger sister into the back.

Her boyfriend put the fish down staring curiously at Sayvonne, "What's up?" he asked with a quirked eyebrow.

She exhaled slightly biting down on her lip and refusing to meet his eyes, "I'm pregnant."

His shoulders dropped as he sighed heavily then ran a hand over his head. He scratched the back of his head, "I thought so. That's why I started pulling in more hours to save up some cash."

Her eyes dart to his face while a smile debated whether or not it wanted to appear or not, "You serious baby?"

"C'mon now baby. What you was thinkin' I was gon' leave you?" he questioned with twinkling eyes and smiling lips as he lifted his girlfriend's chin.

"Don't even think about it," Sayvonne beamed swatting him in the chest.

Her boyfriend broke up what she was about to say and kissed her on the lips. She kissed him back then separated from him. Sayvonne retreated to a corner of the kitchen.

"What's wrong?" he immediately came to her side expressing concern. When Sayvonne didn't respond, he turned her around gently. "Baby, what's wrong?"

Sayvonne bit her lip trying to stop the flow of tears from charging down her face, "I just miss my mama so much," she sobbed into his chest quietly so her brother and sisters wouldn't hear her. "It's just so hard baby. . . I'm not ready for a baby. Rachel's just now getting potty trained. . . Why did God have to take my mama..." Sayvonne broke off her cries with a moan of pain as her mother took over her thoughts. "She'll never see her grandbaby."

The tall broad shouldered man gathered his woman into his arms and stared at Layla who had just walked into the room at lost for words. He cradled her tightly. Layla motioned for him to say something.

While stroking Sayvonne's back and her weeping into his chest he began to murmur, "Baby, calm down beautiful. I know you miss yo' mama but she lookin' down on all of us right now. And she see you baby. You know she up there smilin' in heaven proud of how you taking care of yo' brother and sisters and now a baby of your own. Baby, she see you and I promise you she proud. As far as everything else, don't worry about it. We'll get through it. Everything gon' be okay alright baby?" he took her face into his hands searching her eyes until she nodded. Smiling at her, he wiped the tears off her face. "You ready to tell your brother and sisters?"

She shook her head no.

"Well *I* wanna know," Simone, said walking into the room. "What did you do to my sister? Why she cryin'?" Simone demanded with a six-year-old's authority. "Montae!"

The oldest sibling couldn't help but laugh as she heard her brother come running into the room full speed. He came to a stop next to Layla with Rachel behind him.

"What's up?" Montae questioned looking from Simone to Sayvonne and Tre.

Simone pointed a finger at the couple, "Look. He made her cry."

Montae's eyebrows furrowed together. He stepped in front of his younger sister.

"Hold on lil' man," Layla grabbed Montae's wrist. "I think your sister has something to tell y'all."

Sayvonne gave Layla the finger while her boyfriend nudged her telling her to tell them. She took a deep breath as the two kids looked at her with bated breath and expressions of anger, "Okay you two. What does it mean if Montae you become an uncle? And Simone, Rachel, and you become aunts?"

"You pregnant?" Montae inquired.

Before Sayvonne could answer Simone let out a happy squeal of joy, "I'm gonna be an auntie! Auntie Layla I'm gonna be an auntie now too!" she said excitedly. "Is it a gurl? I bet it's a gurl."

The preteen boy groaned, "Please don't tell me another gurl. Can you at least have a boy?" he pleaded with Sayvonne.

She laughed, "I don't know what the baby will be yet."

"It's a gurl!" Simone announced happily before marching up to Tre. She poked him in the chest, "And you Mister I don't want to see my sister cryin' anymore. You got that?" she poked him again.

"Yeah," Montae said in agreement with his sister. "Now make up right now. Go head do the kiss thing."

Layla laughed watching the kids stand there waiting for their sister and her boyfriend to kiss.

The couple laughed at their audience. As soon as their lips touched one another, a chorus sounded.

"Eww!"

"Gross!"

The room burst into laughter.

Chapter 13

Driving away from her best friend's house Layla sung along with the radio. A smiled crossed over her face when the thought of her being an aunt crossed her mind. She played with the idea of shopping for girl clothes now or later.

Her phone screeched at her from the cup holder causing her to jump. She answered the phone without checking to see who it was, "Hello?"

"Yo," the caller began but was cut off.

"Hey T. I was just thinking about you Daddy. I miss you baby," she cooed seductively into the phone.

The caller smacked her lips together, "Dis ain't T baby," a harsh tone spewed at her, "Dis B mafucka. Da fuck you think I was dat nigga for? What y'all talkin' now?"

"Yeah we is-" admitted Layla rolling her eyes.

"Oh so lemme guess. You ain't down no more since you back dick sharing with the rest?" questioned Brandy.

"First of all, T is all mines. Don't worry about what's going on with me and mines. *We*, me and you, are not together. Worry about that."

She scoffed, "Nah. I think I will worry more about this cash you owe me. You see you got me in a fucked up spot with my connect. So, I needs. So, we can continue and map this shit out or you can put in some work. Yo' choice. You down or nah?"

"Alright Brandy damn. I know I owe yo' fuckin' ass. I really don't though cause you probably would still be locked up if I wouldn't a flushed the shit."

"Right. And it's just so funny how you just skated untouched throughout everything huh? You gon' give me what you owe. One way or a fuckin' nother."

"What you want me to do Brandy?"

"Nah. Tell me if you down for that muthafucka or if you down for me. I ain't got time for yo' ass to be flip-flopping sides when she play yo' ass."

"Obviously, I'm down dummy. I'm still talkin' to you. She ain't no dope boy so how you wanna go about this?"

"Don't worry about it. Just do you when I say its game time."

"Do me and do what? And y'all better not fuckin' touch her!" Layla lashed out pulling into her driveway.

"Don't fuckin' worry about it! Yo' only fuckin' job to keep dat nigga fuckin' distracted when I say so."

"Whatever. Just don't put yo' hands on her. Nobody."

Brandy laughed, "What you a boss bitch now? Don't tell me what da fuck I am and ain't gon' fuckin' do. Yo' ass really then caught feelings fa dis hoe ass nigga huh? Fuck dat nigga. Bitch I made you. I taught you all dat shit you do now. How to be a down ass fuckin' gutta bitch and shit. And you feelin' dis soft ass nigga?" she questioned rhetorically. "Bitch if you ain't down I collect my money another way. You worried about that nigga when dat nigga wasn't worried after she fucked you and left you at da bar to kick it wit' another bitch. Yo' ol' dumb ass fallin' fa every fuckin' trick in da book. Dat nigga playin' yo' ass but I ain't gon' ask yo' retarded ass no damn more. Is you fuckin' in or out?"

Her temper rose and waved furiously at the sting of pain she felt in her chest from Brandy's words, "I ain't never say I wasn't fuckin' game. I was just sayin' cause it's the birthday of one of her fuckin' dead friends, DAMN!"

"Now dats my bitch. Dats what da fuck I wanted to hear. Shit dat nigga can't make you feel how I felt anyway. I was yo' first ma."

She rolled her eyes wishing she could roll them and the creepiness she felt from feeling Brandy's smile over the phone, "Whatever. Don't call me again unless its game time."

"Ha. A'ight ma."

****

"Come on ma," T grumbled under her breath watching her mother struggle to parallel park near Ronnie's gravesite.

Once she was finally barely into the parking spot, T whipped around her and parked in front of Jay's car. She turned the ignition off and sat stiffly in the car with Chantel gazing out at the abundance of head stones surrounding them. Their eyes flickered behind them watching the rest of the family come to a stop at Jay's car. Jay got out of the car heaving a big sigh and sending looks up to the sky. The close-knit group of friends that were family stopped at T's car.

Choking back tears Chantel said, "C'mon bruh. It's our brother birthday. Today a celebration," hollowly she spoke but a wet face and heavyhearted eyes revealed how she really felt.

Her car door opened and Moryah, Ronnie's mother smiled mournfully, "That's right," she took Chantel's hand.

Nodding in agreement T asked, "Lil' Buddy, will you grab the bottles?"

A ghost of smile flashed across her face, "You know it. Lil' Buddy," she laughed, "Who would've guessed that name would stick."

The family walked up to Ronnie's gravesite hands entwined and tears silently dripping off their faces. At her grave they all stopped. One by one, they tossed a red rose down onto her grave. T plopped down first and the family created a half circle around it.

"Well I ain't think it was right. We all here and Kenni ain't. I know we tried to get them a spot together but couldn't," Arianna, Ronnie's sister spoke up. She pulled out a picture of the deceased couple, "But I found this," she showed the group and placed a rock in front of it to hold the picture in place against the headstone.

"Alright now let's pop bottles!" Ma Dukes announced. "Can't break tradition. Y'all been getting loose as a goose since before me and Moryah then known about it. We damn sure ain't stoppin' now," she declared proudly unsheathing a bottle of Grey Goose from her purse.

"Amen to that," Moryah agreed taking out her bottle of Svedka from her purse. .

"Hold up," T stopped them. "We gon' do this right or nah? Birthday boy gotta get a cup of what everybody drinking first."

"Start us off bruh," Jay said with a smile.

Kissing two of her fingers T blew it up to the sky and sent a quick silent prayer up. She poured Hennessy onto Ronnie's grave. Chantel followed up with Jack Daniels and Kim with Nuvo.

"Yo, when you start drinkin' that shit?" Jay broke the melancholy while spilling Patron down.

"Since I bought it and liked it," Kim shot back as both the mothers followed all of their leads ending with Arianna and her bottle of Ciroc.

Peering at the ground as if she could see the mixture of liquor perfectly Ma Dukes commented, "UH-OH! We got somethin' like an Incredible Hulk *Super*. Damn that's light, dark, tequila everything all mixed together. Glad I ain't drinking that," she laughed.

The three studs and Kim caught each other's eye and looked away. Kim began to pass out the cups with a smirk on her face. Chantel put ice in each of their cups.

"Ma if we playin' by tradition we gotta do this right," Jay began.

"First, you get the birthday boy fucked up," Chantel added with a smile.

"But being that we all family and shit. It's important for us to get fucked up too," Kim interjected.

The other three women nodded.

"And?" Moryah posed.

"We all drink what each other drinkin' at da same time," T said simply grinning broadly staring at Ronnie's cheesing face,

"Aww shit," she muttered earning small laughter from the group.

Moryah however shook her head no, "Un uh. Nope. No," she stated furiously as everyone looked at her with laughter etched into their face.

"Ma, what you mean no? I'm down." Arianna said and looked at Ma Dukes. "You down?"

"You know it," Ma Dukes and Arianna high five'd.

"Come on Ma," Arianna pleaded.

Again Moryah shook her head no, "Un uh. No. Where da weed at? I know that's tradition. Let me get some fuck it my system then I said fuck it and drink wit' y'all."

Everyone laughed each woman pulled out a pack of cigarillos and a bag of weed.

"Now hold on now Moryah. Who you den copped from?" Ma Dukes questioned.

"Gurl just cause I don't smoke don't mean I don't know where to get it from," Moryah answered her with a smile.

The two women smacked hands as Arianna looked up from mixing her mother's cup of liquor and her own, "And what's da name a dis game?"

"Simple," Jay said, "We all got different weed right?" she surveyed the weed in everyone's lap.

"Puff," Kim responded.

"Puff," T repeated.

"Blow a shotgun to yo' right," Chantel finished.

Ma Dukes and Moryah guffawed.

"Damn. A'ight. I'm with it," Ma Dukes told them.

Moryah held up one finger while she laughed before tossing back half of her cup's contents back, "C'mon bring it on."

****

"Yo, you think Ron a be mad if we had some hoes here too," Jay wondered out loud two hours later as it was just the crew sitting around Ronnie's grave. "Shit Kim strip fa us. Do that fa yo' brothers. Pop it fa Pimp and Ronnie," Jay laughed.

"Fuck you," Kim slurred.

"Ooh shit fuck me Kim," Jay playfully chided her.

Chantel looked up grinning mischievously, "Shit cut me in or cut it out."

T smiled drunkenly adding, "Ain't no fun if the homies can't get none."

"Fuck all a y'all," responded Kim.

282

"Yo, fuck it. Let s throw a party for my nigga too. We ain't da only one missing her," Chantel mused.

Sprouting up like an erection T stood there staring at Chantel, "Yo, that's a good fuckin' idea Lil' Buddy."

The three friends seated on the ground looked at each other and then at T before bursting out laughing.

"Yo, why da fuck did you stand up fa?" Kim inquired laughing.

She smiled down at them and copped a seat on the grass with them, "I don't know," she shrugged causing everyone to laugh again. "But for real though I like that idea," T stated seriously. "Dig and we doing this shit Saturday. We gotta get the word out. Kim, I want you on da airwaves let everybody know R.I.P. party for our brother Ron. Everybody that knows that nigga, fucked with us, got a shirt made, whatever…gets in free. Everybody else if you wearing a R.I.P. shirt half off admission."

Nodding Kim agreed.

"Lil' Buddy, you gon' be able to make it?" T questioned.

She nodded once, "I wouldn't miss it for the world bruh. I can ask Ma Dukes to watch Dreamz or if she wanna go I can get Mya to stay with him."

"You sure? Cause I'ma need you on cash that night."

"She got him now. Said she missed him. She got him, gon' have him bruh."

"A'ight. Jay, you already know security. I want every nigga on staff there. This my brother shit. We ain't having no bullshit go down. Holla at some of the old crowd we used to run in. Lock them niggas in as extra security. You know niggas always down for rec and to get paid."

"I got it."

"A'ight then foe let's get shit crackin'," T told her family who laughed at her as they stood along with her.

283

****

Layla's stomach churned painfully as she looked around the club. All around her she saw RIP shirts alas she had Kenni's face on hers. Her eyes were locked onto Ronnie's when a voice pulled her away whispering harshly in her ear, "Game time shorty."

She tore her eyes from the picture whipping around angrily, "What? I thought I told you not this fuckin' soon Brandy."

Grinning with malice Brandy sneered, "But it ain't up to you now though Layla. Is it?" she questioned rhetorically. "Its game time baby. Don't be a stupid bitch for this nigga. I swear to God if you fuck up this lick up I'ma fuck yo' life up and that's on everything ma," her ice words sent chills down the young woman and she refused to break eye contact with her.

With frozen insides and eyes running away they halted on a picture of Ronnie hanging over the VIP section. Layla sent her a silent apology spinning around to face Brandy with a quick exhale, "Whatever. I told you I'm fuckin' down. But I swear you better not touch her," she snapped stalking off towards her heartbeat.

****

The club had hit capacity and Layla nervously peered throughout the crowd from her post at T's side. She had started off trying to get T drunk but that goal was achieved already. T was so drunk she seemed like an entirely different person. The drugs she usually used when Brandy and she hit a lick were still in her purse. She was already an accomplice to T getting robbed she didn't want to have to drug her too. Besides that though she was the only female occupying T's time and space that night.

Her stomach pelted. Tonight Colorz wasn't just a LGBT club, tonight's turnout brought out both ends of the spectrum. Hetero and homosexuals were sporting RIP shirts. One of those heterosexuals was her main concern however. In the streets he was Brandy's right hand man. They were like mirrors of one another and their hotheadedness boosted one another's tempers. She licked her lips in an attempt to calm herself.

"Lay, you want a drink ma?" T slurred with low eyes while smoking a blunt.

Layla's full attention surged on T, "Nah. I'm cool baby," she said with a smile.

Sitting up on the loveseat T declared, "Shit. I'ma get a drink. Hell, Ron a want me too."

Tonight had Layla feeling like it was dire but she couldn't help the smile toying at the end of her lips from T's intoxication, "Sit down baby. I'll get it for you."

Relaxing back into the couch T passed the blunt to Kim, "A'ight shorty. I need some Hen! Get me some hen!"

"I got you baby."

Jay dropped down into Layla's now vacant seat. She hit the blunt and stared at her brother and sisters, "Yo, I ain't still ain't heard from Lil' Buddy."

"Da fuck man. She called no texted back me either," snapped T.

"Yeah me either," Kim murmured.

"Yo, I even called Mya. She ain't answering or none either. T you see if Ma Dukes heard from her yet?" Jay asked.

"I'm calling now," said T.

"Bruh, with what phone? Foe you wet as shit. What the fuck man?" laughed Jay.

"I am calling her."

"Lemme see yo' phone bruh," Kim said to her.

"Hold on lemme find it sis."

"I bet I find mines before you find yours," Kim told her rummaging through her purse.

"Found it," T declared proudly holding up the phone. "Hello? Hello?" she looked at the locked screen. "Aww shit," she dialed her mother's number, "Ma…you heard from Lil' Buddy…She ain't call you to watch Dre…She was supposed to been here on cash. Yeah we called her Ma and Jay called Mya. Ain't neither one them answerin'… a'ight…ok…bye," T hung the phone up. "She gon' go by the house," T told her friends.

"What's wrong?" Layla questioned.

"Lil' Buddy MIA," Jay answered her.

Her heart dropped, imagination cranked up on hyperactivity thinking the worst of the worst. She scanned the VIP section for T's youngest brother. She didn't spot her upstairs so she peered over the railing into the main area of the club. Layla's eyes roamed over each person while her imagination toyed with the love she had for T in her heart placing images of Brandy and her goons kidnapping Lil' Buddy and holding her against her will until T brought the money.

She chewed her lip subconsciously. Chantel had a son. The blunt passed between the group with Layla inhaling deeply wondering why Brandy hadn't included her in the plan. No matter what Brandy had always let her know what's up. Layla froze when her eyes caught sight of another one of Brandy's goons. He was known for his itchy trigger finger. If he was here she knew the clique of younger niggas he leaded was in the crowd as well. Layla felt herself panicking as her ears tuned back into the conversation.

Kim laughed, "T you drunk bruh. Just admit it."

T shook her dreads, "I ain't drunk ket Yim."

"What?" Jay and Kim asked in unison before busting out with laughter.

She laughed along with them, "A'ight so I am. Fuck it. Ron a want a nigga to be drunk. She woulda loved dis shit," T's eyes misted over so she turned to Layla. "Shorty, I ain't drunk drunk. I ain't never too drunk to," T held up a finger to indicate one minute while she polished off the rest of her drink. "Shit what was I saying?" Jay and Kim guffawed again but Layla didn't. "Layla, what's wrong? You havin' no fun? I'm sorry. I'm drunk. I'ma get you a drink," T told her one hand on her bouncing leg trying to push herself up.

Layla shook her head no, "I'm fine T. I don't want anything to drink."

The inebriated stud fell back against the chaise, "Den what's wrong ma. I know somethin' wrong," Layla tried to play it off but T leaned up to stare directly into her eyes, "You thinkin' 'bout Kenni?"

At the mention of Kenni's name Layla felt as if a bubble of anger burst inside of her heart. Anger slid through her body from her chest like an ill poison. Layla felt pissed. Pissed at the world, until she felt T's soft lips against her. Layla moaned feeling her anger melt away. T kissed around her neck before making her way up to Layla's ear.

"Dig ma. It's okay. I'm thinking about Ron right now. You can talk to me doe shorty. I got you," T whispered in her ear without the slightest hint of intoxication.

Her words caused Layla's emotions to drop rapidly down to sadness and guilt. She thought about Chantel wondering if Brandy had kidnapped her or got both Chantel and Dreamz. Layla thought about T who had never showed her this much compassion before. She sighed internally nodding to herself. Layla had a job to do and the courage she felt spreading through her gave her the push she needed.

Layla exhaled as her eyes fluttered rapidly, "T something gon' pop off here tonight. Somethin' bad 'bout to go down. I don't know when, but it is," she spoke softly searching T's eyes watching the somber T get replaced with the sober T.

Her eyes hardened as she beckoned Jay and Kim to her who was leaning over the banister laughing and drinking together.

"What?" Kim questioned.

"Dig Jay you handled dat shit wit' da money right?" T inquired running her hand back over the dreads in her face.

Jay nodded as her eyebrows touched each other, "Fa sho. Every hour it's going down."

"A'ight. Peep game I don't know what's up but Layla said something 'bout to pop off. Something bad. It's a lot of our niggas in here get word to them so they ready. Matter fact, Kim you do that. Jay, you tip off security then I want you watchin' B's every fuckin' move. She on my payroll but I still don't trust dat nigga."

Jay and Kim didn't move.

"Where Layla?" Jay inquired.

She spun around and turned back to her family, "Dig don't worry 'bout her or Lil' Buddy right now. Just get on yo' shit," T instructed fiercely. "Ma Dukes, a call about Lil' Buddy."

****

She walked up to Brandy chewing on the inside of her lip and taking deep breaths of reassurance. Layla knew the rules of the dangerous game she was playing and had started but she just couldn't do it. Not tonight, not to T.

"What's up ma," Brandy greeted Layla with a smile.

"B. . . I," her voice faltered staring in the face of her old flame, "I-"

Brandy's face began to twist into a nasty scowl, "What? What da fuck you tryin' to tell me?"

Courage flooded through Layla again she lifted her chin defiantly, "I can't fuckin' do it Brandy," her voice softened. "I caught feelings. I'm in love wit' T."

Her eyes registered Brandy's jaw clamp down onto her tongue flexing viciously but she didn't notice Brandy's hand fly from her side and wrap around her throat squeezing tight.

Chaos erupted at that moment as fights broke out everywhere, bottles flew across the room or at someone's head and gunshots rang out through the club followed by screams and panicking people trying to get the fuck out.

****

Despair ripped through T as she took in her surroundings. The multitude of police cruisers and ambulances not to mention the state of her pride and joy, her club. She walked away from the ambulance that had attended her with her only wounds coming from physical fighting. Her eyes drifted to the sky and she said, "Ronnie, this wasn't da night I planned for you lil' bruh. But thanks for keepin' yo' family safe cuz," T sent her prayer of thanks up and walked to another ambulance to check on Layla. "What's up shorty," she drunk in the sight of her badly body.

Swollen eyes welled with tears met hers, "I'm sorry T."

Sadly T smiled her eyes reviewed the scene again, "How you feelin'?" her eyes roamed over Layla's neck which had fingerprints on it. Blood was on her face and clothes. Her arm was in a sling. A tooth was missing from the front and her hair was in clumps as if a patch or some had been removed.

She matched T's smile, "Kenni, made sure I was safe."

"Good. Ronnie covered us too," her head nodded and she touched Layla's good shoulder prepping to leave. "I gotta see how many other people were hurt."

Her eyes drooped sadly, "Okay T."

From opposite directions T spied Jay and Kim both coming. They met up across the street surveying the scene, "Kim, give me the bad news first. Anybody die?"

Kim let out a long exhale, "No. But Stacy got shot three times covering Layla's ass. She was right there when her and B got into it. A couple other of our folk got shot. Most of the guests got out unharmed fortunately. No one suffered major damage. Most of everyone's damage came from the pandemonium and trying to get the fuck out. "

"A'ight. I'ma take care of our niggas and Stacy's hospital bills on me. Jay, talk money to me. Did they get anything?"

Jay grinned, "Not a damn thing. Shit I'm glad the streets came out. Cuz shit them niggas saved my life yo. Real shit."

"A'ight. In da morning-" T stopped talking as her phone started to ring out, "Ma Dukes. Hello...yeah Mama...what...FUCK!" she roared out punching a wall. "A'ight Ma...we on the way," T hung up the phone turning to her friends who stared at her waiting with bated breath for more sure bad news. "Lil' Buddy locked up. She killed somebody."

****

The trio arrived at Chantel's house and stood transfixed. The windows had been repaired from Mya's act of vandalism however the house now seemed ominously quiet. A glance behind them yielded an unmarked a police cruiser. Chills ran through them as they strode up to the door and was ushered in by Ma Dukes.

"Timothy, what happened?" Ma Dukes solicited. "Kim? Jay?" she looked each of them over one by one.

Unable to respond to her mother straight away T simply looked at her with a set jaw and quivering bottom lip. Tears threatened to betray her cantankerous attitude. Eyebrows settled in with one another. Shoulders slumped as if the weight of the world was on them. Sighing with a heavy heart she replied to her mother, "Ma it's been a long night. All we wanna do right now is find out what's going on with Luh Buddy. We can discuss the other shit later."

Without another word Ma Dukes pulled her into a tight embrace and kissed her cheek. She released her daughter and did the same to Kim.

"I'm fine Ma. What happened?" she mumbled from where she had buried her face in the crook of Ma Dukes neck.

"You'll know soon enough," she replied grimly releasing Kim and turning to Jay. She wrapped her arms around her but Jay's knees buckled and she began to sway. Coming to Ma Dukes assistance Kim and T took ahold of Jay. They assisted their brother to the couch.

"I'm good," Jay told them wincing in pain holding her side.

"You're not. Now move yo' hand so I can see," Ma Dukes snapped out with a smack of her lips. Reluctantly Jay moved her hand. "It look like a bullet clipped you. In and out," Ma Dukes observed glancing back at T and Kim but saying nothing to them.

"What's wrong with Uncle Jay?" Dreamz questioned appearing in the doorway of the living room.

Mya popped up behind him as the other three adults moved in front of Jay shielding Dreamz's innocent eyes. "Dre, come on. Get back to bed. I need to talk to your uncles and Kim," Mya told him taking his hand.

Dreamz snatched his hand back and ran to T. He stood in front of her looking up at her, "Where my mama at?" he looked T and Kim over even closer sneaking glances at Jay. "What happened? Was Ma with y'all? Y'all ok?"

Closing her eyes, T took a deep breath. She rubbed his head, "You come from a family of soldier's lil' man. We good. Chill in yo' room for a minute for me a'ight?"

He opened his mouth to protest but Ma Dukes hissed at him causing him to suck his teeth and go to his room.

"Jay, let me get you bandaged up. C'mon let's go in the other room," Ma Dukes said.

"No, Ma. Not till I hear what happened with my brother," refused Jay and pulling herself into a sitting up position.

Her curious eyes drunk in the sight of her daughter and family wondering what happened to them tonight, "Okay well y'all two pull a chair out the kitchen."

The two did as Ma Dukes said and she began to assist Jay. The room fell silent once Mya reentered the room. All eyes held fast on her.

Standing front and center in front of everyone Mya batted her eyelashes and took a deep breath. "Ok. The night of Chantel's birthday party. Remember how Dreamz was acting out of character?" she paused for the glimmers of reflection to shine forth within them. "Well after I took him upstairs he admitted that one of my staff had been touching him in inappropriate places and that he didn't like it," her

292

eyes were now cast downward as the tears pooled out of the brim of her eyes dropping freely with shame filling her. "I didn't say anything to Chantel that night. I started watching old footage at work and did a more extensive background check on the man Dreamz was talking about. Before I could tell Chantel Dreamz told her the night she came in from Ronnie's birthday. He was cutting up again because he didn't want to come to daycare after school."

Briefly, T locked eyes with Jay and Kim then dropped her head into her hands. Her fingers expanded weaving into her dreads and tugging at the roots of them. Ma Dukes tossed a bag of weed and a cigar into Kim's lap who failed at trying to smile gratefully.

"She was drunk when she came home. We got into a big argument and she pulled out a gun from an old shoebox. I ain't even know she had one but she said she was gon' handle it. She had to. She kissed me, told me she loved me, and was gone. Been gone. I just got the call tonight."

No one uttered a word. It was so quiet you could hear the cherry off the blunt burning. The group sat with wet faces and somber looks. T thought about Ronnie, Chantel who was probably facing death row, and looked at Jay who had a piece of her side blasted away by a bullet that barely missed killing her. T shook her head letting it hang low to hide the tears escaping down her face.

"Who was dude?" Jay questioned pulling her shirt down over her bandaged wound.

Tears cascaded down Mya's face. "A volunteer. He was supposed to be like a gym teacher organizing different games for the older children to do and supervising at the playground. He watched movies with them. All the kids loved him. I didn't know," she cried out beginning to sob helplessly. "I swear I wouldn't have let him around the kids or me."

"It's a'ight ma," Kim consoled her holding her in her arms, "Lil Buddy cool, you know that. Did you talk to the police?"

"I don't know what to say. They want me to come down there but Chantel won't talk to me. The detective told me she hasn't said anything. When they found her she was beating his body with the gun. But she won't say nothing."

Peering up dubiously T asked, "What you mean she won't say nothin'?"

"She just won't talk. The police said she ain't said shit since they picked her up. They ask her questions, she don't answer. She cooperating just won't say shit about nothing. Like she can't talk," Mya said sadly. "I don't know what to do," she cried onto Kim's shoulder.

Standing up Jay made her way over to Mya and lifted her face. "Dig we gon' do somethin'. We gon' hold our nigga down," she looked at T motioning for Ma Dukes and T to come closer before she went on. "We a family and one thing fa sho 'bout this family, is when one of us hurtin' we all is. Y'all my only family left," Jay paused to reflect as she looked at each one of her friends but seeing the blood family that had disowned her one by one because of her drug addiction. Jay blinked, "I love y'all man. We gon' get through this. Together. Everything gon' be alright." Jay and T clapped hands together embracing tightly.

Once the two separated T inhaled deeply. She looked at Mya, "The most important thing to remember is she innocent. Now c'mon let's go down there and see what's up first." T turned to her mother. "Ma, will you stay here with Dreamz?"

Ma Dukes kissed both of the studs' cheeks followed by the feminine woman, "Just come back and tell me what's going on."

The two studs nodded sincerely.

****

After being interrogated by the assigned detectives the group was allowed to visit Chantel. T's hands clammed up with anxiety over the situation as her other brother and sister exited the room with distraught looks. She took a seat across Chantel.

"Lil Buddy, what the fuck man? Tell them what happened so you can come home," T said. No reply came from Chantel who stubbornly stared at T. She sighed, "Lil Buddy, I ain't gon' press you. Just think about Dreamz." She looked around the room then told her, "I think Layla set us up to get robbed tonight at da club." Chantel's averted eyes shot up boring into T's. "Yeah, but she had a change of heart before niggas could shake anything loose. Brandy popped off on Layla though. We went to war in that muthafucka FOE," T told her with a trembling voice. "We good. Layla took one in da arm. B tried to kill her ass though. Stacey took three to the body. She in ICU."

"I want you to raise Dreamz," Chantel interrupted her.

"What?" T stared at her.

"Raise Dreamz for me bruh. Give me yo' word you gon' hold him down fa me while I'm in here. I don't want nothin else from you. Just take care of him, bring him to see me," Chantel repeated with glossy eyes that contained a glint of determination.

T nodded, "I got you. Nephew gon' be straight," they shook hands on it. "Word is bond on that. Shit tell them boys what happened so you can get the fuck outta here." Chantel didn't say any more or register that she even heard the last bit of advice her brother offered. Dejectedly, T sighed with a stand, "Alright. I'ma send Mya in here. She worried 'bout you foe and scared as fuck. I hope she can talk you into it."

Leaving the room T ran into the head detective assigned to the case.

"Nothing to verify your story huh?" the detective rhetorically asked. "Just raise her son huh? Sounds like she's ready to go away for a long time," he sneered. She adopted her youngest brother's state of silence and didn't reply to him opting to walk away. "Hey," he called her back over to him. "You're going to have to sign some things to be that kid's legal guardian and get full custody. I'll send your info to the caseworker assigned to this case and we will need an admission of facts from the child. Otherwise, I'll make sure you don't see your friend for a long time."

"Alright," she told him watching Mya walk up to them.

The detective turned to Mya, "She talk to you?"

Mya flashed a hollow smile staring directly at T, "She told me she loved me and she wants you to raise Dreamz."

Smiling T told her the obvious, "You know I ain't gon' keep him from you lil' sis."

"I know T," she kissed her cheek. "Thanks for being big bruh. Now go home and let one of yo' females tend to you. Or all of them! I know how you is."

She smiled at her words but her insides felt hollow. The fake joy she tried to protrude didn't even flicker within her.

Chapter 14

Stretched out in the bed with Yolanda snoozing on her chest T stared up at the ceiling her mind reeling. *How am I gon' raise a kid?* T questioned herself. *I ain't even got time but I gave her my word doe. Maybe I can push him off on Ma Dukes.* T shook the thought away from her mind.

Yolanda rubbed T's chest, "You still up baby? What's wrong?"

"Just thinkin ma," sighed T.

"Talk to me baby," she said patting her chest.

"Dig a lot of shit popped off tonight. This was supposed to have been a celebration for my lil' brother. I got set up to get robbed by a bitch, my brother got shot, my bartender got shot, I gotta do construction, get all new permits and shit to open my spot back up. Then at the end of the night I get the call that my baby bro killed somebody. Man I'm all fucked up. I'm supposed to be big bruh but all this shit happened on my fuckin' watch. Foe wants me to raise nephew but how can I do a good job at that if I couldn't even protect her or the rest of the fam?"

"Oh," murmured Yolanda rubbing her body against T's.

Quickly the stud's temper flared up in annoyance. *Bitch really just asked me and don't say shit about nothing I just said but I bet she want some dick though,* T thought angrily smiling to herself. She pulled Yolanda closer to her rolling her on her back. Their lips began to dance with one another while her fingers fiddled with her nipples. Yolanda moaned and she fed her, her tongue. Easing a hand down in between her pussy lips she massaged the button. Yolanda moaned out again arching her back as T's finger rubbed a hip hop beat against her clit.

"Shit," Yolanda panted. "Damn T...fuck...I'm 'bout to cum baby!" Yolanda screamed out while her body shivered pleasurably.

"I will be right back ma," muttered T bounding out of the bed.

The dark skinned amazon bit her lip and gave an erotic look at T before she answered, "Ok baby. Hurry up. She waitin' on you now," she placed T's sticky finger in her mouth.

"A'ight ma," she grabbed a blunt off her dresser and didn't look back.

T walked into the living room and sat down on the couch lighting her blunt. She turned the TV on filling her lungs deep with THC. Holding the smoke hostage within her she exhaled slowly wishing the weight of the world would ease off of her shoulders also.

"You good bruh?" Kim questioned coming into the room.

Pushing the rest of the smoke from her lungs T picked up the remote flipping through channels distractedly wishing she could do the same with her life right now, "Yeah. I'm good sis."

"Don't lie to me bruh," Kim rolled her eyes and threw a pillow at her. "You ain't smiled, cracked a joke, or nothing since everything popped off."

Taking the pillow Kim threw at her she passed her sister the blunt and spat out, "What I got to smile or be happy fa? One of my brother's dead, another one my brothers locked up, and we know how much time Lil Buddy can get fa dat shit."

Kim bit her lip looking down, "You think I don't feel that shit T?" she shot at her. "We all do," Kim stated staring into her eyes. "We family, but you usually da one makin' everything so much easier to get through with a laugh or smile." She took the blunt from Kim puffing but not saying anything. Kim sighed. She walked over to T and kissed her cheek, "I love you bruh. Good night."

"Good night sis. I love you too," T said after she had pushed down the twister of emotions.

****

T sat in the waiting area of a government building. She'd received a call that morning requesting a meeting to expedite the process of her becoming Dreamz's legal guardian. First, they wanted to meet her, inspect her home, meet her family, and anyone else the child may come in contact with and dissect everything about their lives. Just thinking about the situation and why she was there had T dropping her head down low battling not to allow the tears to roam from her eyes.

"Timothy Martin," a voice called out bringing her forth from her trance of wallowing in self-pity.

She stood up and followed the woman monotonously not hearing anything that she was saying. The woman directed T into a room, said something, and closed the door. T resumed her position with her head low, fingers tangled in her dreads. Her mind flitted through her brothers feeling as if she had failed to protect them all in some way, shape, or manner. Dimly, her mind registered the door opening, a sharp intake of breath, and then someone sitting across from her.

"Timothy?" a feminine voice questioned softly when T didn't acknowledge the presence.

Slowly, T raised her head, "Yes ma'am. I'm sorry," her words trailed off as she stared into the face of Kiaysha.

"Hey," she said. After an awkward silence she revealed, "I've been assigned to your case. I will be your main contact here."

The stud nodded but declined to respond verbally to her statement.

"You wanna tell me what's going on Timothy?" Kiaysha questioned.

Her hand rose and she made a gesture towards the inches think manila folder on Kiaysha's desk with her name on it. Again, however, she didn't respond.

"Timothy, I'm asking you," said Kiaysha.

"Man," T began but her voice began to constrict and again tears conspired to fall from her green pools. She licked her lips, opened her voice to talk, but couldn't complete the task.

With a glance at her door, Kiaysha swiftly closed the door quietly and locked the door. She came to T rubbing her back as she held onto the stud who was crying softly. "T, what happened? Talk to me, please. I need to hear your side of things."

She sniffled, "Remember I told you Lil Buddy's story was a long story? Well history repeats itself. She killed somebody for molesting her son."

Kiaysha held onto T rubbing her back. She murmured, "Well I can't say I'm mad at her. Why isn't this in my notes however?"

Licking her lips, releasing the pain she felt, T pulled composure around herself draping it across her body, "Because she don't trust the police. She ain't said no words to them or in the presence of them."

"Do they know what you just told me? Did you tell them?"

"Yeah, they know."

"Why don't they believe you?"

Her jaw locked and her shoulders moved up and down stiffly.

"What happened at your club the other night?" questioned Kiaysha.

A sharp breath left T and she rolled her eyes, "Guess that's the reason why," she shook her head in disgust. "It's entirely unrelated."

"What happened?"

She narrowed her eyes at Kiaysha, "It's in ya notes right?" she gestured at the open folder on Kiaysha's desk where she was comparing what was written down and scribbling notes of their discussion.

The light-skinned woman put her pen down. She stared into T's eyes fiercely, "Look I'm here to help you," Kiaysha leaned forward and lowered her voice. "I could easily walk away and it's probably the right thing to do seeing as how we dated. This would be a conflict of interest. However, I would like to help you anyway I can," a twinkle appeared in her eyes. "Besides, you once told me your club was a laid back, chill type of environment. No bullshit, only partying and fun."

Her words brought a smile to T's face, "It is," T replied confidently. "It was," she corrected herself thinking of the last night her club was open. Her smile disappeared turning her lips into drooping lines. "I don't even know what happened for real. It was a celebration of life for anybody that's lost somebody. For me, for my brothers. Unbeknownst to me, somebody else had plotted that night to rob me. I found out early, but shit," her eyes and voice traveled away from the present and fast-forwarded through the memory past. "That ain't stop shit from getting ugly.

Then right after everything settled we got the call about Lil Buddy."

After jotting down all of the information just passed on to her, Kiaysha put her pen down again. She got up from her seat and wrapped her arms around T. When T didn't hug her back, Kiaysha lifted her head up by her chin and grabbed ahold of her green eyes, "Hey. I'm sorry all of this happened but everything will be alright. I'm in your corner. Don't forget that. Everything will be okay."

An ache of some sort pained deep within T. Water clouded her vision. Quickly, she blinked and looked away, "Thanks but you don't know that," she muttered.

****

"Uncle T!" screamed out Dreamz racing towards her and tackling her legs as soon as the tall stud entered through her mother's front door.

"What's up lil' man," greeted T slapping hands with the young child. "Where Ma Dukes?"

"In the kitchen," he announced. Dreamz peeped around T and smiled at Kiaysha, "What's up ma."

Immediately a grin burst forth on Kiaysha's face, "Hey cutie. What's your name?"

"Dreamz but you can call me Dre," he told her with a puffed out chest.

"Okay Dre. My name is Kiaysha Morris."

His eyebrows furrowed together, "Keyasia Morris?"

"Kiaysha Morris."

"Kiaysha Morris," he declared correctly. "Come on in pretty lady," Dreamz welcomed her in and showed her to the living room where he took a seat and patted the area next to him for her to sit.

"Dre, do you know what I'm doing here?" Kiaysha asked him.

302

He looked at his uncle T who was relaxing next to her on the couch with her feet up and a smirk playing on her lips. Dreamz sighed, "Yeah."

"What am I doing here?"

"You breaking my heart because you here with my uncle," answered Dreamz with a solemn face.

The two adults choked out laughter at his statement. Kiaysha stopped laughing and glanced at T who was still chortling away. She patted her leg and turned back to Dreamz, "Your uncle isn't ready for me and besides I'm here for you lil' man."

Dreamz expression changed. Again, his eyebrows knitted together in contemplation, "I ain't never seen you before. Why you here for me?" he questioned with no trace of playfulness.

Before Kiaysha could respond, T jumped into their conversation. She leaned forward looking at her nephew, "Dreamz she ain't here with me like that man. This business. She here to talk to you about what happened."

He nodded, "I believe you, but I ain't telling her nothing. She already got my name."

"Dreamz!" T yelled at him. "This is important man. You think I would bring her back here if I didn't trust her. I say she cool so she cool peoples man. Talk to her man."

"How you know she ain't twelve?" he retorted back using a slang synonym for the police.

"Dreamz," T stated with her last ounce of patience. "She trying to help Lil Buddy a'ight? That's why she here."

"Ma said don't ever talk to da boys. They some snakes so I ain't talking to no lady officer no matter how cute she it."

T shot to her feet shouting out, "Mama!"

Giggling at the exchange between the two Kiaysha slid in front of T, "Calm down T. Chill. Think about it. If

303

his mother is distrustful of law enforcement then naturally he would be too."

"What you want T? How you doing Miss Lady?" Ma Dukes appeared in the living room firing off both questions.

"This is Kiaysha Morris from social services. She trying to help wrap up this situation so I can be the legal guardian," T informed her mother. "And Dreamz ain't cooperating," she glared down at her nephew.

Ma Dukes flicked him in his ear once T was done speaking.

"Ow!" Dreamz cried out whipping around. "What I do?"

"Dreamz!" her finger flew in the air as her scolding began, "Don't you be raising yo' damn voice at me lil' man. Now listen," Ma Dukes collected herself. "Baby, this lady is here to help. She is not the police."

"Say sorry," he demanded holding onto his ear while staring angrily at his grandmother.

Laughing Ma Dukes replied, "Boy, you trippin'."

A brief smile ran across Dreamz's face before fleeing. Kiaysha took that opportune to squat down eye level with Dreamz. "Hey sweetie. My name is Kiaysha Morris just like I told you. I am not the police. My job is to talk with kids and families to make sure that they are okay, being cared for, and showed love. If there is any sign of abuse I will report it. I'm here today to meet you and see if you will tell me what happened to you. I'm also here inspecting your home and your family to make sure they love and will take care of you. If you don't talk to me you won't see your mother for a long time. And the police could take you from T and you might not see anyone else you know for a long time."

Her words froze his feet to the ground. Once the reality of her words kicked in Dreamz shuffled over to stand in front of T. He stared at her, "T? My mama in jail ain't she?"

She breathed heavily and answered honestly, "Yeah man."

"Oh," Dreamz looked down at a loss for words. His head lifted again, "She killed him didn't she?"

Tears stung her eyes as she fought them from falling. T leaned forward rubbing the top of Dreamz's head. She stared into his eyes, "Me and you blessed man. We got mothers that care and that love us. Lil Buddy will die to protect you. Talk to Kiaysha man so that won't have to happen. So, we can bring yo' mama, my brother home alright?"

The sad expression on his face dissipated at T's words. His shoulders squared and Dreamz brushed away the runaway tears that had escaped from his eyes. He went back to standing in front of Kiaysha. Dreamz swallowed the lump in his throat, "I don't want my mama in jail and I don't want her to die. This man, he was a white man that worked at Mya's daycare. He touched me right here," Dreamz pointed to his private area with lowered eyes. "I didn't wanna go back there. I ain't like him touchin' me. Ma said nobody supposed to touch you there but females and doctors. I ain't like that. That's the only reason why I told Ma 'cause I didn't wanna go back there again. I ain't want Ma to get in trouble," he finished with a trembling lip and shaky bravado.

"Hey, keep your head up," Kiaysha lifted his little chin. "Nothing is your fault. Alright? You did the right thing. That man was wrong," when he nodded at her words Kiaysha looked back at T. "Who is Mya?"

"Luh Buddy's girlfriend."

She nodded straightening. Kiaysha began to write down some more notes from this new conversation and Dreamz went to T and whispered in her ear. The two began

305

to smile and laugh while staring at Kiaysha. Kiaysha stopped what she was doing and a hand flew to her hip, "Y'all talking about me?"

The two smiled at each other and simultaneously said, "Nope."

"Y'all come on and get some lunch. Dre, go wash them hands," Ma Dukes called out.

****

Unlocking her front door T led the way up the stairs of her condominium with Kiaysha trailing behind. T hung her keys on her key rack. She maneuvered around the lady to grab a bottle of water out of the refrigerator. She perched on the edge of her bar stool watching Kiaysha admire her living area.

"Damn. This is nice T," observed Kiaysha. "You stay here by yourself?"

Swiftly, T stood guiding the woman out of the way with a light touch on her hips. She went to the hallway. Kim's closed door didn't deter her from knocking on it. She came back into the kitchen and took her seat back. "Nah. My sister in her room probably 'sleep. Kim!" she shouted. "We got company!"

The woman's eyes drunk in T's demeanor. Her usual air of confidence was slightly lacking as if it wasn't as bright as usual. Their exchange was borderline formal, no witty repartee or casual flirting. Thinking back through the day she couldn't remember T smiling; even when she was laughing it was not hearty.

"Timothy, lighten up a little bit. It's not the end of the world," commented Kiaysha with a smile and hands on her hips at her playful demand.

From her spot where she was absentmindedly playing with the label of her water bottle, T looked up at

Kiaysha. Her words registered in her ear and sent a thrill tingling down her body. Her eyes roved over Kiaysha's body while hers in turn remembered the way their bodies communicated with one another. She smiled genuinely.

A pillow smacked T on the side of the face and Kim walked into the view of the other two adults and halted, "Damn my bad bruh. I see why you smiling. Hell I'm smiling now," she said eyes glued on Kiaysha.

"Hey," Kiaysha greeted bashfully.

"How you doing beautiful?" inquired Kim.

"I'm doing good, having fun meeting you all's family. I definitely have a great report to send back to my superiors so far."

Kim's eyes narrowed, "You a police officer?" she guessed.

Laughing Kiaysha shook her head no, "No, I'm not. I'm only a social worker trying to ensure Dreamz is placed in the best custody whether temporary or permanent for him."

"Oh okay. What's your name miss?"

"Kiaysha. Kiaysha Morris."

She nodded eyes widening slowly. Kim looked at T who gave a slight nod and a smile crept across her face. "Your name sounds familiar," she commented slyly.

"Alright Kim," said T standing. "Come on Kiaysha let me show you the rest of the place."

Smiling curiously at the two Kiaysha followed T.

"FOE, I'm headed to the garage," called out Kim.

T didn't respond. She opened every door for Kiaysha to look in and take notice of the well-organized living space she held. When they got to T's bedroom. T walked in and took off her shoes slipping on a pair of house shoes.

"Y'all blood related?" inquired Kiaysha.

"Might as well be. Blood couldn't make us no closer. All of us really friends from back in school days but like I said blood couldn't make us no closer."

Nodding Kiaysha stood staring up at T. They were at a standstill in the doorway. T didn't move to get past her. Kiaysha didn't move to let her past.

"Timothy, I don't have a recorder or anything on me. I'm not wearing a wire. Feel free to be yourself. I only tell them what I want too."

"So, what you saying?"

"You look like you need to smoke a blunt," chuckled Kiaysha bluntly.

With a raised eyebrow, T looked her over thoughtfully then spun on her heel and opened the nightstand next to her bed. "You coming in? I'm closing the door so the smell don't permeate the rest of the spot. We usually don't smoke in our rooms."

She stepped into the room and T closed the door. T went in the bathroom coming back out with a towel and secured it underneath the door. She strode over to her computer desk wheeling the chair to Kiaysha for her to sit in.

T lit her blunt inhaling deeply until the smoke filled every inch of her lungs. She held it in until she couldn't hold it anymore and slowly exhaled through her nose. She toked again in the same manner trying to alleviate the feelings swirling around within her. "You smoking with me?" asked T holding out the joint to Kiaysha.

"No, I'm on the clock," she declined watching the stud who didn't respond back.

Subconsciously, T twisted her dreads. Her mind drifted to her two brothers. Ronnie held in so much pain that T didn't even know was present, didn't even understood how her love for her girlfriend had been so vital. The background of Chantel's life was already so bleak but she had turned it all around. Everything was all good. Why did this cloud of darkness creep into her life again? How could she have not known that Chantel's ex was back in town? T hung her head at the communication she failed to provide between her two brothers, Mya, Dreamz, and even Jay.

Guilt seeped through making her feel if she was more accessible instead of hoeing, a lot of this could have been prevented. Ronnie would still be here, Chantel would have never fucked her ex bitch, which strained her relationship with Mya. Dreamz would've told her first and she could have gotten the police to lock dude up and passed the info to Chantel after the man was in police custody. Which in turn would've prevented her from being locked up, and even now, she made a mental list to reach out to Jay who she hadn't talked too since the night everything was revealed. She didn't want a pop up of Jay's old drug abusing habits with everything going on.

Dimly, somewhere in the recess of her mind she registered someone calling her name. Sifting through the haze of smoke clouding her mind her body realized she was being nudged.

"Hey, you alright?" Kiaysha questioned. "Stand up," she pushed T's arm again.

Before doing so T hit the blunt once more and placed it in her ashtray. She took her time rising to her feet and once done she just stood there silently. Mind still warped not in tune with the present T was taken aback when a soft, sweetness enveloped her squeezing her tight. She looked down into Kiaysha's smiling face.

"Stop stressing, that's not good for you. Everything is going to be fine," Kiaysha told her.

One side of her mouth lifted slightly into a half smile at the woman's campaign to not allow T to be depressed. Thinking about why she was doing so only brought her thoughts back to the forefront and her half smile fled and head dropped.

"Head up," barked out Kiaysha and with gentle fingers she lifted her head by her chin. Gazing into the shimmery green mini-spheres, Kiaysha felt a tug that made her push a tender kiss to T's lips.

Their lips touching one another awakened every nerve ending within the two. The kiss flooded them, heating the two bodies still enclosed in one embrace. One tender kiss led to another until Kiaysha had her hands clenching the chest of T's shirt lips demanding more.

The eros emanating from them dispelled everything else from the room and moved to conquer. With T's torch ignited full blaze she moved from lips to her neck while removing the business jacket from the woman. Her hands wandered until they settled on her nipples flicking and pulling them. Lips moved back to lips and tongues sliding out to frolic without another.

Unabashed Kiaysha stepped back from the stud and shed her layers. In full bloom like a butterfly she came back to her lover kissing her body while undressing her. Laps of passion and pleasure hurdled through T, high jumping into her fingers, running down to tease the pussy in front of her. Two fingers partnered up passing the diamond between her southern lips back and forth. The two fingers dipped out entering her straight away. Her thumb joined the competition massaging her button. Juices coated T's fingers and she sucked them into her mouth.

She kissed T's face sucking on her lips and tongue searching for a drop of her own essence. T pulled back to stand straight up so the woman couldn't catch a taste. Not one to be outdone however the shorter woman jumped wrapping her legs around T's waist.

Smiling, T eased her arms under the thighs and hefted the woman up to her shoulders. She held her in place with a tight grip on her legs. Her tongue snaked out to greet the bare backed pussy sitting proudly in her face. She licked up and down each plump lip and suckled it into her mouth. Her mouth traversed to the pulsating clit and swallowed it whole. T's lips released her bulb and her tongue flattened against her pearl sliding all the way down spinning inside her hole on the way down and way back up.

Hands zoomed and roamed all over T's head and down her shirt scratching her back searching for something of substance to hold onto. "Shit," she cried out feeling the stud swipe her tongue furiously against her clit while alternatively pulling it into her mouth. "We gon' fall, we gon' fall, we gon' fall," Kiaysha stuttered out with curled toes.

Hearing her words T slid her side-to-side responding no with her head. Her hands held on more tightly as she dived deeper. Her nose tantalized Kiaysha's ball of pleasure as her tongue fucked her box.

Kiaysha screamed out from the strokes of T's tongue. "Ooh shit! Fuck!" she hollered as the first round of tremors rocked through her. She humped frantically back on auto pilot. Her body careened itself backward not in effort to run but to hold onto T's legs and get her pussy ate upside down.

With their new position T attacked her jukebox like a fat kid devours his first plate. Her lips, her tongue were everywhere. Sucking on her lips, pulling on her clit, nipping on her clit and tracing her stamp on it. Her tongue zigzagged from one hole to the other and back again.

Her thighs tensed and toes curled as she felt herself riding the wave of an orgasm. She released T's ankles and sat herself up almost lifting her pussy out of T's mouth as she gushed relieving herself of all her sexual potion.

"Damn," Kiaysha looked down at T's wet face and then flipped off of her.

She quickly dressed without looking at T. "Oh my God," she shook her head. "I gotta go T. Fuck," Kiaysha quickly exited the room unnerved.

Six months later

"Damn Ron it's been a long year. It seems like just a week ago I was just sitting here with my bottle reminiscing with you," spoke T from her seat on the ground next to Ronnie's gravesite with a bottle in between her legs. "Shit the last time I left you here I was talking about settling down. Ha," she paused to laugh. "It's funny how you eat yo' words sometimes. I feel like I meant it at that time but at the same time I was full of shit. Now it's like I ain't never wanted a female so bad in my life not even just to have that lil' notch or whatever but I honestly wanna be with her bruh. No other females, no games. She reached me where and when no other bitch could. Hell I ain't even feel alive; I felt like I was just living till she touched me. Enough about that shit though," T took a swig from her bottle.

"Lil Buddy's case today. In a lil' bit actually. I'm fucked up about it brah. You know our court system here ain't shit. I do got a trick for they tough ass though. I made good on that info you slid me awhile back," T paused to reflect and light her blunt. "Yeah fuck you nigga. I know you ain't got over what I said. Real shit though I'm gon' do right by ma. I miss you lil' bruh. Shit I wish you was here physically to meet her." Her cell phone began vibrating in her pocket and T pulled it out. "Speak of the devil. I done talked her ass up," she stood to her feet. "Alright lil bruh

I'm about get up outta here and get on to this shit. Watch over yo' family foe. I love you always."

She whipped out of the parking lot and zoomed into the steady flow of street traffic. Fifteen minutes into the drive T pulled into Mike's parking lot. She pulled a five-dollar bill out of her pocket and got out of the car.

"Hey T," greeted Layla as she pulled into the parking spot on the passenger's side of T's car.

"What's good shorty," T smiled at her. She waited for Layla to get out of the car with the entrance door of the store held open. "How you been? You good?"

"I'm fine. I tried to call you," she added demurely.

"I got a new number."

"Oh okay. Did you ever find out what happened to Luh Buddy?"

Unable to reply with eyes drawn tightly together and tight lipped she merely handed her money to the man behind the register silently. "Yeah," she finally uttered after Layla paid.

"Well? Was she okay?"

She scoffed, "Kind of."

"T what's up? Did something happen to Luh Buddy?"

Her jaw flexed as she spilled the guts of the cigar onto the ground outside of her vehicle, "She killed somebody."

"Who?"

"You don't know 'em."

"Why?"

"Don't matter."

"When did this happen?" asked Layla with genuine concern pushing her weight from foot to foot as she debated whether or not to go to T and console her. Just when she took a step towards T, T answered her.

"Same night everything popped off at the club. I'm on my way to court now," T unlocked her car doors. "You smoking with me or do you got somewhere to be?"

The young woman smiled bashfully, "Nah I ain't got nowhere to be," she settled into the car with the blunt reclining back and staring at T admiring her aura. Layla passed the blunt back to her and watched her turn up her flask taking a huge gulp from it and keeping it tilted. Softly, Layla put the flask down and took it from her. "T you going to court and it's early as hell to be drinking."

Opening her mouth to respond T cut her words short and a finger indicating to hold one minute flew into the air. Her phone was ringing out a new artists' named Mike Vega single. "Hello?"

"Timothy, where are you? You're about to miss check in!" yelled Kiaysha.

"I'm on my way now."

"Alright Timothy. Hurry up."

"A'ight I got you."

"And Timothy please spray something. Jay came in here reeking already."

A trace of a smile flashed across her face, "Yes ma'am. I got some Odor Ban shit for that."

"Okay. I'll see you when you get here."

"A'ight."

"Bye."

"Bye."

She hung up the phone and looked at the flask next to Layla. T turned the music down. "Dig, I gotta get up out here shorty. Go 'head and keep that flask for me though?"

Chewing her lip Layla looked at her with questions in her eyes, "Till when?"

"Until I come get it."

"Okay," she bit her lip hesitantly then pressed a kiss to T's lips. "I love you daddy," she admitted and darted out of the car into her own.

T revved her engine, nodded when Layla looked over at her, and screeched out of the lot.

****

Bristling with anger T sat in the courtroom after being cross-examined by the prosecution and defense. A fleeting smile darted across her face glad she was able to witness Moryah; Ronnie's mother smack the prosecutor with her purse when he disrespected Ma Dukes when she was on the stand. T tuned back into the exchange between Kiaysha on the stand and the prosecutor.

"Ms. Morris, how old is Ms. Thompson's son?"

"Eight."

"And do you believe he knows and understands right from wrong?"

"Yes."

"Why do you think Ms. Thompson will not allow him to take the stand?"

"In my professional opinion the child will feel threatened in this atmosphere as well as embarrassed by having to recall past events which led to his mother's incarceration. He has a distrust of law enforcement as well."

"A distrust of those here to protect and serve? Already at the tender age of eight and guilty feelings about his mother being in jail. So, he would go along to get her out of jail, correct?"

"Objection!" Chantel's lawyer flew to his feet.

"Granted," remarked the judge. "No leading."

The prosecutor shrugged and sneered at Kiaysha.

"My overall opinion of the child is that he is a very bright individual. Both intellectually and what some would say street sense. If he was on the stand he would not lie to protect his mother or tell the truth to protect his mother because he would distrust you. His awareness is very keen. He is very tuned in to what is going on around him. No one would be able to tell him to open up to you because no matter who it was, he would see the disdain written on his family member's faces as they stared at you."

Casually, the prosecutor strolled up to the bench and ran his fingers along the wood. He didn't say anything but continued as if not a care in the world until the judge prompted him. "So, Ms. Morris, why didn't you record this exchange between you and the child?"

"I was unprepared. I was checking out the living quarters of said individual to gain custody of the child. I did not know he would be present and that we would have a discussion right away."

"So, he told you right away? Let me remind you that you are under oath."

"When he was prompted too. He refused. His aunt and grandmother had to beg him and even then I had to gain his trust through my words and identifying myself. It also helped that there was no animosity between his family and I."

"But yet and still he told you upon his first meeting with you."

"Yes."

"But he wouldn't, couldn't tell his tale on the stand?"

"My son ain't taking the stand," growled out Chantel standing angrily from the defense table where her lawyer had a hand on her arm.

"Scared he may forget the story?" sneered the prosecutor walking away from Kiaysha. "No further questions your Honor."

"Next witness," barked out the judge.

The courtroom doors flew open revealing a handcuffed black man with guards flanking his side. He smiled at Chantel standing tall. The burly man took his seat on the witness stand.

"Devonte Thompson present your Honor. I am the defendant's father," he spoke into the mic.

The judge nodded and Chantel's lawyer stood to his feet striding towards him.

"Sir, can you tell us why Chantel distrusts the police and why this issue would be prevalent in her child?"

"Because I was arrested in front of her. In handcuffs she watched police officers beat me while I was helpless to defend myself. At the time of my arrest she was held in cuffs naked. She was ignored when she told the truth."

"What was her truth?"

Devonte's eyes locked with his daughters across the room. He nodded at her. Together the two took a deep breath, "She was raped by the individual I was found guilty of murdering."

Her lawyer resumed his seat next to Chantel, "Counsel rests your Honor."

Immediately the prosecutor hopped to his feet with a smile, "Well, well, well so you are the infamous Mr. Thompson?"

Up and down Devonte looked at the prosecutor with disdain, "Yes."

"Do you know what the police files list about you?"

"No."

"Are you aware that you were under surveillance for many of years before you were detained from drug charges to murder and racketeering? You were quite the slippery fellow until the mishap at which landed you in prison. So, tell me Mr. Thompson what are you imprisoned for?"

"Manslaughter."

"A history of violence passed on," he commented whisking to his table to retrieve papers. "Now let's talk about the facts. I have facts from your case Mr. Thompson that say you murdered a man in cold blood in front of your then fourteen year old daughter," he waved the papers. "Why isn't your story of your daughter being raped present in this police report? Why was it not reported that your daughter was held naked? All of these answers you just supplied to help your daughter is not present in this documentation of your case. Now here we are eight years later with your daughter in the same predicament. She claims, just like you claimed, her son was sodomized, raped, molested with no proof. A man is dead for no reason!" roared the prosecutor slapping his hand down on the counter in front of the jurors. Rushing back to Devonte he snarled at him, "Is this a game to you?"

"No."

"A man is dead, Two men," he reminded the courts fiercely looking at Chantel. "Both for no reason. Neither father nor daughter has showed remorse for the victim. No compassion. Unwilling to even admit for the deceased families' sake that yes I committed this crime. Both of you with fables surrounding this act but nothing to support. What is the purpose between these senseless acts? If we were dealing with animals one bad seed spoils them all. It would be put to death. This is two generations laced with the same uncaring violence. Ms. Thompson, you have a son. If he were an animal I would kill him to break the sick tradition you all are participating in," the prosecution took his seat and waved his hand.

From the witness stand two words, "Baby girl," uttered from Devonte, registered through the stunned room to obtain his daughter's attention. Once their connection was established, he nodded.

Slowly, feeling the anger dissipate and courage coursing through her, Chantel stood.

"Your honor I'd like to testify," Chantel said.

****

"Free our brother, free foe!" Kim exclaimed holding up a drink later on that evening in the basement of Ma Dukes house with her family and Kiaysha.

Everyone held up a drink with her and tossed it back.

"Fuckin' ten years man. The fuckin' max! That's some fuckin' bullshit," spat out Jay, which prompted Arianna to come behind her and begin to massage her shoulders.

T watched them and smiled. She took the blunt from Jay, "You know what though? We going to win this appeal and get her sentence overturned and in the process we gon' get her pops free too."

"How you plan on doing that?" questioned Kiaysha.

She sent a wink her way, "The prosecutor said get proof. We gon' get it."

Inwardly, Kiaysha's heart swelled as she saw the glowing cheerful aura T procreated come back full force. Outwardly, she smiled. "Let me know if I can be of any service."

"You already have," admitted T looking around her family who was watching their exchange of words. "When everything first happened I was lost. I couldn't turn to the females and let them be my cure all. My family couldn't erase this helpless feeling. I couldn't get rid of it but you did. You reached me when nobody else did. You made me smile. You shined some light in the darkness that had enveloped me. I'm grateful and I apologize it took me so long to wake up but I see now and I realize. You the only woman I need. If you will have me that is. I want you and only you to be mine."

Wide eyes and toothy grins gazed at Kiaysha as the family waited for her answer. Time stood still with them watching her sip her drink. Heads cocked and ears perked when her lips split and she began to speak.

"As long as it will only be me. I will only have you," she murmured to the extreme delight of everyone.

Acknowledgements

And we back at it again but you know we gotta go to church first. So, with that said let me give all the praise and glory to my Father. I was blessed with this talent that entertains you and keeps me busy and out of trouble. Thank you Lord for the creative ability bestowed upon me.

A big thank you to Joy Nelson, my editor, that was oh so patient with me during the process. Thank you for your services, advice, feedback EVERYTHING. It was a pleasure to do business with you. You are exactly what I expected from an editor. I hope to do future business with you as well. Kudos.

My man Keith Saunders at Marion Designs! You did it once again and gave me a flyy ass cover. Thanks man and thank you to the models that you hired to grace the cover. I love it.

To my most honest critic, Christiana Parrish, (congrats on your marriage) thank you. Your review lit a fire under my ass and helped to fuel a lot of the extra time spent on this novel.

My top two fans Sonia and Shonetel thank you for your continuous support and feedback. I'm honored to have two remarkable ladies not only as fans but as friends. You've given advice and rocked with me patiently. Thank you so much. Y'all are two of the best fans in the world! Big ups to you! Thank you.

Montaya! Thanks for being my beta reader again lol. Oh the hassle of dealing with my ass and all the questions I want answered. Thanks for everything yo.

Mary Holleran, you know I wasn't gonna leave you out right? Hell it might not had been a Playing Games II if it wasn't for you pushing me to write in high school. Thanks yo.

My Cholo, my woman, thanks baby for being my muse as I recreated this novel. You dealt with all my late nights of writing, my funks over reviews, and everything. Thank you woman! Thank you for supporting my dreams.

Shout out to R-Dub, FOE, my Cincinnati Sizzle family, Spencer, Ward and whatever else is branched off lol. I ain't listing all y'all names. You know if I fuck with you or if I don't.

On another note I must say RIP to Carrie "CC" Cousins and Trina Bridenbaugh. FOE lost these two mothers, these two friends within four months of one another. Your presence is truly missed ladies. Party up FOE.

If you reading these acknowledgements life is too short to not forgive and move forward so make amends. Tell ya loved ones you love them every day mean it and show it. Make every day count.

One more thing before I end this. Please whether you got kids or not, teach them! Instill morals within them that they can carry with them through life. Don't ever give up on them. Let's build these teenagers, kids, children up. They are the future. They need those old school teaching and old school ass whoopings.

Alright I gotta cut myself off. Thanks for buying my book. Please leave a review via Amazon or even on my facebook page. I can be reached at www.facebook.com/AuthorKendraSpencer or flair4writing@yahoo.com. Check out the website www.zoneprince.yolasite.com

Much love to you. Stay up and stay blessed.

Prince #33

About the Author

#BlackLivesMatter #AllLivesMatter
#HandsUpGunsDown

#lesbian #CincinnatiSizzle #FOE #BullyBreedParent
#BlackAndProud

#IworkInTheMentalHealthField
#SometimesIhaveMentalissues

#MusiciansThatHelpedMeWrite
#ChrisBrown #RKelly #TreySongz #JillScott
#AliciaKeys #Aaliyah

#IspeakSailor

#GaryOwenGaveMeThisIdea   #IstoleIt
#YouKnowTheWhiteGuyInKevinHartMovies
#WeBothFromCincinnati

#2Rs3K   #18to80BlindCrippledOrCrazy

#MySisterCallMeTheirHershe
#MyAuntsCallMeTheirNiecephew

#Thanks4theLoveAndSupport
#Ih8ThIs